For my dad, who endured every draft and still loves me.

THE SONGS OF LORALAN

FOR EVERGREENS AND ASPEN TREES

A.L. LORENSEN

CONTENTS

YOUR FREE STORY AWAITS

A quest, a question, a broken boy, and a ruined man. Some endeavor to claim the wish a cursed sword promises; others will do anything to keep them from it.

Get a free copy of the short story
Where Demons Rest here:

www.allwrites.com

The Dragon Scales
The Golden Grove
Monterro
Architect's Heart
Vastet
Caldrech
Lorate
The Phoenix Ridges
Bael
Western Loralan

FOREWORD

Three laws govern the magic of Alchilon:

1. Magic may not be given to those without lest it become a curse upon their heads.
2. Magic bound is magic beaten.
3. The dead must remain with the dead.

These laws were intended to protect the weak and balance the powerful. They were well-intentioned choices made by well-intentioned beings. However, as is often the heartbreaking case, even the best of intentions can be turned against us. In all my years studying the history of this world, the Ancient Laws have caused more pain, sorrow, manipulation, and bloodshed than I believe those original lawmakers ever intended.

-J. Lashton; *The Nature of Enduring Warfare (12th Edition); pg. 3*

PROLOGUE

The waves crashed in overwhelming dissonance, reminiscent of the mourning dragon cries the bard witnessed countless years ago. The smells of ocean salt and iron tangled in the watery light of early morning. Pockets of water riddled the valley, their waves spitting sparks of light and carving deep wounds in their beaches. From the bard's mountain perch amidst shattered rock and uprooted trees, the lakes looked like so many fallen scales. Like the ones she had seen that day of fire and ash so long ago; the day she wished to forget. The bodies scattered across the valley now, staining the lakes crimson, did nothing to banish those memories.

"Too many lives wasted." The jagged scar on the bard's eyelids burned. She half-expected warm arms to draw her close and a chin to rest on her shoulder while deep, soft words of comfort thrummed in her ears. Instead, a bitter wind laughed as it whipped around her and tossed her dust-worn skirt. A stake of loneliness pounded into her chest. The war had cost too much.

The bard waited—humming a tune of better days with eyes

closed—and listened to the thrum of the earth and the beat of the lives upon it. There had to be one voice still out on that bitter battlefield. Just one. And she would wait for it. Despite the songs she sang and stories she told of heroes rushing into battle unfettered, she could not carve that same path. It was her fate and her curse to wait —only wait—until someone reached out to her.

And there, carried across an urgent wind, the call came.

Help him. Someone, help him, please.

She was on her feet in an instant. Jaw set, the bard clasped the strap of her lute close to her chest and slid into the valley. She winced as she tripped over loose roots and trod on shards of debris, but she kept her course to the carnage below. So many dead lay abandoned in the valley. The dead must remain with the dead. She knew *that* better than anyone. But if she could save even one life before death could stake its claim...

When she reached the mountain's base, she removed her boots. The water-logged earth seeped between her toes, cold and sorrowful. The loss and heartbreak swirling in the murk overwhelmed the bard and brought tears to her eyes. She breathed in until her chest ached from the strain, and then let the breath and emotions pass through her until they dissipated. She listened. Three heartbeats throbbed through the earth. Two weak and fading, the other one...

A shudder ran through her. *Seething* was the only way she could describe it; a paltry word that came nowhere near its full presence. She had lost track of the years since she had last felt something so dark. She needed to complete her work before that *thing* overtook her.

She kept careful watch on that presence and focused on the cries she had heard.

Please, if there is a god anywhere, please help him.

She ran, swift as wingbeats, across the crimson ground. She dodged fallen bodies and plunged her feet into icy pockets of sea until she found her. A broken girl, all alone, at the edge of the battlefield. Bodies piled around her like fallen leaves. Her blade was stained with blood almost as deep as the blood flooding the back of her tunic.

The bard approached, not daring to hope the girl was still conscious, but she was mistaken. The girl snatched at the bard's skirts as soon as she saw them.

"Please." A sob tore through her throat. Congealed blood dribbled from her mouth. "Please, help him. He's out there. He...He can't die. I *promised* him."

The bard crouched and put her hand over the girl's. "Shh, all will be well. I will help you and then find your friend."

"*NO!*" The girl's vehemence startled the bard. "*Him* first! He *cannot* die. He *can't!*"

"I understand. I will help you; if you only ask—"

"*No!* I...I don't deserve help!" More sobs wracked her body. "Dead...All dead, because of me. I...I killed them. I killed them all." Her eyes fluttered, her consciousness waning. "Please...Please save him."

The bard's throat hitched in frustration. She could save them both if the girl wasn't so stubborn, but without that critical request for help...She knew her curse's limits all too well. Biting back a retort, she placed her hand on the girl's feverish forehead. "I will help him."

The pain melted from the girl's body. Her eyes finally closed. "Thank you." A last whisper before her body fell still. Not dead, but dancing along its treacherous line.

The bard fought back tears as she stood and searched for the other weakened heartbeat. The only other survivor. Of all the wide-eyed young soldiers around her, only two remained. The ground shuddered, a lingering sob over the lost.

The bard found her target and ran to the other end of the battle-field. She met a gruesome sight at the end of her trail. Despite the countless battlefields she had seen, she would never be used to the gore they left behind. Her stomach churned at the agonized young soldier.

Drenched to his shoulders in his own blood, his breathing was shallow, erratic, and labored. The whites of his eyes shone stark against the crimson as they rolled in his head. His limbs twitched, either reaching for the sword at his side or in the final throes of death. His life-force spilled undeterred from a gaping hole in his head where half his skull had caved in on itself. She suspected a mace to be the culprit.

The bard tucked her legs beneath her and cradled the soldier's head in her lap. He moaned and gurgled blood and spittle. His arms shook to fight her, or so she assumed. The bard hushed him as she would a terrified child and pressed her hand to his skull. Blood dripped between her fingers and left trails down her arms. She tucked him tighter against her, heart aching, and hummed. Gold light illuminated her skin and seeped into the wound.

The instant her magic touched him, a green mist leaped to life and batted the bard's hand away.

She tilted her head and let her magic fade into her bones for a moment. The gold light died. When it did, the mist receded to a spot on the young man's chest beneath his tunic. She pulled back the fabric and found a silver ring on a leather cord. A homemade talisman. It glowed green the closer she came, but its light was fading. The caster was dying. The girl.

"Someone loves you very much." The bard brushed blood-crusted hair from her patient's forehead. "Talismans are no small thing." She touched the ring. It burned bright and hot. At least, it would have for anyone other than herself. She allowed her magic to flow through her fingertips. "*Hush. You have done what you can to protect him,*" she said in the Ancient Tongue, the rich, cadence-like language of magic. It would share her message with its wielder. "*I will do what I can to save him, as I promised.*"

The ring continued to burn bright and fierce, pulsing as fast as an anxious heart. It matched the other heartbeat's tempo she sensed elsewhere on the battlefield.

The bard hummed again and stroked the ring's curve. "*All will be well,*" she said. "*All will be well.*"

The fight left the talisman's caster with a slow and agonizing withdrawal. The ring's glow faded to almost nothing, and the protective mist disappeared.

The bard kissed the ring and wasted no more time. She had a promise to keep.

Golden flames encased her body as she placed her hands on the young man's wound. The song the earth had sung to her through the wind, trees, grass, and soil every night for the past three months tumbled from her lips, focusing her magic.

A ruler will rise
To vanquish the Night.
To bring evil's demise
And bring all to right.

To Death they will fly
And to Earth they return.
The Laws they defy
Before this world burns.

Blood of sorcerer
Blood of saint
Shall become the restorer
And cure Earth's blackest taint.

Thrice failed
Is thrice cursed.
If good does not prevail
Then Earth shall see its worst.

MOVEMENT INTERRUPTED HER. Stumbling, shuffling; the air thick with the stench of defeat and vengeance. Seething hatred washed from the lakes' mist and solidified into a single presence. It had returned. Fine hairs along the bard's spine stood on end.

You must leave, Sister Earth whispered to her. *You cannot be lost.*

A thick shield of fog rolled in. The bard suspected it came as a gift from her worried friend.

She checked her patient. Though still bleeding, his skull had been repaired. He breathed deep and even, and his limbs had quieted. Although not fully healed, she had gotten him through the worst of it. He would live.

Whatever vile thing headed her way continued to shuffle closer. She hesitated, unwilling to leave the young man behind, but Sister Earth urged her away, echoing her words to the nameless caster.

All will be well. All will be well.

Her friend had yet to steer her wrong.

She departed, melting back into the mountainside and leaving the grisly battlefield behind her. As she picked her way back up the mountainside, she chanced one last glance back. The seething presence crouched beside her charge, examining his face and checking for signs of life. Frustration. Fury. Desperate opportunity. They all flowed from the presence—the *man*, though only just—as inexorably as the waves against their shores.

He stood and looked across the battlefield, and at that moment the bard saw a flash of bone-white blade—a sword strapped at his waist.

Dread thrummed through the bard and summoned goose-flesh along her arms. She had not seen that sword for centuries; knew it had been too much to ask to never see it again.

Leave, the Earth begged. *Leave before it claims your soul.*

The sword-wielder gathered the boy in his arms like he might a sack of flour for barter and limped away from the battlefield. The bard closed her eyes, heart aching, resenting her inability to intervene.

All will be well, the Earth whispered to her once more. *All will be well.*

PART ONE

LORATE

CHAPTER

ONE

Gentle with the precious cargo! I can't afford any mistakes!

A laugh. Trinkets clanked together and an orange glow came from somewhere.

Of all people, you dare to lecture me on mistakes? After the carnage you left behind? You're beyond fortunate that Osmen didn't add you to the body count.

He furrowed his brow and moaned. The voices raked jagged claws across his throbbing head. Fevers wracked his body and tied him to disjointed dreams that fractured further from the voices floating around him.

It wasn't my fault! Someone said. Gruff, assertive, yet shaken.

Charging after the entirety of the rebellion without a plan 'wasn't your fault'? another responded in deep, resonant tones that dripped with contempt.

The sword it...it told me everything would be all right. That I could win if I acted quickly.

Silence. The orange glow faded for a moment.

Perhaps I should relieve you of that sword. It does terrible things to an untrained mind.

NO. If my ancestors were good enough to wield it, then so am I.

And now you are the first in your family to be banished to a useless fort in the King's Army. I'm sure they are all very pleased.

Blessed silence took over. Animosity spread like fog through the quiet, but he didn't care. The throbbing in his head grew numb. Sleep brushed the edges of his mind.

How long will whatever you're doing take? Gruff asked Contempt.

Tell me what happened to the ambushers at the Dragon Scales instead of asking stupid questions, Contempt responded.

Phantom branches whipped past him, shattered and bent against the moonless sky. Waves crashed in terrible cacophony. Lakes scattered across a barren valley, surging against their shores like a shattered ocean. The stars glittered across their waves.

Screams. So many screams. A sliver of the night sky swinging in long, beautiful arcs. A white blade meeting it. Sparks shrieking into the night. A head of dark curls. Pain splitting his skull. The ground— his eyes—stained scarlet.

...thought we had them, but their leader was...unearthly.

They escaped? Contempt asked, sounding as if he already knew the answer.

No. All dead, at too great a cost.

His heart clenched. He moaned and fought his sheets. They tightened around him. Long, bony fingers pressed against his forehead. He couldn't force his eyes open.

This ring will help. Contempt again. *Be sure he keeps it close. For all your failings, you are regrettably in the best position to keep him safe. For now.*

Your faith astounds me, Sedick.

Consciousness—*sound*—faded away. Only memories remained, swirling into nothingness. Glimpses of a smile and green eyes faded too fast for him to catch. A woman wreathed in golden flames, humming to him.

All will be well.

All will be well.

His head throbbed. The pressure nearly drove his eyes from their sockets. The musky candles on the dining table and dusty hearth fire only exacerbated the pounding in his head. He shifted on his makeshift bed and twisted the two rings strung around his neck to distract himself.

The only relief was a cool whisper of a breeze between the warped wooden slats of the nearby window. It brushed the bandages pulled tight around his head and cooled the sweat beneath them. He itched to uncover the window entirely—let the air soothe every bit of him, from the top of his head to the burn scars across his torso— but he refrained. The frosty air might make Linae sick.

As if on cue, a wail sounded from the hallway. Hasty footsteps went to Linae's aid.

"Hush, my love," a woman said. "What is all this fuss about?"

Lady Vinea crept past the dining room, her tiny daughter cradled against her chest. She bounced Linae as she wove between the myriad of trunks, sacks, and other belongings scattered across the floor. Her well-worn silk skirts brushed the dust from the floor in swirling clouds. She hummed softly as she tucked blankets more tightly around the infant.

He had developed a deep respect toward the lady of the house over the few days he had regained consciousness. She had a warmth and a sort of...familial comfort about her.

The humming stopped when she looked up and saw him. She peered at him for a few moments before she drew back. "Oh! I didn't realize you were awake! Your bandages make it hard to..." She stopped herself and shook her head. "I'm sorry. Did Linae wake you?" She should have been more worried about her own sleep rather than his, judging by the dark circles beneath her eyes. But she wasn't. She cared more for a stranger than she did herself.

He shook his head at her question and immediately regretted it. Arcs of pain crackled through his spine and behind his eyes. He blinked them back as best he could. "Don't worry about me." He winced at his voice; it sounded like he had eaten glass.

Lady Vinea watched him with a small smile on her face. "You've come into my care on the verge of death and with no memories. I can't help but worry."

His stomach twisted at the reminder.

She gestured with an elbow to the rings around his neck. "Does that help?"

A smile pulled too tight on his cheeks. "Not yet," he said. He touched the larger ring, thick and gold and gaudy, centered around an ugly black stone. Lady Vinea's husband, General Laire, had told him one of the king's warlocks had made it; a man named Sedick that specialized in memory magic, whatever that meant. It was supposed to help recover his memories so long as he kept it around his neck. Skepticism and a hint of unease lingered with him at the prospect, though. Nightmares of whispered words and shattered visions still plagued him. And new monsters haunted him in the night, leaving him breathless and petrified. Surely a magic ring meant to help would not leave him so utterly terrified. But he was desperate enough to try anything, no matter the nightmares. A lifetime's worth of memories was too precious to sacrifice to fear.

He absently toyed with the leather strap around his neck until the smaller ring fell into his palm, a silver band with simple filigree across it and curling words on the inner rim. He couldn't read the language, though. According to Lady Vinea, Laire had found him with it. Touching it calmed the night terrors.

Lady Vinea tapped his foot with hers. "Don't fret. Lord Sedick is an odious man by nature, but Laire and I can both attest to his magic's effectiveness." She brushed the side of her palm around Linae's face, her eyes warm with adoration.

"I have to agree, much to my chagrin." General Laire Baison entered the room.

He got to his feet and nodded, blinking back the spots that swam in his eyes. Uneasy trepidation laced his veins, but he fought it back. This man had *saved* him. Lady Vinea tried to get him to sit again, worried about his injuries, but he assured her he was fine. He greeted General Laire with a small bow.

Laire stood a good head and shoulder above his wife and stooped to kiss her. He then cooed at his daughter. Linae squealed in delight and pulled on his short, silver-flecked beard. Laire chuckled. Linae curled her fist around his finger. "I'm happy to see you up and about, my boy," Laire said to his guest. "Mace wounds are serious business and have killed more men than I can count. You're lucky to be alive. How do you feel?"

He shuffled his feet and touched the bandages on his head, trying to pull a smile. Why couldn't he look him in the eyes? "Sore, sir."

Laire straightened and looked at him fully. "Is that all?"

He glanced between Laire and Vinea, not sure how to respond. They had both been so kind. How could he say it? Did he *want* to say it? He stretched a smile in his aching cheeks. "I'm not sure I know what else there *could* be. A man with no name can't ask for much." He chuckled, but it sounded hollow even to his own ears.

"What about Tristan?"

Both men looked at Lady Vinea with surprise. Laire's shock mingled with...something else. He put a hand on her arm in a silent signal, but she ignored him. She shifted Linae and smiled. "What if we call you Tristan? It's what we would have named our son if we had one."

His mouth fell open. A thousand emotions clamored for space all at once. He glanced to Laire for guidance on how he should answer, but Laire's expression was unreadable. "Why—What have I done to deserve such an honor?"

Lady Vinea took his hand and squeezed it. "No one deserves to be alone. We may not be the most well-to-do family, but we can be yours if you'll have us."

He didn't know how to respond. His gut squirmed with discomfort, even as tears of gratitude filled his eyes. A new family? He hadn't grieved the loss of his old one, if he even had one. Deep down, he wanted to believe he still did; that they were doing everything they could to find him. But belief was a shadow of reality. Kind, generous people wanted to be part of his life. *Now.* In the real world. Did he dare push that aside for only a sliver of hope?

He brushed the moisture from his eyes. "I'm...*honored.* But I couldn't possibly take the name. If you have a son, then what—"

"We won't." Lady Vinea curled Linae closer to her. She stroked the infant's fine hairs. "One was miracle enough."

He didn't know what else to say. He was quickly running out of polite excuses. *Why* did he need excuses? He couldn't say. Something filled him with unease as if he were treading places he didn't belong. But did someone with no memory belong anywhere?

General Laire must have sensed his hesitation and cleared his throat. "Take the name." He clapped a hand on his shoulder. "You'll need one if you plan to become a soldier here."

He recoiled. "A *soldier*?"

Linae fussed in her blankets. Lady Vinea bounced her and excused herself to their back rooms, casting her husband a parting, questioning glance.

He—*Tristan,* he supposed he should start calling himself, since they were so insistent—looked at General Laire in consternation, trying not to let his unease win out. More indiscernible emotions swept through him. He didn't belong here. He didn't belong with Laire. Something not quite right swirled about the general—he couldn't place what—but it made him want to *get out.* He shoved the feelings aside. His battered mind had already played too many games with him. "You want *me* to be a soldier?" Tristan asked. "When I don't even know who I am? Or what you fight for?"

"That part's easy." Laire waved his hand dismissively. "We fight for freedom from the monsters that walk among us. We will rid Loralan of the Ancient Races' evils and their foul magic." Laire looked at him with somber kindness. "And what better way to find out who you are than in fulfilling a purpose?"

Tristan rubbed his thumb over the silver ring, trying to ignore the rushing in his ears. Too fast. This was all too much, too fast. "I'm sure there could be other ways—"

"What else did you plan to do?"

"I...well..." An excellent question that he should have had a response to. Vague snippets of something floated through his mind. "I was hoping to find out who I was. See if those memories are still out there somewhere. Maybe."

Laire leaned against a wall, arms folded and face unreadable again. "Where would you start?"

"Maybe you could tell me about the Dragon Scales?" Tristan couldn't say why that name had stuck with him, but it floated ever present in the back of his mind. Someone had mentioned it. And he could have sworn it had been Laire.

A shadow crossed Laire's face, and his brow furrowed. "The Dragon Scales? As in the fairy tale?"

All the breath fled from Tristan's lungs. No. It *couldn't* be a fairy tale. "The what?" He kept his voice light, but inside his stomach churned.

"The Dragon Scales is a place of lore that doesn't exist. Said to be the safest, fastest path between the Ancient Lands and Loralan's capital. It's a wide valley littered with pockets of the sea, scattered about like so many fallen dragon scales."

Something leaped in Tristan. Voices and images that he couldn't quite see or hear. A deeper ache settled on his bandaged head, and orange-tinged dread settled in with his hope. He fumbled with his rings. They were both hot to the touch. The Dragon Scales *had* to be what he was looking for.

"Only problem with the place is the unholy storm that shields it from outsiders all but one week out of the year. Manifestation of some goddess' wrath or some nonsense like that." He picked at his teeth. "All too convenient an excuse for why nobody's found it if you ask me."

Tristan rubbed his forearm, trying to play off the desperation building in his stomach. "So it's not real?"

"No more real than an elf's love." Laire spat at the floor and ground it out with his boot. "And I know all too well that *that* is nothing but fantasy." He pushed himself away from the wall. "I'm sorry I couldn't be more help on that front. But my offer still stands. You are welcome to stay here at Lorate."

Tristan curled his rings in his fingers, his head spinning, and said nothing. He couldn't articulate the emotions swirling through him like a building storm.

Laire placed a warm hand on his shoulder and grounded him from his panic. At least for a moment. "Let me reword it this way; family is hard to find. When you have it, never let go." His focus slipped to somewhere far beyond the fort, lost in a world Tristan couldn't see.

Tristan knew he was trying to help, and he was grateful for it, but Laire's words drilled deep into his chest, carving more wounds on his heart.

Laire blinked and returned to the moment. "Vinea and I only transferred a few days ago. It's a temporary placement, but it will be home to us for a while." A yawn leeched itself from his throat. "I can't attest to the men yet, but I can attest to myself. I will give you a home and a purpose and a family here." He stood in the doorway, the picture of strength and benevolence. "Besides, where else could you go?"

Those words shot Tristan in the chest as true as any arrow. He staggered from their force. A lump formed in his throat. He looked at the dusty floors, at the footprints and scuff marks and swirls from the wind blowing through doors and windows. Even the floor knew its past better than he did. He couldn't bring himself to respond to General Laire's question, even though he knew there could only be one answer. What good was choice when he had only one option, anyway?

General Laire nodded once as if taking his silence for consent. "Come on." He glanced through the window slat gaps. "It's late, but I'm sure men will be in the mess hall. Let's have you meet the rest of your new family."

Laire strode into the night. Tristan followed, wishing he could go back to an hour ago when he still had power over his life. He winced at how ungrateful those thoughts sounded.

The breeze that had teased him through the dining window slats washed over him the moment he stepped outside, ruffling his dark hair not pinned down by bandages and plucking his tunic. He imagined being somewhere—anywhere—else. A place he felt at home; where he knew himself and could make his own choices.

General Laire crossed the fort yard to a squat, ramshackle building. Lantern light glowed through the rough-hewn wooden wall's gaps. Tristan followed, unsure if the light seemed inviting or like the glint of an ancient, many-eyed monster ready to swallow him.

The room inside was sparse but clean. Rows of simple wooden benches and tables lined the wall. A small fireplace crackled in the back. Ten men huddled around it while another lounged in the corner. They nursed drinks and chatted amongst themselves. Quiet chuckles rumbled through the room. The one in the corner—a narrow-waisted, broad-shouldered man who even sitting towered over the other men —seemed content to watch from beneath his mane of sandy hair. The warmth and calm enveloped Tristan. *Could* this become home?

His hope fizzled the moment the men caught sight of him and Laire in the doorway. The temperature dropped as all conversations stopped. They only stared. Cold. Unfeeling. Barely veiled hostility. Tristan's mouth ran dry. His gut shrunk. He wanted nothing more than to disappear.

Laire straightened to his full height and met their stares. "I have not officially introduced myself yet. I am General Laire Baison. As I'm sure you're aware, King Osmen has transferred me to replace General Tal Hasson."

They said nothing.

General Laire seemed unfazed. "I trust we'll know each other better in time. I must return to help get my family settled, so I can't join you tonight, but this man will." He dropped his hand on Tristan's shoulder. "He is a fighter. Please take good care of him." He leaned closer to Tristan and spoke only to him. "You'll be all right. You can't survive what you have without the grit to survive more." With that, he left.

Tristan nodded to the room with a tight smile and tripped into a seat, wishing he could vanish. He hadn't been prepared to be thrown to the wolves all on his own.

The murmuring began.

"The invader has a pet, does he?"

"General Tal would never pick favorites."

"Bet the bandages are so he can spy on us better. I can't hardly see his eyes."

"That's the stupidest thing I've ever heard. That's not how spying works."

"*You* tell me who he is, then!"

"Bet you he's one of those monsters in disguise."

"An Ancient One wouldn't want us!"

"How do you know? They're *monsters*! They do what they want!"

Tristan tried to ignore them. Sister Earth, he tried. But their words pounded on his head like the mace that nearly killed him. Who was he? Who *was* he? He didn't know. He could be anything. That was the terror of nothingness. The images of his dreams marched through his mind like a parade of horror. An empty wasteland. Howls and shrieks. Black, soulless eyes as wide as his face. Rows upon rows of teeth. Spindle-like fingers reaching for his throat.

Who are you? They hissed in time with the surrounding murmurs. *Who are you?*

He didn't know. *He didn't know!*

Tristan put his head in his hands, trying not to shake. He tugged feverishly at the gaudy gold ring. It had to show him something. It had to.

Nothing.

The rush of hissing inner voices grew with the surrounding chatter. *Spy. Assassin. Murderer. Enemy. Monster.* The words swirled in his mind until he heard nothing else.

Someone clattered into the seat across from him. It jolted the table and broke him from his spiral.

He looked up. The loner from earlier—the sandy-haired young man with shoulders nearly as wide as the bench—had sat across from him. He munched slowly on a piece of toasted bread and studied Tristan.

Tristan fidgeted in his seat. What did the newcomer want? What did *any*one want from him? He had nothing to offer himself, much less anyone else. Couldn't they let him wallow in peace?

"So, who are you?" the man asked.

Tristan broke.

"I don't *know!*" He slammed his hands on the table. "Why don't you ask everyone else since they're so keen to pass judgment?" The room fell silent. His mind did not. He glared at the watching men as their lingering whispers plowed wounds in his thoughts. They averted their gazes, shoulders hunched. He gained no small satisfaction from their discomfort. "My memory's gone. Taken. I don't know anything." The barbs in his voice didn't mask the brokenness. He studied his palms, where he had calluses at the base of each finger. He didn't know where he'd gotten them. Such a small, stupid thing he wished he knew.

The man across from him kicked his feet up. "If *you* don't know anything about yourself," he ate another bite, crumbs spewing like sparks, "what makes you think these idiots do?"

Tristan gaped at him. He opened and closed his mouth like some demented fish as his halted thoughts tried to form words with no success. "What?"

The man smiled. "You are the only person who knows you the best. Don't let them choose who you are. You're capable enough to do that yourself."

Tristan could only sit there with his jaw dangled open. The silence stretched on as his thoughts collided to process the man's words.

A deranged laugh spilled from his mouth. He couldn't help himself. The stranger's notion had been so unexpected. So needed. All his pent-up emotions and uncertainty tumbled out in an instant. Once he started, he couldn't stop. Rolling, choking from his throat, the laughter washed away the dark thoughts swirling in his mind. Tears pricked his eyes. From relief or mirth, he couldn't tell. "You... you sound like an eighty-year-old man," he wheezed. He couldn't say anything else. Could not express the other emotions fizzing through his body.

"And you sound like a lunatic." The man grinned. "Just my kind of person." He brushed the crumbs off his tunic and extended his hand. "I'm Styrax Glanson. Traveling sage. Resident water enthusiast. Collector of lost souls." He raised an eyebrow. "And you are?"

"I'm...not a sage. Or a lunatic. Maybe." Tristan flicked the moisture from his eyes. "Still trying to figure the rest out." He shook Styrax's hand with a wan smile. "They call me Tristan."

CHAPTER
TWO

A roar of triumph swelled from General Shadowalker's soldiers as the golden canopies of the Golden Grove came into view, bathed in the mist of azure waterfalls. Swarms of pygmy dragons took to the sky from their wildflower nests, glittering in a riot of jewel tones. They winged through the Golden Grove's ancient trunks, dodging through doors and windows that had been grown inside the gold and silver-veined wood. One of the last bastions of magic left. If it were to fall, the thrice-accursed war would be lost.

The anticipation and excitement resonated so deeply through the soldiers they practically hummed. Another victory. Another haul of food for the rebellion and all those that relied on it. The parties alone would last well into the night, flooded with cheap ale and high spirits.

Aspen leaned against her saddle pommel and watched her troops. They eyed her beneath their leather helms, awaiting that final order before they could consider their mission complete. None of them broke formation, but their longing was palpable. She let the silence drag on, seeing if any of them would break. They didn't.

Aspen's heart swelled with pride, and she allowed herself a small smile. "Go on, then," she said.

The deluge would have been no greater if she had thrown open a dam. The soldiers' whoops knocked birds scattering into the fading evening sky and rattled the trees' golden leaves. Even though she had released them of duty, they each stopped first to salute her, two fingers to their lips, before making their way into the village. Elves—mostly elderly with stooped backs and white hair, or children clutching to the hems of robes—poured from their homes and welcomed the soldiers back with hugs and cheers and offerings of food. None of the soldiers accepted the food—it was too precious a commodity to take from their own people—but the gesture was appreciated.

Aspen watched as groups laughed together and pantomimed their success. Her heart warmed in her chest. Twenty years of war had taken many things, but it was moments like that that made her remember their sacrifice was worth it.

"They're a little livelier than usual tonight, wouldn't you say?"

Aspen turned to her cousin, Ash, who had sidled her mount beside hers. The trees' golden glow haloed her honey-blonde braid and small face smudged with dirt from their journey. Her gray-green eyes were nearly the same color as the feather fletches on the quiver of arrows she carried across her back. Aspen's mount, Stormbreaker —a massive, dapple-gray unicorn—shifted beneath her, snorting and tossing his head in greeting to Ash's.

Aspen scratched him beneath his mane. "As they should be. A victory against the soldiers at Bael is no small feat."

"Helped in no small part by the legendary General Shadowalker, of course." Ash looked at her with an impish grin and waggled an eyebrow.

Aspen rolled her eyes. "Perhaps. But now *Aspen Tanner* is going to bed."

"Good. If you wake up before noon tomorrow, I'll tie you to the bed until you get some proper rest."

"I don't doubt it." Aspen clicked to Stormbreaker and away they went. She waved to Ash over her shoulder.

She followed the outskirts of the Golden Grove proper, nodding to elves as she passed. The older ones eyed her with disdain and stepped back a few paces as if she might taint them. Whispers of *half-blood curse* and *coward* followed in their wake. The children waved and offered hay to Stormbreaker. They gave Aspen hope.

She stopped at a small hut nestled just outside of the golden tree line. Vines climbed their way up the walls and had nestled beneath the shingles, and cobwebs had gathered in the corners of the windows and doorway.

A hollow pit formed in Aspen's stomach even as relief washed through her. She was home, but it was an empty one devoid of the life and color that had once filled every corner of the clearing.

Aspen dismounted and unsaddled Stormbreaker. She gave him a thorough brush down until his silver coat shimmered and then sent him on his way to roam where he pleased. He whiffled at her cheek before trotting into the trees to find his herd.

Aspen watched him go and then waited for the moment she had watched from her bedroom window nearly every night of her life.

The sun dipped behind the Architect's Heart, the mountain range shaped in a protective ring around the Golden Grove, and a great sigh went up from the trees. The leaves shimmered and rustled, and their golden light dimmed. A few moments later, the first moonbeams caressed the trees, and the leaves shed their golden coats. Golden hues faded to silver in the moon's embrace and drowned the grove in their brilliance.

Whenever you're here to see the leaves turn from gold to silver, you'll know you're home.

Aspen rubbed the base of her left thumb, the mark beneath her bracer burning. She remembered the boy that had told her that. Remembered the promise they had made to each other.

And how she had shattered that promise.

Aspen trudged through her door, knapsack weighing on her

shoulders and sword heavy at her side as the nostalgia turned bitter in her mouth.

The silver leaves gilded every edge of her cottage. Dazzling specks of dust were wisping away from the open door. She grimaced and slammed the door against the light, drew the curtains tight, and basked in the blessed dark. She could forget for a moment the dust that had built up over her months of absence, that she had left a dish or two in the sink, and that she was alone in a home that had once been full of life.

Aspen unbuckled her sword from its sheath and hung it in its place against the wall. Her knapsack she dropped to the floor without preamble, and then she slumped into her chair next to the cold hearth. She *could* have lit it. She could have lit a candle, at the very least, but the night was warm, the hour too late, and the price of getting up was far too great.

Now that she had settled in, though, the ache of battle crept through her bones. The jagged wound that ran from her right shoulder to her left hip throbbed. She'd have to have Ash help her with some salve eventually.

Aspen flexed her shoulders and stretched her neck. Despite her soldiers' success, a worm of worry crept at the corners of her mind. She tried to shake it off. The ambush at Bael had been as fruitful as she had hoped. They had secured more supplies for the rebellion, caused some mayhem, and had gotten away with no casualties. On either side. A perfect mission.

And yet, the worry remained. She had a knapsack weighed down by snatches of paper, clustered together from correspondents across Loralan. Nothing significant. Nothing alarming. Save for a single name woven through them. Lorate. A nothing fort in a tiny village, unimportant to the rest of the world.

Weariness settled across Aspen's bones. "We'll settle it tomorrow," she said to herself.

She hummed to herself as the blanket of sleep hovered over her eyes. When was the last time she slept? She couldn't remember. She ought to get into a proper bed. It wouldn't do to be sore for roll-call the following morning. She had to...

Sleep...

She was nearly there when someone rapped on her door. "Aspen?"

Aspen rolled her eyes to the ceiling and curbed a sigh. Maybe if she didn't move, they'd look for her somewhere else and leave her in peace.

Another knock. "I know you can't let a mouse by without waking up, Aspen. I hate to interrupt you, but we have to talk."

Aspen padded to the door with a groan. "Ash, you're *absolutely certain* this couldn't have waited until morning?"

Ash folded her arms and raised an eyebrow. "Considering I usually have to *force* you to sleep, you think I would do this if it was avoidable?"

Aspen opened the door wider with another sigh. "I *suppose* you can come in, then."

"As if you could stop me." Ash slid past her with a smile. "I'd light a fire to brighten up this den of yours, but we don't have time for that." She lit a few candles and sat down. The cheeriness melted from her face the moment Aspen closed the door. Concern pulled tight around her mouth and eyes.

Aspen edged into the seat across from her, a thousand thoughts circling through her mind. "What's wrong?"

Ash steepled her fingers and pressed them against her lips. She watched Aspen, eyes darting back and forth. Studying her for who knew what. Aspen had long since learned the art of silence, but something about Ash's piercing, gray-green gaze was always too much for her. She shifted in her chair as much as she could stand before finally snapping.

"*What?*"

Ash leaned forward, covering her face with her hands. "There's really no good way to tell you," she said into her palms. She slid her hands away from her face and pulled her hair back tight. "There's been another prince sighting."

Aspen's heart plummeted to her seat. She didn't move. Didn't breathe. A lump caught in her throat and choked her. Stars swam in her vision as her ears rang and blood fled from her face. All thoughts of sleep vanished in a second.

"*No,*" she said, not realizing it had been audible. Not again. She couldn't do this again. How many times now? Five? Six? She had lost count against the raw, aching heartache that drained the lifeblood from her veins. She couldn't look at another pair of too-blue eyes— another smile not quite crooked enough. Each hope dashed to pieces against the bitter rocks of reality. "He's dead, Ash." The croak finally made it from her constricted throat. "Haven't we been through enough to know? Haven't *I*?"

"Aspen, I know. Sweet Sister Earth, I know." Ash leaned back in her chair, eyes cloudy as she watched the candles' dancing flames. "I hate to bring this to you. Especially when the last one was so..." She glanced at Aspen, searching for a word. Probably one that would best spare her feelings.

Aspen was too old to be coddled. "Disastrous? Horrific? Catastrophic in every way because I let my desperation cloud my judgment?"

"I suppose that's...several ways to put it," Ash said.

Aspen massaged the bridge of her nose, a dull ache settling in behind her right eye. "Have them send someone else. Or better yet, no one at all. Can't they let his memory finally rest in peace?" She bit back the emotion that threatened to reach her voice.

"He's the only one that can lay claim to the throne and give us legitimacy," Ash said with regret. "We have to take any chance we can to find him." She looked at Aspen. Aspen's inner hurt was reflected in her face. "And you are the only one we can trust with certainty to get it right."

Aspen shut her eyes; closed out the world for two moments. The only moments she could spare. She cursed to herself. "I won't do it, Ash. If someone wants to bring him to me, fine."

Ash closed her eyes, the pain evident on her face. "You know that's not how this works."

"Make due, then." Aspen knew she was putting Ash in an impossible position. She knew this wasn't her fault. But Aspen could not do it anymore. To herself or anyone else. "I have soldiers to train here, and I'm sure orders will come from Dallowyn any day now of where he wants us next."

"They could do without you for a few days. Lorate's only a three day's ride at—"

"*Lorate?*" Aspen's stomach plummeted. Not Lorate again. That had been another dread she had hoped to bury. Aspen crossed the room to her knapsack, despite her aching joints, and retrieved her satchel of messenger pigeon scrolls. She dug through them until she retrieved a bundle tied together. All in various handwriting. She sat down again and studied them in the candlelight. "Why does that place keep coming up?"

Ash craned her neck to see. "What is it?"

"Messages from the scouts. Several of them have made passing remarks about Lorate; said that it's come up in several conversations across the kingdom. Nothing substantial or out of the ordinary, but this many at once…"

Ash crouched next to her and ran her fingers over the scrolls. "Maybe it's a sign?"

Aspen snorted. "Doubtful. But it warrants some extra study, at least."

"I'd say quite a *lot* of things require further study, namely your ability to control your soldiers, oh *esteemed* General."

Aspen shut her eyes and inhaled deeply. She needed to employ a guard dog. Or twelve.

"Elder Inula, to what do we owe your visit?" Aspen asked as she glanced to the doorway where a new visitor had emerged.

The tall, regal elf glowered beneath the copper circlet on her brow. The flaxen tresses combed past her knees stood in stark relief against her deep green robes, and she clasped her long, graceful fingers in front of her. "I thought you ought to know already," she said, her green eyes dim with aloof disgust. "General Shadowalker has eyes and ears everywhere, does she not?"

"None where your oversized nose can't reach, apparently," Ash grumbled to herself.

Inula's eyes narrowed. "Did you have something you wished to share, Ash?"

Ash beamed a dazzling mockery of a smile. "Nothing at all, mother, except to tell you how radiantly spiteful you look this evening."

Inula's grasped hands tightened. "I told you never to call me that."

"Radiant?" Ash asked airily.

"*Mother.*"

"Oh, but I thought you were all about titles?" Ash placed her hand on her chest, her face screwed up in exaggerated apology. "Or is that only for ones you feel you've earned?"

Aspen withheld a snort.

"Enough, *whelp*," Inula said. "You are lucky I allow your presence here at all after your banishment." She turned to Aspen, cutting Ash out of the conversation. Ash made a face and a few unsavory gestures. "You are to go to Lorate at once," Inula said.

A new wave of dread settled over Aspen. That place again. Her reluctant resolve to go doubled, but she couldn't let Inula know that. "My apologies, but I am otherwise detained. Unless these are orders from General Dallowyn, I'm afraid—"

"They are." Inula handed her a ribbon-bound scroll with a smirk. "His network has uncovered a plan for Lorate to invade the Golden Grove. Heard some fool nobles discussing it over dinner." She brushed an errant strand of hair over her shoulder. "We don't know when or how, but anticipate it will be in the next few months. Although my personal force is formidable, and your soldiers are...*adequate*, they will not match the numbers Osmen will send after us. We must request aid from the Midnight Fens while their gateway is active in Lorate."

Aspen's mouth went dry. An invasion. Already, her mind buzzed with preparations that had to be made. She would have to appoint someone to oversee training and general management while she was gone. Her soldiers would have to give up some of their accommodations to provide room for the Midnight Fens' forces. Food would need to be reallocated—

She shook her head. All that in time. Right now, Lorate was their only path forward. Aspen nodded and took the scroll from Inula. She felt the buzz of protective magic around it. Duplication spell, most likely, in case something were to happen to it.

"We will ride at once," Aspen said, the words dull and lifeless in her mouth.

"No mounts," Inula said.

"You can't be serious!" Ash leaped to her feet, cheeks flushed with outrage. "That's a two-week journey by foot!"

"The Midnight Fens do not tolerate beasts of burden of any kind. It will already be a miracle if they let half-bloods such as *you* in." She looked Aspen and Ash up and down with contempt. "Besides, your mounts have just returned from a long journey. They require their rest."

Ash clenched her fists, her lips pressed tight. "Ah, yes, but the half-bloods are disposable, is that right?"

Aspen clamped a hand around Ash's arm before she could say anything else. "We will leave immediately." She bowed to Inula, the movement stiff and reluctant, and forced Ash out the door.

"Oh, and *General.*"

Aspen stopped with a masterfully concealed sigh but didn't turn around.

"Your purpose here is based solely on your ability to perform. Don't fail us again."

The words fell like death knells on Aspen's ears.

CHAPTER

THREE

The sun shone bright and dirty across Lorate as men trundled about, polishing weapons, sweeping beneath beds, and dusting every surface. Plumes of dust wafted into the sky and swirled with orders and general complaints.

Tristan sat on the stoop of his barracks, scrubbing his saddle. Styrax and a line of five other men sat next to him, all bent to their tasks of scrubbing leather down. Some saddles, some boots, others leather breastplates in various levels of decay.

"Don't understand why we put this show on every six months," one said, splashing a little bit of spittle onto the leather and scrubbing it out. "We all know this place has gone to the roaches."

"Have to impress his *highness* Sedick somehow, don't we?"

"More like his *lowness*," Tristan muttered out of the corner of his mouth to Styrax. "Can't be taller than my hip, can he?"

Styrax snorted and huddled closer over his saddle, trying to hide his laughter.

"No," someone else responded to the original question. "I'd just as soon throw him under a plow and bury him in manure."

They all laughed at that but quieted as one of the captains

strolled by to check their work. Once the captain left, they warmed back to their topic.

"What's he supposed to expect from folks like us, anyway? We all know we're a token fort a nothing more." The other soldier straightened his back and peered down his nose, frowning with mock imperiousness. "Bringing 'hope to the common folk' and becoming 'heroes to the people'," he said in an affected drawl. He dropped the act with a scoff. "What a stinking pile of manure *those* promises were."

Tristan shrugged in reluctant agreement. In the five years he'd been at Lorate, they had not seen a single moment of action. No battles, no rebels; not even a rogue highwayman. Those were reserved for nobles and knights and career soldiers. Not a bunch of rag-tag farmers and merchants. They hadn't been much of anything except a joke to the rest of the King's Men. Their fort inspector, Lord Sedick, always made that abundantly clear when he made his visit every six months. The people of Lorate were supportive and kind, but the rest of the kingdom...Fort Lorate did nothing to help their waning hopes. Tristan couldn't help but wonder why King Osmen had created Lorate in the first place.

"Wet that for me, would you please?" One of the men asked, handing a brush to Styrax. Styrax handed it back sopping wet in the blink of an eye. Tristan couldn't remember seeing him put it in the soap bucket. The other man didn't seem to care that it dripped all over his trousers and went back to work. "You know, when I found out that General Laire used to lead the Vanguard, I was actually *excited.* I thought maybe I *could* learn something. Look where that got me, scrubbing boots that'll never be clean." He motioned to the boots, covered in dust and grime and mold.

"There are better things than learning how to fight," Styrax said, taking a drink from his water skin. "I consider it a blessing that we have that luxury."

"The old sage strikes again," Tristan said with a smirk.

Styrax rolled his eyes.

"I agree with Styrax," one of the others piped in. "I'm *all for* not having to fight a war I didn't start, so long as I and my family get paid for it. There are worse things that could happen."

"Exactly!" the one on the end crowed, setting a breastplate down and moving to the next one. It almost crumbled in his hands. "Like getting caught in General Shadowalker's clutches."

The man with the boots scoffed. "I don't think he exists. What kind of general's never been seen on a battlefield?"

"A coward."

"Nah," the man with the breastplates said, giving up on his pointless task. "He's been plenty successful over the past few years to prove he's real. Did you hear what happened at Gravaym?"

"That's got nothing to do with it! It's all that filthy magic they've got. No wonder they turned on us and started this whole war. We were easy targets!"

Styrax stiffened at Tristan's side. It looked like he meant to say something, but he shook his head and mumbled to himself. "Everyone loves to conveniently forget Brahmon."

Tristan furrowed his brow. "What's Brahmon?"

"A half-blood village. Or it was, until Osmen burned it to the ground. *That* was the start of the war."

Tristan looked askance at Styrax. "How do you know these things?"

Styrax shrugged, his focus far away as he scrubbed aimless circles on his saddle. "I've been around the kingdom a time or two."

The other men continued with their tirade. "It's not fair, them talking through trees and addling people's minds and whatnot. I mean, look at Tristan and what they've done to him! What kind of sane person believes in the Dragon Scales?"

"A smarter one than you, old man!" Tristan threw a rag at his face.

"Tristan! Catch me!"

Tristan hardly had time to register the words before a small blonde girl launched herself into his arms. His freshly cleaned saddle crashed to the dirt, cleaning supplies and all, as he tried to keep her from the same fate. She squealed with glee. That sound alone kept Tristan from begrudging her the two hours of wasted work. He grinned and swung her around a few more times, much to her delight.

The men scoffed at the saddle in the dirt. "Never would have gotten away with that with General Tal around," one of them said, but he still smiled at Tristan and Linae.

Styrax whacked the man over the head with a wet rag. "He wouldn't have let you be a lazy sod, either, so you take your pick!"

"Linae!" Lady Vinea strode across the fort yard as quickly as her skirts allowed, her lips pressed together in the worried sort of irritation only mothers seemed to possess.

"Uh-oh," Tristan said, his hand cupped to Linae's ear conspiratorially. "We might be in trouble."

Linae nodded. "Uh-huh."

Tristan bit back a chuckle and set Linae down.

"Hello, Tristan," Lady Vinea said with a harried smile.

Tristan bowed his head. "Lady Vinea."

She waved her hand. "You know you don't have to call me that." Without skipping a beat, she frowned at her daughter. "Linae, how many times have I told you not to run off?"

"But mama, I—"

"How. Many. Times?"

Linae scuffed her shoe and swished her skirts. "A lot," she grumbled.

"That's right. And do you see the weapons and big animals and people running?"

Tristan saw a much different Fort Lorate than Lady Vinea did; at least the one she tried to portray to her daughter. The "sharp" objects were nothing but a collection of hunting daggers fashioned into a passable warrior's weapon. The soldiers had repurposed their farm horses as battle steeds. Shaggy and sway-backed, some of them might have been big, but they didn't have a mean or rebellious bone in their bodies. And the men...well, he wouldn't bet a copper coin on any foot-races. The fort itself posed more danger than its occupants. Draped in an unholy stench fueled by mounds of manure and other waste, it crawled with rats, mice, roaches, and feral cats. The years hadn't been kind to Fort Lorate.

"This is no place for running wild," Lady Vinea continued. "I need to keep you safe. Now, will you *please* listen to me?"

Linae nodded, her bottom lip quivering. She balled the seam of Tristan's pant leg into her fist.

Lady Vinea sighed, gathered her skirts about her knees, and crouched to meet Linae's eyes. "Do you remember the surprise?"

Linae lit up like a gold coin in the summer sun. She tugged on Tristan's trouser leg. "Mama says you have to come to town with us!" She produced a wilted, half-smashed crown of braided dandelions. "And you have to wear this!"

Lady Vinea passed a hand across her eyes and stood. "I said we would *ask* him if he would come." She looked ruefully at Tristan. "We thought it might be a welcome break from preparations for the esteemed Lord Sedick."

Tristan grimaced. "My lady, I've heard it's best not to invoke such wrathful spirits."

She chuckled. "You are right. Talking about him will only bring him to Lorate faster."

"A fate we all hope to avoid, I'm sure." He bowed his head. "I'd be happy to escort you to town, m'lady." He took the crown from Linae and affixed it atop his head. "And I would be honored to accept this gift, my lady."

Linae beamed with pride.

Tristan smiled and turned back to Lady Vinea. "Would you like for me to invite Styrax as well?"

She hesitated a moment, thoughts flashing through her eyes faster than Tristan could read them. Finally, she splayed her hands and donned another smile. "I don't see why not. He would be welcome. Thank you."

"Of course!" Tristan grinned at Linae and hoisted her onto his shoulder. "Will you help me call for him?"

Linae giggled and nodded.

Tristan cupped one hand around his mouth while he kept Linae steady with the other. She cupped both hands around hers. "Hey, fish boy!" Their shouts floated across the fort yard. Linae broke into more giggles.

Styrax rose from his perch with a world-weary sigh. "What do you two hooligans want? I don't think they quite heard you three towns over."

Tristan waved him over. "We're escorting Lady Vinea and Linae into town. Let's go!"

"Do I have to go with *you*?" Styrax trotted to them with a grin. Styrax was still the only one that actually appeared to belong on a military base, and Tristan tried not to feel too woefully inadequate as he stood next to him.

"Seeing as how they requested me first, I'd say yes, you do," Tristan said. He sniffed in mock disdain and nearly choked on himself.

Styrax elbowed him. "Careful! Don't want to hurt yourself!"

Tristan rolled his eyes and fought back a grin. "My apologies, Lady Vinea, for this empty-headed simpleton. He's not much for educated conversation, but he'll be the perfect sacrifice if we run into any danger."

Styrax bowed low and kissed the back of Linae's hand. She accepted the gesture with the dignity only a five-year-old could muster. Styrax winked at her. He bowed to her mother and offered to take the shopping basket slung over her arm.

Off they went—a grand procession through the rancor of Fort Lorate—with Tristan's saddle and other chores abandoned in the dust. They could wait a few more hours. While Linae giggled on his shoulders, arms outstretched to take in the sun and the sky, Tristan could almost forget the piles of manure and refuse, the rats and roaches in every dark corner, and the omnipresent stench.

Almost.

Tristan, Styrax, and the two ladies left the fort into the soft, broad-leafed forest around it. There was no hint of a breeze, but the trees provided a gentle liveliness. Leaf edges caught the sun's glint, and the drops of light they failed to catch speckled the ground below. The grass sparkled with dew that dampened the squirrels foraging for seeds. They scampered back to the waving canopies, where the melodies of bird-song met in light harmonies that faded into the still sky. The embrace of the Phoenix Ridge mountains surrounded Lorate's valley on every side, and, if the breeze blew just right, the scent of the sea on the southern side of the mountains carried over their peaks.

As the minutes grew long, Linae slumped against Tristan in boredom. When it seemed she couldn't take it any longer, she tugged on tufts of Tristan's dark hair. "Tell me about how Papa found you!"

"Linae," Lady Vinea said, voice sharp with reproach. "It's unkind to demand things, and that story is too violent."

"But, Mama!" Linae protested. "I want to hear about Papa being a hero! You always say he is!"

Lady Vinea watched her with pursed lips and raised eyebrows. A single corner of her mouth twitched, as if she fought back a smile. "You could make an excellent negotiator one day." She brushed back an errant strand of hair with a sigh and brushed dust from her skirts. "You may only hear the story if you ask Tristan *politely*, and only if he agrees to tell it."

Linae craned her neck to look at Tristan upside down. "*Please?*"

Styrax laughed. "How can you say no to that?"

"It is difficult," Lady Vinea said with a wry look.

"How does this sound, oh great mistress, so none of us get in trouble?" Tristan asked Linae as he swooped low under a branch to her delight. "Why don't *you* tell the story?"

"Okay! I'm better at telling it, anyway."

"Linae!" Lady Vinea said with mild horror.

Linae ignored her and puffed up self-importantly. "You were on a secret mission to the most magical place of all—the Dragon Scales! You had to fight *hundreds* of elves, dwarves, and other monsters to protect the kingdom, and you were beating them all!"

Tristan walked a little taller. He liked this version.

"But one snuck up and hit you on the head. You almost died!" She bounced with excitement as she warmed to her favorite part. "But Papa saved the day! He fought them away and brought you home to get better. And now you'll live with us forever and ever!"

"Maybe!" He lifted her from his shoulders. Her foot caught the leather strap around his neck and pulled the two rings it carried from beneath his tunic. "I couldn't have told it better myself! You should be a bard someday." Linae tried to protest her unceremonious dismount, but Tristan told her she was so big and grown up now that she made his shoulders ache. She seemed grudgingly content with his answer and trotted to hold her mother's hand.

"*That* was different," Styrax said with a crooked grin. "I seem to recall fewer 'evil things' and less fighting on your end."

Tristan laughed, keeping the bitterness at bay. "You're lucky you recall anything at all! Better than an empty-headed sap like me." Much as he tried, he couldn't keep all the bitterness from his voice. The scar on the crown of his head burned. He toyed with the rings around his neck. "All I have about that night is whatever Laire told me. That and the Dragon Scales, which he *refuses* to mention."

Styrax gave him a sideways glance. "Are you all right?"

Tristan sighed. Five years around Styrax and his observation skills still surprised him. The knucklehead. "It's stupid."

"Are we ever *not* stupid?"

"No, really. You don't need to worry about it. I'll be fine."

"Tristan," Styrax faced him, walking sideways. "I met you when you were more bandage than face with little improvement since. You can stop the dignified act and just tell me what's wrong."

Tristan rolled his eyes with a self-deprecating smile. "You'll laugh."

"It's my favorite pastime, second only to swimming. Go on."

Tristan rubbed his forehead. "I just..." He shook his head and sighed. "It really is stupid, but when Linae suggested staying forever, it—" he waved abstractly, fishing for the correct word. He didn't find it. "I can't stay here forever. I *can't*. But I also can't help but feel that may be all I'm meant to do."

A squeal from Linae fractured their conversation. "Look, we made it!" She pointed to the smoke and dust rising above the forest canopy. Amiable clatter bounced through the trees.

"This isn't the best time to have a lengthy conversation," Styrax said as his attention darted between Lady Vinea and Linae and Tristan. "But two quick thoughts. One, listening to what everyone says you're 'meant' to do is almost always wrong. Two, don't worry about where you'll end up. You've never been one to settle for mediocrity."

Tristan smiled at him. "Do you practice your sageness, or does it come naturally?"

Styrax bowed with a great sweep of his arms. "Would that I could tell you, but alas, my secrets are mine alone to bear."

Tristan rolled his eyes. "Someday I'll figure it out. You can't hide everything forever."

Styrax smiled, a knowing look behind his eyes. "We'll see."

They trotted to catch up with their charges.

Though smaller than most in Loralan, Lorate's town bustled with all the fervor of a community three times its size. Tristan attributed it to the townsfolk's nature. Descended from Phoenix Ridge miners, Lorate's villagers knew how to enjoy their time in the sun. Luthiers and ale makers rivaled the farmers in numbers. Anything from weddings to blown dandelions could become an excuse for a town-wide celebration. Cheap drinks and even cheaper food flowed in abundance.

At least, that was the Lorate Tristan used to know. Over the past five years, although the bustle and busyness remained, the tone had shifted. Laughter rarely punctuated conversations. The wellsprings of food and drink had faded to occasional trickles. Celebrations became fewer each year.

Linae brushed past Tristan as she ran to the center market of town in pursuit of a group of children chasing a honey-colored squirrel. Lady Vinea tried to call her back to no avail. Tristan snapped from his haze.

"I'll keep close to her," Tristan assured Lady Vinea, trying to dismiss the unsettled feeling in his stomach. "Styrax can help with your shopping."

"What if *I* wanted to watch Linae?"

"No!" Lady Vinea glanced around the square and up at the rooftops, eyes darting from one building to the next. After a few moments, she realized Tristan and Styrax were watching her, taken aback by her tone. "Oh! I apologize. Styrax, I hope you know that that was not a reflection on your character at all." She touched his shoulder briefly in apology. "I would just so appreciate it if you could come help me, and if Tristan stayed here in the square."

Tristan and Styrax shared confused looks but shrugged at each other.

"Absolutely, my lady," Styrax said. "Whatever you need."

Lady Vinea smiled. "Thank you." She turned to Tristan. "And thank you, too. I'm sorry she insists on being such a whirlwind. Just stay in the square, and I'm sure she'll be fine."

"Not to worry." Tristan waved and loped after Linae, smirking at Styrax's silent dismay at being the pack-mule.

Shop owners called to him as he passed.

"Morning, Tristan!"

"Good to see you!"

"Any luck finding the Dragon Scales? I heard it's hiding out with a group of friendly elves." Uproarious laughter followed the remark.

Tristan smiled and waved. "Not as much luck as you have finding the bottom of your tankard!"

Another roar of laughter from onlookers as the man sulked.

Tristan found Linae entrenched in a passionate debate between tag or hide and seek. She clenched the squirrel to her chest as it tried to escape. The poor thing's eyes looked ready to pop from its skull. Linae nuzzled her face into it, blissfully unaware of its plight.

Tristan leaned against a nearby building to watch. Linae was fine. No point in interfering with her fun.

"...Don't understand why it's gone on so long."

The voices of two women—probably hawkers for the stall by how well their voices carried—drifted to Tristan as he sat at the wall. He glanced their way. One younger woman with a riot of freckles across her face brushed the dust from her vegetables as she chatted with the portly, graying baker beside her.

"Twenty-years since the Day of Bluest Blood... I'm not sure how many more times I can raise my prices before people accuse me of robbery!"

The baker wiped the hair from her face, leaving a smudge of flour on her temple. "We've all had to adjust to the war. If you need anyone to blame, blame the rebellion! Their prince died in battle years ago. They don't even have a claim to the throne anymore, but they still fight anyway and prolong this mess. Stupid beasts, the lot of them."

"Finest potatoes this side of the Phoenix Ridges! A dozen per copper!" The freckled woman frowned and put her potato back in its stacks while a group of people passed her by. "They never found the prince's body, though."

"They're just saying that to keep us guessing," the baker said through smiling teeth as she accepted a coin from a passerby and handed him a loaf of bread. "They're trying to hold out long enough to wear us out."

"They're doing a good job of it." She nodded to the group of children Linae played with. Her freckles creased. "I'd sign a peace treaty right now if it kept those little ones away from war."

"Just wait until you met the Ancient Races in person. You wouldn't be so eager to have anything to do with them, then."

Their chatter fell away to mild-mannered bickering. Tristan relaxed the hand he didn't know he'd clenched.

King Osmen had established Fort Lorate as a morale boost for Loralan's commoners. But a single gesture couldn't erase twenty years of pain. These people needed more. They needed an end to the bloodshed. Tristan wished he could do more than sit in a useless, backwater fort and play soldier.

He stewed over that, watching Linae play through the merchant stalls, until Lady Vinea and Styrax—overburdened with fresh food and yards of textiles—came to fetch them. Lady Vinea smiled until she saw Linae. "*What* is in your hand?"

"A squirrel!"

While Lady Vinea haggled with her daughter to let the rodent go, Tristan helped divide Styrax's load. Styrax made grand theatrics of his broken back and splayed knees from all the work he'd done. Tristan rolled his eyes.

Lady Vinea's and Linae's argument ended when the squirrel finally extricated itself from the girl's clutches and scurried off. Lady Vinea snatched Linae's hand before she could chase it, and away they went. Tristan and Styrax hurried to catch up.

As they left, Tristan brushed against someone in the crowd. He turned to apologize, but the words froze in his throat. A pair of green eyes framed by dark curls looked back at him, stunned. His heart clenched. The crowd continued to part around him, but for a moment, time froze for him. Not moving. Not breathing. An inexplicable feeling came over him as if he'd watched the world turn from silver to gold in an instant. A feeling of *home* washed over him.

"Who—?" Before the word finished, she was gone. She'd slipped into the crowd and away from him. "Wait!"

Useless. She had already disappeared from view. He stood in the crowd, staring at the spot he had last seen her. No. No, she couldn't be gone. There had been *something* there. Nostalgia. A memory? His heart leapt to his throat at the thought. He had to find her. For the first time in five years, something from his past stirred within him. He couldn't let her go so easily.

He was about to dive back into the crowd when a tiny hand grabbed his. "Tristan, come on! Momma says it's time to go!"

"But...I..." Tristan scoured the crowd again, his heart feeling like it might shatter. The blood drained from his face. How could he have lost something so important so quickly? He couldn't have imagined it, could he?

"Tristan, come on!"

He nodded mutely, looking one last time. Nothing.

"Tristan!"

He looked at her and smiled, even though it felt hollow. "All right. All right, I'm coming. Let's go home." He left, feeling like he had abandoned a piece of himself in that square that he would never get back.

FOUR

Aspen drummed her fingers on a rock outcropping as she looked across the sleepy town below. Nestled snugly in rolling fields, with jagged, barren mountains as sentinels on three sides, she could see why the war had failed to extend its reach here. So secluded. Laughter filtered through the treetops as smoke from cooking fires mingled with the skies overhead. The clouds seemed a little brighter than the ones over the front lines, ripe with smoke and blood. She wondered how long this little town would stay that way.

The sun warmed her back and a cool wind brushed across her face. She closed her eyes and basked in the quiet she knew could not last. It seemed the war would leave no village unspoiled.

Ash rose to her feet behind Aspen, arrows rattling in her quiver as she strung her bow on her back. "Chaedra's here," she said.

Aspen rose just as the woman crested the hill. Dark-skinned and light-eyed, Chaedra blended well with the rest of the townsfolk on this side of Loralan. Her quick smile made her welcoming, her attentiveness trustworthy, and her loyalty to the Prince's Rebellion deadly.

Chaedra hugged Ash and moved to do the same for Aspen but stopped. Aspen nodded a greeting and her thanks.

Chaedra returned the gesture. "It's *so good* to see you both." She withdrew some scones from her apron and handed them to Ash and Aspen. They were still warm. No matter how delicious they smelled, though, Aspen couldn't stomach a bite. Too much turmoil to think of food. "I heard about Bael," Chaedra said. "Masterful work, as always, General Shadowalker."

Aspen smiled faintly and bobbed her head. "I would be nothing without all the good soldiers crazy enough to listen to me," she said, patting her on the shoulder. "You've done great work here. How are you?"

Chaedra pulled her dark coils from her face, eyes bright. "I'm well. These are good people here." Her smile turned to frown. "Which is what makes your reason for being here even more disturbing." She fumbled through her apron and produced a letter. She handed it to Aspen. "My informant knew nothing about ulterior plans Osmen and his men may have. She gave me this letter, though. The tone is...concerning, to say the least, which is why I contacted you before this whole invasion business, but I couldn't find anything specific in it." She folded her arms across her chest, brows furrowed in concern. "Maybe you'll see something I didn't?"

Aspen took the parchment. "Thank you, Chaedra. And you're sure you can trust this informant?"

"I am. She knows what it's like to lose family to this war. We all do." Chaedra twisted a faded silver band on her finger. "She wants it to end just as much as the rest of us." Chaedra caught Aspen watching her fidget and stopped.

Aspen placed a hand over Chaedra's. Chaedra's promise band—gifted by her fiancé before the King's Men had slaughtered him—was warm against Aspen's palm. "I trust your judgment."

Chaedra nodded. "Thank you, General."

Aspen nodded and tapped the letter. "If I may, I'd like some time to look this over before we head to the village. Might give me a better idea of what I'll be looking for there."

"Oh, uh..." Chaedra cast a sideways glance at Ash. Ash shook her head almost imperceptibly, and then coughed into her fist when she noticed Aspen watching her.

Aspen arched an eyebrow, her stomach already coiling in dread. Ash wouldn't. Not after the conversation they'd had in the Golden Grove. "Is there something I should be aware of, Ash?"

Ash smiled blithely, her eyes never quite meeting Aspen's. "Not at all. It's nothing I haven't already told you."

Apparently, Ash *would*.

Aspen's throat clenched, and she ground her teeth. Her heart beat faster as it sunk to her toes. "I thought I made it *abundantly* clear that we were not to pursue this?"

Ash finally met her gaze, her face forced into neutrality. But Aspen could see regret in the tightness of her jaw. "You did. But I chose to ignore that. For your sake, and for the rebellion's."

Aspen let out a bark of laughter, a shallow husk of a thing that grated on her throat. "*My* sake? Do I not get my own say in the matter?"

Ash sighed and rubbed her brow. "Of course you do, Aspen," she said. "I'm just trying to help."

"Then stop it," Aspen said, more venomous than she had intended. "I don't need that kind of help."

Chaedra had been following the conversation, eyes darting between the two of them as they argued. "If this is about the prin—"

Aspen cast her a look that cut off the words in an instant. She rounded back on Ash. "I am *not* doing this, Ash. Not again."

"You think I would make you do this if I didn't have to?" Ash asked, the words nearly a hiss through clenched teeth. "What other options do we have?"

"*Plenty.*"

Ash shook her head. "No, we don't. Chaedra and I already have it arranged, and—"

Aspen threw her hands up, casting an accusatory look at Chaedra. "Not you, too."

Chaedra lifted her chin but crossed her arms over her chest as if to protect herself. "My informant helped coordinate it. I can't let her risk be pointless. She'll be bringing him to town any moment for you to see him and make your judgment. He'll be wearing a dandelion crown."

Before Aspen could retort, Ash jumped in from the other side. "Four seconds, Aspen. Four seconds for you to say yes or no, and then we—"

"I'll save you those seconds," Aspen said through gritted teeth, blood roaring in her ears. "*No.*"

Ash and Chaedra both fell silent, but Aspen sensed the lingering, stubborn fight in them. That was not a battle she was willing to lose.

"The prince is dead," she said. "No look-alike impostor will change that."

Ash tried again. "Aspen—"

"*No*! No more of this nonsense. We go to town to find what we can about the invasion, and then we *leave*. We will leave ghosts in the past where they belong."

Ash opened her mouth one more time, but Aspen cut her off. "Ash, don't make me pull rank," she said, hating how tired she sounded. "I will if I have to. This is not something I'm willing to negotiate."

Ash pursed her lips, hands clenched around her bow. Chaedra shuffled her feet and fidgeted with her ring. Aspen knew that was as close to a concession as she would get from them. She sighed. "I'm here to do one job, and one job only." She gestured to Chaedra. "Lead on. The sooner we get this over with, the sooner we can work on protecting the Golden Grove."

Chaedra nodded, her jaw tight. "Yes, General."

Aspen inwardly winced. Perhaps she had been too harsh.

Chaedra led them down to the village single file, traversing long-forgotten goat trails. As they shuffled across loose shale and hugged the edge of the mountainside, Ash sidled up to Aspen.

"Aspen, you know I never do anything to hurt you, right?"

"I do." Aspen leapt across a gap in the trail that dropped straight down the mountain to a cluster of pine trees waiting to skewer unsuspecting travelers. "But you know that doesn't keep me from speaking my mind."

"Sister Earth *forbid* you ever stop doing that." Ash followed her across the gap with a rueful smile. "I just can't help but think; what if this next one *was* him? It would make a world of difference for the rebellion and, most importantly, for *you*."

Aspen clenched her teeth against the surge of hope in her chest. Of *course*, it would make a difference. The rebellion would have its legitimacy back. She would have *him* back. Her best friend. The only man she had ever loved. But it was not to be. Five years of bone-aching, mind-numbing heartbreak had taught her that. "I don't have that kind of faith anymore."

She left it at that. Ash's sadness radiated off her, but Aspen ignored it. The silence between them dragged on until they reached the base of the mountain.

"I won't be able to come into the village with you," Chaedra said, brushing dust and leaves from her skirts. "The seamstress is expecting me, and it might draw suspicion for me to accompany you down. Go to the main square. The market gathers there, and it's where you'll find the loosest tongues." She gave Ash one more hug and saluted Aspen, two fingers to her lips. "Go in luck. I will be ready for when you need me again." She left them.

Aspen nodded to Ash, and they separated, one to the eastern part of the village, the other to the west. They'd go from the outer edges and work their way in. Better to divide the workload that way

Aspen tapped her fingers on her thigh as she wound her way through the little fort town. Every so often, she touched the hem of her cowl to keep it in place. It wouldn't do to flash her pointed ears in a place like this. Lorate was too small for a stranger to go completely unnoticed—the whispers and less-than-subtle glances made that all too clear—but the townsfolk played it off as best they could. The market stall owners called a little louder as she passed, their eyes searching for hidden pouches of gold. The regular folk drew further away, their glances taking in her sword and shadowed face. The war might not have sunk its teeth into this tiny corner of the kingdom, but its rumors and worries were still felt.

Whispers followed Aspen as she passed.

"Where's she from?"

"A sorcerer, do you think?"

"What would a sorcerer be doing in a place like this?"

"What do sorcerers do *anywhere?* Still can't understand why his Highness tolerates them. They've got the same magic as all the rest of the beasts."

"But they're *human.* Mostly, anyway, I think. And I'd rather have a human with magic than an elf with one any day."

Aspen flexed her fingers beneath her cloak. *Wonder how they'd feel about something like me with magic?*

She let the thought and the whispers slip from her mind as she crossed through alleyways and stalls. She had to find someone willing to talk to her. This excursion would have all been for nothing if she scared them all away. She had to understand why Osmen would send *this* fort, of all of them, to invade the Golden Grove. And once she understood why, she could stop it. Every step made her thoughts spin faster, exploring plans and options and battling back the anxiety that rippled through her chest like a raging ocean.

"Is there something we can help you with, dear?"

Aspen broke from her thoughts like a drowning man gasping for air. She blinked, and her whirling thoughts subsided for a moment. "Pardon?"

"I'm afraid if you walk one more circle in front of my stall, you might fall over."

Aspen smiled at the portly woman behind the bread counter and her companion in the next stall over. Her cheeks ached as she stretched them into a smile she didn't believe. "My apologies," she said as she approached their stalls. "I wander when I think."

"Ale! Flagon of ale for the lady? Only a sample of what you'll find at the Black Leech, Lorate's finest tavern!" A man in another stall tried to push a flagon to Aspen. She waved it off, but he persisted. "It'll clear those wandering thoughts of yours!"

"Leave the girl alone, Brogan," the older woman said. "Save your energy for the inspector's men." She rolled her eyes. "Never can seem to do anything *but* drink."

Brogan frowned. "You never let me have any fun, Grimmel."

"Not when it comes at the expense of a young lady!"

Aspen's smile softened to something a bit more genuine. She liked this Grimmel. She plunked a coin down and took a loaf of bread from her stall.

"I can't imagine what would have you so deep in thought," Grimmel's stall neighbor, a young woman with dainty freckles dusted across her face, said. "If I had looks like you, all I'd try to do is get some handsome soldier to notice me."

Grimmel gave her a sideways look. "Is that right, Bren?"

Bren's face darkened beneath her freckles. "If I weren't already married, of course." She organized her already tidy potatoes.

Aspen tucked her dark hair deeper into her cloak and fidgeted with the bread in her hand. She tore a piece and took a bite. It melted in her mouth. Her eyelids fluttered as she savored the taste. "Did you say the fort inspector's coming today?"

"Ah, yes. The great Lord Sedick comes to grace us with his *noble* presence," Bren said. She snapped a carrot in half and spit.

A flame of fury roared to life in Aspen's chest. She ground her teeth and tapped the dagger hidden beneath her tunic. What she wouldn't give to sink it into Sedick's unsavory places.

"Hush, Bren." Grimmel's attention darted to Aspen. Perhaps the war had touched them more than she originally thought. "A member of the king's court in our village is a blessing."

Bren scoffed, and her nose curled in disgust. "I'd feel more blessed if he actually paid. And left my sisters alone," she said.

Aspen's lip curled. Sedick left a trail of abominations wherever he went. She listened closely as the women bickered, but nothing useful came from it. She took another bite of her bread and scanned the square, wondering where Ash had gotten to. Ash had to have better luck with her information gathering. But could Lorate *really* be a threat to the Golden Grove, no matter the information they found? Aspen doubted it. But then why send them at all if that was really what Osmen intended to do? There had to be more than just—

All thoughts vanished the moment a man brushed past her. Dark hair, firm jaw, straight nose with a slight bend at the bridge, and a smile that pulled higher at the right than the left. A crown of wilted dandelions rested against his brow. His stride, his smell, his *presence*, felt as familiar as watching the Golden Grove leaves change from silver to gold. A breath of home that flooded her senses. Aspen's heart stopped beating when he turned to look at her. He stopped, confusion flashing across his face.

"Who—?"

No. *No.* Aspen darted behind a crowd of people passing and hid behind Grimmel's stall.

"Wait!" he called.

Aspen didn't respond, her breath ragged in her throat. He looked —He looked just like—

NO. She had told Ash not even an hour ago that she would not do this again. He was dead. He was dead. He was *dead*. No crown of dandelions—no impostors, no matter how convincing—would ever replace him. No matter the stirring in her bones. No matter how desperately she wanted to look again, follow him, and never let him leave her sight. She shook her head. Not now. She couldn't do this now. She had to meet back up with Ash and Chaedra. Had to come up with a plan. She willed—*begged*—him to leave.

Aspen watched him through a slit in stall's wooden planks. He searched the crowd, his expression almost... *broken*. It looked like he might tear through the crowd after her, but a tiny blonde girl appeared and took his hand. She tugged him away, and after a few minutes of coaxing, he finally left, glancing back every few steps, his face ashen.

When he had disappeared into the crowd, Grimmel chuckled and lifted Aspen by the elbow. "I see you've found Fort Lorate's most eligible soldier. Haven't seen someone so overwhelmed by him before, but s'pose everyone's got their limit," she said with a smile. "Best prepare for a fight if you're after him. Every young unmarried woman in town is after him and his friend, Styrax." She cast another sideways look at Bren. "*Married* ones, too."

Bren flushed and crunched a bite off her broken carrot.

"Soldier?" Aspen rasped. Her heart still thudded in her chest and echoed in her ears. Much as she tried not to, she caught herself looking into the crowd for one more glimpse of him. If it really was *him,* he wouldn't be a soldier. Couldn't be. He would rather wallow in the Pit for the rest of eternity.

"I know they don't look the part—no crests or swords—but Tristan and Styrax are the best and brightest. They all are." Her chest had swollen with pride.

"You're sure it's just the *young* ladies with their hearts turned, Grimmel?" Bren asked.

"Oh, you fiend!"

The two women bandied words between them, but Aspen heard none of it. Instead, she stood rooted to the spot, every hair and muscle and fiber electrified. Her tongue swelled in her mouth and nearly choked her. Her arms hung limp and useless at her sides, and locked knees were the only things that kept her legs from collapsing. That and pure force of will. Tristan. That was his name. Of course not *him.* No matter how much they looked alike.

Aspen grit her teeth until they ached. No more of this. She would have no more of it. She turned to the insistent ale hawker, her mouth dry as the soldier's face swam in her eyes. She plunked a coin on his counter. "I'd like that drink now."

He readily obliged and watched open-mouthed as she downed the tankard in one go.

A honey-colored squirrel chittered as it dodged between boots and skirts until it reached Aspen. It crawled the length of Aspen's cloak to her shoulder and settled by her ear.

"What kind of beast is that?" Grimmel asked, eyes wide. "Never seen fur quite like that!"

Aspen smiled again, her cheeks feeling like lead. "She's got a terrible mind disease. Makes her fur this way."

The squirrel squawked in protest and smacked Aspen with its tail. Aspen's smile didn't falter. "Thank you again for the bread and the company. Both were a treat." She tossed another coin each to Bren and Grimmel with shaking hands and then wound her way into the crowd before they could say anything else. When she found a window in the crowd, she slipped into a back alley and swept the squirrel off her shoulder. "It certainly took you long enough."

The squirrel changed, growing and stretching into Ash's corded frame with her honey-colored hair pulled away from her pointed ears, and her bow strapped across her back. "*Mind disease?* Really?"

Aspen shrugged, wishing her fingers would stop trembling.

Ash noticed. "What—?" she stopped herself, her eyes growing wide. "You saw *him*, didn't you?"

"*No!*" Aspen snarled. Too quick.

"You *did*." Ash leaned close and gripped Aspen's arms. "Does he—I mean, is it possible that—?"

"I already told you, *no*." She wrested herself from Ash's grip, wishing she could just as easily break the images from her mind. "Did you hear anything about the invasion?"

Ash sighed and leaned back against the alley wall. She folded her arms as she watched the villagers pass by. "Nothing of value. There's talk of a fort inspection, but it seems a routine thing."

"Did you hear who the inspector is?" Aspen asked, grateful for the distraction.

Ash clenched her fingers around her arms, her fingernails digging furrows in her skin. "My good friend Sedick."

Aspen's righteous fury rose again as she took in the silvery scars along Ash's arms. She knew how many more were hidden beneath her clothes; had seen them as fresh wounds when Ash had escaped Sedick's dungeons. "I wouldn't stop you if you wanted to pay him an unfriendly visit."

"I wouldn't *let* you stop me," Ash said. She smiled, but it never reached her eyes. She leaned against the alley wall and fidgeted with the hem of her cloak. "But it can wait. I have plans for him later." She looked at Aspen. "You're certain it's *this* fort that's assigned the invasion?"

"No, I'm not, and can't fathom why Inula and Dallowyn *are.*" Aspen picked at her thumbnail. "But if neither Chaedra nor her source could refute it, the only option I have is to assume Lorate does intend to invade the Golden Grove."

"Maybe the town is trying to keep it secret?"

"Not likely. These are farmers and common folk." She thought of Grimmel and Bren, their faces so warm and bright as they watched those—she swallowed—those *soldiers.* "They're too proud of those soldiers to keep something like that secret for long."

Ash slid down the wall, resting on her haunches, arms relaxed on her knees. "Then what do we do?"

Aspen gave up on her ragged fingernail. With the proper time, she would have been able to make plans to get the information without unnecessary risks. But time was a long-forgotten luxury. The Midnight Fens' entrance would close any day now, and they needed proper information for their petition.

"I'll have to infiltrate the fort to search for their plans. Their general will have them."

Ash snapped her attention to Aspen. "I'm sorry. I must have misheard you. You must mean *we'll* have to infiltrate?"

Aspen shook her head. "I won't put your life at risk unnecessarily."

Ash pursed her lips. "I'm fairly certain finding plans to protect a defenseless settlement is a necessary risk. Even if it weren't, you think I'll stand by and let you risk *your* life alone?"

"What other choices do we have?"

"*Plenty!*"

Aspen grit her teeth as her words were shot back at her. Ash gave her a look that made it clear that had been her intention. Aspen held up her hands to stave off the tirade she knew Ash was building to. "One is all we can spare. If they catch one of us, the other can still go to the Midnight Fens."

"So let *me* go! I have *years* of experience getting into things I shouldn't!"

Aspen pinched the bridge of her nose. Her head throbbed. "I've fought with you once already today. Please don't make me do it again."

"Well, then, it might do you some good to *listen* every once and a while."

"I am your general, and this is my idea. I have to take the risk."

"No, you don—"

"Ash!" Aspen shrank deeper into the alleyway as passing villagers peered in at them. She waved Ash closer to the shadows. "I'm going. And that's my final decision."

Ash clenched her jaw and looked away. She hated it. Aspen *knew* she hated it. But she couldn't risk her life for a half-baked idea. She couldn't have another death on her conscience.

"I'm following you to the gate, then," Ash said, jaw set tight.

Aspen went to retort, but Ash cut her off. "That is not something I am willing to compromise. I'm *going*, and you can punish me for insubordination all you want."

Aspen shut her eyes, willing her headache to go away. "Fine. I'll allow it. You've gotten away with so much anyway that I'm not sure punishment would do you any good at this point."

"Good. I'm glad we're in agreement." Ash stood, adjusting her bow across her back and brushing off her trousers. "And the *moment* something goes wrong, I'm coming in after you."

Aspen paled. "*No,* you're not. That will be *my* mistake that I need to deal with on my own."

"Nope. It's decided, and you can't stop me," Ash said with a smile.

"I *won't* let you do that."

Ash leaned closed. She clenched Aspen's wrist as if afraid to let go, even as she smiled. "Then don't get caught, and we won't have a problem."

FIVE

It took Tristan hours before he could fall asleep that night. The rest of his day had been spent in a daze trying to understand the phantom woman from the village. Who was she? Why did she seem so familiar? Where had she gone?

And, most importantly, why hadn't he torn the village apart trying to find her?

He had thought to talk to Styrax about it, but something held him back. It felt too sacred, somehow. Like he had to protect every shred of that experience with his very life.

So he did. He went to bed that night with his head still racing until fevered sleep finally took him over, and he drifted into disjointed dreams.

Death called *to him from the waves.*

Crashing. Churning. The waves sang to him by the thousands, their tune rich in wishes and the promise of memories long since forgotten. Glittering and enticing and deadly, they shielded numberless figures— dark and shiftless with no faces to mark them by—from view in their sound. The figures waited, silent and watching, for him to approach. They made no move to approach him, but he knew. He knew they wanted him dead.

His heart thundered against his chest. Frantic. Frightened. Stars bloomed in his vision from soundless flashes of lightning streaking across the sky. Unable to determine why, he searched the hazy grayness for something, anything, to help him against the figures waiting in the waves. Nothing and everything surrounded him at once. And it wanted him obliterated.

His hands shook around a sword hilt. Did he know how to use it? Would it make a difference if he did? Adrenaline roared in his ears and drowned out the sound of his own breath, but never the sound of the waves. They were inevitable. Taunting. Sneering.

Waiting.

A scream cut through the waves. His vision blurred to nothing but shapes and streaks of scarlet. His head split. Pain engulfed him. He battled the death the waves offered, but it was a battle he knew he'd lose.

Something brushed against his vision, stark in its detail against the blurred world. A strand of long dark hair. The corner of an embroidered cloak. A black sliver of stars.

For evergreens and aspen trees.

Calm whispered through his veins—a spring breeze through a winter-barren field. Warmth bloomed in his chest and the nameless foes and implacable waves lay forgotten. He was not alone. Someone knew him, cared for him, and wanted to help. A promise hung on his lips as it played in his ears.

The enemies in the waves charged as one, a force as roiling as the waves, no longer faceless swathes of black. Terrible. Pale as bone. Eyes wide —black and unblinking—and starving. Howls ripped through their gaping mouths, filled with rows of rotting teeth.

He braced himself against his ally, prepared to fight as one against the horde. Together they would prevail. Together, they could do anything they put their minds—

But they were no longer there.

He was alone. His ally had vanished as quickly as they had appeared. He had no way of calling them back. His chest caved in on itself and his courage fled. Tears of regret, loneliness, and longing carved wounds in his cheeks as he met his end.

Alone.

"TRISTAN!"

Tristan bolted awake, chest heaving. He tried to scream when he saw a pair of wide eyes staring through the dark, but it strangled in his throat. He flailed at the creature.

Whatever he swung at caught Tristan's fist. It moved into the narrow shafts of moonlight creeping through the gaps of the barrack walls. Wisps of bedraggled sandy hair. His golden eyes glinted against the silver night.

Tristan's breath shuddered in relief. Styrax.

"Listen," Styrax said as he dropped Tristan's fist. "I'm not rich, and I'm not particularly bright. Please refrain from damaging my face. It's the only thing I've got going for me."

Tristan blinked the last dregs of horror-stricken sleep from his eyes. The monsters and waves melted away, leaving him back in the barracks with men snoring around him as the moon forced its way through the cracks in their walls. He sank back and pressed the heels of his palms to his brow. "Sorry, I almost took your nose off," he said. "I was talking again, wasn't I?"

"Something about...trees? Though why you would be so scared of trees is beyond me." Styrax picked an errant thread from his hair and leaned forward, hands clasped between his knees. His tone softened. "Do you remember anything this time?"

Tristan threw his hands to the ceiling in a hopeless gesture, the lump in his throat too big to speak around.

"Fancy a trip to the roof, then?"

Tristan nodded.

Without a word, Styrax grabbed his boots, tucked in his night-shirt, and crept past the other sleeping bodies. Tristan followed suit, even though he knew the caution was a wasted gesture. Since most of Lorate's men had grown up as heavy laborers, they knew the value of sleep and wrung it out of every minute they could. Nothing short of a dragon or the sun could wake them up.

Outside, the night breeze washed over Tristan, its lullaby stark against the crash of phantom waves against his skull. Crickets chirped while bats swooped low to snatch passing moths. The moon's burnished silver draped over Tristan like a blanket. Warm. Gentle. Real. Far from his nightmare's hazy shores.

Styrax gave Tristan a boost to the barrack eaves and then helped himself up. Together, they pried up the loose roof board they had discovered after a bad summer storm years before. Underneath was a leaf and mortar alcove they had made. They pulled their hidden trea-sures from it. For Tristan, a leather-bound book and bedraggled goose-feather quill. For Styrax, a small vial of water.

Tristan perched on the edge of the roof and cracked open the book to the first blank page. Styrax settled to the roof as Tristan wrote every feeling and image he could remember from the dream. A cloak and a black sliver of stars. A phrase...something. *Something!* He clenched his jaw as hard as he clenched his pen. It was almost there. At the nib of the quill. He toyed with the rings around his neck as he tried to force the words into being. But then an orange haze filled his vision, and the words vanished as quickly as dew in midsummer sun. All that remained of the dream was one vivid, horrifying image; the monsters coming for his throat. Although they were one of the few things he actually wanted to forget, he wrote every excruciating detail. He had too few memories to be selective with them.

When he finished putting every detail down—to the last cancerous tooth—Tristan put the quill down and thumbed through the pages he had already filled. All splattered with maddeningly brief snippets of ideas that faded to nothing. All ending with the same nightmare. Something had happened to him that night before his memories ended. Something with those horrible beasts. And he would need to face that someday if he wanted his memories back. Of that, he was certain.

Tristan curled his fingers around the leather cover until his knuckles turned white. The thought of abandoning even those small flecks of himself made his stomach roil. He would do anything for the full story, no matter the outcome.

With a sigh, he put the book away and stared across the fort yard. It was quiet except for the gate guards' snoring. The moon cast silver shafts of light across the eclectic patches of vegetable gardens and fruit trees speckled across the dust. Scraps of wood and cloth designated which patch belonged to whom. Tristan didn't know how the gardens survived on Lorate's barren soil. He supposed war could only steal so much. People's natures would prevail no matter where they ended up. The other soldiers had even taught him how to cultivate his own windowsill plant—a red-blossomed pea plant. Lorate had its faults, but occasionally it felt somewhat like home. But it wasn't enough. He wanted, *needed,* the rest of his story.

A flash caught Tristan's eye, and he turned. He watched Styrax tilt his vial of water end-over-end. The liquid caught the moonlight and glittered silver.

"Tell me about that vial again?" he asked. "I need a distraction."

"You're almost as bad as Linae." Styrax held the vial against the light, turning it to diamond for an instant. "My stretch of river," he said with a smile in his voice. "Home. My own piece of Loralan and near perfection on earth."

Tristan tried not to envy him his home and memories. "Why leave for a place like this?"

Styrax laughed. "I don't know what on Mother *Night* you could mean." He flopped on his stomach and looked at Tristan with a crooked smile. "Lorate is perfection incarnate."

Most nights Tristan would laugh and leave it at that. But something about tonight—about the terror of being left alone with his thoughts—made him press for more. "No really, Styrax, why? You can tell me anything. I'll most likely forget about it by morning, anyway."

He expected at least a chuckle out of that, but Styrax simply looked at him, propped up on his elbows. There was something otherworldly in the moon silver mixed with his golden eyes. He let out a heavy sigh and laid back on the shingles with the vial resting on his chest.

"I didn't have much choice in the matter."

"Someone forced you out?"

Styrax nodded but offered no further explanation.

Tristan shifted his seat, not sure how to proceed. "Did you kill someone?" he asked, waggling his eyebrows.

Again, he expected Styrax to laugh, but he just toyed with the shingle grooves beneath him. "More the opposite, actually."

"You...fathered an illegitimate child?"

That finally got Styrax to laugh, a bark that dispelled the tension in his shoulders. "I'm so glad to know you hold such a high opinion of me." He choked back more laughter. "And you better be careful, otherwise we'll wake up the night guards and *both* be in trouble." They both paused and checked for night guards. Snores rumbled, but little else.

"What am I *supposed* to think of all your cryptic nonsense?" Tristan puffed out his chest with faux bluster before he deflated with sputtering chuckles.

They sat like that for a moment, taking in the stars and cats crashing through garbage piles while they chased mice in equal appreciation. The quiet stretched on, and Tristan yawned as his eyelids began to droop.

Styrax broke the silence first. "What would you do if you met an Ancient One?"

That woke Tristan up. He looked at Styrax like he had grown horns. "What kind of question is *that*?"

Styrax shrugged. "Humor me." He swirled the vial in his palm. "You've run into an Ancient One, a user of magic and supposed enemy to the kingdom. What do you do?"

Still reeling from the question, Tristan defaulted to the answer he knew best. "Turn them over to General Laire, I suppose."

Styrax quirked an eyebrow. "Tristan, it's just me up here. You can speak your mind. You're far too curious a person to just let someone else handle it. What would *you* do?"

"What does it matter? We're never going to meet one out here, anyway."

Styrax said nothing. Only waited.

Tristan knew Styrax wouldn't let him off the hook without a proper answer. He was stubborn like that. What *would* he do? He would ask them if they knew about the Dragon Scales at bare minimum. If they knew anything about the night he lost everything. Laire refused to tell him about the place; no clues on its whereabouts or if it actually existed. The townsfolk made it quite clear it was a fairy tale. Someone else *had* to know, didn't they?

He toyed with the rings around his neck. But what if the Ancient Ones refused to help? What if *they* were the ones that tried to kill him that night? Would he be able to defend himself? Would they try to finish what they started? The monsters from his dreams reared their ugly heads, grinning like wolves. His thoughts turned orange-tinged and hazy.

Monsters.

He clenched his hand tighter around the rings. "I'd kill them. It's the only thing they deserve." Bile rose in his throat, from fear or something else he couldn't tell. The words had fallen out before he could stop them. His stomach roiled.

Styrax didn't look at him. "Are those your words? Or Laire's?"

Tristan threw out his hands in disbelief, the orange haze blurring his vision. "They nearly *killed* me, Styrax! I have the scars to prove it!" He gestured to his head; to the burns that engulfed most of his torso. "What else do you want me to say?" The words burned like poison on his tongue. His chest and throat constricted. Even though in his mind he knew he was right, his body rejected the answer.

Styrax looked at him with a smile, but it seemed...off, somehow. He didn't move, but it was as if a gulf had opened between them. "You're right. Of course, you're right." He looked away, brought his knees to his chest, and traced the ridges of the roof with a finger.

Some of Tristan's steam drained from his ears. He released a long, calming breath and waited for his heart rate to return to normal before he laid back on the roof. "Was there something you were getting at with all these questions?" he asked carefully.

Styrax shrugged. "Just curious." He rubbed his arms, and for the first time, Tristan noticed tiny, silvery scars peppered across Styrax's skin. Small enough to hardly be worth noting, but there were *hundreds* of them. Spaced evenly and each the same size. Tristan had never seen anything like it.

"Those scars...where did you get them?"

Styrax shrugged and said nothing.

There was only one thing Tristan couldn't get him to talk about. "Are those from when you lost your home?"

Styrax's fingers tightened around his arms. But then he smiled at Tristan. "Sweet Mother Night, can you believe how late it is? We should get to bed. Fort Inspection starts bright and early tomorrow."

"Wait, can't you tell me—"

Styrax stood, brushed his trousers off, and put his vial back into their hidden compartment. "I've lived long enough to know that there are times and places for unhappy memories, but it doesn't help anyone to live in them. Better to move on, move forward, and make better ones." He offered Tristan a hand. "Or find the happy ones we lost along the way."

Tristan let him pull him to his feet. He put his book back and sealed the compartment. Styrax had made it clear he didn't want to talk about his past anymore, so Tristan filled the silence with his own. "Do you really think I *can* find my memories?" he asked. "Happy or not?" He wasn't sure if he was asking Styrax, or himself.

"Not here, you won't."

Tristan balked at his bluntness. But he also couldn't disagree. Five years at Lorate had gotten him nowhere. Something in his gut stirred. If he wanted to find his memories, he would have to leave Lorate, and soon. He let himself off the roof. "Where would I even start, though?"

Styrax landed next to him. "What about this Dragon Scales place you're always talking about?"

Tristan scoffed and ran his hands through his hair. "Right. Chasing fairy tales. That'll get me places in a hurry."

Styrax gave him a look that seemed to pierce to his very soul. "Have you ever considered *why* Laire doesn't tell you more about it?"

Tristan shrugged off his unease. "All the time. But then I feel like a terrible person for doubting him. He *saved* me. Who am I to question anything he does?" He shoved his hands in his pockets as they walked back to their barracks. "Besides, he doesn't have anything useful to gain from willfully keeping me in the dark."

"Other than having another soldier to fill his ranks," Styrax said, eyebrows raised.

Tristan rolled his eyes. "A *terrible* soldier."

"I won't argue with you there."

Tristan chuckled, but the sound had a bite to it.

Styrax must have noticed. He bumped shoulders with Tristan. "Whenever you're ready to go on your grand adventure, say the word and I'll be right there with you."

"Thanks, Styrax."

"Anytime."

Tristan bit the inside of his cheek as he moved his delicate pea plant into the sunshine. He almost imagined the leaves and vines stretching like a toddler just out of bed. The red blossoms bobbed their heads, and he smiled at them.

"I'm telling you the Fernite strain grows better."

Tristan sighed and poured a drizzle of water on the plant. "Good morning, Boff."

Boff appeared next to him and peered at the vines. He had a stooped back and permanently squinted eyes from years of labor in the fields. Tristan suspected his daughter ran one of the vegetable stalls in town. The spatter of freckles across his nose—barely visible against his leathered skin—seemed all too familiar. "Yep. Fernite strand'll serve you fine. Vines are sturdier and they'll produce more peas. 'Sides, isn't natural for pea blossoms to be red."

Tristan scooted the plant farther from Boff's critical gaze and patted the older man on the shoulder. "I appreciate your input, Boff, but I prefer the Monterro strand. I like the red blossoms."

Boff shook his head and shambled off, muttering something

about young people never listening to common sense. Tristan rolled his eyes.

"It would make things easier if you just grew his strain, too," Styrax said while he rubbed crusted sleep from his eyes.

"Absolutely not, based solely on principle." Tristan tugged off his nightshirt and pulled on a clean tunic. "If I give in to the man that has to start every morning with the same argument, I'll never hear the end of it."

"You *already* don't hear the end of it." Styrax combed his fingers through his hair. He winced anytime he hit a tangle. "I'm just saying it's a lot of trouble for one pea plant."

Tristan frowned and touched the delicate leaves. He couldn't say why he had grown so attached to the little thing. He picked a bug out of the pot, eyes losing focus as his mind slipped to someplace else. Some place he couldn't see or hear or touch, but he somehow still *knew*. A taste at the tip of his tongue as nostalgia slipped through his muscles like silken thread.

"Tristan, you all right?" Styrax asked. Tristan's trance shattered, and he flicked the bug away.

Styrax sat on his bed and peered at Tristan. "You've been quiet, which, although a blessing to my poor abused eardrums, is unusual for you. Is something wrong?"

"Ha-ha." Tristan moved to leave, but Styrax stuck out his foot. Tristan heaved a sigh. "Styrax, I'm fine."

Styrax raised his eyebrows and cocked his head. "Tristan."

Tristan rubbed his brows. "I need you to stop being so observant for maybe two seconds. *Please*."

"Absolutely not. It's what I do best, and I won't apologize for it. How else do you think I've lived this long with the mouth I have?"

Tristan rolled his eyes. "You say that like you've lived a thousand lifetimes or something."

Styrax grinned and tossed his head. "How else would I become so sagely?" He leaned forward, smirking. "Now stop stalling and tell me what's going on."

Tristan gave in. There was no escape from Styrax. He sat on the edge of his bed and glanced around the room. Empty. Everyone had already left for the mess hall and other morning chores. Tristan leaned forward and clasped his hands between his knees, glancing around one more time. "You have to promise that this conversation *stays* just a conversation, and doesn't go anywhere else."

"Well, drat. There go my plans for the rest of the day. Boff will be so heartbroken not to hear the daily gossip."

"Styrax, really. I'm serious."

Styrax's joking smile faded. He mirrored Tristan's posture and nodded. "Okay, then. Tell me."

Tristan scratched his head, almost hoping someone would come interrupt them. How did he even begin to say what had been on his mind? "Do you—do you ever think about leaving this place?"

"All the time."

Tristan shut his eyes and shook his head. "No, I don't think you understand. Not leaving Lorate when the war is over. I mean *right now.* Just packing up and leaving and never coming back. The kind that gets people imprisoned or worse for desertion." The words tumbled out in a pile of nonsense. Once he started, he couldn't stop them, like a dam that had burst. "I know it sounds crazy, and it would be the *worst* way to repay Laire and Vinea for everything they've done for me, but I think I've done everything I need to do here. I need to get out and find my memories. I've been sitting here doing nothing for five years, and it's time for me to finally do something." Tristan sucked in a gasp as he realized he had forgotten to breathe. Stars wavering on the edges of his vision, he looked at Styrax. "Do you? Ever think about that?" he finished lamely.

Styrax leaned forward, golden eyes suddenly very, *very* serious. "I repeat: All. The. Time."

Tristan blinked, gap-mouthed, at him for several minutes. Styrax? The only one in all of Lorate that could pass as a soldier? *He* wanted to leave, too? "Really?"

Before Styrax could answer, Linae popped in.

"Tristan, Styrax!" Her blonde head of curls bobbed through the maze of beds. "Papa says he needs you!"

Tristan shared a look with Styrax and was grateful when he saw an assurance that this conversation was not done. They followed Linae out into the fort yard.

Once there, all thoughts of desertion and memory seeking had fled. The bustle and preparations had turned to utter silence. All the men stood at attention, silent as dead trees. Laire stood among them near the entrance, dressed in his finest breeches and embroidered coat. It felt as if they had stumbled upon a funeral.

"Is Sedick here, do you think?" Tristan asked Styrax from the side of his mouth.

"Feels just like his type of party."

Tristan snorted.

"Papa!" Linae cared little for somber occasions. She ran to Laire and flung herself at him. He caught her and hugged her close.

"How is my warrior today? Did you vanquish all the beasts?"

"Of course!"

The rest of the soldiers relaxed as they watched the exchange, but remained at their stations. Lady Vinea appeared from her quarters and approached. She smoothed her hair and greeted her husband with a peck on the cheek. "What is all this?"

"The men caught sight of Sedick's entourage on the road. I thought I might surprise him with a formal welcome, as he so seldom gives us proper warning."

Lady Vinea plucked a thread off his shoulder with a crooked, knowing smile. "I don't suppose you've left him any...less pleasant surprises?"

"No, but I definitely considered it." He leaned forward with raised eyebrows. "But perhaps you had something in mind?"

She chuckled and took Linae from him. "The fact that he has to stoop so low as to associate with the likes of us is punishment enough for him." She licked her thumb and ribbed dirt of Linae's cheek. "Come, my wild thing. We cannot let your father outshine us for such an esteemed guest." They disappeared into the general's quarters.

Laire watched them go. "I am a lucky, lucky man." With a sigh and a smile, he turned and clapped Tristan on the shoulder. "All right today?"

Tristan smiled and shook his hand. "Yes, sir."

"I heard Linae made you tell that Dragon Scales story again yesterday?"

"As always."

Laire winced. "Maybe tell her 'no' every once in a while. I think she's already aiming to marry you, and this old heart can't take that."

Tristan shrugged. "I'm afraid I can't do that, sir. You once told me you would never ask me to do something you yourself wouldn't do." He grinned at Laire. "Lady Vinea *is* always complaining that you can't refuse Linae anything."

Laire attempted to look peeved, but he had a soft, indulgent look in his eyes. "You've got me there, I suppose," he grumbled. "You've got to spoil your children while you still have them." A shadow crossed his face, but then he blinked and it was gone. He gave Tristan a sideways look. "When did I teach you to be so insubordinate?"

Tristan smiled and patted him on the shoulder. "I learn by example, sir."

Laire laughed. "I suppose I've been a poor teacher, particularly when it comes to our *esteemed* guest we're expecting today." He shook his head as they walked further into the yard. "You ready for this song and dance with Sedick?"

Tristan sighed from deep in his chest. The sound gargled in his throat. "About as ready as I always am."

"You're a better man than I am. I'm not as patient with his shenanigans."

Tristan shrugged. "He's trying to help me get my memory back and has never asked for payment. I don't appreciate his approach to it, but the least I can be is cordial."

"Hmm…" Laire nodded to the strap around Tristan's neck. "Is the ring helping at all?"

An uninvited lump swelled in Tristan's throat. He inwardly cursed and swallowed it back. "I couldn't say, sir. I know I have… dreams, but I forget them as soon as I wake up." He pulled absently on the strap, worry swirling through his mind. He shook it off and stood tall. "But I'm sure it will come with time."

"You may be better off without it."

Tristan reeled back, eyes wide. "Pardon, sir?"

Laire placed a hand on Tristan's shoulder. "Hard as it may be to hear, forgetting is often a mercy. Wish that I could forget a few painful memories myself."

Tristan stared blankly at him, words refusing to form themselves. How could he say that? How could he say that, knowing that Tristan had *nothing*?

If Laire noticed he had touched a nerve, he didn't show it. He glanced at the sky, watching the white clouds scud by overhead. "Well, I'm sure Sedick will have something to say about it when he gets here. You know how particular he gets about his pet projects."

"Horses approaching!" someone called from the watchtowers.

A scowl flitted across Laire's face. "Ahh. Speak of the devil and he will come."

THE BOY SHIFTED in his saddle, sweaty and tired beneath his dark cowl. He'd lost count of how many hours he'd been in the saddle, but his rump felt swollen and stiff all at once. He couldn't remember much of anything, really. Only snippets floating through the orange haze of his mind; whispers that never fully formed. But it didn't matter. He was Lord Sedick's servant—a shadow meant to bend to his every whim. He didn't need memories. Didn't need a name. He lived only for his next order.

That was what his mind told him, at least. His body protested mightily. Hunger gurgled in his stomach, and each of his horse's steps drove him deeper into the saddle. Despite his exhaustion, nervous anxiety raced through him as the fort came into view. He shifted back and forth and stood in his stirrups. The memories he had been permitted to keep were the ones related to his service to Lord Sedick. He had been to so many forts with his master over the years, but somehow this one was...different. He couldn't say why. But his magic roared in his veins and kept him from settling.

He considered asking Lord Sedick about it. He eyed his master, whose orange robes dazzled to the point of blinding in the sunlight, and decided against it. The bruise on his cheek had still not healed from the last time he had spoken needlessly. He could wait.

"Boy!"

He jumped. Had Lord Sedick read his thoughts? He worried at the silver stud embedded in his ear and urged his horse to ride alongside Lord Sedick's mount. His body trembled in his master's presence, and he couldn't look him in the eye. Instead, he watched the golden bangles around his master's arms as they bounced with the horses' gait. The feeling of magic—a buzzing, innervating feeling that sent shivers down his back—radiated from them. Lord Sedick had no magic of his own, but he found other ways to wield power.

"This is the first time I've let you accompany me to Lorate, is it not?" Sedick asked, watching the fort grow closer with each step.

"Yes, my lord," he said.

"Hmm." Sedick dabbed sweat from his brow. "Heed me well, boy. First, if the Lady of the Fort tries to speak with you, you must keep it brief. Avoid her if you can. You will receive a lashing any time this order is not followed."

The gates loomed over them. Bugles sounded, and the gates opened wide, dust curling around them and blinding them all.

Sedick's voice floated to him through the dust. "Second, there is something here that will entice you to act out, to use the magic so graciously born to you. Do *not*, under any circumstances, let your magic run free. The time is not yet; but you will get to make your kill eventually. I'll make sure of it."

LAIRE NODDED to the gate guards. They opened the main gate on protesting hinges that made Tristan grit his jaw against the pain. Dust swirled into the air from beneath the doors, and once it settled, the shapes of a caravan came into view. As they drew closer, Tristan made out the shapes of six horsemen, a cart filled with shriveled weeds, and Sedick's signature entourage shrouded in gray cloaks embroidered with his personal signet. All were warlocks under the patronage of Sedick's own master, by some accounts. One of them couldn't have been more than sixteen, which surprised Tristan. Sedick had never had an acolyte so young before.

At the forefront of them all rode Sedick Kandral himself, Warlock head of the King's Inquisitors, and part-time Fort Inspector. Gold and silver bangles and talismans dripped down his arms and neck, clattering together in a frenzy with every step his mount took. Gaudy, orange silk robes embroidered in silver billowed around him like demented butterfly wings. He barely concealed a sneer as he passed the Lorate soldiers, his pale blue eyes glinting nearly as brightly as his bald scalp.

"Banners, attention!"

The King's Men banner, a silver crown encircled by golden flames —representative of the flames Osmen used to end the previous royal family's rule on the Day of Bluest Blood—snapped to attention beside Lorate's banner, a purple potato speared through the heart by a hunting dagger. The moment the banners opened, the bugle players blared to life, belting discordant fanfare long and loud. Soldiers beat their fists to their chests as one, somber as men on their way to battle.

Tristan choked back a laugh as he tried to keep a straight face. The whole welcome was more fit for a king's military procession than an eight-man entourage. It came across as mockery rather than respect. And by the gleam in Laire's eyes, he knew that all too well.

Sedick halted in the center of the fort yard and curled his lip. "General Laire, it appears someone informed you of my early arrival." The voice that rumbled from his chest did not match his slight frame. Rich and silken, it was the voice of an orator. Tristan hated it. "I thank you for your most generous welcome. I hope you did not go through too much trouble for it." His tone had all the sickly sweetness of a silver-tongued snake.

Laire grinned wide and bright, an expression that never reached his eyes. "On the contrary! I find nothing is ever enough for your magnanimousness."

Sedick's nose twitched—nearly sending his spectacles flying— but he chose not to retaliate. "I bring you gifts," he said instead. "Since so few others care enough to contribute."

At that moment, Lady Vinea emerged with Linae, each in their oldest, most threadbare silks. Vinea held her head proud, eyes glinting with quiet rebellion. They paled almost comically against Sedick's loud atrocity. Tristan saw a small smile turn up the ends of Laire's mouth.

Sedick smiled so tightly that his lips nearly disappeared. "Ahh, the treasures of Lorate," Sedick bowed his head.

Lady Vinea curtsied. "May you find all the comforts you deserve in our home, Lord Sedick."

"Mmm-hmm."

Linae tugged on Vinea's dress, and dust wafted from the folds. Linae pointed to the young acolyte beside Sedick. "Who's that boy, mama?"

"I'm sure that's just—" Lady Vinea straightened, all pretenses and coolness gone. She smiled, and her rigid spine softened. "Sorren! What an unexpected surprise. Look how you've grown!"

The boy's eyes nearly popped from his skull. He glanced at Sedick, fear in his eyes. Sedick did not return the look, but his jaw tightened. The boy's face paled, and he tugged at a silver stud in his earlobe. He drew his cloak tighter about him and ducked his head. "The-the lady has me confused with someone else."

Vinea's brows furrowed. She stood beside Laire to get a better look, Linae clutched close to her. "Of course, I don't. How could I—"

Laire placed a hand on her arm and shook his head nearly imperceptibly, casting another glare at Sedick. Vinea gave him a guarded, questioning look, and he shook his head again. Tristan squinted for a better look at the boy. Who *was* he to garner such attention?

"You said you bring offerings, Lord Sedick?" Laire asked.

"Indeed." Sedick brushed road dust from his shoulders. "The gift comes directly from King Osmen, following an embarrassing defeat at Bael. General Shadowwalker caught them unawares, and they paid the price for it."

Sedick loved to hear himself talk far more than Tristan cared to listen, but that name caught his attention. A flurry of whispers washed through the crowd at Sedick's words.

"Bael? *The* Bael?"

"They're our front line guards! They couldn't have beaten them!"

"It's the magic. The Ancient Races never fight fair."

Sedick listened to the murmurs with feigned surprise. "Oh, had you not heard, Laire? I thought since you used to lead the Vanguard, you would have kept some of your old connections."

Laire said nothing, but the veins on his jaw stood out as the muscles clenched.

"Well, I won't hold you in suspense," Sedick said with a smile that could freeze fire. "I do not exaggerate when I say it was an embarrassment. Not a single casualty. Caught with their trousers down, as so many others have put it. All their supplies were stolen or burned and, as always, General Shadowalker got away with no one seeing him." He pulled an apple from his saddlebags, took one bite, and then tossed it on the ground, juices still dribbling down his chin. "The front lines will suffer without those supplies, but I suppose that's their own fault for being idiots."

The fort had fallen silent. Tristan's stomach clenched. They all stared at the fallen apple, now beset with starving flies, as Sedick's words sank in. None of the towns or cities he knew of could spare food. Soldiers would die pointlessly for that theft, and Sedick couldn't bring himself to show them even basic decency.

Sedick reveled in their shock. "Because of that failure, the king has commanded that all his soldiers be granted access to serpent root. And make no mistake, this kindness cost him more gold than *many* of you," he glanced at Tristan, "are worth." He motioned his cart forward. Even upon closer inspection, it still looked to be full of nothing but dried, shriveled weeds.

"And what good will those do us?" Tristan asked no one in particular.

Styrax made a strangled noise in the back of his throat in response. "A lot more than you think," he said, voice strained.

"These are the best defensive weapon we have against the Ancient Races." Sedick flourished almost mockingly to them. The look on his face showed he knew how ridiculous and pointless they looked to everyone. "Please keep them accessible at all times. General Laire, I trust you will distribute these appropriately. I will know if there is an error. I counted them myself."

Laire stretched his lips in a smile so tight they were almost transparent. "Of course." He turned to the soldiers and motioned them to the carts. "Captains! Collect your bundles and distribute them to your men!"

The captains distributed the serpent root without incident, all save for one strand left in the cart. One too many. Tristan watched with no small amount of pleasure as Sedick fumed. He hoped Sedick would explode into a fiery, passionate rage over the fact that his perfect counting had gone awry. He'd love to see a few popped blood vessels. But, unfortunately, Sedick kept himself from a complete meltdown. He rolled his eyes back in his head, exhaled, and carried on.

"One last thing for you all," he said before the masses parted. "I am going to forgo my usual inspection this week."

Another silence rang through the fort, and then a cheer swelled and shook the birds from their perches. Tristan clapped and whooped with the rest of them.

Sedick held up a hand, his lips pressed in an irritated but somehow smug look. A wild look danced in his beady eyes. "King Osmen is not so far distant as you might think. He has watched your efforts, and you have impressed him. Never has he met common folk so dedicated to his cause."

Quiet scoffs and mutters.

"It is for this reason that he has picked you to march against the final elven stronghold, the Golden Grove."

All sound ceased in a breath. The soldiers gaped at Sedick, faces pale and bloodless as parchment. Tristan's heart crumpled in his chest. The Golden Grove? *The* Golden Grove? The elven stronghold protected by a forest that had eaten hundreds of men whole, and inhabited by the rebellion's most fearsome warriors? Why? Why on Mother Night's grave send *these* men to invade? No matter what Sedick said, Tristan knew the king couldn't have been watching them. If he had, he would have known these men were not warriors meant to fight the kingdom's greatest foes. These men weren't killers. They were farmers and builders and craftsmen. Husbands, fathers, brothers. Friends. And they would all die.

Lady Vinea clutched at Laire's arm. He said nothing. Tristan had no feeling in his hands and feet. Styrax's jaw gaped open. His face was so pale it was almost translucent.

"In lieu of my inspection, I shall oversee preparations for your new assignment." Sedick could hardly keep the cheeriness from his voice. "You have limited time, and there is much to be done."

Without another word, he bowed to the crowd, and then he and his men trundled to the guest quarters.

An unmoving, airless crowd of dead men trembled in his wake.

SEVEN

Vinea was quiet when Laire returned to his quarters. The whole fort was quiet, really. All their voices were cut by fear and shock. He had known this day would come the moment he stepped foot on Lorate soil, but it didn't lessen the anticipation thrilling through his stomach. His five years of torment were almost over. He'd be able to take his family back to the capital—back to where they belonged—as soon as this ordeal was finished. The Golden Grove's den of murderers would fall, and his family would prosper in the rebellion's defeat.

Laire settled himself into his chair at the table with a small smile. Soon, very soon, everything would be as it should be.

Vinea had set out a cup of his favorite herbal tea next to a vase of fresh lavender. She would collect it in the mornings with Linae, and always smelled of it. Laire's smile deepened at the thought of Vinea and Linae traversing the extensive palace gardens in Monterro soon, able to collect more flowers than they knew what to do with.

He went to take the cup, but something in the swirl of dark liquid reflected back an elven face. His first love. Smiling, crooning sweet nothings, and then drenched in blood as she held a small figure in her lap. Laire bit back a cry and shoved the cup away from him. It had been years since that face had haunted him. Did she know, somehow, what he intended to do to her kin? He shook his head to rid himself of the thoughts. No. The Pit had her, and there she would stay.

He folded shaking hands in his lap and focused on the beauty of the woman before him rather than the menace of the one behind. "Is Linae asleep?" he asked, ignoring the slight tremor in his voice.

"For now," Vinea said, scrubbing a little too vigorously at a wooden bowl. "Though I imagine it won't be for long." She clattered the bowl against others as she set it aside to dry. "She's too excited about her father and Tristan going off to fight the monsters."

Laire heard the barbs in her voice. Noticed that she kept her attention trained on anything but him.

He crossed the room and put his arms around her waist. He drew her to his chest, her hair mingling with his beard. She smelled of soap and flour, too lowly for her station but still so, *so* lovely. He pressed her to him, soaking in her soft warmth. She resisted at first, but slowly softened and let herself lean back into him.

"Talk to me, my darling." His lips brushed against her hair. He kissed the nape of her neck.

"How long have you known about this assignment?"

Laire exhaled as his gut clenched. He rested his chin on her head, unsure how to answer. But he knew his silence was answer enough. She had always been too perceptive.

Vinea went stiff in his arms. "You've always said this was only a temporary placement." She pulled herself away and faced him. "All day I've told myself that there was no way you could have known. That you wouldn't let us bring Linae here—wouldn't let us be *happy* —if you had known this would be the outcome." She crossed her arms, eyes blazing. "But I was wrong. You've known all along that we've been making a home in a-a—" She cast her hands about her head. Laire watched so many words tie themselves to her tongue before she found the one she must have been looking for. "*Slaughterhouse!*"

He tried to go to her. "That may be extreme—"

"Is it?" She took a step away from him and gestured to the window. "Look me in the eye and tell me you expect any of those men to return to their families after their ordeal." She didn't give him time to answer. "They are not your Vanguard, Laire."

Laire clenched his jaw, a wave of guilt and anger and failure shooting through his veins. "You're right. They're not, because *my* Vanguard died." Images of a young woman with a black blade wavered across his mind. He clenched his fists. Even five years later, the hatred and anger still ran deep. Killing her once was not enough.

Vinea pressed her palm to her brow. "Laire, I understand that you want to do everything you can to prove yourself to Osmen again, but this is not the way to do it. These men have never seen a battlefield in their lives, and yet you've chosen to bury them there."

"Vinea," Laire took her face in his hands—brushed a few stray curls from her face—searching for a shred of understanding. "You forget I can't act on my own. I did once, which nearly killed me and got us transferred to this wasteland."

She pulled away again. "But you are *complicit* in it! It's the same thing!"

"*Vinea!*" The word thundered through the kitchen. She recoiled, eyes wide with shock. His heart twisted into knots. He had not meant that. He sank to the table again, hands clasped in front of him. "My love, look at me and tell me you think I would knowingly send men off to slaughter."

"The man I love *wouldn't*, which is why I'm so *angry* with you." Vinea's voice was barely above a whisper but carried all the venom of a pit viper. She turned her back on him went and about cleaning their already spotless kitchen.

Laire took a few deep breaths, trying to settle the anger swelling in his chest. She didn't know. She didn't see the full picture of what he was doing for all of them. He wanted—*needed*—her on his side.

He wouldn't be able to go on without her. He could tell her just enough to keep her satisfied without making her complicit in case something went wrong.

"The Vanguard will be with them."

The words hung like a blade across the room. Vinea froze, her shoulders seizing and her hands going still. The clatter of cleaning fell silent. Laire heard only the rush of the night air outside. "What?" Vinea asked, breathless, the word nearly strangled in her throat.

"You cannot tell a *soul,* Vinea. No one can know." He leaned back in his chair, the secrets he had kept for so long spilling out in a rush. "While our men fight the front lines, the Vanguard will flank the Golden Grove and finish them." It was like an anvil had lifted from his chest. He had loathed every second of keeping things from her, but it had to be done. She would understand, in time, even when the rest of the story unfolded.

Vinea didn't move for a moment. Didn't look at him. Her body trembled, and she clenched her hands in the rag, twisting it in impossible knots. She was quiet for so long Laire began to wonder if she had heard him, but then she exhaled heavily. All the tension left her body. She set her rag down and sat beside him at the table. "Thank Mother Night." Tears welled in her eyes. She dabbed at them and laughed hoarsely. "I thought I was going to lose you, too."

He hugged her. "I'm sorry I scared you."

She buried her face in his chest. "You *should* be." Her hands still shook in her lap.

They sat at the table together in silence. Vinea poured a cup of tea for herself and nursed it, leaning against Laire and tracing her fingers over the back of his hand. "Why the subterfuge? Why send these men at all?"

Laire scoffed. "Sedick knows better than I do," he said.

"That vile—" Vinea slammed her mug on the table. Droplets of tea splatted like bloodstains on the wood. "He *would* think of something like this. Just to see how many people he can hurt." She gnawed on her lower lip. "And what he did to Sorren? How *dare* he? I cannot abide that odious, myopic—" she cast her hands about her again, "*monster's* presence here any longer!"

Laire took her hands in his and kissed her knuckles. "I'm as unhappy about it as you are, but there's not much we can do considering the debt we owe him."

"If I didn't know any better, I'd almost think you regret what I gave you." Sedick sent them a simpering smile from the doorway.

Vinea's face turned white. She stood up so quickly her chair threatened to topple. She clutched at the neck of her dress and glanced to Linae's room. As if on cue, Linae emerged.

"Mama, I'm not sleepy." She saw Laire and her eyes immediately lit up. "Papa!" She ran to him and flung herself into his lap. "Are you going to stop all the monsters?"

Laire glanced between Vinea and Sedick, the tension in his own chest rising. "Of course I will," he said without looking at Linae. "I'm a hero, aren't I?"

"I knew it!" She threw her arms around Laire's neck, and he kissed her forehead, still watching Sedick with caution. Sedick curled his lip in disgust.

"Pardon her, Lord Sedick." Vinea extricated Linae from Laire. Her hands were clammy against his skin. "If you'll excuse us, I have a daughter that needs to go back to sleep."

"Yes, I'm sure you do." Sedick waved her off without so much as a glance in her direction. Laire shot him a glower, which Sedick seemed to take great pleasure in.

Vinea's eyes burned bright. She glanced at Laire, who motioned her to the bedroom and safety with a look. She clenched her jaw, straightened, and nodded stiffly before stalking off with Linae. Linae stuck her tongue out at Sedick over Vinea's shoulder before Vinea closed the door behind them.

Sedick commandeered a chair across from Laire and draped his robes across any surface available to him. The bangles around his wrists clinked together and set Laire's teeth on edge.

Laire gripped his cup so tightly he thought it might break. "I would appreciate it if you didn't speak to my wife that way."

"And I would appreciate it if you didn't *speak*. Yet here we are, both unsatisfied." Sedick took a sip from Vinea's cup. He watched Laire pointedly, daring him to say something.

Laire smiled thinly and grabbed his own tea. It had gotten cold and sour, but he chugged it down.

"Have you tired of your sword yet?" Sedick asked, licking tea drops from his fingers. "You know I will pay you a handsome price for it."

Laire wanted nothing more than to be rid of the bone-white, cursed sword his family had protected for generations. Its voice always hovered at the edge of his mind, whispering in nonsensical gibberish that brooded with darkness in his heart. But he could never let Sedick know that. He enjoyed disappointing him far too much.

He put his teacup back in its saucer. "How is Milaia? Does she know what you've done to her son?"

Sedick's lip twitched in disgust at the mention of his wife. "He was *my* son, too. Before her fool notions got in his head and he betrayed me." He nodded to the doorway Vinea had disappeared through. "Your prize has fire in her. It may be attractive now, but be careful she doesn't turn it on you."

Laire itched to punch Sedick in his smug face. "Leave my *wife* out of your thoughts."

Sedick took another sip, unperturbed. "Although, I suppose I don't have to warn you, do I? You've already lived that heartbreak once, haven't you?"

Some of the color drained from Laire's face as his first wife's images played through his head again. "I *won't* let that happen again."

Sedick smiled thinly. "We'll see." He set the tea down and leaned forward, bangles clanking and threatening another headache for

Laire. "But enough of the past. Why don't we discuss your pet project instead?"

Laire cocked his head, curbing the malice that raced through his veins the longer he had to stare at Sedick's face. "What is there to discuss?"

"He says he has dreams."

"Everyone does."

"Memory dreams, you dolt." He removed one of his bangles and passed it back and forth between his hands. It glowed a hazy orange. "My talisman has kept him subdued this long. But if he continues to have these dreams, there's no telling what could happen."

"Are you finally admitting your incompetence?"

Sedick slammed his palm on the table. The teacups leapt from their saucers, spewing more bloody droplets, before setting back into place. "*I* risked myself for *you*! I will not have you insult me so!"

Laire leaned forward, resting on his elbows as a smirk spread across his face. "*I* did nothing. You're stuck with me because the king ordered you to be. And if *you* fail, I will not be dragged down with you."

Sedick tilted his chin back and stared down his nose at Laire, his eyes glinting with loathing. "I have driven greater men than you to madness," he said slowly, a growl deep in his chest. "Watch your tone. I need not remind you that of the two of us *you* are the failure. This fort of yours is proof of that."

They sat that way in silence for moments that stretched to minutes, each boiling in mutual hatred. Finally, Laire leaned back, face set in stony lines. "Is there a chance he'll get his memories back?"

Sedick laughed with self-righteous indignation. "I am not so careless. No, he will not get his memories back. Not fully, anyway. The closer he gets to them, the more the talisman will fight him. He could lose his mind completely if we're not careful."

Laire stewed on this, chewing the inside of his cheek as he thought.

"It won't make much of a difference, though, will it?" Sedick asked, plucking a loose thread from his robes. "Not if he's going to die anyway."

"*No,*" Laire said, his heart plummeting to his toes. "No, we have to make it look like he went willingly. It won't be as effective any other way."

"You and your melodrama." Sedick leaned back with a sigh, folding his arms across his skinny chest. "Ludicrous as I think it is, King Osmen is quite eager to see your plan through, drama and all. He says he might consider reinstating you to your post if all goes without a hitch." He cast Laire a smug sideways glance. "Although, considering your failure at the Dragon Scales, I wouldn't put too much stock in this plan shaping up to anything other than disaster."

Laire bristled. "That failure is what got us here, isn't it?"

"Yes. I can hardly contain my gratitude." Sedick curled his nose at the fort. "Just remember, your family may not be so lucky a second time around. Osmen does not take kindly to repeat abject failures."

Laire's heart tightened. He knew that. The only suffering Vinea and Linae had been put through was being uprooted to Lorate. If he failed again, the consequences could be much more dire. He toasted to Sedick with his cold tea, a too-tight smile tearing at his cheeks. "I suppose I'll have to take his right-hand failure's word for it."

Sedick's face tightened. "Just see that Tristan dies in that battle, and then maybe we'll both keep our heads."

EIGHT

It didn't take long for Linae to fall asleep again. She might have been stubborn, but she was still only five, and tiredness always won out in the end. Vinea smiled and brushed a curl away from Linae's face before kissing her forehead. "Goodnight, my meadowlark."

Laire's and Sedick's voices carried from the dining room. Vinea's mouth tightened. Considering the announcement from this morning, their conversation couldn't be anything but doom for the men of Lorate.

She left Linae asleep and crept to the door, avoiding the creaking floorboards Laire endlessly griped about. "Once we leave this place, I'll have nothing but stone for floors. They don't whimper like kicked dogs every time you walk over them," he'd say.

Vinea frowned. Now, even those small moments felt tainted. He'd known all along that this place was doomed. Even with the Vanguard, the Golden Grove was no foe to take lightly, and so many lives would be lost. Unless she could stop it.

She crouched and pressed her ear to the door.

"...suppose I'll have to take his right-hand failure's word for it," Laire said.

Vinea smiled. She could imagine the look of barely suppressed outrage on Sedick's face. He deserved it.

"Just see that Tristan dies in that battle, and then maybe we'll both keep our heads."

Vinea's heart plummeted. All traces of a smile vanished. What did Tristan have to do with any of this?

Vinea expected Laire to say something—*anything*. He wouldn't let a comment like that stand. Tristan was family. Laire loved him as much as Vinea and Linae did. He wouldn't purposely put him in harm's way.

But the silence drew on for far too long. Eventually, chairs shifted and they moved on to other topics. They said nothing else about it.

Vinea drew back from the door, a shaking hand over her mouth. "*No.*" She staggered a few more steps, unable to draw in a full breath. "Laire you *wouldn't*. What has Sedick put into your head?"

The walls closed in around her, and her chest threatened to burst. Memories of a different night, almost a lifetime ago, played through her mind. A night when she had heard whispers through the walls. Snatches of conversations. Plans to overthrow King Salaith and Queen Eden. Plans to murder Vinea's family—the Vastir—for being too close to the royal family. She had tried to warn the royal household, but it was too late. Osmen had slaughtered them all on the day of Bluest Blood and burned nearly half the capital down with it. The guilt still haunted Vinea through the night.

Sobs built in Vinea's throat. Osmen the Flameslayer had come for the Vastirs next. She had been able to get them to flee, but Osmen's agents were faster. Her father speared through the heart. Her mother drowned. All of her siblings...all gone. All slaughtered.

And now, Osmen had come for her family again. Sedick wanted Tristan dead. She would not believe Laire had a hand in it. Not the kind, sensitive heart that doted on her and Linae, and would do anything to protect his family. Not the man that had saved her from wretchedness and had kept her secret all these years. He would never lie to her this way. Not intentionally.

He lied about the Golden Grove.

Tears filled her eyes. Frustrated. Terrified.

Enraged.

Vinea lifted her skirts and crept outside. It didn't matter what part Laire had in it. Now *she* had a part, and she would not fail again. Tristan would not die. Not while she had breath in her lungs and a heart in her breast. The family that had entrusted her to protect their legacy would never forgive her, and neither would she. She had to get Tristan out. *Tonight.* And she needed help. She swiped the coin purse she kept beneath her bed and headed out into the night.

The walk from her quarters to the bunkhouses seemed like the longest Vinea had ever taken in her life, and she had escaped the palace on the Day of Bluest Blood. Any moment, she expected a guard, Laire, or Sedick to leap from the shadows and haul her to the stocks where she belonged, but they never did. The moon was her only spectator, casting long rivers of silver across the dust and grime. Vinea remembered the time when she lived in palaces gilded in the purest silver. She'd come a long way from all those years ago. The entire kingdom had.

Vinea made it to the bunkhouses without incident. There was an odd gurgling sound inside, like water bubbling from a spring. She opened the door, and her heart leaped to her throat as the door squealed on aching hinges. She expected the entire bunkhouse to be up with cries of alarm, weapons drawn and ready to cut down the traitor she was. She waited, breath caught in her chest, but no one stirred.

"Lady Vinea?"

Vinea bit back a scream and leapt back. Styrax loomed over her in the doorway, a sopping wet knapsack over his shoulders. For a moment, it seemed as though the rim of his irises glowed white. She took a step forward to see it better, but it vanished. He stepped back into the barracks, his face guarded.

"What are you doing here?"

Vinea put a finger to her lips, her hands shaking from the adrenaline roaring through her, and motioned him outside. He glanced around the barracks and followed her, albeit reluctantly.

"What's this about?" he asked when Vinea closed the door behind him. He stood away from her, arms crossed and hugging the shadows.

Vinea had never seen relaxed, dependable Styrax so on edge. She shook her head. The entire *fort* would be on edge. It wasn't every day men were told they were being sent to their deaths. She ignored Styrax's question. "Where's Tristan?"

Styrax furrowed his brow. His shoulders sagged as though with relief. The knapsack dripped water on the ground beneath him. "On the roof, I think."

She gripped Styrax by the arm. "Find him." He was cool to the touch, like the brush of currents over her skin as she dipped her feet in creeks. Her fingertips crackled and fizzed on his skin. She released him with a gasp. "You have—"

He blanched white. His limbs tightened to his sides, and he glanced around them in a panic. "Lady Vinea, whatever you're thinking—"

She held up a hand. "You don't have to explain anything to me. We *all* have our secrets."

He gaped at her, unblinking. "I—" he shook his head, as if unable to find the words, and simply nodded, his lower lip quivering.

Vinea sighed and nodded back. "This might make things easier."

Styrax furrowed his brow. "What do you mean?"

"I don't have time to explain everything, but I have an impossible favor to ask you."

Styrax waited for her to finish, shoulders tight.

"I need you to take Tristan and get as far away from here as possible. It's not safe for him to be here anymore." She rummaged through her skirts for her coin pouch. "You'll be deserters, but I can promise that's a far better fate than what awaits you here. I can pay you—"

Styrax stopped her. "I'll do it. You don't need to pay me anything. Your trust despite—" he chuckled thickly and motioned abstractly in the air. "Means more than you know."

"Are you sure? I'm asking so much—"

"It's nothing I haven't considered already." He gestured to the knapsack. "More times than I can count."

Vinea's heart broke for him. "Thank you, Styrax," she said. "Keep him safe. He's more precious than you could know. May we *all* meet under better circumstances one day."

Styrax bowed his head. "Thank *you*, Lady Vinea. Stay safe."

Vinea patted him on the arm, another pulse of electrifying energy flowing through her arm. The streets had once been overrun with people like him and the air charged with their presence. That was the Loralan she remembered; and the Loralan she hoped to see again.

Vinea left Styrax. She wanted to heave a sigh of relief but couldn't bring herself to yet. She had someone she could rely on, but he and Tristan still had to get out of the fort alive. She would inform Chaedra to look for them when she could sneak away again. For now, though, she had to get back home without being spotted—in a fort full of people with the moon shining down like a traitorous beacon.

Vinea steeled herself and crept back to her quarters. Every sound was an alarm bell in her ears. A cat chasing a roach became footsteps coming after her. She crossed into the alleyways. The creaking beds behind the barrack walls were the squeal of shackles around her wrists. Would Laire protect her? She had to believe he would, even though she knew a betrayal from another wife would be worse than a knife to his back. And what would happen to Linae?

As her thoughts spiraled, she caught movement near Laire's office. She froze, heart pounding, thinking that her end had come. Instead, it was simply a streak of blonde curls disappearing through the doorway. Vinea sighed, moving her shaking hand to her heart. She smiled wanly, equally relieved and exasperated. She would never get that girl to stay in bed. Jogging to catch up, she followed her daughter through the doorway to Laire's office, and heard her talking.

Vinea frowned. Nobody but the night guards should be out this late. At least, nobody with good intentions. She picked up the pace. "Linae, who are you talking to?" She rounded the corner.

In a moment, she saw her daughter framed in the moonlight through the open window, head held proud and arms crossed over her chest. And there by her husband's desk was a dark figure with a weapon at its side—a shadow, a phantom, a *nightmare*—studying her daughter. Vinea's retribution had come for her daughter instead.

Vinea screamed, and the night shattered.

LAIRE ERUPTED from the table at the scream, the blood draining from his face, replaced by raging, horrified adrenaline. His chair crashed to the floor behind him. He knew that scream; that *voice. Vinea.*

He was out of the room in two steps, flying through the hallway to his bedroom. Sedick followed in his wake.

Laire ground his teeth but ignored him. He ripped a scabbard from off his wall and drew the sword. The bone white blade—one side straight and razor-edged, the other as jagged as dragon's teeth—sapped the light from the room. The sapphire eyes inside the dragon-headed hilt gleamed, and the twisted unicorn horn grip glowed. No matter how beautiful the weapon, though, Laire grimaced at the numb, buzzing sensation it sent through his fingers and up his arm. The weight dragged at his shoulder and the indiscernible whispers shivered through his ears. He had never been fond of the blade, but it killed who he needed to kill, and that was all it needed to do.

Sedick's voice strangled in his throat. "You—" For once, he was at a loss for words. "You keep *that sword* as a...*wall* decoration?" Spittle flew from his mouth in his outrage. "Do you *know* what that weapon is?"

Laire shoved Sedick aside and sprinted to his office. He had his wife to save and *nothing* would keep him from that.

CHAPTER

NINE

Tristan escaped to the roof again that night. The air hung heavy and stagnant. Unmoving. Unbreathing. Just like the rest of the fort. No one dared speak. Their fears, anxieties, and tears—all ill-suited for *respectable* King's Men, whatever that meant—were liable to spill out at once, and they couldn't have that. Their silent, unfocused stares as they packed and polished gear and followed Sedick's asinine orders spoke more volumes than any words could. That frozen, dream-like state had remained even as they had all trickled off to bed.

Tristan hadn't even tried to sleep. He had too many emotions jumbled in horrible knots in his stomach. Even if he had managed to quiet his thoughts long enough to sleep for an hour or so, he knew what waited for him. Impending doom seemed to be an ingredient ripe for the most horrific nightmares of his life. He'd take a pass on those tonight.

The longer he sat, the more resentment built up in his gut. For the war. For the Ancient Ones that made it necessary. For Sedick. *Especially* for Sedick. Tristan clenched his hands as an interaction from earlier resurfaced, gnawing at his already flourishing worry.

Sedick had approached Tristan after most of the soldiers had dispersed following his announcement. "A word with you?" he asked. "If Laire's pet can spare a precious moment of his time?"

Tristan peeled the corners of his lips into a tight, close-mouthed smile, his heart thudding in his chest. He had wanted to say that no, he could not spare *any* of his time, seeing as how he was now expected to prepare for an invasion that would likely get them all killed, but he refrained. He also refrained from bowing. "What can I do for you, my lord?"

Sedick's lip curled at Tristan's small rebellion, and it made Tristan's smile feel a little more genuine. Sedick inspected his fingernails. "I have so many better things to do with my time than swapping pleasantries, particularly when I know no pleasantness is intended." He cast Tristan a mockery of his own smile. "I will get straight to the point. Have my limited resources and time helped you, or are you still as empty-headed as the day I met you?"

A hollow pit formed in Tristan's stomach. "Perhaps—" his voice cracked. He licked his suddenly dry lips, glancing at the soldiers watching the exchange from the corners of their eyes.

"You all right?" one mouthed to him.

Tristan nodded and tried again. "Perhaps you would like to discuss this somewhere more *private*, my lord?"

"In case you have not noticed, boy, I am a busy man and do not have time to gallivant about the fort as you all seem prone to do. You should be grateful I have taken as much time as I already have." Sedick folded his arms within his voluminous sleeves and waited, a smirk prowling the edges of his face.

Tristan's chest puffed up and his fists clenched. The other soldiers grumbled, casting dirty looks and gestures at Sedick while he wasn't looking. Styrax took a step closer to Tristan, covering his back. Tristan deflated. Sedick boasted the bigger ego between them, and Tristan didn't have the energy to fight it. At least he knew that, despite whatever Sedick had to say, the soldiers of Lorate had Tristan's back.

"I have dreams, my lord." He tried to put as much feeling behind the words, make Sedick understand that they were *more* than just every-day dreams—that there was *something* to them—but it was a wasted effort.

Sedick quirked an eyebrow and sighed. "Oh?"

Tristan pressed on, even as he saw Sedick's interest waning. "I see...*things*."

"You have a stunning way with words, truly," Sedick said with a sneer.

"I don't know how to explain them, but I know they're *important* things. When I wake up, though, they're gone."

The sneer had dropped from Sedick's face. Instead, he was impassive, but there was an odd tightness about his lips now. "Go on."

Tristan glanced around again. The rest of the soldiers had lost interest, thank Mother Night. He lowered his voice and leaned toward Sedick. "There are monsters. Pale ones with wide, dark eyes and rows of rotting teeth. They're not human...but seem like maybe they had been at one point?"

Sedick nodded, a gleam in his eyes. The tightness around his mouth vanished. "It seems my magic is working, then."

"*What?*" A lingering dread clawed its way up Tristan's throat. "But your spells are supposed to help with my memories. Surely that can't—" He swallowed dryly and nearly choked. "What about a home? My family?"

"It's *your* past, boy. I could no more change your memories than I could give a barren man a child." He wiped dirt off the hem of his sleeve. "If you're concerned about it, see me after my announcement at the end of inspection, and perhaps I may strengthen the wards on the ring to see if that helps."

He smiled as sweetly as any weasel. "Until then, I shall forget your presence entirely. Good day."

Tristan paced the roof once before he sat down again, letting the night air cool the steam from his ears. That conversation still left

Tristan with a gaping hole in his chest and rage searing through his veins. His life couldn't be simply monsters and dread. It couldn't be true. It *wasn't* true. And yet the dread that had perched on his shoulders the moment Laire gave him a name dug its claws a little deeper. He shook it away. No. There was more to it. He would accept nothing less.

His mind drifted back to the future, hung low over Lorate like an executioner's blade. An attack on the Golden Grove. The thought settled in his stomach like curdled milk. Had he ever been to war before? Would latent skills resurface from before he could remember? None of his skills from Lorate would be of any help. Planting crops was all fine and good, but a pea plant couldn't shield him from a sword. If he and the rest of Lorate didn't come up with something fast, they'd be nothing but arrow fodder. He rubbed his rings, and a tired orange haze settled around his eyes. What a waste the past five years had been. He had nothing to show for them.

Styrax's voice floated through his mind. *Whenever you're ready to go on your grand adventure, say the word and I'll be right there with you.*

Tristan had shrugged the thought away before. What could two runaways accomplish?But the more he pondered it, a new, frenetic kind of excitement built in his chest. He had a little money saved up. Not much, but it'd be enough to get him a few towns over, with some extra for a map or two. He could work for his keep as he traveled or just live off the land. He could make it work. And if Styrax came like he said he would, that would be extra hands and extra company. Extra guidance, really.

But a knot twisted in his gut. Could he leave the rest of the fort behind with clear conscience, knowing what the others would face? These men had homes and families, and he had nothing—just a pea plant on a windowsill. Wouldn't it be better for him to put himself in danger if he could save even one other man?

He slumped back against the roof. The leaves swirled and hissed in harmony with his battling thoughts. Bouncing. Shimmering. Whispers and syllables of a long-forgotten language that was alien and familiar all at once. Tristan closed his eyes and listened, wishing they would give him some idea of where he should go from here. And then they coalesced into one voice.

Be careful. One on the roof.

Tristan froze, his heart hammering. What... What was *that*?

I see him.

There it was again. A new tree. Another tone. An unfamiliar voice, rich and feminine, with a lilt he couldn't place. What was happening?

Chills raced down Tristan's spine. The world stopped save for the whispering trees around him. The hairs on his neck stood on end as his heart raced. He waited to hear the voice again. Moments stretched to minutes. Nothing. He had almost convinced himself that it had been trauma and sleep deprivation—just him wishing to hear something that didn't exist.

And then it happened again.

What do you see?

Tristan's heart nearly shot through his throat. He tried to swallow it back without success. He couldn't deny it anymore; he'd *heard* something and that thought formed a deep pit in his chest. He closed his eyes and prayed that it was simply a trick of the night breeze, carrying conversations closer than they normally would be.

Nothing so far.

But then, where was the breeze? The air had been stagnant all night. Tristan's limbs numbed with fear and his throat turned to paste.

Barracks are clear. I've found the general's office. I'll check there and let you know what I find.

"Tristan?"

Tristan started so badly he nearly slipped off the roof. Cursing under his breath, he righted himself and glanced at the ground below. "Styrax! Wh-what are you doing over here? Aren't you supposed to be asleep?"

Styrax looked at him in a way he never had before.. "I came to check on you."

Tristan mashed his lips together. He didn't have time for a chat. "I'm fine." *Please leave.*

Apparently, Styrax missed the unspoken part. He leaned against the building and stared into the fort yard. He kept his face impassive. "The Golden Grove, huh?"

"So I've heard." Tristan swung off the roof, ears strained for any more messages and only half paying attention.

"How do you feel about it?"

Tristan ran a hand through his hair, his leg bouncing. After a few breaths, he looked blankly at his hands. "I'm going to die, aren't I?" He looked at Styrax, the finality of it all settling over his shoulders again. All emotion seeped from him at that moment. For a second, the voices sat forgotten.

Styrax drew closer. "You don't have to die a martyr, Tristan."

Tristan sighed. "You're going to be sagely and say 'my choice is my destiny' or something like that, aren't you?"

"No."

Tristan blinked in consternation. He had never heard Styrax so serious. "What?"

"No, I won't tell you that. I'm going to tell you that we can get out of here right now."

Tristan took a step back, his heart thudding in his chest. His face flushed and froze all at once. "You don't mean...*leaving*, do you?"

"That's exactly what I mean." Styrax tossed something to him— his knapsack, packed and ready to go. "I've told you, you won't find your memories here. What better time to leave and start looking for them?"

Tristan looked at the knapsack in his hands as if it were some indescribable creature. "But what about the others? What about Vinea, Linae, and Laire?" Dread jolted through him as he said their names. The voices! Someone was going straight for the general's quarters. All three of them were in danger. He had to leave *now* to make sure they were safe. They had saved him, and now it was his turn to return the favor.

"If they're smart, they'll leave, too."

Tristan slung the knapsack over his shoulder to appease Styrax, but his mind was no longer on the conversation. "Can I... Can I think about it?"

"Tristan, there's a time for thinking, and a time for doing. We have to *do* something, now, before it's too late for either of us."

Tristan took a step back. He had never seen Styrax so anxious before. His gaze slid to Laire's office. Was that a figure slipping in through the front door? Or his imagination? "Styrax, I'm sorry, but I can't make a decision like that without thinking it over. I just can't."

Styrax maneuvered so that Tristan was looking at him face-to-face again. "Is something wrong?"

"There's—" Tristan stopped himself. His gut twisted in on itself. What if he was wrong? What if there was no one there, and he had just been hearing things? He couldn't drag Styrax into that. Couldn't risk Sedick's ridicule falling on the both of them. "It's nothing. I have to go. I'll think on it and come find you."

Styrax pressed his lips together as if to protest but nodded instead. "Hurry, though. If we're going to leave, we have to do it tonight."

"I understand."

"Don't forget your journal. I haven't been up there to grab it yet."

"Thank you."

Styrax looked at him with suspicion but left him on his own. Tristan waited for ten steps.

When Styrax disappeared, Tristan squared his shoulders and set his sights on Laire's office. He didn't see any activity, but he supposed any self-respecting elf wouldn't do much to betray their presence. Setting his shoulders and praying he'd be able to put his own advice into practice without dying, Tristan set off through the shadows to face the enemy.

TEN

Aspen crouched against the fort wall. Her cloak bled into the long shadows that cut the silver swathes of moonlight into shards. The tree she had climbed brushed her back as she surveyed the yard.

It was certainly the most eclectic fort yard she had ever seen. Instead of lounge awnings and gambling circles, small garden plots and carefully pruned fruit trees took up most of the space, sprinkled about in a system she assumed *someone* must understand. Each plot had a haphazard name-plate next to it made from scraps of wood or fabric.

It almost made Aspen smile to see the gardens. The men were still just men, with interests and pet projects and lives outside the war. But she could not ignore the wards and symbols etched around each door and window, marked in charcoal or ragged dye. The scraps of twigs and cloth shaped into stars and moons hanging from the windows—talismans made by desperate men. Any kinship or sympathy she might have felt toward these men stopped at those signs. Although useless and simply the result of superstitious rumors, talismans left one obvious message. She and others like her were not welcome here. Here, or anywhere else. They never would be, so long as the false king sat on his stolen throne.

The surrounding trees rustled without a breeze with whispers shaking from their leaves. The sound shivered up the tree at Aspen's back, the shimmering leaves brushing together in unison into a single voice. Ash's voice.

Be careful. One on the roof.

Aspen glanced across the yard again. For all the life in those little garden beds, none seemed to be anywhere else. No movement. No guards. Just the whistle of a soft snore somewhere in the night.

And one man stretched across the top of a roof. From afar, he looked almost like...A pang of nostalgia blossomed in Aspen's chest.

She squashed it.

She put her hand on a nearby branch and spoke back to it. "I see him." The leaves sighed her message in a single breath, sweeping from branch to tree to forest beyond as it made its way to Ash.

Message sent, Aspen crept across the fence, looking for a place to get down without breaking her legs. She glanced back to the roof, but the man hadn't moved. She would have to keep an eye out for him, but for now, she was safe.

Aspen leapt across the divide between the fort wall and an outlying building, light as a fallen leaf. From the smell leaching through the building's roof, it could only be the waste disposal facility or the mess hall. Her bet was on the mess hall. Trying not the breathe in the toxic fumes, Aspen let herself off the roof and made her way deeper into the fort.

Away from lamps and fires of the bigger cities she'd snuck through, the stars dazzled overhead in great swathes of blue and green. Their brilliance gilded the fort in soft silver. If Aspen wasn't spending most of her time dodging piles of unnamed refuse, it almost could have been beautiful. That, and if it weren't filled with people eager to kill her if given the chance.

What do you see? Ash's voice was fainter this time, carried to a single apple tree across the fort yard. Aspen picked her way to it, sliding from one patch of shadows to the next. She placed her hand on the smooth bark, crouching beneath the low-hanging, fruit-laden branches. She stepped on a slimy, rotting apple that had fallen and grimaced. "Nothing so far."

Hidden in shadow and tucked as close as it could come to a wall, the apple tree was a relatively safe vantage point for the moment, so Aspen stayed, surveying the rest of the buildings. All of them were too rough-shod to be what she was looking for. If this fort was like any of the others she had been to, she needed the biggest, nicest—

Ah. There it was. The general's quarters. Lording over the heart of the fort, and with a smaller detached building just off to the side. The most likely place for a private office. A single light was on in the larger building, but the smaller was dark. Perfect.

"They make this too easy," Aspen said to herself. She touched the tree again. "Barracks are clear. I've found the general's office. I'll check there and let you know what I find."

Getting to the general's quarters was a simple matter. No guards. No towers. No traps. Every step she took reminded her that these men were not soldiers. They didn't think like them—hadn't grown up fighting the shadows Osmen had told them lurked around every corner. If they really intended to invade the Golden Grove, they'd have no chance of success. She had trained her men too well. If the rumors were true then by Sister Earth what was Osmen *thinking*?

The office door resisted entry, but a small dagger in the lock did the trick. Aspen lifted the door from the bottom as she inched it open so it wouldn't squeal on its hinges. She closed it the same way and then turned to the interior of the office. "Oh, sweet Sister Earth."

A menagerie of very dead animals leered at her from nearly every surface. Their glass eyes stared bleakly into her soul, their fangs bared in frozen snarls. The shadows they cast clawed their way up the walls and across the floor, almost alive in their grotesqueness. Nightmares.

Aspen bowed to them, both to sympathize and to appease any vengeful spirits that might have taken residence. She picked her way further inside, careful not to knock one over. With how big and packed in they were, the ensuing racket would bring the whole fort on top of her.

Interspersed among the stuffed corpses were an array of weapons. She glanced over them as she passed, and her scalp prickled. They were dwarven and elven made. Weapons from the Ancient Races. Trophies. It was a dark reminder of why she was here. She would have no more deaths on her conscience.

She found what she had been looking for tucked away in a corner beneath a small window. An oaken desk, thankfully clear of dead animals. It had a single wide drawer with a small lock. Too small for a dagger to be much good against it. Aspen tested the drawer, hoping the general had forgotten to lock it. No such luck. With a sigh, she withdrew a small vial from her cloak and unstopped it. A puff of moisture followed the cork, and a tiny green shoot poked its head out.

Aspen closed her eyes and controlled her breathing. This had never come easily to her. She spoke to the vine in the Ancient Tongue, the syllables slow and precise. The blood in her veins buzzed and throbbed, awakened by the magic within. She opened her eyes to watch the plant stretch toward the lock and tried to ignore the green, telltale mist of magic that bled from her skin. She had spent years trying to control it to no avail. There was nothing she could do about it now, no matter how much strength it leached from her.

The vine picked through the lock mechanisms until Aspen heard it turn. Thankfully, it didn't take more than a minute. Aspen called the vine back to its vial and stoppered it again. The mist dissipated. Her fatigue did not. Cursing her drooping eyelids and leaden limbs, Aspen did her best to ignore them and opened the drawer. Her heart leapt at the contents. Documents. So many documents. If there was anything to find about the invasion, it would be here.

She rifled through the stack, careful not to disturb its order or placement too much. The less evidence she left of her presence, the better.

"What are you doing with papa's work?" A voice. Imperious. Young. Scared.

Aspen's body tensed like a bowstring ready to snap. *By the Architects.* She slowly looked over her shoulder. A young girl framed by golden curls glowered at her from the safety of a stuffed lion in the corner.

"Linae, who are you talking to?" A woman walked through the doorway—the spitting image of the girl.

Aspen wished she could have somehow stopped time, but no magic could touch it. The smile on the woman's face melted the moment she caught sight of Aspen—the monster in the night—in the same room as her daughter. She screamed and snatched her daughter to her chest. The shock must have frightened the poor girl because she began to cry. "Who are you?" the woman asked, taking steps toward the door. "Why are you—?" She stopped as she gave Aspen a once over. "You're-you're with the rebellion, aren't you?"

Aspen glanced for escape routes. The woman had the door blocked. There was a single window behind the desk. But lantern light began to flare in the yard. The window would lead her right into the spotlights if she didn't hurry.

"You're with Chaedra, aren't you?" the woman asked.

Aspen froze. How did she—?

The woman clamped a hand over her mouth in horror when her eyes focused on Aspen. "Oh, Mother Night, what have I done?"

"She was…getting into papa's drawers!" The little girl sobbed.

The woman covered her daughter's ears tightly. "Everything's going to be all right." She looked to Aspen. "I told Chaedra I would bring Tristan to *you,* not the other way around. Where *were* you yesterday?"

Aspen's heart stopped. *She* was their informant? The lady of the fort? But why—? Aspen shook her head. It didn't matter. What mattered was the sound of people rousing and the clatter of weapons. She had to get out. Now.

The informant grabbed her by the arm. Vice-like. Desperate. "You have to take him away. Get Tristan out safe. *Tonight.*"

"What was that?"

"Lady Vinea? Are you all right?"

Voices. People spilling into the fort yard. Aspen had to *leave*. "I'm not in a position to—"

The woman's grip on her tightened. She pulled Aspen close, desperation hissing through her teeth. "He has been recognized by the last remnants of the Vastir family. You *must* get him out."

Aspen's heart stopped. She watched the woman, wide-eyed. The Vastir? The late Queen's—? It couldn't be. Osmen had hunted them to extinction decades ago. But if some *had* survived, and they recognized this Tristan as—

No. *No!* She could not do it.

"Find Tristan, and go through the south gate," Lady Vinea said. "It's never guarded. It's not safe for him anymore."

Aspen swallowed. She saw the terror on the woman's face. Not of her, but for someone she cared deeply for. No matter how much she wanted to, she could not turn that down. "I will do what I can."

"Thank you." The woman released her with a heavy sigh of relief. "Go, and may the winds carry you far from this forsaken place." She hiked Linae higher on her hip. "Unfortunately, we all have lives and identities to protect, so I am going to scream again. *Run.*"

She didn't give Aspen time to respond. She shrieked and tore out of the office. "LAIRE!"

Aspen cursed. She flung a handful of parchment into her knapsack and vaulted out the window. An alarm bell, strident and frantic, shattered the quiet. Lanterns flickered to life and men poked their heads out of doorways. Aspen grit her teeth and dodged the squares of light. They grew in number with every toll of the bell and soon swarmed with men like moths to candles. The longer she stayed, her chances of escape dimmed.

...don't get caught.

Aspen cursed again. Ash would kill her for this.

As the darkness drowned to its last breath in the soldiers' lights, silver-tinged fog rolled in like a phantom. It shrouded everything; trapped the men and light inside their barracks. The fog electrified Aspen's skin and made the fine hairs on her arms stand on end. *Magic* energized it. Not hers, and not Ash's. Someone else was here that shouldn't be.

Amidst the cries and curses of confused soldiers, Aspen said a prayer of thanks to her unseen savior. She ran off through the mist to find the wall and escape.

The only wall she found, though, was flesh and bone as she collided with someone. They grappled arms and legs as they both tried to keep themselves upright. Aspen snatched a handful of tunic. They seized her shoulders. Both came to a standstill, heaving and trying to wrench from each other's grips.

"*You're* the one!"

Aspen jolted. No. *No.* Anything but that voice. Anyone but the person it belonged to.

His face swam through the fog, illuminated by stray shafts of moonlight. A wraith. A memory. A dagger to her chest. "What have you done?" He blinked, and a film of confusion fell over his eyes. "Who are you?"

Aspen grit her teeth, hatred swelling in her veins. "I am *no one.* Release me." She jarred her shoulders away from him. He released her without a fight.

She wrapped her cloak tighter about her and turned to run. The Pit have him and everything he touched. She would not traverse that poisoned road of false hope again. She had a different mission to fulfill, and by Sister Earth, they w*ould not* capture her here.

And then those four words drifted to her across the eddies of fog. "Do I...know you?"

Aspen paused. Only for a moment. Her duty kept her from running. Her hope made her turn, pausing for the barest instant to entertain the thought that maybe...just maybe...

And that was the end.

Pain ripped through her back, following the familiar, jagged trail from shoulder to hip. Flashes of another night—of blood spilt and roaring waves—flashed through her mind. A gasp rent from her throat. She staggered to her knees, sweat pouring from her face as she shook. How? *Why?* Why was this happening *now*?

The fool that had distracted her had questions of the same vein. "What-what's happening? Why are you—?"

"Good catch, Tristan. This beast nearly killed Vinea and Linea." A voice swirling in the fog. A voice Aspen could never forget.

Aspen's limbs seized; her heart clenched. Fear trickled down her spine in the wake of that voice. That nightmare she could never banish. Every second brought it closer. Every step sent more pain razing through her veins. It drove her farther into the dirt. Flooded her mouth with bile. Turned her vision nearly black. But she clenched her jaw and dug her nails into her palms. She would not fall. Could not.

The sword appeared through the mist. White as bone. Smooth and sharp as glass on one edge. Jagged as dragon's teeth on the others. She felt as she did when it had first wounded her. Torn in half.

Stupid, stupid idiot! She should have known—should have checked to see who lorded over the fort. She had made the same mistake that had nearly killed her the first time. The same one that *had* killed so many others.

The man—*Laire*—stopped when he saw Aspen. He cast his eyes across her. She prayed he wouldn't recognize her; that maybe he had forgotten the night that she could not.

"*You!*" His eyes widened.

"General Laire, are Lady Vinea and Linae all right?" Tristan asked, eyes flicking between Laire and Aspen.

"Tristan, get away from her," Laire barked, an odd light of fear in his eyes.

"Sir, *what* is hap—?"

"*Now!*"

Tristan didn't move. He seemed rooted to the spot, knees locked and shoulders tight. Aspen tried to force herself to her knees, trying to mask the gasping, ragged breaths the effort tore from her. They could argue all they wanted. She had to *leave*.

Tristan clenched his fists and took a step in front of Aspen. "Sir, if Vinea and Linae are all right, can we withhold judgment? I think I may know this—"

"You will do as you're *told*, soldier!"

Tristan flinched.

"I will remove you myself." Laire stormed over and shoved Tristan out of the way. Laire glowered down at Aspen. Powerless. Unable to move. Battling to stay conscious. And he grinned. "I've already killed you once."

No. *No.* It would not end like this. She bared her teeth in a feral grin with a confidence she never felt. "Well, you did a rotten job of it, didn't you?"

His grin faded. "You won't destroy my plans. Not this time. Your time has run out, monster."

The words pounded in Aspen's chest, echoes of that night so many years ago. If only it had been so simple then.

Laire raised his sword to strike. Aspen couldn't draw her own. Not in such close quarters. She needed something smaller. She gripped the hilt of her hidden dagger as the sword came down and tried to dodge, but a wave of pain flooded her. Dulled her senses. Slowed her down. She cursed the sword even as it came to end her.

"Sir, wait! Please!"

A moment's hesitation, that's all it took. The blade skated off a cobblestone, a hair's breadth from Aspen's back. She leaped for the thing nearest her as she drew her dagger. She collided with Tristan. Far enough away that she could now stand, she forced Tristan up with her, gripping her arm around his chest and pulling his back to her. Tristan stiffened in horror when she pressed her dagger against his throat.

"Move and he dies." This was stupid. This was desperate. The

Laire she knew and dreaded would never value his soldiers' lives above a kill. But this was the only way she could put distance between herself and that cursed sword. And fulfill her promises.

By some miracle, Laire halted in his tracks. His palpable rage practically evaporated the surrounding mist. "You don't know what you're doing."

"I believe that's for me to decide." Aspen took careful steps back into the mist, attention never leaving Laire or the sword. Tristan didn't fight, but his limbs were tense—whether from anger or fear, she couldn't tell.

"You've made an enemy of a dangerous man," Laire said.

"I have many enemies. One more makes no difference to me." The mist finally enveloped them and blotted Laire from her sight. She darted as quickly as she could to the south gate with her hostage in tow, gaining strength with each step away from that wretched sword.

CHAPTER

ELEVEN

Tristan couldn't get his mind to stop spinning. Nausea followed it, flowing through his limbs and stomach and making bile flood his mouth. Phantom memories wafted off the smell of the elf's hair. Nightmares flowed from Laire's bone-white blade.

Tristan bit his lip. None of that mattered right now. He was being held at knife point. An enemy had infiltrated the fort. He had to be a soldier right now. The rest would come with time.

Distraction. He needed a distraction.

"You don't think the mist's a bit overkill?" Tristan asked her as the foamy shroud rolled through the alleyways.

"*Hush.*" She dug the knife tighter against his throat but didn't draw blood.

He wondered if he could run. She seemed distracted enough by trying to find her way through the fog, squinting into the curling eddies. But he had seen how quickly she could move. He didn't want to take his chances with that unless he absolutely had to.

"What exactly is your plan here? Using me as a hostage won't do you any good. I'm not worth anything."

"Your general seems to disagree."

"Well, I…" She had him there. Why *had* Laire given in so easily? She was the *enemy* and could hurt hundreds more people. Wouldn't it have been better to capture her, even if it meant he might die? "Regardless, you're surrounded. Sure, the fog has bought you some time, but it won't be long until Laire's caught up to you." Tristan didn't know why he was antagonizing her. Nerves, probably? He had not been prepared to contemplate death at the end of an elven knife when he woke up this morning.

"Is there a point to this?" The knife blade dug a little harder.

"There's certainly a point to that knife," he said to himself, fighting back the urge to cackle like a maniac. He had lost his mind. Goading someone with a blade to his throat wouldn't win him any awards for brilliance, but he had to do *something*. "All I'm saying is —" his voice cracked. He cleared his throat. "I really hope you didn't waste more than a few seconds coming up with this, because this is a *horrible* exit strategy."

She dug her nails into Tristan's arm until he could have sworn she drew blood. The dagger never wavered from his neck. "You are very bold for someone being held at knifepoint." She said nothing else, and neither did Tristan.

The distraction had been useless. Instead, he cast around for something he could use to defend himself. He was a *soldier*, for Mother's sake! Sure, his training had been paltry at best and he hadn't picked up a sword in five years, but if he and the others were going to survive the campaign against the Golden Grove, he had to do something *now*.

But, no matter how much he tried, there was nothing for him to do. The elf's grip was too strong, her blade pressed too close to his jugular. She had no weapons in her belt that would do him any good. No other daggers. Only a sword, which would be impossible to use in such close quarters. Unless…

Not entirely sure what his plan was other than to get away, Tristan craned his wrist and wrenched the sword out of its scabbard.

It didn't come all the way free, but he didn't need it to. He twisted it and jammed the exposed part of the blade into the elf's hip. She grunted and muttered a curse. Tristan felt her blood skimming over his hand. Before he could do anything else, she kneed him in the small of the back. He gasped and jerked away. The sword came free of her side and slid back into its sheath.

She tightened her grip on him, her breath hot and ragged in his ear. "Give me one more reason to slit your throat."

Tristan grit his teeth and glared at her from the corner of his eye. "I'm sure you have plenty, so what are you waiting for?"

Figures emerged from the mist, rumpled and carrying an assortment of misused weapons in their hands. Tristan's heart stopped. No. No, they couldn't be here. She'd kill them all.

"Who's out there?" one of the soldiers called before lantern light illuminated them all. Boff. His crinkled eyes grew wide at the sight of Tristan and the elf. "What's going on here?" He lifted the light higher. "Tristan, you all right?"

"Boff, stay back!" Tristan threw his weight against the elf and tried to shove her farther into the mist away from the others. He wanted—needed—help, but these were not the men to do it. They'd get themselves killed. "Go back inside!"

Boff didn't listen. He gripped his weapon—a rusted pitchfork—tighter in shaking hands and motioned the others forward. "Tristan, hold on. We'll get you—"

Something shrieked through the air and pierced the lantern, dousing the flame and shattering the glass. Tristan saw a glimpse of silver-green fletching before the light went out. An *arrow*. Boff screamed, and so did the men with him as more arrows rained from the heavens. Weapons were shot from their hands. Others hissed past their ears and the space between their arms and torsos. The men scattered.

Tristan's heart thumped adrenaline through his body and his face lost all color. "GET INSIDE!" The words nearly split through his chest as he strained against the elf. "GET TO COVER!"

Aspen, GO! The trees shouted in ragged dissonance.

"Sweet Sister Earth, Ash, I told you to *stay away*," The elf, Aspen, said, her tone dark and bitter. She dragged Tristan away from the chaos as he fought against her.

"You've killed them!" he snarled, digging his heels in and frantically searching for signs of life. "They've done nothing wrong and you *killed* them!"

Aspen shook him and boxed one of his ears. Stars spiraled through his sight as the ear rang. "They're not dead!" she said. "That archer can shoot a flea off a dog. If she wanted them dead, they wouldn't have a chance to scream." She hauled him away with her again. "She'll make sure your friends survive the night. She knows who the real enemy is."

Before Tristan had a chance to ask what that meant, the fog solidified in front of them and they collided with a solid wall. Aspen cursed and whirled in a different direction.

"Let him go!"

Tristan sagged in relief. He knew that voice. Someone that would be able to help. "Styrax! Thank Mother Night!"

Aspen cuffed him but didn't stop moving. "I don't take demands from shadows."

The mist parted like a swirling curtain being drawn aside and Styrax stepped through. Any relief Tristan might have felt withered. His chest clenched and his mouth ran dry. The Styrax that stepped out was not the brother, mentor, and friend he knew. Something lurked in the way he carried himself. The rims of his irises glowed white, and the air snapped and singed around him.

Aspen tried to keep retreating, but Styrax lifted a hand and spoke in a language that gurgled and rushed like a mountain stream. The mist turned into a solid sheet of ice, blocking Aspen's path.

Tristan couldn't breathe. The blood drained from his face. Danger. *Magic.*

"Let my friend go," Styrax said again, his voice slow and even as he watched the knife at Tristan's throat.

Aspen's grip on the knife didn't change. "No. Too many people depend on me."

"Then why on Mother Night would you come *here*?" Tristan asked before he could stop himself.

She didn't say anything, but her grip tightened on the dagger, and he felt her jaw tighten.

Voices loomed and ebbed through the swirling fog. Styrax muttered something under his breath and the surrounding mist thickened. Sweat droplets formed on his forehead. "Release him, and I'll help you escape."

"And why should I trust a naiad working under a murderer's banner?"

A *naiad*? What in Mother Night was that?

Styrax balled his hands in fists and threw his shoulders back. "Considering I'm most likely your only way out, I'd say you don't have much choice."

Aspen's teeth ground in Tristan's ear. His head throbbed, and his gut roiled. Styrax not only had magic, but he was *helping the enemy*? The one that currently had his life at the end of a blade? Rage, frustration, and hurt billowed through his chest in a torrent of questions. Why? How? What did he hope to accomplish? How could he betray him like this?

Aspen hesitated a moment longer. Her grip on the dagger loosened, but not enough for Tristan to escape. He felt her heart pounding against his back.

"They all have serpent root," Styrax said. "The longer you spend here, the less time you have to warn your people."

Her body went completely rigid, and her knuckles turned white against the dagger hilt. "*What?*" Dangerous. Full of dread. The blade pressed a little too deep into Tristan's neck and cut off his airflow. He tried to pull it away, but her grip was like iron.

Styrax noticed and his face paled. He took a step closer, the white rims of his irises glowing bright and fierce against the gold. "I have my own gripes with the Ancient Races, but I know this is no way to win a war."

The soldier's voices drew ever closer, shouting as more arrows whizzed through the mist. Aspen growled, and her hand shook. "Fine." She flung Tristan to Styrax, and her hand went to her sword hilt. "Your Lady Vinea has warned me that this place isn't safe. You should both leave before things get uglier than they already are."

Styrax helped Tristan to his feet and muttered a few more of his strange words. The ice wall melted, and a tunnel parted in the mist. "That will get you to the wall. The rest is up to you."

Aspen left with only a single glance back at Tristan. "Don't follow me. It will end badly for you." She disappeared into the mist.

Tristan shoved Styrax away, his hand at his throat. The sensation of the blade still whispered across his skin. He dry-heaved, body trembling. He wanted to say something—*anything*—to Styrax, but no words came. Too much. It was all too much.

Styrax broke the silence first. "Are you hurt?"

Tristan shook his head.

"Good." Styrax's shoulders drooped. He wicked sweat from his brow and clutched a shaking hand on his knapsack strap. His eyes still glowed, but only faintly. "Then let's get out of here."

"*What?*" Tristan croaked.

The shouts were nearly on top of them. Tristan could have sworn he saw the white haze of Laire's sword parting the mist as it knocked arrows aside. Styrax spoke more words of magic and the fog thickened nearly to stone walls. Styrax grimaced, his face pale and drawn. "I can't stay here, Tristan, not after Sedick gave out that serpent root, and *especially* not after this. And you—you've said yourself you'll never find your memories here. Come *with* me, and we can find them together."

"You want me to—" Tristan staggered back a pace, his mind reeling. He grabbed at his rings to calm himself. Sedick's settled into his palm. Orange-tinted, searing rage blasted through his mind like fire devouring a mountainside. He nearly staggered back from the sheer, sudden force of it. It sucked the blood from his face. The ring burned in his palm. "She almost *killed* me! And you helped her escape!" The words came out so sharp they nearly split his lips.

"Keep your voice down! They'll find us!"

"And now you want me to *leave* with you? The *enemy?*" He didn't know where the ferocity came from, but fear continued to fuel it as the ring pulsed in his palm.

Styrax's face blanched. "Tristan, whatever you think I may be, I've never been your enemy." He reached for his shoulder.

Tristan wrenched it from him. "You nearly got me *killed*, Styrax!"

"I *saved* you! And I'm trying to do it again! You heard what the elf said about Lady Vinea. Something's not *right* here, Tristan! They'll never let you find your memories as long as you're here." He moved toward him.

Still clutching his ring, Tristan took a step away from him and whipped the serpent root from his pocket. "Why should I trust *anything* either of you say? You *lied* to me! For *five years!*"

It was as if Styrax's face shattered. "Tristan, *please.*"

Tristan couldn't get enough breath in his lungs. Soldiers were closing in from every side, still distracted by arrows, but drawing in with every step. His head throbbed. The feeling of the knife at his throat dug deeper into his skin. And now the one person he thought cared about him...It had been nothing but a lie. "What was I to you? A game?" He hated how vulnerable and pathetic he sounded.

"You *are* my friend, Tristan," Styrax said, eyes darting to the shadows lurking in the mist. "That is something I would never lie to you about. And I'll explain everything else later, I promise." He reached for him again.

An image flashed in Tristan's eyes. Styrax was no longer Styrax. His gold eyes melted to black obsidian; lidless, soulless eyes that reflected Tristan back at him. His mouth split into rows of teeth inside a jaw dripping with rotting flesh. His skin stretched so tight across his body it was made nearly translucent, the veins writhing like worms beneath it. A nightmare made real. Tristan screamed and threw the serpent root.

It struck at Styrax like an angry viper and wound around his chest and arms. Barbs sprang from their stems and anchored onto his skin. The stems bloated, glowing bright white.

Styrax's screams were unlike anything Tristan had ever heard. They tore at his ears and clawed at his chest, wrenched from deep in Styrax's chest. Styrax collapsed, and the fog vanished in an instant. His eyes no longer glowed.

Tristan let the ring go from his palm, and the anger and fear drifted away. Tears welled up in his eyes as Styrax writhed in breathless agony. His chest heaved heavier and faster, pulling in even less oxygen than before. Spots swam in his vision. Guilt crushed his chest. Monsters howled in his mind. "What...what have I done? What do I do?"

Soldiers had taken notice of Styrax's screams and were approaching. Laire followed in their wake. Another shower of arrows stopped them in their tracks, but it wouldn't keep them there for long. Tristan had to act fast. Otherwise Styrax would die.

Styrax had already nearly screamed himself hoarse when Tristan crouched. Tears cut deep tracks across his cheeks and his eyes were clouded over in misery. He looked at Tristan; reached for his hem. "Tristan, please," he sobbed. "Help me."

"Styrax, I'm sorry. I'm so sorry!" He tried to yank the plant off, but it was stuck fast. "It won't come off!"

"Some-Someone like...me. They'll know how to help."

"Like the elf?" Tristan asked, his voice shrill. "The same one that just tried to kill me?"

But Styrax's eyes had already rolled back into his head.

The blood drained from Tristan's face. The world heaved and swayed. Styrax's words flew through his mind like wooden tops. They bashed against the monsters and ricocheted in his skull. Tristan staggered to his feet, stars of orange pain dancing through his eyes. Leave? Desert the only home he'd ever known? Go after someone that would kill him the first chance she got?

But what was the alternative? Watching his best friend die? Knowing he had been the one to cause it?

The soldiers weren't on them yet, but they would be soon. He pawed at the rings around his neck with trembling fingers and caught the smaller of the two, holding it tight to him. He ran his thumb over the unintelligible words etched around it.

Help, he wept internally at the memories it kept from him. *Tell me what to do.*

Warmth flooded through him. It coaxed life back into his limbs and chased the orange-tinged haze from his vision.

For evergreens and aspen trees.

A whisper. Barely a thought. But there just the same. The words spread like a warm blanket across his shoulders. Comforting. Secure. A flood of relief stilled the trembling in his limbs and smoothed the anguish from his brow. The monsters in his mind fell silent.

You're not one to be content with mediocrity. Styrax's words from only a few days ago. Mother Night, it felt like a lifetime.

He clutched the ring so tight it left a mark on his palm. He dried his tears and wiped his mouth. Without another thought, without another moment to hesitate and change his mind, he threw Styrax over his shoulder. "Don't worry. I'll get you out of here. You've still got a lot of explaining to do, remember?"

Soldiers were shouting at him—he even heard one that sounded like Laire—but he blocked them out. "I'm sorry," he said. To Laire. To Vinea and Linae. And to Styrax.

He ran toward the gate.

TWELVE

Laire watched Tristan and Styrax disappear into the night. Gone. Tristan was gone. The insurance he'd kept for five years. The prize he'd groomed, nurtured, and developed; the one that would give his family the life he'd once had and lost. His world—his plans—shattered in an instant. All because an elf with a black sword had appeared where she didn't belong. An elf that had died five years ago. And now she had foiled Laire's best-laid plans. Again. And he had to keep Tristan away from her.

He screamed and grabbed the man nearest to him, throwing him after them. "Go after them!"

The man scrambled to his feet, his face pale. "Sir, we...we're not equipped to handle an elf. None of us have swords, and we...we've never seen..."

"By the Architects." Another man crumpled to his knees, tears streaming down his face. "We're all going to die. We can't face *one* elf! How are we supposed to fight an entire *army* of them?"

"Get off the ground, you worms!" Laire spat. "That is an *order*! Go find Tristan *now*."

None of them listened. They simply stared, listless and useless.

Laire roared and took off toward his quarters. They would not get away. Not again. He could deal with his insubordinate men later.

He smashed his front door open and marched to his bedroom. The walls closed in around him. His ears rung and crescendoed into a chorus of death tolls. *Gone. Gone. Gone.*

He snatched an emergency knapsack from beneath his bed and tightened his sword belt. He didn't want this out-of-hand spiral to run its course for more than a few hours, but he had to expect the worst. He might be gone for a very, very long time. Whatever it took to bring things back to order, and to finish off that elf he'd left for dead. Vinea appeared in the doorway just as he put on his coat, arms crossed tight across her chest as she stood tall and stiff.

"What happened?" her voice trembled, but only just. Keeping it together for his sake and Linae's.

"They're all gone."

"*Who* are?"

"The elf. Tristan. Styrax. They all left together."

"*What?*" Vinea dug her fingernails into her palm, her face swirling with conflicted emotions. "Tristan is gone?" Something in the way she asked seemed off. Almost... relieved?

He straightened and watched her. "I saw it with my own eyes. But I will make it right."

Vinea glanced to Linae's room, almost subconsciously. "You're going after them, then?" She wrapped her arms around herself.

"Monsters have kidnapped one of my men. Why wouldn't I go?"

"Why are *you* going?" She sat on the bed as she watched him finish his packing. An extra pair of boots. Crossbow and bolts. A length of serpent root.

Laire grunted as he shoved the pack closed. "Because I'm surrounded by cowards."

"And yet you still want to send those men to the Golden Grove?"

"VINEA!" Laire whirled on her, eyes blazing and chest heaving. Indiscernible whispers crawled through his mind. Red tinged his vision. "This is *not* the time for this! Everything I have done I have done *for us*, and I will not have you question me again!"

Vinea drew herself to her full height, chin tilted back as she met Laire's eyes. Regal. Imperious. Furious. "I will not have you speak to me that way again. I am your *wife*." She glanced to the sword at his hip. "Put the sword away."

Some of the blazing fury ebbed from Laire's pounding head. "Vinea, I'm sorry. I don't have time for this right now, I—" He took a step toward her, but she shoved him back.

"Laire Baison, remove that sword *right now*. I will not speak to you with it on. You know I hate what it does to you."

"Vinea…"

She folded her arms and waited, lips pressed tightly together while her eyes swam with moisture.

"My love, I'm sorry." Laire unbuckled his scabbard and dropped it on the bed. "I'm sorry I hurt you. But I have to go. Tristan needs me."

"*I* need you, too, Laire," she said, her voice wavering. She took his hand in hers. "Search parties can be sent after Tristan. Stay with Linae and me. Retire from this war you're so desperate to fight. *Please*."

Laire watched her closely. Traced the freckles on the bridge of her nose. Counted the wrinkles he knew he had given her. What harm would it do to tell her? To explain what he was doing and why? To quiet her fears? She had been his partner in everything for more than ten years. Surely she of all people deserved an explanation. He opened his mouth with the words ready to tumble from his lips, but he stopped them. Dammed them inside his throat. If he told her, then whatever fate befell him would be hers as well. She would have no escape. He couldn't do that to her; couldn't rob Linae of two parents instead of one.

Instead, he brushed Vinea's cheek with his palm. "I can't. And you will understand why when this is all over. I promise." He kissed her, held her to his chest for a moment, and then left her on their bed. He buckled his sword back to his waist as he left.

Sedick waited for Laire just outside the door, and his young acolyte stood tucked away in the shadows. "A shame to leave such a beautiful creature behind. Rest assured, she will be safe in my care."

Vinea bristled. "I have taken care of myself long before I met you, Lord Sedick, and I will continue to do so long after you are gone." She slammed the door in their faces. Laire heard a stifled sob behind the door.

Laire stared at Sedick, long and piercing, trying not to let his own heart break. "I trust you as much as the elf that murdered my son. Touch my family, and you will spend the rest of your short life counting the atrocities I commit against you. They will be many."

Sedick grinned. "I do so love to see that vim of yours."

Laire leaned over him, hand resting on the pommel of his sword and air burning hot through his nose. "You seem so interested in my family's sword. How would you like to see it through your gut?" He walked away.

"Not so fast, *General,*" Sedick said, not the least perturbed by Laire's threat. "You will want to know how to tame the boy if he's gone...*feral* by the time you find him."

Laire laughed, a bark with no mirth. "*Why* would I listen to you? It's *your* magic that should have kept this from happening in the first place!"

"I only promised to keep his memories locked away. His behaviors fall on you. You elected to be his caretaker, after all." He smiled, smug as any viper with fresh prey.

Laire breathed in every fiber of patience he could find in the air because he had none left of his own and looked back at Sedick. "What do I need to do?"

"Speak a single word." He withdrew a scrap of parchment from his robes with a flourish that set Laire's teeth on edge and handed it to Laire.

Laire glanced at it briefly and curled his lip. "This is gibberish."

"That *gibberish* is a warlock word." Sedick turned it right side round and whispered the pronunciation to Laire, careful to keep it out of his acolyte's hearing range. "If the boy becomes too difficult to handle, say it, and all his fight will vanish."

"How does it work?"

"As long as my curse has any residual tethers to him, simply hearing the word will activate it," Sedick said. He grinned, his black eyes gleaming with triumph. "Touch will be your most foolproof option. But be wary, oh noble warrior—the farther he drifts from this...ahem...*hallowed* place, the less likely he will be to welcome you with open arms."

Laire curled his fist around the fine silks at Sedick's throat and drew him close. The acolyte swept from the shadows and stood behind Sedick, eyes glowing purple. Sedick waved him away.

"Beware your smug jokes, Sedick," Laire said. "Remember that you are as entrenched in this as I am. If I go down, I'm dragging you to the Pit with me." He shoved him away and stormed out the door.

SEDICK RUBBED his neck and watched Laire leave. He bit back the words he wanted to say. No use in arguing anymore, even though his skin burned at Laire's parting threat. How *dare* he?

And more importantly, how dare he so casually carry the sword that had been Sedick's life's journey for the past twenty years? The sword that had only been sung about as a nighttime horror story to keep children in bed and a siren song for those seeking power for the past four hundred years. The sword that had driven his benefactor mad. The sword that would grant Sedick's every wish.

Sedick flexed his fingers, burning with rage. That fool had no idea what he had. Sedick had watched Laire misuse and neglect the sword for over ten years, completely horrifically oblivious to the power and history he held. He had been patient then, waiting for Laire to slip. He could be patient now. It was only a matter of time before Laire died on one of his hare-brained schemes, and then Sedick could collect his prize at his leisure.

He heard Lady Vinea shuffling around in her quarters and smiled to himself. There was nothing against him enjoying the wait.

He snapped his finger at his shadow, and the boy appeared at his side. "Go check on the woman and her child."

The boy dithered. "Lord Sedick, you said I should not associate—"

Sedick backhanded him. "*Go!* Never dare to question me again."

The boy bowed and left without another word.

THIRTEEN

Vinea rocked Linae back and forth as Linae sobbed in her arms. "But *why* is papa gone?" she asked, smearing her tears across her face. "And why didn't he...he take...me?" She heaved with broken-hearted wails and buried herself deeper into Vinea.

Vinea stroked Linae's hair, trying desperately to battle back her own anger. She couldn't put that on Linae. Her father was her hero, and Vinea intended to keep it that way for as long as she could. No matter how undeserving he was of it at the moment. "He's off on an important mission, my love. He thinks he's doing the right thing and is going to find Tristan." She brushed damp strands of hair away from her daughter's face and kissed her cheeks. "But that's not nearly as important as the fort. He needs his big, strong girl to look after it while he's gone."

Linae pulled herself away, five-year-old fury raging behind her eyes. "But I don't *want* to stay here! I want to go with him to find Tristan! I have to save my brother!"

Tears welled in Vinea's eyes. "And you make me very proud for wanting to do that." She kissed Linae's forehead and helped her lay her head back down on her shoulder. "That's all mama wants to do, too," she said into her hair, rubbing her back.

They sat that way for a while, both quiet in their private misery. As Linae's body started to relax and her sobs quiet, Vinea leaned back against the wall and asked, "Do you want to sing a song?"

Linae's body tightened again. She scrunched her fingers on Linae's dress. "*No!*"

"Well, can *I* sing it, then?"

Linae wiped her nose on the back of her sleeve. "Okay. But I'm *not* singing."

"All right, I won't make you sing." Vinea snuggled Linae closer to her and looked out at the stars through their open window, remembering the nights when her mother would sing their lullaby to her and her sisters. Remembering when she had passed it on to them to sing to her future grandchildren, as it had been passed on to her by mothers past. For a long time, Vinea had thought she would never get a chance to sing it. She thanked the gods every day for the miracle that was Linae, even when that miracle had been brought about by Sedick's ugly magic.

> Hush now my child
> My young meadowlark
> Do not fear the dark
> Your mother is watching,
> My darling, my dear
> And all will be well 'til you wake.

Linae's tight, grief-stricken body relaxed. She twirled a single finger in Vinea's hair and sang the rest in a tired, breathy voice, despite her earlier protests.

> For I am the night
> And I am the stars
> That guard you my baby

Where'er you are
So sleep now in peace
Let all worries cease
For your mother shall ever stay near.

Linae's voice trailed off before the last line and she slumped against Vinea, completely asleep. Vinea maneuvered out from under her and realized with a pang how big Linae had gotten. She gave her a kiss on the forehead and tucked her in. She was about to leave when she caught sight of Sorren in the doorway. He was watching them, face soft and broken-hearted. The moment he realized he'd been caught, fear flashed across his face. He fled, tattered gray cloak emblazoned with Sedick's crest fluttering behind him.

Vinea wanted to call him back but didn't. If he had been able to sneak out from Sedick's watchful eye, that meant his master was distracted. And that gave Vinea all the chance she needed. She already had her messages, and now she could get out to send them. She crept out the doors and into the night.

Vinea couldn't stand how the silence loomed over the fort, like a funeral shroud over an open casket. She had seen too many of those in her lifetime; watched too many family members disappear beneath its folds. This war had to stop before the entire kingdom fell to it. No matter the cost to herself. She would protect Linae, and she would protect Laire, even if it was from himself.

Vinea pulled her cloak tighter about her as gooseflesh appeared on her arms. With Sedick's temporary charge of the fort, she knew it was dangerous to be out here. She also knew, though, that this could be her last opportunity to sneak away. If she didn't take this chance now, she doubted she would get it again. She had a feeling Sedick wouldn't let her out of his sight again. The thought made her blood rankle

After squinting into the surrounding darkness, Vinea determined no one had followed her and pulled back an overgrown corner hedge. A cage of three pigeons cooed in welcome.

"Hello, my loves." Vinea withdrew two leather cylinders from her cloak. Messages for Chaedra. One berating her for sending someone into the fort. They had *all* been in danger. The second was a warning about Lorate and the Vanguard. Guilt panged at her chest for betraying Laire's trust, even when he had betrayed hers, but it had to be done. If the Golden Grove fell, then the man that murdered her family would forever stay on Loralan's throne.

"What an odd time for a walk, my lady."

Vinea's heart leapt to her throat. Her fingers shook and her face paled, the world swimming around her in dizzying circles. No. No, no, *no*. Not him. Not now. She should have waited. Bile rose to her mouth and black horror closed in on her vision, but she choked it back. She took a breath and forced herself to be passive. Not to react. Not to run like her body told her to. She tucked her messages into her sleeve and turned. "Lord Sedick, I did not see you."

"No, I suppose you didn't." He peeled himself from a nearby wall and approached her, an oil stain in the moonlight. "It's dangerous to be out here alone. Haven't you heard? There are elves about tonight." He peered at the cage and stroked one of the birds with a long, claw-like finger. "Odd pets for a lady of your stature."

Shivers ran up and down Vinea's spine. She hated this man. Hated him like a snake hiding in the grass. Hated his crooning, silken voice that wrapped around her throat like a lovely noose. His eyes that strayed too far. "Perhaps, but I do love them so." She tried to take a step back—he was too close and was likely to smell her fear—but she stumbled on a thick, deep-rooted weed. She righted herself, but not before her scrolls slipped from their hiding place and rolled to Sedick's feet.

"Oh? What's this?" He raised an eyebrow at her. "Sending notes to your beloved already?"

Vinea couldn't speak. Her mouth had run too dry. Her voice had fled as more blood drained from her face.

"I hope you don't mind. I wonder what people write to one another when they're in love." He didn't wait for any pretense of permission. Vinea couldn't feel her heartbeat. With each line, Sedick's smirk grew wider. Vinea couldn't remember the last time she had breathed.

Sedick rolled the messages and stuffed them into a pocket in his robes. "I'm afraid I shall have to keep these with me, even if they are nonsense." He looked at her pointedly, his eyes glittering beetle-bright. "The Vanguard has no ties with this campaign against the Golden Grove. They have far better things to do than coddle peasants." He clasped his hands behind his back, rocking on the balls of his feet as if simply enjoying the night air. "And the *prince*. What a notion! He has been dead for so long that I had nearly forgotten he existed." Dropping his affected pleasantries, he gave her a stony look. "And he has *stayed* dead."

Vinea knew he was lying—*he* knew he was lying—but he was still remarkably calm, which somehow terrified her more than his anger would have. She should run, but she couldn't pry her feet from the ground. Even if she could, she *would not* leave Linae behind with this horrifying creature.

"No matter how faulty your information is, you still intended treason. Heartbreaking though it may be, for that reason I'm afraid I shall have to *do* something about you." He gave her a feral grin that made her skin crawl and her blood turn to ice. "What would your poor husband think?"

He beckoned her to follow him, and she did so with leaden limbs.

As Vinea followed him back to her quarters, her body shook, and her head spun. She couldn't breathe. Couldn't think. She barely put one foot in front of the other. Now that Laire was gone, she had no one to protect her. Although, in light of what she had done, she doubted Laire would want anything to do with her. What would Sedick do to her? What would he do to Linae? Her daughter had done nothing wrong, but Vinea knew what they did to the families of those they called traitors. All too well. A sob welled up in her throat at the thought, but she bit it back. She couldn't let Sedick see her that way. He thrived off weakness and vulnerability, and she refused to give him any fodder.

Sedick didn't speak to her until they entered Laire's office. He settled behind Laire's desk and raised an eyebrow at her to see if she would protest. She did not. That was not a fight worth dying for.

Sedick sighed. "Terrible thing, treason." He kicked his feet up on the desk and crossed his hands across his narrow chest. "I see so many traitors come through my doors every day. Get to pick apart their brains until there's nothing left, and then send them to die mad and alone in a dungeon somewhere." He picked at his thumbnail. "I adore my duties, but everything has its downfalls. Do you want to know the worst part of what I do?"

Vinea didn't but imagined there was no escaping it.

"Not *one* of my victims was intelligent." He waved his hand about his face in disgust. "Just being obstinate for the sake of it. I can't stand a person without a cause." The golden embroidery in his robes flashed as he leaned forward, eyes glittering. "But you are not like them, my lady. It would be such a waste to lose your mind over something like this." A wicked smile curved at the corner of his mouth. "Especially after all the time and magic I put into helping you and your husband conceive such a *lovely* little girl."

Vinea resisted the urge to tear that smile off his face for taking that tone of voice about her daughter. "I'm not..." she cleared the hoarseness from her voice. "I'm not sure there's any other option, is there?" Her hands trembled at her sides, but she kept her chin firm.

"If I were a King's Guard, that would be the case. Fortunately, my position in the court grants me certain...liberties. And I am, after all, a merciful man."

Vinea's eyes darted to Sedick's shadow, Sorren, pressed so deeply into the back corner he almost disappeared. Where had been the mercy for him?

"I have a proposition for you, my lady," Sedick said with suppressed glee. Vinea's stomach squirmed at the possibilities. "You find your husband and bring me his sword, and I will forget this unsavoriness."

Vinea blinked, unsure if she had heard him right. "I beg your pardon?"

"Give me your husband's sword, and I shall forget this whole matter."

Vinea eyed Sedick skeptically. That couldn't be all there was. All she had to do was get rid of the sword she hated, and he wouldn't tell another soul about her treachery? There was more to it. There had to be. Sedick always found a nuance that suited him best. The problem was that she couldn't think of him gaining any benefit other than the sword itself. And he could barely lift a finger for himself, so a weapon would do him no good.

"What about my daughter?"

Sedick grinned, an expression that never belonged on his face. "She will stay here under my protection," he said.

Vinea blanched, her motherly instincts roaring to life. Tearing his mouth from his face sounded better with every passing moment. "Absolutely not."

Sedick placed a dainty hand over his heart. "Vinea, I am hurt. My magic helped you conceive the child. What makes you think I would harm her?"

Vinea said nothing. She had no bargaining power here. But she would rot in the Pit for all eternity before she let Sedick lay one finger on Linae.

Sedick continued to talk, enjoying himself far more than he should have. "I am nothing but generous, though, my dear. I will send my servant with you, and should you choose to, you can ask him to 'show me', and you will see through my eyes exactly as I do."

Sorren stepped forward at a wave from Sedick. Vinea's heart broke for the boy. She remembered him so full of life and joy and wonder. Now, he was nothing but an empty puppet for his master. She took his hands in hers, watching his eyes for any hint of recognition. Nothing. Just a glaze.

"Show me," she said.

The rims around Sorren's irises turned orange, and suddenly Vinea was no longer looking at him, but herself from behind the desk, holding Sorren's hands. Pale and terrified. Blonde hair starting to show strands of silver. When had she gotten so old?

She released Sorren's hands, and the vision ended. She scowled at Sedick. "I assume this works both ways, and you'll be able to see me, too?"

Sedick spread his hands. "But of course. One can never be too cautious around traitors."

Vinea didn't rise to his bait. "If I see one hair on Linae out of place, our agreement ends."

"In every sense of the word," he said, grinning like a cat with an injured bird.

Vinea bowed stiffly, understanding his meaning. If she put one toe out of place, made one comment or talked to one wrong person, Sedick would turn her in as a traitor. She would be hunted and killed just as the rest of her family had been, and there would be no more protection for Linae. "I will need time to pack and say goodbye to my daughter."

"Of course. My servant will accompany you."

So it had already begun. She would not be free of this man until Laire's sword was in his hands. So be it. She nodded once and exited the office, her extra shadow in tow.

"Wait, boy."

He stopped and waited for Sedick to approach him. Lady Vinea left and disappeared around the corner. Sedick pointed to the boy's earring. "*Elesare.*"

His brain fog lifted, and he blinked at Sedick in wide-eyed shock. "What—?"

"Silence!" Sedick gripped his arm and leaned close. "I still own you, wretch, but I've loosened your tethers." He handed him a set of daggers. "If you see the man named Tristan, kill him on sight. I will not be dragged through Laire's game any longer." He shook him. "I don't care if it even takes your life to do it. Just kill him."

He nodded. The terror racing through him didn't matter. Not the hope and prayer that it would never come to that. Not the fear of shedding blood or of having to die to do it.

All that mattered was his master's bidding. And he would destroy himself and the world over to fulfill it. He had no choice.

PART TWO

THE DRAGON SCALES

FOURTEEN

Stupid, stupid, stupid, STUPID! What were you THINKING?

Aspen dodged trees and leapt over roots as she put as much distance between herself and her nightmares as she could. Her wounded hip throbbed almost as terribly as her head. Think. She had to *think*. All that loomed in her mind was that awful, wretched sword. Get away. Run. Hide. *Fight*.

Aspen clenched her jaw. No. *Think*. Fear and desperation had gotten her into this mess. She couldn't afford the same mistake again.

Assets. She no longer had a hostage. A very *noisy* hostage. Why had she had to grab *him*, of all people? With his shouting in *that* voice?

No. Assets. Mist from an unknown source. Sword. Knives. No hostage. Ash.

Ash! Where was she? Had she gotten away?

"I told you not to get *caught!*" Ash appeared from the darkened trees, bow drawn and eyes narrowed in worried anger. She fell into step alongside Aspen as they ran through the forest away from Lorate.

"I didn't *get* caught," Aspen said

"Caught enough to take a *hostage!*"

Voices floated to them through the fog. Haphazard orders. Cries and shouts for backup. Yelps as men ran into each other through the haze.

"And you've brought the whole of Lorate down on us. *Wonderful!*"

"Perhaps we can discuss this at a different time?" Aspen asked through gritted teeth. "We have to get to the Gatekeeper *now* before this forest floods with soldiers."

"It wouldn't *flood* if—" Ash stopped. Peered closer at Aspen. "What happened in there? You're afraid."

Aspen bit her lip until it bled and fought past the tightness in her chest. She could never figure out how Ash read her so well. "We need to go. *Now.*"

A scream shattered the night, and the mist evaporated in an instant.

Ash went white and looked at Aspen. "What on Sister Earth was that?"

"I have one guess," Aspen's immediate thoughts went to the naiad. Something must have happened to him. And there were very few things that could elicit a scream like that. "Serpent root."

Ash covered her mouth, eyes wide and hollow with horror. "You can't be serious."

"I am."

Ash stopped, leaning on a tree for support as she processed. "That will *kill* everyone." She strung her bow across her back, hands shaking and face set in grim lines. "How many have it?"

Aspen's stomach churned, wishing she had an answer that could set Ash's mind at ease. "The whole fort."

Ash staggered back a pace. Aspen nodded and pushed past her. Ash followed without another word, and they sped off into the night.

Aspen felt Ash's concerned look on the center of her back as they trekked through the forest. Her cousin's palpable worry bashed against the back of her head and made it throb. Well, throb *more*. She tried to ignore it. Sister Earth, she tried. Even as the tension swelled in the space between them and made it impossible to move without feeling it. Trying was not the same as succeeding, though.

She had hoped Ash would pick up on her not-so-subtle hints to leave her alone—minimal eye contact, increased physical distance, hand clenched around her sword like she might lop off a stray tongue—but Ash was adept at ignoring them. "What are you not telling me, Aspen? You look like something out of a nightmare."

Aspen glowered at the patches of stars through the trees. Was she not allowed a moment of peace? Her glower softened a little. No. She wasn't. Not when others' lives were also at stake. She could swallow her demons for them. "Sedick wasn't our only old friend in Lorate tonight. General Laire runs the place."

"The man that nearly *killed* you?"

Aspen rubbed the base of her left thumb, hidden beneath her leather bracer. Three faces swam in her vision. "Yes."

"Did he recognize you?"

"Yes." Aspen's back ached at the thought of it.

"And that soldier we saw in the village?"

Aspen missed a step. Missed a heartbeat. That soldier—Tristan—danced about the edges of her mind, trying to dig past her barriers. Should she tell Ash? Let her know of the roiling, burning emotions terrorizing her body and logic?

"No." No. She could not. Would not. That would make the possibility real. She would not reopen that heart wound again. Aspen pushed on through the forest.

Ash followed silently behind. Aspen couldn't tell her thoughts this time and couldn't decide if that was more or less distracting to her.

They had no signs of pursuers as they trekked from the fort. The sounds of shouts and general panic subsided into the distance, and their own unease subsided as well. Aspen waited to breathe a sigh of relief, though. They would be safe once they were back beneath the canopy of the Golden Grove.

An owl floated overhead on silent wings, and the tops of the trees soughed with air currents that didn't reach the lower branches. Aspen watched the progression of the moon across the sky. Their window of time shrank with every step they took. Aspen's mind already spun with alternate plans if they missed their opportunity, all of them feverish and desperate and doomed to fail. Aspen pushed them aside. She *wouldn't* miss the opportunity. She would make certain of that.

The time passed in silence until they broke through the tree line into what the locals had deemed Scrub Valley. It grew a grand total of three scrub bushes dropped like some misbegotten children's toys. A narrow river chugged a lazy, uneven course just off-center in a mud-congealed bed. A deer's old carcass buzzed with flies at the base of one bush.

Ash wrinkled her nose. "They couldn't have found anything more inconspicuous, could they?"

"Probably not," Aspen said, her attention drawn to a free-standing stone arch on the other side of the river. Vines with silver-flecked black leaves twined their way around the weathered marble. The stone glowed moon-white with ancient magic, and the space within the arch wavered and spun like eddies of fog.

Ash made Aspen bandage her hip before they made their way to the archway. They skirted past clumps of weed and the deer carcass. Aspen leapt over the shallow river with ease. Ash didn't have quite the same luck. She yanked her boots out of the muck with a sickening squelch, grumbling about short legs. She hobbled behind Aspen, dragging the tops of her boots across the grass as best she could to get the mud off.

Aspen stopped before the arch, her mind harrowed up with all the ways this meeting could go wrong. Ash sidled up beside her and withdrew a tied scroll of parchment from her knapsack. Aspen took it, nodded to Ash, and then called out to the archway, "We are Ash

Inulasdoter and Aspen Tanner of the Golden Grove, representatives of the Prince's Rebellion under order from Commanding General Dallowyn Grerson. We approach on this, your one day of condescension, to speak with your Council of Elders regarding a matter of utmost urgency."

The words drifted across the clearing until they fell and died, leaving Ash and Aspen alone in the silence. They waited. And watched. And waited some more. Nothing stirred. The flies around the deer carcass continued to buzz. The river gurgled in its shallow course.

Aspen shared a look with Ash, who shrugged. Aspen opened her mouth to repeat her request. A bored, simpering voice cut her off before she could start. "Don't start all over with that tripe. I heard you the first time." A long, lithe elf strode out of the arch, making the murky space beneath it swirl. He towered over Ash and Aspen, with long red tresses down to his waist. An ash-shafted spear strapped to his back glinted with the same hostility as his wide-set green eyes. "I am the gatekeeper for the Midnight Fens. All pleas for entry must go through me."

Aspen exhaled as irritation rose in her chest. She had to remain calm. As asinine as all the bowing and scraping could be, she would endure it if it meant getting what she needed. She began again, "I am Aspen, and this is Ash. We are here as—"

The gatekeeper held up a hand. "They have assigned me as the one that chooses who may enter and who may not. Whom I listen to is under my discretion." He picked at his teeth with a sneer. "I refuse to listen to a pair of filthy half-bloods spewing lies of self-importance. Good day." He pirouetted on his heel and made to leave.

"You may not *wish* to see us," Ash said, cutting Aspen's mounting retort with a withering glare, "but you are duty-bound to hear any messengers from the Prince's Rebellion. That is whom we represent."

"You could be the *oh so great* General Shadowalker," the gatekeeper jeered, "or even General Dallowyn himself! We still will not see you."

Aspen straightened her shoulders and met the elf's gaze with all the intensity she could muster. She had dealt with defiant contempt often. He did not cow her. "I have in my hand a copy of an Agreement of Alliance that says otherwise. Your Council of Elders signed it at the start of the war, and it is still in effect."

"Precisely." The gatekeeper combed his fingers through his hair, bored. "Our *Elders* signed it. We did not. We have since dethroned those old fools, and now serve under our illustrious queen. Your Agreement no longer holds water with us."

"A *queen?*" Ash asked. "Oh, Inula is going to have a fit. A break from tradition? And she could have been a queen all along?"

"Hush, Ash." Aspen remained unfazed. She had read the Agreement. She knew what it said. "This Agreement states that 'As the current acting Council of Elders, we sign this agreement of wartime allies, in good faith, on behalf of ourselves and all current *and future citizens of the Midnight Fens*, so long as Osmen the Flameslayer reigns over the kingdom of Loralan.'" She tilted her head. "That sounds to me as if your people *did*, in fact, sign it."

The gatekeeper's face paled with rage. "If you will not leave this place of your own free will, then I shall remove you by force." He drew his spear and lunged at her.

"Aspen!" Ash's bow flew off her shoulder as she drew it.

Aspen gaged the situation as the spear came for her midsection. His balance was flawless, his stroke powerful and precise. The weapon honed to perfection. He had the advantage of reach. Her sword wouldn't get anywhere near him before he skewered her.

Aspen swayed to one side. The spear tore through her tunic but missed her body. The elf had been so certain he'd hit her that he had let his guard down. He staggered forward a half-step, off-balance, but it was enough. Aspen stepped in toward the weapon and latched onto the spear shaft. "Well, *that* was dramatic, wasn't it?" she asked. Using all her shoulder, back, and thigh muscles, she heaved on the weapon.

The gatekeeper staggered forward a few more steps, his eyes

wide. In a panic, as he saw himself being drawn closer to Aspen's own weapon, he released the spear and backpedaled, falling on his rump. Aspen used the added momentum to spin and hurl the spear into the trees across the river. The spearhead sank itself deep into the heart of one of the tree trunks, where it stayed, quivering from the force of the impact.

Satisfied that the weapon would no longer be an issue, Aspen turned back to the gatekeeper, who gaped at his spear.

"Aspen, are you all right?" Ash asked, her bow still trained on the gatekeeper.

Aspen's body screamed at her for the strain. Her knees threatened to collapse beneath her. She elected to ignore it. "Relatively speaking." She offered a hand to the fallen elf. "We're not here to pick fights. We are allies, after all." The elf smacked her hand away and stood up on his own. Aspen's face hardened. "But if you continue to bar our way, we may have no other choice. Lives are at stake."

The gatekeeper brushed himself off and sniffed. "Please. As if I haven't heard that before."

"I'm sure you have," Aspen said, trying not to snap. "But would you let people die for the sake of your pride?"

The gatekeeper glowered at her but said nothing.

"Are we going to have a civil conversation about this, or will I need to throw *you* into a tree this time?" Aspen's jaw ached from the strain of not saying more.

The gatekeeper bristled. "I would like to see you try."

Aspen remained silent, watching him with one raised eyebrow. Much as he might want her to, and much as she would *love* to send him after his spear, she would not rise to his bait.

He waited for what felt like an eternity for an answer. Ash lowered her bow but kept an arrow knocked. If he tried anything else, he'd end up with that arrow through his throat before he could even scream.

It seemed the gatekeeper realized he had lost his advantage, if he'd ever had one at all. The fight left his eyes, but he still puffed out his chest. "May I see the document?"

"Of course." Aspen handed it to him.

The gatekeeper scowled and looked over the scroll. His scowl deepened and he cleared his throat when he reached the end of it. "Amazingly, your paperwork all seems to be in order. I *suppose* you may have *brief* entry."

"How incredibly generous of you," Aspen said.

The gatekeeper's face paled in fury. "*But,* you must do as I say, *when* I say to do it, understand?"

Aspen wanted to shake him. Maybe it would dislodge some of his misbegotten ego. But she refrained. Barely. "Lead the way."

The elf harrumphed with a fleeting, cloying smile on his face, tossed his mane over his shoulder, and glided into the archway. He vanished the moment he entered. Aspen's gut dropped. Something was not right.

"Do you think he wants his spear back?" Ash asked.

"We'll let him figure that out later," Aspen said. "You should stay here." Without another word, she followed the gatekeeper into the arch, unease twisting in her stomach. Her hand hovered close to the pommel of her sword. This felt very much like a trap.

She emerged into a dark cavern. The only thing she could discern in the dark was a blue glowing key set on a table. The light pulsed faintly, like a tiny heart.

"What is this?" Aspen asked.

The gatekeeper chuckled with mirthless satisfaction somewhere in the dark. "When our queen took the throne, precautions had to be made against those that were still loyal to the Council. I am required to tell you that that is the key to the new entrance to the Midnight Fens, but that is all you will get from me."

Aspen's blood froze and boiled at once. A new entrance. More time. It would require more time that they simply *did not* have.

She clenched her fists, digging furrows into her palms with her nails. "Where?"

"Ahh, see, that's information reserved for those that lay their hands on the key."

Aspen felt, rather than saw, the blade coming for her. She threw her body forward into a roll as something scythed above her head. Another spear. She drew her sword, its black galatite blade imperceptible in the dark. The spear came for her again. She swung. The spearhead clattered behind her, its shaft cleaved in two.

The gatekeeper fell into a shocked, fuming silence. Aspen sheathed her weapon and collected the key. She faced the darkness around her and found the whites of the gatekeeper's eyes. He blocked her path back to the entrance.

She displayed the key in her hand. "*Where?*"

"I cannot allow half-bloods to tread our city's holy ground!"

A dim, narrow shadow lashed out at Aspen's midsection. The spear staff. She sidestepped and caught the staff in one hand. The wood burned and scraped into her palm, but she ignored it. She rammed it back into the gatekeeper's stomach. He doubled over with an "oof" of breath forced from his chest. "I will not play your games. The lives of my people, *our people*, are at stake."

"*You* are not my people," he ground out. "And neither are the people of the Golden Grove. They have taken our holy land, and we will not aid them until we get it back!" He leapt and snatched the key from her hand.

An arrow shrieked through the darkness and knocked the key from his grasp. It skewered it to the ground where it stayed, still pulsing faintly.

"Just like old times, eh Aspen?" Ash's voice drifted through the darkness. "I always love a good heist."

Aspen wrenched the broken spear from the gatekeeper's hands and threw it into the darkness. She marched to him and threw him to the ground before he had time to process what she had done. He fought and snarled against her, but her years of upward battle kept him pinned. Her battered body screamed and wailed at her for the continued abuse she put it through, but, again, she ignored it.

The gate-guard continued to spit profanities and landed a blow across her jaw. Aspen lifted his torso and slammed him to the ground again for good measure, applying pressure to his windpipe with her forearm. "I will not turn this into the long, 'glorious' battle you want. You will not go home a hero." He tried to get up, but she slammed him back down. His eyes bugged from his skull. "You *will* tell me where to take this key before I'm forced to drag your half-lifeless carcass across the entire kingdom, and you can *personally* tell the children and elderly of the Golden Grove why the help they needed never came."

"Take them all... to the Pit with you," he said with a wheeze.

Aspen gripped his forehead in her palm. "Last chance. Half-bloods have trained in the art of the mind. I could just force it from you. But I'm afraid I lack a certain finesse to it. You might forget how to walk. Or breathe. I have no control over what I destroy."

The gatekeeper's struggling stopped. "You're bluffing."

"Am I?"

He fell silent. Aspen allowed some of her fear, worry, and anguish to run through her veins. Her magic poured from her skin in green mist, enveloping the both of them. She felt his breath, hot and fast, against her arm. She whispered guttural nonsense under her breath, but just loud enough for him to hear. She used her other hand to drive her thumb into the point just behind his jaw where his head met his neck. His head would start to swim, and stars would dance in his eyes. Perfect substitutes for actual magic.

He caved. "The Dragon Scales! You'll find the entrance during the week of calm."

The world stopped for Aspen. The gatekeeper's words pounded against her chest like a battering ram. She couldn't breathe. *There? There, of all places?* "Are you lying?" she asked in a whisper, hoping it sounded more intimidating than terrified.

"By the Architects, no! Get your filthy half-blood magic away from me!"

Aspen slammed him to the ground again. "Are there any *other* surprises I should know about?"

"Only that the dragon will seek the bearer of the key."

"Dragons died out ages ago."

"The great dragons, yes. But lesser creatures live on."

Aspen released him and stood on unsteady feet. She held the key so tightly in her hand that it grated against her bones. Her magic still clung to her, but she tried to force it back. Her arms and legs shook. She straightened her shoulders and looked the gatekeeper in the face. "Thank you. May we never meet again." She left without another word. She thought her heart might have stopped beating.

Ash followed her out. "What happened? What's next?"

Aspen looked past her and strode away, her back blade straight. "We're going to the Dragon Scales."

Sister Earth, *why* couldn't she keep the tremor out of her voice?

FIFTEEN

Tristan hadn't expected how heavy Styrax would be. He hobbled beneath his weight, trying not to crush everything around him and leave a trail for the soldiers to follow. Sweat poured off his face in torrents. His chest heaved beneath the strain, and a knot the size of a workhorse clawed at his side.

Styrax faded in and out of consciousness, moaning one moment and deathly silent the next. Tristan hated both of them equally—the groans for the reminder of the pain he had caused, the silence for the fear that Styrax had died.

Tristan didn't know how long he had been walking before his foot sunk deep into a sinkhole. His other knee buckled, and he toppled. Styrax rolled off his back with a groan.

"Styrax!" Tristan wrenched his foot from the hole, his knee and ankle throbbing. He tried to lift him again, but his trembling arms gave out. He looked around, heart thundering, hoping no one had seen them yet. The moon burned bright and fierce on him as if coaxing their pursuers to him. He didn't know how they hadn't found them already. He worried at the rings around his neck, almost hoping they would speak to him again— give him words of wisdom and comfort. They said nothing, but the small one seemed to glow and almost burn in his palm. Had the undergrowth been this dense when he had first passed through? It seemed to have grown a meter at least in the last few minutes. He couldn't even tell where they had come from anymore.

But he had to keep going. He had no other choice. *Styrax* had no other choice. Grasping at desperate straws, Tristan hooked his arms beneath Styrax's shoulders and half-dragged, half-carried him to an upright position. He shook him awake. "Styrax. Styrax!"

Styrax's eyes struggled open, crusted with milky pain. "Wha—?"

"Styrax, Ancient Races can sense when other Ancient Races are nearby, right?"

Styrax's gaze gained a little more focus. "How do you... know that?" His eyes clouded again and threatened to roll back.

Tristan shook him again. "Where are the elves, Styrax? Where can I find them so I can take you to them?"

Styrax whispered something unintelligible.

Tristan leaned in closer. "What?"

"East...near scrubs." And that was it. Tristan had lost him to unconsciousness again.

Tristan maneuvered Styrax onto his back, trying not to groan from the weight, said a prayer to whatever gods would listen that no one would find them, and headed east. He couldn't say exactly where Styrax had meant to send him, but the only place he knew of with scrub brush was Scrub Valley. What any elf would want over there was beyond him, but he had to trust Styrax. It was the only lead he had, and he certainly couldn't trust his own judgment right now. That had almost gotten Styrax killed.

As he made his way through the brush, careful to listen for soldiers coming after them, a nagging thought kept coming back. Styrax's question. How *did* he know Ancient Races could find each other? Laire had never taught him. The other soldiers and villagers had said nothing about it. The only other option was that it was from...

He shook it away and pressed on. He would have time enough to stew over that when Styrax was back on his feet.

No one ever came. He saw no soldiers and no patrols, and he and Styrax made it to their destination without incident.

He had fully expected to find nothing at Scrub Valley. Nothingness seemed to be its perpetual state, and that also would have been in harmony with how the rest of this horrific night had gone for him. But there they were in counsel with a third party. A traitor? Didn't matter. He only needed their skills. He should have known he could trust Styrax. It made his predicament all the more gut-wrenching.

He knew it had all been too easy when Aspen hurled the spear into the tree above him and nearly scalped him. He dropped to undergrowth with a curse, Styrax tumbling from his back, and waited.

Five.

They were going to kill him.

Ten.

All this suffering had been for nothing. The gods hated him.

Fifteen. Styrax was going to die alone and helpless without Tristan, and no one would be the wiser.

Twenty.

Nothing.

Tristan hazarded a glance above his cover. No one was coming his way. Instead, Aspen disappeared into a free-standing archway. Completely, totally vanished. Tristan blinked at the archway, his mind aching from the effort to comprehend it. Where had it come from? Why was it *here*, of all places? How had they known about it? And how had she just—? He rubbed his face. He had to stop before he combusted. All that could wait. Styrax mattered most right now.

Tristan inched his way toward the other elf. She paced irritably, scuffing the dust with her boots and glowering at the archway. As Tristan approached, he caught her grumbling incoherently under her breath. Tristan settled into place, trying to work up the courage to ask her about Styrax. Every time he thought he'd steeled his nerves, though, the moonlight caught the glint off her massive recurve bow and the double-knives at her sides. He melted back into the shadows to try again.

Before he could approach her, the elf threw her hands in the air. "Architects have it!" she dove into the archway and vanished as well.

Tristan's heart leapt to his throat. No. *No!* He'd been too late! They were gone, and he wouldn't be able to get them back. Horrified, frozen tears welled in his eyes. He hadn't been fast enough. He had sentenced Styrax to death.

But then Aspen stumbled back through the archway, clutching a glowing key with a haunted look in her eyes. Ash followed suit, shouldering a bow. They had *definitely* killed the other elf. Tristan didn't know what to do. He couldn't ask *murderers* to save Styrax.

"What now?" the blonde elf asked.

"We're going to the Dragon Scales."

Aspen's announcement was like a gong in Tristan's ears. *The Dragon Scales,* he thought in a daze. *They're going to the Dragon Scales.*

In a moment of either bravery or sheer stupidity—and Tristan was fairly certain he knew which—he leapt out of the underbrush. "Wait!" he called, trying not to sound desperate.

The elves turned as if on a pin, weapons drawn faster than Tristan could process.

"I thought I told you not to follow me," Aspen growled, smoldering rage and hatred in her eyes. Behind it, though, he could tell her thoughts were not fully present. They were somewhere else far, far away. Somewhere that terrified her. Her face paled, and she pressed her hand to her wounded hip. "I don't have any more time to waste on you." She sheathed her sword and moved to step around him.

Tristan threw out his hands to stop her.

Tristan didn't think she could have been in any fouler of a mood. She managed. "I certainly hope you know what you're doing."

He didn't. He really, truly didn't, but that didn't stop him from blurting, "I...I need your help. Please." The request faded to barely a squeak.

Aspen seemed just as stunned. She looked at Tristan as if his brains had fallen out of his ears. Now that Tristan considered it, perhaps they had. "*You* want *our* help?"

"Yes." Tristan's certainty was quickly leaving him. But Styrax swam in his mind again. "Please. My friend is dying. They used serpent root, and..."

"Out of the question." Aspen pulled up to her full height. "We don't have the time for this. We have other lives at stake."

Rage turned Tristan's veins to fire. "So it's fine to leave one of your own out there to die a horrible, agonizing death? You really are just heartless monsters!"

Aspen took a step too close to him, her breath hot on his cheeks. A strand of her dark hair brushed his chin. "Need I remind you who put him in that situation in the first place?"

"Enough!" Aspen's companion pushed her way between them. The end of her bow bashed against Tristan's nose. She shoved Aspen to one side and Tristan to the other. She was incredibly strong for her tiny frame. "My name is Ash, and I am her cousin." She nodded to Aspen. "*I* will help your friend, but we have to go *now*. Take me to him."

"*Ash,*" Aspen said, a growl in her voice.

"A stranger helped me when I needed it most. It would be a poor repayment to leave someone else to the same fate."

Aspen clenched her jaw, obviously unhappy but unwilling to argue. "Just *hurry*."

Relief washed through Tristan. "You'll help him?"

"She won't be of much help if you keep stalling," Aspen snapped.

Tristan ignored her. "He's over here."

They found Styrax where Tristan had left him. Tristan had begun to wonder why no soldiers seemed to be in pursuit at all. The forest was deathly quiet. No sounds from anywhere, not even the trees. It was odd, and the hairs on the back of his neck inexplicably stood on end. Aspen seemed just as uneasy as he did. She posted at the edge of their little clearing, her attention never staying one place for long and her hand on the hilt of her sword.

Tristan helped Ash maneuver Styrax into a more accessible position. Styrax's breathing had turned to little huffs of shallow breaths every few moments. He was fading fast.

Tristan did as she requested and laid Styrax out flat. He had never seen someone so pale. Even the color from Styrax's hair seemed to have leeched away. It terrified Tristan.

"I've never seen it this bad," Ash said in a horrified whisper.

Tristan's heart sank deeper into his stomach. "What do you mean?"

"The serpent root shouldn't incapacitate him so quickly...unless he's had this happen before."

Tristan remembered the hundreds of small, silvery scars along Styrax's arms. Horrible guilt struck him. Just how little did he know about the man he called his best friend? "I think he has."

Ash nodded and said no more. She pulled a small vial from her knapsack. When she opened it, a vile smell punched Tristan square in the face. He recoiled, but Ash seemed unperturbed. She collected a pinch of the odious red powder and sprinkled it over the serpent root. The vine hissed and recoiled, withering at the powder's touch. It maintained its thorned grip on Styrax, though.

"Grab the roots, please," Ash said. "Pull when I tell you to."

Before Tristan could, Aspen stiffened. She crouched and motioned for Ash and Tristan to do the same. "Get down! *He's* here."

Ash didn't ask who she meant.

Tristan wouldn't tolerate such games. "Who is?"

"Did I *ask* you to speak?" Aspen shot him a glare that could freeze the summer sun.

Tristan was about to snap back, but then he saw him through the trees. Laire. A knapsack on his back and his white sword at his side. Tristan didn't know how a normally welcome sight could become so dread inducing in a single night. It reminded him of those first few weeks with Laire. There was something...not quite right in Laire's eyes. He *seethed* with dangerous energy, something that made Tristan's heart pound so frantically he feared someone would hear it. The scar on his scalp ached. He almost heard voices screaming in his head. Death clung to Laire like a cloak tonight.

Laire went to leave, but stopped and cocked his head. He turned back around, and Tristan could have sworn he looked him right in the eye.

Oh, Mother Night.

Laire took a few more steps closer, crouching to the ground.

Don't blink, don't blink! Don't make a sound. Don't even breathe.

A few more steps and Laire would be right on top of them.

Aspen whispered something under her breath, and a chorus of leaves sprang to life. They waved and whirred together, the movement rushing away like someone running through the underbrush. Laire's attention snapped away, and he followed the sound into the darkness.

They all breathed a collective sigh of relief when Laire was gone.

"How many were there?" Ash asked. She had been too short to see over the bushes.

"Just one," Aspen said, her words labored. "If we're careful, we should be able to make it past him."

"No time to waste, then." Ash waved Tristan back to Styrax and drew a short sword at her side. She looked at Tristan and motioned to the serpent root. "Are you ready?"

"I think so?" he said, grabbing hold of it.

She shoved a rag in Styrax's mouth. "All right, then *pull!*"

Tristan heaved on the root with all his might. It pulled away from Styrax's skin, but the thorns clung fast, digging into his flesh almost like talons. Styrax arched his back, a scream stretching his lips away from his teeth, but muffled by the rag.

Ash muttered unintelligibly and her sword glowed silver-gray, the same color that glowed on the outer rim of her irises. She slashed the sword forward, cutting the thorns at their base. They shriveled and vanished in a puff of smoke, but more sprang from the vine.

"Throw it away once it's free!" Ash hissed between clenched teeth, battling off the fresh growth.

Tristan bunched his shoulders and heaved it away, shocked at how heavy it had become from gorging on Styrax's magic. It landed with a sickening thud but sprung to life and tried to slither back.

"What do we do now?" Tristan asked, watching in horror as it writhed closer.

A flash of star-flecked black whirled past his vision, and the root belched out its stolen magic, its stem slashed into fine shards. Tristan looked at Aspen with wide eyes as she slid her sword back into her sheath. He hadn't even seen her move.

The magic swirled aimlessly in the underbrush before it inched back to Styrax and settled into his skin. A little color returned to his cheeks, and he stirred.

"Well hello, handsome," Ash said when Styrax opened his eyes. "Nice to see you awake."

Styrax scrambled back, his face pink. "I, uh—" He saw Tristan. "Tristan! Thank Sister Earth!"

Tristan helped him to his feet. Although his color had returned, he still leaned heavily on Tristan for most of his support. "I'm glad they left you in one piece."

"Barely," Aspen said, shoulders thrown back. "He won't be so lucky again. We wish you both the best, and now we take our leave."

"W-wait!" Tristan couldn't say what drove him this time, but she had said the name—the name he'd tried to find for five years. "Let us come with you. To...to the Dragon Scales," his voice cracked. What was he *thinking*? Even if the Pit threatened to swallow her up, there would be no way under the stars Aspen would let him go with them. And did he *really* want to travel with a volatile monster, anyway?

Aspen seemed just as stunned. "*Excuse* me?"

"*What?*" Styrax hissed, casting sideways glances at Tristan.

Tristan straightened. This was his one chance. Now or never. "Take us with you to the Dragon Scales."

"The *audacity*—" Aspen paced toward him, shaking her head. "You nearly get me caught, nearly get your friend killed, and endanger our lives further with your need for damage control, and now you expect me to *let you come with us,* dragging your half-dead friend along with us?"

"Hey!" Styrax protested.

"Yes," Tristan said with a squeak. It sounded insane even to his own ears, and he knew it, but he still had to try. Much as he and Aspen both hated it, he had the feeling she might be his only chance to get to the Dragon Scales. He had to take the chance when it presented itself.

Aspen laughed, a hollow sound brittle with thorns. "You are absolutely *shameless!*" She paced in a small loop, running her hand through her hair. "I refuse."

The words pounded against Tristan like a battering ram, but he stood his ground. "You don't understand; I *have* to go."

Aspen looked at him with a cold, raised eyebrow. "Is that so? Why?"

"I..." How could he put it? How could he say, "*I lost my mind and need it back*" without sounding like a maniac? "I just do. I'll pay any price."

The moment the words left his mouth, he regretted them. *Anything* meant a great deal more to those with magic. They could just as easily ask for his soul or firstborn child as they could money. But it was too late. The damage had been done. Styrax looked at him like he had taken leave of his senses.

Something spread across Aspen's face. Something not quite a smile, but still just as pleased. "*Any* price, you say?"

Tristan winced. He knew it would have been too much to ask for her to overlook that.

She turned her back on him and took two paces away. She appeared to be thinking. But then, in the time it took to blink, she had whipped her sword from its sheath and charged at him. Silent. Deadly. In complete control.

"Tristan!" Styrax cried out in warning.

Without a thought, he dropped Styrax and snatched Ash's short sword from her. He dodged Aspen's first blow. There was only the barest flicker of movement before her second came. The crash of steel against steel grated against his ears as he met her. His sword slid down Aspen's blade nearly halfway before she deflected him to the side. As he staggered for balance, Aspen struck him on his back with the flat of her sword.

He whirled on her. The sword snaked forward and bit into Aspen's arm. Tristan looked at the blade, eyes wide. A thin line of scarlet blood glinted in the moonlight.

Aspen raised an eyebrow and leapt at him, her sword whirling in treacherous arcs. Tristan gave ground beneath her ferocious attack. Adrenaline rushed through his veins, and blood pumped in his ears until he heard nothing but the crash of their weapons. Aspen battered against him in a flurry that left his head spinning. Ash's sword took the punishment, but his elbows did not. They creaked and threatened to break at any moment. His shoulders and arms were ablaze from the exertion. It took all his concentration and energy to meet Aspen's blows. He had no way to go to the offensive, but he could not die here. Would not. Not when he was so close. He ground his teeth and concentrated on blocking everything out but the next blow.

But something...*something* hovered on the edge of his mind. Directions on how to move and what to watch for. Where to put his feet and where to throw his weight. Were they...*memories*?

The thought was the distraction that led to his downfall. One moment, his sword shrieked against the black metal of Aspen's. The next, it was on the ground, and he was on his knees, staring down the tip of that black blade.

Tristan's heart leapt to his throat alongside the lump of emotion forming there. He'd...he'd *lost*. Just as he'd thought he might be on track to find his memories life, had snatched it from him.

Aspen's chest heaved as she held Tristan at sword-point. A strand of hair waved in and out of her face with every breath. A mix of emotions roiled in her eyes. Tristan had never stood a chance.

They sat that way for a moment in complete silence, but then Aspen retracted. She sheathed her sword and gave him a hard look. "You are arrogant, bigoted, vindictive, and a nuisance. However, you can hold your own in a fight, and that counts for something. I will most likely regret it later, but if you still wish to come, you may."

CHAPTER

SIXTEEN

Tristan handed Ash her sword back and picked Styrax up in a daze. Ash nodded once and went to Aspen. Wordlessly, Tristan moved to follow, still trying to grasp all that had happened, but Styrax remained motionless.

"Styrax, what—?"

Styrax ignored him. "And what about me?" he asked Aspen. "Do I have to fight for a place as well?" He had a bitter edge to his voice. An edge honed over years of experience. It cut Tristan to his core.

"I wouldn't have much fun fighting an ailing naiad, would I?" Aspen asked, arms crossed.

Tristan clenched his jaw. "He could take you on and tear you limb from limb if he wanted! Did you *see* that fog—?"

"I'm not a monster, Tristan," Styrax said, bitterness and resentment turning the words to daggers.

Tristan nearly took a step back. He had never heard Styrax so...so *hardened.*

And who made him that way? a small voice asked.

Styrax's eyes widened, as if he'd surprised himself with his vehemence. He passed a hand over his face and left it there, shoulders slumped in defeat. "I'm a naiad, a spirit of rivers and streams," he said. He chuckled emptily, as if at a long-overused joke. "At least, I used to be. I'm really not sure what I am anymore."

Aspen pressed her hand to her eyes as if trying to shove them to the back of her skull. "Sister Earth, what did I do to deserve this?" She gave them both an accusing look. "What you are is of no concern to anyone right now," she said, "Ash and I have places to be. War waits for no one, especially not for those that wish it to." She jabbed a finger at Tristan. "If you are coming to the Dragon Scales, you are coming now. Understand?" She gestured to Styrax. "The same goes for you." She left without another word.

Ash cast a glance over her shoulder at her retreating cousin. "Don't worry. She was like that with me when we first met, too," she said. "It'll ease up eventually...maybe."

"Ash!" Aspen barked.

"Coming!" Ash bounded after Aspen.

Tristan looked at Styrax. "Well, I know I'm crazy, but I'm choosing to follow them. You...you can come with me if you'd like." He waited, suddenly feeling inadequate. How could he possibly say anything to make up for what he'd done? There was no way under the stars Styrax would want *anything* to do with him.

"Not sure I have any other choice at the moment," Styrax said, not looking Tristan in the eyes.

Tristan had no right to feel this way, but relief flooded through his chest. He didn't know what he would have done if Styrax had chosen to stay. Together they walked away from the only home he had ever known.

All was silent as they marched through the night, except for their ragged breaths that plumed in the air. Tristan shivered as they walked. The march kept his blood circulating, but a stiff night wind cut through his body, and his fingers and toes felt like ice.

The sky had just tinged gray with the first hints of sunlight when Aspen called for a quick break.

Tristan wanted to sink to the ground immediately. His legs felt as flimsy as wet parchment, and his stomach protested his lack of food. But he saw how both Ash and Aspen hardly seemed winded—as if they'd just taken a scroll through a town square rather than hiked up half a mountain. He forced himself to stay standing. If they could do it, so could he.

"Here," Ash handed them a handful of nuts and dried berries. "It's not much for now, but don't worry. I'll make sure we eat well tonight." She stretched her arms overhead and yawned. "Any preferences? Seasoned roast meat? Rabbit stew? Pheasant and potatoes."

Tristan's stomach growled. *Yes to everything.*

Ignoring the saliva that had built up in his mouth at the mere mention of food, Tristan inspected the nuts and berries in his hand. "Aren't we still technically your enemies? Why are you feeding us?"

Ash cocked her head. "Not particularly. You asked to come; we accepted. We're not heartless monsters in the business of eating companions, contrary to popular belief." She winked at him and smiled. Her face darkened when she took in Styrax's wounds. "Though I can't say the same for those in Lorate."

Tristan had no response to that.

Aspen glanced to the sky, seeming to judge the growing light. "Fifteen minutes is up. Let's move." She didn't turn around, but simply marched off without waiting for a response. Ash followed her without question.

Tristan followed close behind. As they'd walked, he'd jumped too far into thoughts of the rebellion, how it was run, and what part Ash and Aspen played in it to let the conversation drop. He had to ask. "Which general do you serve under?" He didn't know why he'd asked it that way. The only two he really knew of were the commanding general, Dallowyn, and General Shadowalker. Any other answer would be meaningless to him.

Ash cast her eyes to Aspen, who continued to forge ahead, seemingly oblivious to the conversation behind her. "I serve under General Shadowalker."

Tristan's jaw nearly dropped off his skull. *The* General Shadowalker? So many questions tumbled through his mind that he didn't know what to do with them all. What was the general like? Where was he at now? How had she and Aspen become part of his army? Did he really just send his servants and concubines to do all his work for him? That question got him thinking about the stories some of the Lorate soldiers had spread about a ten-foot-tall woman with horns and a long, scaly tail mowing down lines of men with a black sword twice as tall as any man. Sans the horns and tail—though with her cheery demeanor, he could see the confusion—and the exaggerated size, could that have been Aspen? She was the only woman he had ever seen with a black sword.

As he stewed on that, another thought came to mind. He wasn't sure if he should voice it, but ended up deciding that his situation couldn't get much worse either way. "What does General Shadowalker want with Lorate?"

Ash shook her head, her lips pressed in thin lines of worry. "That's what we'd like to know."

She didn't seem willing to be forthcoming with any more questions, so he let the silence drag on. If he was honest with himself, he had been using Ash as a distraction to keep from talking to Styrax. Guilt corroded its way through his heart and stomach. He couldn't think of a suitable way to address what he had done to him. All that played through his mind was Styrax's silent plea to leave with him before things got worse. And what had he done? Waited, and watched as Styrax almost died. Even after Styrax had befriended him, encouraged him, and defended him. A shiver ran down his spine. He had come too close to losing Styrax forever. He absently touched the rings around his neck.

But he's a monster! The incessant voice raged.

I don't want to hear it from you! Tristan snapped back.

He glanced at Styrax. Styrax shuffled head down, shoulders slumped. He watched the ground go by with a sightless gaze, trailing along beside Tristan as he tried his best to carry his own weight. Tristan had never seen him look so defeated.

Tristan knew he needed to say something. Exactly *what* was an entirely different matter. What did one say after such a twisted, horrible betrayal?

HE betrayed YOU! Not the other way around!

Tristan shoved the voice aside to as deep a corner of his mind as he could. He opened his mouth to speak, but the words fizzled out in his throat. He shut his mouth again. What could he do? What could he say? Everything felt so trite and inadequate.

"How far do you think we are from Lorate?" He inwardly cringed. Why? Why, by sweet Mother Night, did he have to be this way? Could he not hold a normal conversation with someone for *once*?

"Pretty far," Styrax responded. He didn't look up from his feet.

At least Tristan had gotten *something* out of his pathetic attempt at an apology. "Yeah?"

"Yeah."

They stayed that way for several more minutes, casting uncomfortable glances and clearing their throats. Neither of them said another word to the other.

"Sweet Sister Earth! Will you two just kiss and make up already?" Ash piped in, startling them both. "Your awful communication skills are putting my teeth on edge! You're friends, right? Act like it! It shouldn't be that difficult!"

Tristan opened his mouth to say something, but Styrax cut him off. "*Are* we still friends, Tristan?"

Those words cut deep. Tristan looked at him. He saw the hurt, the pain, the anger, and the betrayal all cross Styrax's face at once. But, underneath it all, he saw deep-rooted loneliness and a desire for connection without danger attached. It must have been an agonizing road to walk as an Ancient One amidst a kingdom turned against you.

"Yeah, Styrax. We're still friends. If you'll have me."

It looked as if the sky had lifted from Styrax's shoulders. His entire body unclenched and a ghost of a relieved smile crossed his face. "Thank you, Tristan. That means a lot more to me than you could understand."

The voice in Tristan's head raged against him, but he batted it aside. It seemed a much easier feat than it had been only an hour before. He was grateful for that.

He had one question left to ask. "Why didn't you tell me before they forced your secret out like that in front of everyone?"

"Admittedly, that wasn't the best way for you to find out," Styrax conceded. "But, let me ask you this; what would you have done if I *had* told you?"

Tristan went to respond with something like "I wouldn't have cared!" but he faltered, remembering their conversation on the roof.

"I almost told you so many times," Styrax said. "I wanted to trust you, but there's a genuine fear that comes with living as someone that's different. And am I wrong to say that fear wasn't unfounded?"

Tristan took in the wounds along Styrax's arms and chest. It was his turn to drop his gaze. "No. I...I wish I hadn't turned into your worst fear. You are my best friend, and I should have known better."

"I forgive you, Tristan," Styrax said almost immediately.

Tristan rocked back on his heels at how quickly the forgiveness had come. "But, I—"

Styrax held up a hand. "You're my friend, Tristan, and a mortal. We all make mistakes, and I'm not willing to give up the one friend I have over one." He smirked lop-sidedly, more like the Styrax that Tristan knew. "Besides, you're still young—practically still an infant. I can't hold that against you in good conscience."

Tristan's knees nearly gave out on him, and his chest felt it might burst. He hadn't realized how dependent he was on Styrax's friendship and support. And then he registered Styrax's jab. "An *infant*? You're only a year or two older than me, at best. You don't have room to talk."

Styrax winced dramatically. "Try again, my friend. It's closer to a few centuries."

Tristan blinked uncomprehendingly. "What?"

Styrax puffed out his chest. "Yep! I've graced this world with my presence for two-hundred and seventy-six years, and I've got several hundred left in me."

Tristan reared back. "That's not true."

"It is!" Ash chimed in. "You didn't think 'Ancient Ones' was simply a title, did you? I'm two-hundred and fifty-three, myself."

"No." Tristan glanced between the two of them. Both young and healthy—in the absolute prime of their lives. Yet, he saw the wisdom of lifetimes in their eyes. They had seen things change and grow and pass away that he couldn't fathom. "No?" he said again in a smaller voice. Maybe they were telling the truth after all.

He glanced to Aspen, still plodding ahead, oblivious to everything else except for whatever world she had escaped to in her mind. "How old is Aspen, then?" She acted far too crotchety to be anything younger than five hundred.

"Twenty-three," Ash said, her voice quiet. "Only twenty-three. But sometimes, I feel like she's had a longer life than the rest of us combined."

The silence after Ash's statement sat heavily on Tristan's ears.

When Tristan had envisioned finally embarking on his grand adventure to find his memories, he had imagined feeling excited, powerful, and full of possibilities. If not that, he certainly hadn't imagined marching up switch-backed, barely there mountain trails dragging a half-dead man next to him while they followed two fugitive elves. Everything ached. Every breath. Every step. Every look back toward the fort that had been his home. They stopped every few hours, mostly when his breath got ragged enough for everyone else to hear.

"When did you get so heavy?" he griped at Styrax.

"I bear the weight of my people's sins."

Ash snorted at that.

Aspen poorly concealed her frustration every time they had to stop. She checked the sky like a mouse watching for hawks and ground her teeth at the sun's relentless progression. She didn't sit when they paused for a rest. Instead, she circled restlessly, studying a crumpled roll of parchment and making notes on a separate one, eyes narrow as she tapped her finger on her lips. After a moment she'd crumple the parchment again, shake her head, and resume pacing.

Ash tried on a few separate occasions to get her to snack on dried berries or change her bandages, but Aspen waved it all away. Tristan wondered what had her so distracted. Of course, he couldn't voice the question. He preferred to *not* have his head bitten off. He had enough to worry about on his own, like how to keep his legs from falling off out of sheer exhaustion.

It seemed a miracle when Aspen finally called for a full stop for the night. Without pause, Tristan dropped to the nearest spot of somewhat flat ground. Tremors coursed the length of his legs. At least they were still attached. His raw hands bled from catching rocks and brush to keep himself from sliding back down the mountain. His lungs wanted to burst from his chest and his cheeks ached from his constant panting and wheezing. He wanted to melt into the ground and never come back.

"Next time I see you...dragged off by elves...remind me not to come after you," Styrax wheezed, arms akimbo, one foot propped on a jagged stump.

Tristan nodded and gulped in more air. "Remind me not to be... stupid enough to ask to go...with them."

"You've got it."

Tristan almost fell asleep in that instant, but footsteps clomped toward him, and a boot nudged his shoulder.

"Get up," Aspen said. Clipped. Imperious. Accustomed to giving orders and having them followed.

Tristan cracked one eye open and glared blearily at her. "What do you want?"

"Do you want a fire or not?"

"A fire sounds lovely, thanks." He closed his eyes again and draped an arm over his face.

She dug her boot deeper into his shoulder. "We need firewood. Go collect some. Consider it payback for slowing me down all day."

Tristan laid his head back and groaned. "You realize it's partially your own fault I'm here, right?" he asked. "You could have easily told me I couldn't come."

"Well, if you aren't one for gratitude!" Aspen said, eyebrows up and shoulders thrown back. "I thought I'd done you a favor. Would your life have been too terribly horrible if you had left me alone?"

"Maybe." He sounded petulant. He knew it and inwardly winced.

Aspen folded her arms, a smile pulled tight against her teeth. She waited in silence, goading him to say something else.

Tristan glowered at her. He hated everything about the situation but had no way to get around it. He rose to his feet, his joints shrieking in protest, and bowed stiffly to her, a mocking scowl on his face. "Anything else I can do for you, my lady?" he asked.

She massaged the bridge of her nose. Her shoulders sagged. "No. Just...go." She waved her hand vaguely at Styrax. "Take him with you. Bring back water or something."

Tristan pulled Styrax to his feet and turned to leave, but Aspen called a final warning. "Ash and I have spent our entire lives in forests. Don't think we couldn't track you if you choose to run and tell your friends where we are. It won't be much of a chase with the sorry state you're both in. Simply a waste of my time."

Tristan whirled, "We're *prisoners* now?"

Aspen was unfazed. "For now. Earn my trust and then we might negotiate."

Tristan gaped wordlessly. The *nerve*! He stormed off, fists clenched at his sides. "Maybe I *will* try to run if you put it like that." He and Styrax limped off together to do her errands. Despite the rancor Aspen's words left in his mouth, he knew she was right. In their current state, he and Styrax would look like tired old men with arthritic joints if they tried to escape. That didn't mean he didn't want to try out of spite.

Safely out of Aspen's earshot, Tristan said to Styrax, "I genuinely hate that woman."

Styrax shook his head. "You think she feels the same about you? I couldn't quite tell."

Tristan growled in resignation. "We might as well split the slave labor. Do you want firewood or water?"

Styrax smirked. "I'll take water." He spread his hands, and the rims of his eyes glowed white. Water droplets burnished gold from the sunset formed in midair and condensed into a globe twice as big as Tristan's head. Styrax raised his eyebrows at him as he held the water aloft. "You think that will be enough?"

Tristan shifted on his feet, still not quite certain how to feel about the whole magic thing. At least it had uses beyond harming or capturing people. "Show off," he grumbled.

Styrax grinned.

THE MOMENT TRISTAN and Styrax were out of sight, Aspen's body gave out on her. She collapsed where she stood. She tried to move her arms to catch herself but couldn't get them to respond. *That's all right,* the morbid thought trudged through her mind as the ground came to meet her. *I don't really need my face, anyway.*

"Aspen!" Ash leapt to her aid and caught her before she made impact. "By Sister Earth's moldy bread crust, you're going to *kill* yourself!" She looped one of Aspen's limp arms over her shoulders and helped her to the nearest log, where she sat her down and helped her lean back against it. Aspen winced when the rough bark brushed against her back.

"*Moldy bread crust*, huh?" Aspen slurred. "Haven't heard that one before."

"This is not a time for jokes, Aspen." Ash yanked her knapsack to her, lips mashed together. She dug through her pack and retrieved a water skin and the dried nuts and fruits she'd tried to give to Aspen all day. "Take that."

Aspen complied meekly. She knew she should have accepted them earlier in the day when Ash had offered them—perhaps she wouldn't have been in as poor a state now—but she'd had too much on her mind to worry about such things. How on Sweet Mother Earth could she protect the Golden Grove from the impending attack if they couldn't get to the Dragon Scales in time? Any plan she'd tried to formulate throughout the day seemed more like last-ditch suicide than anything plausible. There had to be *something*! No matter how much she tried to coerce it, though, her mind refused to supply an answer.

"Aspen, I gave you food to *eat*, not just to sit in your hand." Ash crouched in front of Aspen, a salve box in her hand. "You're going to let me take care of your wounds now." It wasn't a question. "Back, or this other mess first?" She gestured at the rest of Aspen's wounds.

Aspen shifted her body to assess the damage. Despite her back wound's severity, she'd learned to manage the pain over the years. The smaller ones were more at risk of infection. "My back can wait," she responded. She grabbed a piece of dried fruit at random and bit into it. The sweet flavor of strawberry settled on her tongue. She closed her eyes and sucked the fruit, savoring it. What she wouldn't do for a piece of her mother's strawberry tart.

Tears sprang unbidden in her eyes. She dashed them away and pinched the bridge of her nose. She knew exhaustion had settled too deep if she was crying over a little food.

Ash unwrapped the bandages around Aspen's hip. She paused when she saw the damage and clenched her jaw. Her hands shook, but she said nothing. Ash scooped some salve out and went to work. Aspen sucked in a hissing breath through clenched teeth when the salve touched the wound. It stung as badly as the time she'd fallen into a nettle patch as a child. Eventually, the soothing effects took over, and she relaxed.

The cousins sat in silence, Ash intent on her ministrations and Aspen nibbling on her nuts and fruits. The surrounding trees creaked and rustled like old women telling their years-old stories. Pine needles snapped and cracked in gentle undertones. Crickets chirruped and owls called for one another through the trees.

The lull settled deep into Aspen's chest. Her limbs deadened and her eyelids drooped. Too tired to fight, she let it wash over her, even though she knew better.

The trees' quiet cadence grew to the crash of dozens of sets of waves. The owls turned to cries of men as they shouted at each other. The crickets became the clash of swords and the creak of leather in a desperate battle. Death called to her from the waves.

Aspen jolted awake, her heart drilling a hole through her chest. Cold sweat stuck to her hairline and the base of her neck. Her gaze darted around the camp, searching for the specters that never left her side. She strained to hear the ghostly waves' roar. Nothing. Just the trees' whispers. Only Ash as she re-bandaged the last of her wounds.

A dream, Aspen realized with relief. *Just another dream.* She rubbed a shaking hand over her eyes. "How long was I asleep?"

"About twenty minutes." Ash cinched another bandage hard enough to make Aspen wince.

"That long?" It had only felt like seconds

"Yes. Imagine that. Your body needs sleep." Ash clapped the salve box closed and moved behind the log, jaw tight and arms tensed. "Sit on here and lean forward."

Aspen complied, her thoughts still lost in her nightmare, no matter how much she tried to turn them toward something else. Why? Why couldn't those memories leave her in peace?

Ash lifted the back of Aspen's tunic and froze. "Aspen?" she asked in a measured voice. Too measured. "How long has it been since you treated this?"

"Three days," she responded without thinking. She winced, realizing too late the tirade that was about to follow. She should have lied.

Ash dropped the back of the tunic and marched around the log until she faced Aspen, her face white with fury. "You mean to tell me you had us full-march all day in *this* condition?" She gestured to Aspen's back. "*Why?* We would have stopped for you!"

"We don't have *time* to stop!" Stress turned Aspen's words fierce. "There's too much at stake to worry about a single person. Hundreds —if not *thousands*—of innocent lives depend on us to get back as quickly as possible. That duty comes before all else."

"Aspen!" Ash crouched and took one of Aspen's hands in both of hers, her eyes desperate. "You're right. Lives depend on you, but there's not a lot of good you can do for them when you're dead!"

Aspen snatched her hand away with a scoff. "I'm not entirely sure that's true," she said. The words bubbled out before she could stop them. She cursed and bit her lip, turning from Ash.

Ash squeezed Aspen's knee, soft and earnest. "Don't let Inula get in your head. General Dallowyn wouldn't have given you your position unless he thought you could do some good."

People make mistakes. Aspen didn't voice that thought.

"If you won't take care of yourself for *you*, will you at least do it for me?" Ash asked, bending until she forced Aspen to make eye contact. "*Please?* You're the only family I really have left. I would fall apart if I lost you, too."

Aspen withheld a sigh. Tired. She was just...so tired. She wanted nothing more than to fall asleep and never wake up. Leave the world's madness behind her. But Ash needed her. Hundreds of others needed her. She would not abandon them like she had been abandoned. She could leave when the war ended. For better or worse. "If you insist."

Ash hugged Aspen, who tried not to flinch under her touch on her back. "Thank you."

She released Aspen and went back to her ministrations, massaging the ointment into the long, jagged wound that crossed from Aspen's right shoulder to her left hip.

Aspen swallowed back the pain and sat in silence, remembering her life without Ash. It had certainly been quieter, but barren of her bubbly love and energy. Aspen would have stayed in a dark place for a long time, and she wouldn't have been able to claw herself out of it without Ash's tough love. Or cooking. She half-smiled to herself.

"Ash, thank you," Aspen said, hoping Ash realized it was for more than the medical help. She'd never been exceptional with words.

Ash stopped. She gaped at Aspen. "You *thanked* me? Have I died without realizing it?"

Aspen rolled her eyes heavenward. "Oh, Sister Earth, I'm sorry I said it."

"It's just so *unlike* you, Aspen," Ash went back to work. Aspen felt her infuriating grin through the back of her head. "I hardly know what to do with myself."

"If *certain individuals* wouldn't make such a fuss about it when I did it, maybe I would say thank you more often!"

"Maybe these 'certain individuals,' who sound *so* lovely, talented, and intelligent, by the way, wouldn't fuss about it if you did it more often. What do you think of that?"

Aspen opened her mouth to respond, but then shut it again. She had no retort, so she turned to silence.

"You've relented *twice* in one day? I'm not sure if I should celebrate or check you for a fever." Ash put her hand to Aspen's forehead.

Aspen swatted it away. "Hardee har har."

They fell silent again, this one comfortable and companionable. Aspen stretched her neck and rolled her shoulders as the pain eased through her back. Bliss.

"You're welcome," Ash said. She combed her fingers through

Aspen's hair and pulled it back in a braid for her. "So, Tristan...do you think...?"

Aspen's body tensed again. "No," she said. Too forced. Too harsh.

Ash tied off Aspen's braid and sat next to her with a sigh, massaging her feet. "I mean, you said he intrigued you. I could only assume that meant—"

Aspen clenched and unclenched her hands, hoping to dispel the turmoil inside. It didn't help. "I told you. He's dead, and I'm not entertaining any other possibilities." She held up a hand to ward off the other questions waiting on Ash's tongue. "The only thing I will say is that something does not feel right here."

"Are you sure it's not just you wanting to leave the sick dog where he lay?"

Aspen bristled. "Of *course*, I want to leave it! But the only reason I came in the first place is because I value my duty over myself. You *know* that!"

Ash put a hand on her arm, and Aspen immediately regretted her outburst. She saw the hurt in Ash's eyes. "I know that. I'm sorry I suggested otherwise."

Aspen massaged her brows. "No, *I'm* sorry. I shouldn't have put that on you." She leaned forward on her knees, her exhaustion catching up with her again. "The short of it really is that Tristan is not the man you want him to be. That man is dead."

Ash fed her another handful of nuts and then resumed her ministrations on Aspen's back. "We'll just have to see, won't we?"

SEVENTEEN

Tristan blinked sweat from his eyes as he lugged an armful of deadfall back to camp. He panted as he tried to keep the wood scraps balanced on top of each other. The top one wobbled precariously. Tristan froze. If one stick fell in his meticulous monstrosity, all the others would, and then he'd have to pile them again. For the fifth time.

Styrax whistled to himself as he meandered behind Tristan. His water ball bobbed behind him in time to the beat. "Are you sure you don't need any help?" he asked.

"Yup," Tristan said with a grunt. He didn't know why he chose to be stubborn about it. He *would* appreciate the help. But Tristan wanted to prove he could be just as useful as magic. Or so he told himself as he cast bitter looks at Styrax's orb.

Styrax allowed for another pause, making Tristan's labored wheezing abundantly clear. "You're *certain* you don't need any help?"

Tristan heard the infuriating smirk in Styrax's voice and refused to turn to see it. "Listen here, mister...I-can-use...magic...to-solve-all-my-problems," he strangled out. "Some of us have to live life...the hard way, and we...*like* it."

"I can see that."

Tristan cast him a side-eyed glare. "Are you *trying* to upset me?"

Styrax gasped. "Wha—*me*? I would *never!*"

Tristan rolled his eyes and grunted again. "And you wonder why humans don't like you," he said.

The sound of Styrax's footsteps stopped. "Tristan, shut up."

Tristan craned his neck over his shoulder. "What? Is your magical ego so fragile?"

"No, really, be quiet!" Styrax said with a hiss.

Tristan stopped and looked. He regretted it. He recoiled in shock, his eyes and mouth wide. He wanted to articulate his horror but couldn't find the words or sound to do so. "Wha—how—what *is* that?" he forced out.

Styrax shook his head and shrugged wordlessly. He couldn't tear his attention from the scene.

Ash and Aspen had their back to Tristan and Styrax. Ash had lifted the back of Aspen's tunic and applied a yellow-green salve to the most horrifying wound Tristan had ever seen. It looked like someone had tried to cut her in half and failed. Black veins spider-webbed away from the inflamed, puckered edges. Pus and other fluids oozed from the center. Tristan could almost feel the pain on his own back from the mere sight of it. He tried to look away but couldn't bring himself to.

"How is she still alive?" he asked himself.

Styrax responded with another mute, useless shrug.

Questions tumbled through Tristan's mind like leaves in a summer gale. What gave her something like that? It couldn't have been too long ago. Was there a monster roaming around, tearing people to shreds? Was it nearby? For the sake of stealth, he kept his questions to himself, but his body filled to bursting with them and the hairs on the back of his neck stood on end.

Ash finished her ministrations and let Aspen's tunic fall back into place. She said something quietly to her and put the salve in her pack. As she bent, her gaze locked onto Styrax and Tristan. Her eyes widened, and her shoulders tightened.

"Uh-oh," Styrax shrunk deeper into the brush.

Ash's face tightened. "I wonder when those two will be back," she said loudly enough to carry to Tristan and Styrax. She gave them a pointed look. "I'd sure like to get dinner started."

"Why are you talking like that?" Aspen groused.

Tristan and Styrax scrambled away. Tristan gathered as many of his fallen sticks as he could find. Styrax grabbed the rest while his water globe looped around his head in dizzying arcs, its edges spiked like the fur on a startled cat. Tristan's heart pounded against his ribcage and made him feel like an escaped convict. He tried to shake it off. They hadn't done anything wrong. It had been an accident!

Even so, he snuck glances over his shoulder, waiting for the vengeful embodiment of Aspen's wrath to fly from the trees and tear him limb from limb.

"How much did you see?"

Tristan leapt ten meters out of his skin as Ash materialized from nowhere. His re-stacked sticks catapulted from his arms. "Mother *Night!*"

"*Quiet!*" Ash dragged Tristan and Styrax back into the underbrush. She peeked through the bushes toward the camp. Aspen sat with her back straight and swept her attention across the camp's perimeter. Her hand rested on her sword's pommel, ready to lop off the head of any intruders. Or terrified prisoners hidden in the bushes. "Ash? That you?"

"She knows we're here," Ash hissed.

"Is that a bad thing?" Tristan asked, his heart pounding for no good reason. They hadn't done anything *wrong!*

Ash looked at him like he was an idiot. "She's one of the most renowned generals in the rebellion. You tell me!" She ushered them deeper into the underbrush, glancing over her shoulder again. Her eyes widened in horror. "Oh, by the Architects."

Tristan and Styrax saw it at the same time. Aspen had vanished from camp.

Ash whipped around. "Where did she—"

The black blur came from nowhere, gleaming like the hide of a viper as it arced through the trees. A wraith wielded it in unperturbed silence. Tristan had no time to react. It'd cut him in two, straight through the middle. *So much for figuring out your life,* his internal voice sneered.

"Aspen, wait!" Ash shouted.

"*Sweet Sister—!*" The blur shifted, and the flat of the blade bowled Tristan over as it slammed into his midsection. He toppled with a gasping grunt of surprise, the wind blown out of him. He crumpled, curling into a ball and wheezing like a donkey with a stuffed nose.

"Sister Earth, you nearly killed him!" Styrax crouched next to Tristan and helped him sit. Tristan saw stars but stayed at least semi-conscious.

"I nearly killed *all* of you!" Aspen tore at her hair. "Why, on Sister Earth's name, were you sneaking around like a bunch of bandits?"

"Sticks," Tristan wheezed.

Aspen furrowed her brow. "What?"

Ash embraced the excuse. "We were looking for more wood for the fire. Tristan found quite a bit, but apparently is too clumsy to keep them all in his arms at one time."

If Tristan hadn't been occupied with trying to get breath back in his body, he would have resented that.

Aspen arched her eyebrow at Ash. "Uh-huh."

Ash smiled disarmingly.

Aspen sighed and crouched next to Tristan. He thought he almost saw *compassion* in her eyes? "Ash, you and Styrax get dinner started. I'll get this radish sack back to camp." She slung Tristan's arm over her shoulder and hauled him to his feet with surprising ease, waving Styrax away as he hovered close by. "Go on. I won't eat him."

That you felt the need to mention that is cause for concern! the voice in Tristan's head wailed.

Styrax hesitated another moment. Tristan silently willed him to stay. He couldn't be left alone with the maniac that had nearly chopped him in half. Styrax shrugged helplessly and left.

A real loyal 'friend' that one, Tristan's inner voice grumbled as his stomach churned. *Absolutely worth risking your life for.* A headache manifested itself as if the voice had kicked the back of Tristan's right eyebrow repeatedly to show its displeasure.

"All right, come on, you sad sack." Aspen hoisted Tristan a little higher on her shoulders and proceeded to half-drag him back to camp. Tristan tried to get his feet under him so he could refuse her help, but his battered chest and sides protested, and he was still light-headed enough that he'd fall if left to stand on his own. So, he begrudgingly accepted her aid for the moment.

"How are your ribs?"

"They...function...when they haven't been...*bashed in*," he wheezed.

"Perhaps this will teach you not to skulk in bushes around people accustomed to being ambushed," she said.

"What is it with you people...beating on a man...when he's down?"

"I beg your pardon?" Aspen asked.

Tristan sighed, which filled him with nothing but immediate regret. He grimaced at the fresh pain flaring in his sides. "Nothing. Never mind." He shrugged himself away from her. "I can walk on my own now. Thanks." It took him all of one step before he snagged his foot in a bush and toppled. He decided to lie there forever and accept his fate.

"Sweet Sister Earth's *sake*," Aspen grumbled as she picked him back up. "You stubborn idiot, let someone help you."

Tristan bristled. "*Forgive me* if I don't want help from the person who nearly cut me in half! Seems all your kind wants to do is hack people to pieces!"

Aspen shook her head. "You people that choose to live in constant fear over rumors and nay-sayers baffle me."

"It wasn't a nay-sayer that just about gutted me!" Tristan shot back. He grimaced. Why on Mother Night were all his muscles attached to his bruised ribs? "Besides, you can't tell me there's no truth to any of those stories. There's too many for that to be the case."

Aspen stopped. Her gaze burrow into him, and Tristan couldn't help but return it. His eyes met hers. He hadn't realized how *green* they were, like ageless evergreens standing sentinel on mountain precipices.

For evergreens and aspen trees.

The words stirred in his chest and curled warmth into his fingers and toes. He unconsciously reached for the leather strap around his neck.

"I won't lie to you and say we're blameless in this war," Aspen said quietly. "Both sides have committed atrocities that should never have happened. What I can say, though, is this; *I* do not fight a war of right and wrong between them. I fight only for peace." At that moment, she didn't see Tristan. She saw something beyond him, through the mountains and trees, to what he didn't know. But then she blinked. Her eyes widened fractionally as if she hadn't realized she'd spoken out loud. She looked away and started walking again without another word.

Tristan followed in her silence. There had been such a depth and gravity to her words. His heart sat a little heavier in his chest. The world simultaneously expanded and contracted around him.

Peace. Such a small word, but it hung in the air. Peace? Could there really be such a thing?

Absolutely not! The words clawed through Tristan's body like a starving beast. *They have done nothing but slaughter and torture and toy with us. Pretty words won't change that!* The voice pounded and ricocheted through Tristan's mind like rocks slung into a slot canyon. *Ask her this; was our only atrocity the scar on her back? It seems a pittance of repayment for the damage they've done.*

Only when Aspen stopped dead in her tracks did Tristan realize he'd asked out loud.

Aspen threw her shoulders back and looked him square in the eye. Snatches of moonlight shone off her eyes like bolts of lightning in a thunderstorm. She smiled without her teeth, her lips pulled as tight as a loaded bowstring. The words that escaped them shot as sharp and true as any arrow. "Much as I know you would love to claim that minor triumph, the blame for my scar lies solely with me." She dropped him where he stood and marched back to camp, her hands balled into fists.

Tristan dragged himself to his feet and grimaced the entire way.

Rotten, foul woman, the voice snarled. *Good riddance to her.*

"Shut up," Tristan said to it with a groan. He limped back to camp. Every step loosened his taught, shocked abdominal muscles, but he still ached. When he finally plopped beside the fire, it felt as if a bitter winter frost had settled over the camp. Aspen sat straight and poised, the epitome of cool politeness. The quiet, perfectly controlled rage behind her eyes was terrifying. She pointedly refused to acknowledge Tristan's presence. Ash sensed the tension and maintained a stony silence while she stirred a bubbling, fragrant concoction. Styrax looked to Tristan with an unspoken question, clearly baffled.

Tristan shrugged. Inside, though, his gut squirmed with guilt.

She wrote off the fact that she nearly split you in two like it was nothing. You are perfectly justified.

Tristan could get behind that, mostly. It didn't keep him from fearing for his life, though. The storms in Aspen's eyes had been too real. He'd have to be careful. No telling when she might completely snap and turn full monster on him.

Ash silently divvied the soup between them. She cast glances at Aspen the entire time. Tristan accepted his portion with caution. The smell of simmering vegetables and seasoned meat practically drove him to tears with how hungry he was, but he waited. He wouldn't put it past Aspen to poison him after their spat. She seemed the vindictive type. Ash's furtive glances in her direction did nothing but confirm his suspicions.

After a few minutes of silence as they ate their food, Aspen set her bowl down and leaned forward, eying Tristan and Styrax as if she could see straight through to their souls. Tristan's face burned and his skin itched. He wanted to fidget beneath her gaze, but he couldn't give her the satisfaction. So, he sat, eyes boring back into hers, rump sweating.

Aspen quirked an eyebrow at him, a smirk hovering on the corner of her lips, as if she knew his internal struggle. "Let's talk," she said.

"If we're prisoners, we won't say anything to you," Tristan said.

"That so?" Aspen asked him. Before he could respond, she turned to Styrax. "A naiad presence in a backwater fort concerns me. The naiads haven't changed their stance on neutrality in this war, have they?"

To his credit, Styrax sobered from his food rapture, at least somewhat. His smile remained, but Tristan saw the guarded look in his eyes. "I wouldn't know. I haven't spoken to another naiad in eighty years."

"What were you doing in Lorate, then?"

"Not one for mincing words, are you?"

"No."

Tristan snorted. Styrax puffed out his cheeks and let them pop. "I'd been on the run for too many decades. I needed a quiet place to cool my heels for a while."

"So you chose a *King's Fort*? A place actively fighting against magic?"

"*Active* is a very strong word for Lorate," Styrax said with a small smile. He looked at Aspen, eyes flinty. "Besides, I didn't exactly see any havens of magic jumping at the chance to accept a riverless naiad into their fold."

Tristan clamped his jaw. So the Ancient Races really *were* as bad as he'd heard. They'd even reject one of their own in a time of need. One word circled in his mind, though. Riverless? What did he mean by that?

Aspen acknowledged Styrax's jab with a nod. "Wish that I could deny that, but knowing how they treat half-bloods, I can't imagine your reception has been any better."

Styrax nodded, his jaw tight. Ash cast him a sympathetic look.

"Half-bloods?" Tristan asked before he could stop himself.

"Ahh, so the prisoner *has* spoken after all," Aspen said, her voice dripping with vicious sarcasm. "Welcome to the conversation."

Tristan could have bitten off his own tongue with hate and regret. Why couldn't he just stay *quiet*?

"To answer your ignorance, half-bloods" Aspen gestured to herself and Ash. "Half elf, half dwarf." Ash scrunched her nose and waved. "Half elf, half human." Aspen tapped herself on the shoulder.

Tristan unconsciously curled his lip in disgust. Aspen sighed. "I know. All very *shocking* that a pious human could stoop so low as to fall in love with an elf, the sin of all the earth. But here I am, a testament to heresy." She gave Tristan a burning, hateful look, and turned back to Styrax without another word. "You're certain your presence at Lorate has nothing to do with an attack on the Golden Grove?"

All anger and malice toward Aspen fled in an instant, replaced with cold, dead fear. Tristan blanched. His heart pounded so hard against his ribs that he could have sworn Ash and Aspen could hear it. Blood rushed through his ears, and the night air turned stagnant against his skin. How had they known?

Tristan watched Styrax, hoping—*pleading*—for him to lie. Deny anything about it. Any hope the men of Lorate had of surviving would be snuffed out in an instant if Ash and Aspen found out. They'd take it back to General Shadowalker, and then it all would be over before it even began.

Styrax leaned back, eyes wide. "We were only told about that yesterday. How did you already know?"

As good as a confession.

Tristan leapt to his feet with an involuntary cry. "You've killed them!" he said.

"No, he hasn't. Sit down," Aspen said, her face white and intent on Styrax. "When?"

"I—"

"You *would* say that, wouldn't you?" Tristan shoved his way between them and pointed an accusing finger at Aspen. "You and all your fake nobleness. You'll mow them all down without a second thought, and you only say you have no intention of killing them to appease your own conscience!"

Aspen stood as well, her shoulders thrown back and her eyes smoldering fire. "No, I say that because I command the soldiers stationed in the Golden Grove, and I am accustomed to being obeyed. Now *sit. Down.*"

He did, though he couldn't say why. But he did it with a sneer as his mind raced. She commanded them? But they served under...his attention slid to Ash as pieces fell into place. *She* served under General Shadowalker. But Aspen...

He laughed, cold and cruel, the sound digging barbs into his throat. "You're not General Shadowalker. I know you're not."

Aspen rubbed her face and sat down again, suddenly looking exhausted. "Oh, for Sister's *sake*! I don't have time for this!" she said. She glowered at him between her fingers. "Please, tell me, what else do you know about me, oh mighty one?"

"First, you're arrogant and self-righteous with a wicked tongue and a power complex."

"Oh, is that all?"

Tristan grit his teeth. "You are physically incapable of saying no to Ash."

Ash beamed at that. Aspen clacked her knee against hers.

"You don't like people, and use empty threats to keep them at bay."

"I assure you, they're not empty."

"You can't *stand* when people call you out, and you have to correct them even when they're right." Tristan held up a hand before she could get in another cutting remark. "But none of that really matters because you're simply a monster, just like all the stories say. I can make exceptions for Styrax and maybe Ash, but you, *you* fit the bill perfectly. Heartless, cowardly, and ruthless."

Aspen smiled with her mouth, but not her eyes. Never her eyes. "You'll have to try harder than that to hurt my apparently non-existent feelings. I've heard much worse," she said

"But you don't really matter, do you?" Tristan asked, smugness oozing through his chest. "General Shadowalker does. And I *know* you're not him because he's never been wounded in battle. So, do you want to tell me where you got your scar on your back, then?"

All the breath from the group snuffed out at once. No one moved. No one made a sound as Tristan's challenge settled on them. The silence rang in Tristan's ears. He felt the daggers of Styrax's warning glare on his back and registered Ash's gaping mouth, but he only had eyes for Aspen. The storms had returned in cold, dead, unwavering fury.

Tristan nearly took a step back. Everything in his body screamed at him to walk away. Everything except for one very loud, vindictive voice. "Well?" it goaded with his voice.

Aspen's cheeks pulled tight against her teeth, lips never parting, her back straight as an arrow. "If you'd really like to know, I was wounded by a sword fabled to steal souls—a sword wielded by your General Laire. So, if I seem a little soulless to you, it's because I am."

Tristan took a step back. Some of the air and rage shifted to horror.

"He was too scared of an eighteen-year-old girl to take her head on," she said.

Tristan shook his head. "You're lying. General Laire is the bravest man I know. He would never—"

"Answer me this, then. If he's so brave, why is he turning a blind eye to his *own men* being sent on a suicide mission?"

Tristan had no answer for that. He had seen the way Laire had looked at the announcement. Almost as if he had detached from the situation. As if he had *known* and had expected it. But *was* that cowardice?

Aspen tossed the rest of her stew broth into the fire, where it hissed and fizzed. Ash pressed her lips together in annoyance but said nothing. "I'll take first watch," Aspen said. "I've got some thinking to do. Everyone else get some rest. It'll be a long day tomorrow. You—" she pointed at Styrax. "Come with me. I have more questions."

Tristan opened his mouth to protest. Aspen pointed a finger at him. "Say one more word, and you'll have a scar to rival my own. Go. To. Bed."

Tristan snapped his mouth shut and crawled into his bedroll, fuming.

EIGHTEEN

S moke engulfed him. Coated every edge of his vision. Screams ricocheted through the blackness. He kept one hand against rough stone walls, letting them guide him through the murk. Someone tightly clenched the other in a soft hand.

"Never you worry," her whisper disappeared into the smoke with a hacking cough. "We'll be all right. We'll make it through this. I'll keep you safe, I promise."

His racing heart settled at her voice, its warmth wrapping him in a blanket of comfort. He called her name.

Roaring screams swallowed the word. The monsters had returned in their wretched, naked forms.

The hand was ripped from his grasp. He stumbled forward with a cry, scrabbling for the woman's comfort. And then the world split. The smoke evaporated and left shadowy figures in its place. People he should have known. Family. Friends. So close he could almost breathe in their familiar scents, but they were just out of reach—their faces shrouded in forgetfulness. They smiled. Waved. Called a name that echoed hollowly in his ears. They needed him. Wanted him. Their eyes lit up as he approached.

It took only a moment for that joy to melt from their faces. For horror to replace it.

The monsters had not come for him.

He tried to fight. Tried to flee. Tried to look away. But all for naught. He remained frozen in place as the monsters devoured them shred by shred. Saw their blood pool around their feet and smelled the acrid, copper scent of it as it left a sharp taste in his mouth. He heard the moment their unending screams finally stopped.

The monsters reared their heads and grinned at him with their blood-stained teeth. "Monsters," they said, repeating the word that thrummed through his mind as he watched them, wide-eyed.

The sound thrashed him like a stone thrown in a pond. Tremors raced the length of his spine. He hadn't known they could speak. Hadn't expected something so merciless to be able to.

"Remember." Their voices tripped over each other, a cascade of rasping tongues, "Remember which monsters have done this. Remember, they are the ones you released!"

Tristan flung himself from his bedroll, shivering even as sweat dripped down his back. Where—? Where was—?

He remembered. As the night air chilled his flesh and stars stared from their perch, he remembered. He had left the fort. Abandoned his home. His family.

To right a wrong, he reminded himself, though the effort was half-hearted. *To save Styrax.*

So you did more wrong?

Tristan massaged the scar on his scalp, hoping to drive the guilt-ridden voice out of it, turn it into nothing but a bad dream.

A dream...Dream. *Dream!* He'd had a dream! Patting his tunic, he floundered through his bedroll. He needed his...

His...

His journal.

His vision shattered. His ears rung. Blood fled from his face. He had forgotten it. Even after Styrax had told him not to.

One after the other, the events of the past day collapsed on the crown of his skull like stakes driven into fractured wood. It drove him to the ground, head in his hands, as if that would protect him from the onslaught. Everything. He had forfeited absolutely everything. His home. His family. Safety and protection and familiarity. And now even the small scraps of memory he had collected over so many years. All just gone. No way to get them back. Ever. He hadn't had time to think or say goodbye. He'd lost them forever.

Tristan ground his teeth as a sob built in his throat and bile roiled in his stomach. He took clumps of hair into his fists. Why? Why did he have to lose himself over and over and over again? Was he not allowed a life? Not allowed to belong? Not allowed peace?

A sound coaxed him from his aching thoughts. A soft lullaby, floating to him from the trees and caressing each leaf as the rich, low notes dripped from their branches.

> Hush now my child
> My young meadowlark
> Do not fear the dark
> Your mother is watching,
> My darling, my dear
> And all will be well 'til you wake.

Tristan's muscles relaxed. His hands unclenched from his hair. Without thinking, he mouthed along to the words.

> For I am the night
> And I am the stars
> That guard you, my baby

Where'er you are
So sleep now in peace
Let all worries cease
For your mother shall ever stay near.

Exhaustion bloomed in every muscle and turned Tristan to sinking stone as a familiar sort of warmth eased the ache in his soul. He collapsed onto his bedroll. Tears spilled thick and free down his cheeks. He let them fall, too tired to stop them. Too tired to wonder where he had heard that song before. Peace and belonging would come. It had to. With time. He would make it so.

ASPEN WATCHED Tristan fall back asleep as the last note of the lullaby faded in her throat. She didn't know what had prompted her to sing it in the first place. It was an old song from her childhood, sung by her best friend's father every night before they fell asleep. Mist filled her eyes at the memory.

Despite herself, she wondered what haunted Tristan. What could rip him so quickly from sleep like that? His explosion had nearly knocked her from her perch in the trees. She had thought they were under attack. Maybe he had been.

Aspen regarded the moon, the stars, and the black expanse of the sky, wondering how many gods were watching and cared about Tristan's terrors. Her terrors. Wondered if the gods even existed at all.

"You don't care about how damaged you leave people in your wake, do you?" she asked the nothingness.

She got nothing in response.

Aspen didn't know what she had expected. She scoffed and settled back against the trunk of her perch, focusing again on the letter Chaedra had given her. She had lost count of how many times she had read it, but she still couldn't decipher what it was supposed to mean. She had asked Styrax about it as well after she had sent Tristan to sleep, but he had nothing to contribute. She tapped it on her knee and read it again.

General,

I write to you as the King's Men, whom I once served with all the conviction I possessed, take me to either rot in Monterro's dungeons or meet my fate from the executioner's blade.

I will not pretend to be a man of many words, so I will get straight to the point. This kingdom has failed. It has been built to fall, and it will fall. Mercilessly far. I do not understand why Osmen has chosen this path or all he has in store, but I do know that the price for his ambitions is too great. Too many lives will be unwilling sacrifices. And it will start with the men of Lorate, and the true purpose for its founding.

Please, as a broken, condemned man, I am begging you. Do not follow through with the fate—the execution—the kingdom has set for these men. Whatever prize or promise you seek is a mockery. Nothing but lies. You will bring about the start of Loralan's ruin, if it is not already upon us. Do better in the post I am being forced from. Listen, watch, and rebel when the time is right. And, most importantly, please treat the men of Lorate as family. They were mine.

General Tal

Aspen placed the letter against her forehead as if that would somehow channel its meaning to her. She could tell why Chaedra and Lady Vinea had found it concerning. The wording was as ominous as it came. But she couldn't figure out what could have had the previous general so worried—couldn't figure out what knowledge could slate him for execution. Lorate was as far from the battlefield as it could get. Its true purposes were limited. It made no sense. Not for Lorate. Not for Osmen. He was a blood-thirsty murderer, but he was a calculating one. There was something more to it. There had to be. He never did anything without reason. But what purpose could a fort of ill-trained farmers serve?

Aspen folded the letter with pursed lips and tucked it back into her pocket. It would come to her. Eventually.

Just hopefully not before it was too late.

The next few days passed in a blur for Tristan, filled with nothing but hiking, eating, and collapsing into bedrolls at the end of the day. He was pleased, though, that his sore muscles eased with every passing hour, and he didn't breath as heavily with the exertion as he had at the start of their journey. It had only been a few days, so the change was minimal, but at least it was progress.

Aspen maintained her stoic aloofness throughout their trek, but Ash had fallen into step with Styrax and Tristan for most of it, sharing stories and bandying jokes. She brought a happy ease with her that calmed Tristan but only seemed to fluster Styrax, much to her apparent delight. Tristan shared in that delight only because he so seldom saw Styrax tongue-tied.

Tristan was not entirely immune to her, though. She had also worn him down enough for him to tell her about his memory loss and why he wanted to go to the Dragon Scales. He had been hesitant about what her response would be, but it had gone over much better than he had anticipated. She asked clarifying questions about time lines and locations, and listened intently as he gave her as much information as he could. It was refreshing to see her genuine interest in the topic rather than the mocking—gentle though it might have been—from the others in Lorate. Tristan felt some of the weight lift from his shoulders to have another person know and care about his plight.

The lifted weight from his shoulders did not lighten the load from his eyelids, though, which dropped like lead weights the moment he settled into his bedroll for another night. Unfortunately, his sleep didn't last as long as he would have hoped.

Tristan woke up dazed and sweating. Another nightmare, this one filled with golden light and rows upon rows of Monterro pea vines. Their blossoms dripped blood as the monsters prowled through the rows, feasting on faceless shadow people. Tears cut deep tracks down Tristan's cheeks as he remembered. He wiped them away. No use crying over something he wouldn't remember in the next hour anyway. He couldn't even write it down to try to decipher later...

His eyes were drawn to the glow of firelight—of Aspen huddled around a stack of parchment and assorted writing utensils. He clenched his teeth and exhaled a breath. If he wanted a favor, he'd have to swallow his pride. He just hoped he wouldn't lose any appendages in the process.

He pulled himself from his bedroll, shivering in the night air. Too tired to care about appearances, he bundled a blanket around his shoulders, shoved his feet into his boots, and shuffled to the fire.

Aspen didn't look up from her pile of scratches and maps. Notes scrawled across the margins of every page with sloppy ink splatters smudging some of the words. Tristan didn't know how anyone could read them. Aspen shuffled them closer to the firelight, tapping the end of her quill to her lips. "Ash, I'm all right for another few hours. You can sleep for awhile more and swap me out later."

Tristan shuffled on his feet, trying to keep the blanket tucked around him. "I'm fairly certain Ash wouldn't be a fan of that arrangement."

Aspen's grip tightened around her quill. She straightened her shoulders and gave him a thin smile. "I thought you'd be asleep by now."

"I was." He sat down, not sure how to proceed and wondering if this was a good idea at all.

"Couldn't sleep?" Aspen asked, as if sensing his uncertainty. She stirred the coals in front of her, the smoke swirling through her hair.

Tristan shook his head.

"Me either." She leaned back with a sigh and watched the stars. "I used to enjoy sleep once."

Tristan indulged her. It was the best way he could think to distract himself while he tried to figure out the best way to ask his favor. "What changed?"

"My dreams."

The silence fell back on Tristan's shoulders as his own dreams flooded his thoughts. Could he talk to her about them? *Should* he talk to her about them? Would she even listen? "What do you dream about?"

Her hand curled into a fist, scraping shards of grass into her palm. "Nightmares. The same ones, night after night." Tristan got the feeling she wasn't really talking to him, but rather cursing—or questioning?—some higher power.

"Me, too," he said. He couldn't bring himself to say anything else about them, but as his dream faded away, he knew he had to say something now before he lost the dream forever. "This is going to sound stupid."

"Probably," Aspen said, dipping her quill.

Tristan pressed his lips together, remembering why he hadn't wanted to ask her to begin with. *Push through, Tristan. Push through.* "Be that as it may, can I have some of your parchment? And a quill?"

"That was not at all where I expected that to go." Aspen gave him an intrigued look but didn't ask any questions about his request. "I supposed some ink and paper won't hurt." She offered him a few sheets and a short, battered quill. He went to take them, but she pulled them back at the last moment with a skeptical look. "You won't send messages regarding our location, will you?"

Tristan rolled his eyes. "How in Mother Night would I do that? And *why?* I'm a deserter."

"Both excellent questions," she said with a pointed look.

Tristan sighed. "You rebels and your overly active suspicions." He snatched the parchment from her. "I'm using them for a journal. Is that a suitable enough answer for you?"

Aspen cocked her head. "That's an odd way to keep a journal."

Tristan bristled, already beyond done with the conversation. What did it matter to her? "I had a bound one, but I—" his voice cracked, and he leaned back, horrified. He couldn't get emotional in front of *Aspen.* "I left it. Goodnight. Thank you for the parchment." He moved to scurry off, but Aspen called him back.

"It'll be easier to see what you're doing by the fire," she said. "Eyesight is too precious a commodity to risk."

Tristan blinked a few times, not sure what was happening. Just a few nights ago she seemed to have burned at the very thought of his presence, and now she wanted him to sit with her around the fire? "I won't be a bother?"

"The night air and a warm fire are things that belong to everyone. I won't be bothered as long as you're quiet."

Still unsure of what was happening, Tristan inched his way back beside the fire and sat down. Aspen had gone back to her own work, and it was as if Tristan didn't exist anymore. He settled in, watching Aspen out of the corner of his eyes to see if she made any sudden lunges for him. She didn't.

He let out a long, slow breath and began to write. The outside world faded away as the words spilled from the quill. For the first time in a while, the effort came easily to him. The details stayed clear and fresh. As more and more words filled the page, though, the monsters from the nightmare seemed to close in. Their rancid breath coated his spine. Their claws curled around his throat as their whispers filled his ears.

Finally, he could do it no more. He stuffed the parchment into his trouser pocket, and the monsters receded. Tristan rubbed his brows, bundled the blanket closer to him, and watched the fire for a while. He wished the flames had some way to speak. They always seemed to hold secrets far greater than he could ever hope to understand. Maybe they would tell him where to get his memories back.

He stretched with a groan and handed Aspen her quill. "Thank you."

"Keep it," she said off-handedly, putting her parchment in a pile and stirring the fire again. "Judging by how intent you were on that last passage, I imagine you'll be needing more use out of that quill."

"Th-thank you," he said, caught off-guard at the kind gesture. He turned the quill over in his hands. Now that he wasn't so intent on writing with it, he noticed indents all along the shaft of the quill and mangled bits of feather. He smiled despite himself. "Do you bite your quills?"

Aspen went pink across her nose. He noticed similar bite marks across the additional quill she had in her hand. "It's a filthy, nervous habit. You don't have to keep the quill if you don't want it." She tried to grab it back, but Tristan snatched it away from her.

"Are you often nervous, General Shadowalker?" he goaded.

She went quiet, settling back into her seat with a serious look. "Far too often. That's what happens when the weight of the kingdom falls on too few shoulders."

"Oh." Tristan twirled the quill in his fingers, not sure what else to say. Discomfort filled the space between them.

Aspen sighed and ran her fingers through her hair. "I never asked," she said. She looked at him, eyes bright in the firelight "What do *you* dream about?"

Tristan tried to gauge her intentions. If he wanted to talk about his dream with someone else to see if they could make sense of it, now was his opportunity. But he took the coward's way out. "Peas."

She chuckled, the sound unexpectedly warm and rich. It buzzed in his ears and sent tingles through his fingers. "You sound like Gan."

"Who?"

A sad sort of fondness crept into her eyes. "My best friend's father. I think you two would get along."

Tristan leaned forward, entranced by Aspen's rare openness. He had never thought he'd see the day. He *certainly* didn't deserve it. But he didn't dare pass up the opportunity. What was it about late nights around a campfire that made it so much easier to just talk? "Tell me about him?"

Aspen smiled, her expression soft. "He's a pea farmer by choice. He could have held practically any position he wanted, but that called to him, I suppose. Don't ask me why, because I couldn't tell you." She folded her arms across her chest and settled deeper in her seat. Her eyes focused on the memories brought to life. "You have to be careful not to bring peas up when you've got places to be. He'll go on for hours about the varieties and best growing methods. You'd think he'd been doing it all his life."

Tristan smiled with her, remembering his many morning arguments with Boff at Lorate. He wondered if Gan preferred white or red blooms. "Had he not been planting peas before?"

"No. He was on the previous king's counsel, appointed by Queen Eden herself. They were old friends."

Tristan gaped at her. "He went from *that* to *peas*? How did he survive the—um—" There was no polite way to say it.

Aspen had no such qualms. "The massacre?" she asked with steely eyes. "It's all right to call the Day of Bluest Blood what it is. Both sides have been guilty of them, and the more we hide from the fact, the less likely we are to change it." She swirled the embers with a long stick. "Gan had excused himself from the council meeting that day over a disagreement, so he missed the poisoned drinks. He heard the screams, though, as Osmen's men invaded."

Tristan gripped one fist in the other. The monsters that plagued his dreams gave him an idea of what that must have sounded like. How petrifying and eerie that must have been. "Did he have any family in the city?"

"He did."

"What...what happened to them?"

"His wife died in his arms. He was too late to save her." Aspen threw her stick into the fire. "When he lost her, he did what he could to help everyone else. He tried to save the queen and her six children, but only found the youngest prince, trapped beneath the queen's corpse."

Tristan watched the sparks dance across the logs, his eyes not fully focused. A sound echoed faintly in the back of his mind. As the rest of the world slipped deeper into his exhaustion, the sound grew into the sobs of a soul clinging to the last piece of happiness they had left. A woman, begging for mercy for her son, screaming his name. Tristan's heart raced, aching for whomever the voice belonged to. The flames of the campfire leapt to new heights, flooding his vision. They devoured everything in sight; the camp, the forest, the stone walls. A golden crown.

Aspen brought him back to the present. "Gan saved the prince from the flames that had engulfed the lower levels of the castle and stole a horse from the stables. He rode for three days and nights until he reached the Golden Grove. Our healers saved the prince, and Gan chose to remain with us to raise him."

Tristan's eyes had misted over. His breath caught slightly in his chest. "He sounds like an amazing man."

Aspen's face had softened again. "He is."

Tristan brushed his eyes, hoping it looked like he was only clearing smoke from them. "Where did your best friend come into the picture?"

Aspen knit her brows. "How do you mean?"

"You said he was your best friend's father, but you only said he took the prince to safety, and his wife died..."

Aspen rubbed her face and sighed. "Oh, sweet Sister Earth." She looked at him with exasperation. "He *was* the prince."

Well, now Tristan just felt like an idiot. "Right. Sorry." He twiddled his thumbs, not sure what to do with his hands. His burns ached, but he resisted the urge to scratch them. "Are... are the rumors true about the prince? Is he—?"

"He's dead." Aspen said with no expression. She didn't look him in the eye. "No matter how much I wish he weren't."

They fell into long silence, Tristan mentally kicking himself. He shouldn't have asked. Mother Night, why couldn't he keep his questions to himself?

Just when he thought their silence might be permanent, Aspen spoke again. "Do you really have no memories at all?"

Tristan winced. "Did Ash tell you?"

"She did."

Tristan clasped his hands in his lap. "Well, then to answer your question: none."

Aspen said nothing. They watched the stars in silence. A breeze drew whispers from the trees. Tristan had never breathed air so crisp. Ash said something to Styrax somewhere out in the dark, and he laughed. The person Tristan had been at Lorate seemed such a distant memory. Would there be a time that all of this would be forgotten again, and he would be nothing but an empty shell once more? Would he survive having all that taken from him again?

Aspen watched him closely. "I never thought I'd say this, but I don't enjoy your unusual silence.

Tristan scoffed and pushed his fingers against each other. "Can I...tell you something?"

Aspen leaned back and regarded the stars. "It seems tonight's the perfect time for stories and secrets."

Tristan took that as a 'yes'. He sighed and rubbed his face. "I'm afraid that none of these memories will stay."

"What do you mean by that?"

Tristan ran a hand through his hair—felt the scar beneath it. "The only thing I really know about my memory loss is from what my general told me, and even that was just an educated guess." He tossed a pebble into the fire and watched the ashes collapse off the wood. "Who's to say it's not something else? What if it happens all the time? What if it's me, or..." He swallowed hard, remembering his conversation with Styrax. "Or a spell, or a *curse*? I don't know if I would be able to survive that again. I might go insane or hurt someone else or *die* or—"

Aspen's hand on his knee stopped the flood of words. His spiral into panic had been so complete that he didn't realize she had moved. The simple touch squelched the raging thoughts in his head. He looked her in the eyes — soft, green, and vibrant — and was enveloped in the peace of summer dusk.

"We each have something to fight for." She removed her hand on his knee, but her eyes never wavered. "Are your memories worth that fight?"

Tristan had to force his answer past the lump in his throat. "Yes."

She nodded once. "Then I will help you win that fight."

Tristan's small, breathless "Thank you," hardly felt adequate enough. How could she take on such a burden so easily? And with such quiet confidence? How could she do that for a man that had fought and derided her at every turn? One that had almost gotten her killed?

And how was it that her simple phrase had made him feel lighter than he had in years?

Aspen smiled in understanding. Tristan doubted he had been able to communicate the full depth of his feeling, but it seemed she had at least gathered some of it.

She scooted a few inches away and stoked the fire again. "Don't think me entirely unselfish," she said in a voice that sounded like it should be teasing, but had a hint too much truth in it. "You'll be helping me, too."

"Oh? How's that?"

"If, while I'm helping you, I'm able to learn how to willfully forget something, you will have paid any debt you may owe me a hundred times over." She no longer focused on the fire, but something deeper in it. Something only she could see.

Tristan had seen that look from her before. Something haunted her in the darkest parts of her mind. He wished he could help her the same way she had offered to help him. "What would you forget?"

Aspen's eyes refocused. She looked at him with quirked eyebrow, but shadows still lurked on her face. "That's the hard part. The more I talk about it, the less likely I am to forget." She stood and brushed off her trousers. "It's late. I think all this talk has finally lulled me to sleep." She smiled at him again. Not full and not entirely happy, but warm. Tristan's heart pattered in his ribs. "Goodnight, Tristan."

"Good...good night." He watched her walk away, his heart inexplicably beating in time with her footsteps. "Aspen?"

"Hmm?"

"Could we...maybe do this again some time?"

She was silent for a moment. She didn't look at him, but he could have sworn he saw a touch of pink on her ears. "I might be able to arrange that."

CHAPTER
TWENTY

A few mornings later, Tristan woke up to a new leather notebook laying next to his boots. He turned it over in his hands, admiring the deep blue cover as a fuzzy sort of warmth spread to his fingers and toes. He smiled, not sure what he had done to deserve the gift, and looked around for Aspen. He didn't find her, but Ash waved him over.

"I'm going into town! You're coming with me, and you have no choice in the matter. Your clothes are too rank to save!"

Tristan took an indignant sniff at himself and then had to grudgingly agree. He tucked his journal carefully into his knapsack and followed her.

While they were out, Tristan grabbed himself a sword from a seedy merchant at a cheap price. The blade itself had more dents and dings than an actual blade and shed rust whenever Tristan drew it, and it looked like an apprentice might have overseen the metal tempering. It had left uneven, sloppy waves on the surface, and someone had sharpened the blade so poorly that the top had moved off-center and dragged Tristan's arm down with it. It would be more of a danger to him than anyone else if he ever had to use it in combat. But it was his, and it was something.

The problem was that Aspen took one look at it and confiscated it on the spot. No amount of snarling protest could change her mind. Tristan felt like a scolded child and hated every moment he saw his weapon around her waist. He forgot to thank her for the journal.

The next night, Aspen called for their nightly stop as the sun disappeared behind the mountains. How many nights had it been now? Four? Twelve? They all blurred together.

Aspen had adopted the habit of wandering into the forest to mutter and pace incoherently after they all pitched camp, rolling and unrolling a slip of parchment. Tristan couldn't imagine what sort of purpose that served, but he supposed crazy begat crazy.

Tonight, though, Aspen shirked her frantic ramble and approached Tristan. "You, come with me."

"I've already gathered enough firewood to last through the night," he said with a goading smirk as he settled himself deliberately next to the fire. "And I made sure Styrax collected water and Ash had everything she needed for dinner. We set the tents. Campsite's cleared. Any would-be predators have been scared away. I don't believe there's anything else that should keep me from enjoying it."

Aspen pinched her lips together in a mocking smile, one eyebrow cocked. She bowed deep enough for her hair to touch the ground. "Forgive me, *your lordship*, I did not realize basic chores were such a *hardship* for you." She straightened. "I can only imagine that someone as beleaguered as you would not want the additional responsibility of a sword." She left in a swish of hair and leather without giving Tristan time to respond.

Tristan knew it was a setup. He knew she'd baited him to serve her own agenda. But, *Mother Night,* his curiosity would be the death of him one day.

Tristan followed Aspen, grumbling at himself for letting her win every step of the way. "You don't actually plan on giving me a sword, do you?"

Aspen said nothing until they reached the edge of camp. A river rushed nearby, and the firelight cast the barest of amber glows on Aspen's face. She smiled like a cat watching a maimed bird. She unbuckled his sword from around her waist. "You want this sword back, do you?"

Tristan already hated this game he had allowed himself to walk into. He grit his teeth. "Yes, I do."

Aspen raised an eyebrow. "You want *this* sword?"

Tristan knew she was up to something—he heard it in the goading tone of her voice, and simply because she was *Aspen*—but just couldn't figure out *what*. He slid his feet a shoulder-width apart, ready for whatever she threw at him. Unless it was magic. He couldn't do much to brace for magic. "Yes, that one." What was she getting at? There weren't other swords lying about to be picked up on a whim, unless she intended to give him hers, which he doubted. She'd practically growled at him when he'd tried to sneak a better look.

One corner of Aspen's mouth twitched in what could be mistaken for a smile. Dread pitted Tristan's stomach. Something was not right here. Aspen twisted her body and lobbed the sword—*his sword!*—into the nearby river. Tristan lunged too late for it. It hit a hidden boulder, snapped in two, and sank into the dark, swirling current.

Tristan gaped. "You...I..."

Aspen brushed her hands, her nose curled in disgust as rust flakes rained on the grass. "I wouldn't give that sword to anyone as a fire-stoker, much less an actual weapon. I promise you're much safer without it." She looked at him, a glimmer of...*humor* in her eyes? "Let's get you trained, and maybe you'll earn the chance to own a *real* sword, yeah?"

Tristan still reeled. Sure, the rust had eaten it to almost nothing and its crooked blade had terrible balance, but that had been his first sword. "You threw my—" he stopped. Something finally registered. "Did you...offer to *train* me?"

"Little slow on the uptake, aren't you?"

Tristan narrowed his eyes and ignored the jab. "Why? This isn't an excuse to beat on me all you want, is it?"

"That's a side benefit." Aspen folded her arms with a quirked eyebrow. "You have been rather insufferable."

"Is that so?" Tristan mirrored her stance with a crooked smirk. "I could say the same about you."

Aspen bowed. "Forgive me, oh high and mighty one, for hurting your tender feelings."

Tristan mashed his lips together. He couldn't contend with that without walking further into a trap, no matter how much she deserved a snarky comeback. Or three.

"I see you've learned some manners and the art of silence. Well done!" Aspen applauded. Tristan's ego took each clap as a direct attack. Before he could think of anything to fire back at her, she tossed a smooth, carved branch to him. "Take that. Your training starts now."

Tristan hefted the branch. Aspen had carved off all the nubs and rough bark and tapered it to a comfortable balance. When had she found the time? No matter the answer, it was leaps and bounds better than the poor excuse of a weapon languishing at the river bottom. He hated to admit that. "You still haven't told me why you're doing this."

Aspen smirked and picked up another carved branch. She twirled it around her wrist. "I'll let you figure that out for yourself. Shall we begin?"

As was her primary form of communication, Aspen did what she liked without giving him any time to respond. She lashed out with her stick and whacked the ball of his wrist. He yelped and dropped his weapon. "At least give me a chance to be ready!" He wrung his throbbing hand.

Aspen scoffed. "Your enemies won't give you time to prepare. I thought you would know that by now."

"It's true, they won't." Ash plopped herself in front of the nearest tree trunk to use as a backrest. She munched on the nut mix she always carried with her.

Tristan groaned. "Aren't there better things you could do with your time?" he asked Ash.

She shrugged. "Probably, but none as exciting as this." She winked and crushed another nut between her teeth.

"What's going on over here?"

Tristan pinched the bridge of his nose. Not Styrax, too.

Ash made room for Styrax at her tree. "We're watching Tristan change colors. I hear he specializes in black and blue." She offered Styrax some of her snack.

"I didn't know Tristan could do magic." Styrax took a few nuts and sat beside Ash. "Tristan, why didn't you tell me?"

Tristan pointed an accusing finger at him, which only made Styrax grin more. Mother Night curse him. "*You* have no room to—"

Aspen snapped her staff on his wrist again.

He recoiled and whirled on her. "*Ow!*"

"I don't think that's how you're supposed to do it!" Styrax called.

Tristan jabbed a finger at him again. "I've heard enough from you!"

Styrax chuckled.

"Eyes up here!" Aspen jammed Tristan's ribs. "Those two don't matter right now."

"I resent that!" Ash said good-naturedly.

Aspen ignored her. "If you want to live, the only person who matters is the person swinging a weapon at you." She struck him again. Tristan narrowly dodged it. She twisted her wrist at the last moment and tagged the bony part of his hip. "Now pick up your weapon and let's get serious about this."

With his bruises and pride smarting, Tristan bent to pick up his branch.

Aspen cracked her staff against his tailbone. He shot straight up in shock with a yelp, and she jabbed his chest. He staggered back a pace or two.

"What's the matter?" Aspen batted wide eyes. "I said pick up your weapon." The barest hint of a smile hovered on her lips and in the brightness of her eyes.

Walk away, Tristan, his voice of reason begged. *You don't have to play her sadistic game. WALK AWAY.*

He wanted to. Mother Night, he wanted to *so badly*. But her smugness *rankled* deep in the pit of his stomach. He couldn't walk away until he put her in her place.

Tristan watched Aspen. She didn't move. Didn't even seem to breathe. If Tristan didn't already know she was there, he might not have seen her at all. But a certain energy hummed around her, waiting—anticipating—like the air before the first storm cloud rolled in.

Tristan kept eye contact while he bent to retrieve his so-called 'weapon.' He waited for Aspen to move as he inched closer. Waiting for any sort of hint to where she might go next. No such luck. Maybe she intended to let him get it this time? No. She took too much pleasure in toying with him. She could never let it be that easy.

Aspen's attention flicked right. Just for an instant.

Tristan seized the opportunity. He lunged left, away from where she had indicated she'd go.

And fell right into her trap.

She set her staff in motion before he took his first step. It smashed into his shoulder with the help of his own momentum. His fingers missed his stick by a hair's breadth. He hobbled away, cradling his shoulder. "Stop *doing* that!"

Aspen smirked. "Stop being predictable, and perhaps I might."

Tristan glared. He took in the clearing, trying to plan how best to get past Aspen's impossible defense. Nothing. Absolutely nothing. No rocks. No other branches. No hidden weapons or tricks of any kind. Just an impenetrable wall and a hopeless situation.

The tension and resolve eked from Tristan's muscles. Why fight anymore? Aspen had never intended to teach him. She only wanted to humiliate him. Well, mission accomplished. She'd already taken too much of his dignity. He wouldn't play along anymore.

"Come on, Tristan!" Styrax called. "You fought harder for your pea plants than this!"

Ash scrunched her brows. "Pea plant?"

"He used to keep one on his windowsill. Awfully protective of the thing."

"Aww, sweet baby."

Something stirred in Tristan at Styrax's goading. A whisper of *something* someone had once taught him somewhere. The warmth of a kind presence sent a flood of comfort and pride through his chest. He saw no face and heard no voice, but the feelings' familiarity ached deep in his soul.

He glanced at the staff on the ground. Maybe...maybe he could try *one* more time.

Aspen cocked her head as if she sensed the change in him. "Are you ready to get serious now?"

Tristan said nothing. She'd have to see, wouldn't she?

To be fair, he knew just as much as she did about how this would turn out. But what was in the details?

Before he could second-guess himself, Tristan broke into a full, pell-mell tilt toward his fallen staff. No rhyme. No reason. Just pure mad-dash. Blood and adrenaline surged through him. The ground churned beneath his feet. The edges of his vision blurred as he focused on a single point. The stick.

If nothing else seems to work, barrel through your enemies like a battering ram. They'll never expect it.

The words came like echoes to Tristan's mind. He couldn't place the voice, other than he *knew* it. That thought—that *glimmer*—of any faint memory fueled every step. He *had* become a battering ram. He had never felt so powerful in his life.

The feeling died as quickly as his appetite when he saw Lorate's mess hall food.

Everything happened so fast he couldn't catch it all. All he knew was his intention to bowl Aspen over failed spectacularly. He slammed into a stone wall. Her body was denser than it looked. Limbs flailed. The earth turned on its head. The stars in his eyes obscured the stars overhead as he lay flat on his back. His mouth gaped open as he tried to suck in the air forced from his lungs.

Aspen leaned over him. "That was...absolutely terrible." She offered him a hand and helped him up. "A friend of mine used to pull stunts like that." Aspen gestured to the churned earth from his ill-advised charge. "The result was about the same, so don't feel too bad."

"I suppose that's what I get for being more pod than pea." Tristan froze as soon as the words left his mouth. The garbage brain vomit of words that somehow warmed his heart. He couldn't remember thinking them. They just came out, as if he'd heard them and said them all his life. The warmth deepened in his chest.

Aspen watched him, her body still and her eyes guarded. Tristan couldn't tell if she was breathing or not. "An old, dear friend says that," she said, her words slow and precise. "He and his son are the only two people I've heard say it."

Tristan shrugged, uneasy with the tension that had sprung from nowhere. Why did it feel like she stared straight into his soul? "Must be a regional thing."

Aspen regarded him with narrowed eyes and tight lips. "And what region would that be, exactly?"

Tristan winced. She'd caught him. What did Aspen do to liars? He didn't want to find out, but couldn't bring himself to fess up, either. Why, oh why, had he dug his grave over something so meaningless? "I...uhh..."

Aspen watched him flounder. Her eyebrows traveled farther and farther up her forehead. Mother Night have it all. He'd cornered himself.

"He couldn't tell you, even if he wanted to," Styrax offered, his tone cautious. "He doesn't like to talk about it, but Tristan doesn't know where he's from."

Aspen peered closer at Tristan. "You told me you remember nothing about your past, but I never asked; how did that happen?"

Tristan stopped and really looked at her for a moment. She watched him with a steady gaze, no skepticism or waiting for the next opportunity to crack a joke at his expense. Odd how such a simple question could stoke a warmth in his chest that trickled to his hands and feet. It softened pains and worries and ill feelings. He had already told her so much. How could he tell her anything but the truth now?

"I was attacked." He brushed his hand along the scar on his head. "La—" he stopped. She probably wouldn't want to hear any story about Laire. "The man that found me said a blow to my head is probably what caused the memory loss."

Aspen set her staff down, her skin gray. A faint green aura surrounded her. "May I see it?"

Tristan furrowed his brow. "My...my head?"

"Yes."

Mystified, Tristan obliged. He parted his hair for her to see. She traced gentle, featherlight fingers across his scalp. Over the divot in his skull and the puncture scars. Her hands trembled. The green aura grew.

"These look like mace marks."

Ash stood, her face pale and her eyes wide. "Aspen, are you *sure*?"

Tristan looked at Ash, lost. Sure? Sure about *what*?

Aspen didn't answer her. She balled her hands at her sides. Wafts of green magic curled off her and swept away with the breeze. "Why do you want to go to the Dragon Scales?"

Tristan met her gaze. He saw it there. She *knew*. She knew *something* about him, or at least something that could get him started. He toyed with the strap around his neck. The single phrase that had sent him on his journey to begin with played through his mind.

For evergreens and aspen trees.

He opened his mouth to respond, to answer truthfully, and finally, *finally* get answers in return, but the words strangled in his throat. Before his eyes, Aspen transformed. A bald, pale monster watched him with lifeless, lidless black eyes that consumed nearly its entire face. It grinned at him with a gaping mouth. A thick black tongue ran across its rows of rotted, serrated teeth.

Tristan's heart seized in his chest. His head pounded with blood and his body quivered. One of his rings burned a circle on his chest. He couldn't breathe. He couldn't move. He could only stare, his mind a complete blank of nothing but horrific agony. No escape. No safety. Only the monster in his eyes.

Tristan flung himself back and threw his hands up to shield himself. "I won't tell a monster like you anything!" Heaving, clutching one hand at the burning ring around his neck, he glared at Aspen. She had returned to her 'normal' self, but he knew her true form now. He had seen it for himself. "You won't get *anything* from me," he said with a hiss.

Ash and Styrax leapt to their feet. They shouldered between Aspen and Tristan.

"Tristan, what's wrong?" Styrax put a hand on his shoulder.

Tristan wrenched his shoulder from Styrax and backed farther away from them all. His heart pounded in his throat and ears. His head buzzed. Styrax looked at him with wide eyes, a jumble of concern and hurt.

Aspen watched him without a word. Tristan saw several things run through her mind at once. A stony shroud fell over her face. She brushed away her hair and picked up both staffs, sheathing them in her belt. "Training will resume whenever you'd like." She looked Tristan square in the eyes. Cold. Distant. "In the meantime, I suggest you consider whether you plan to continue on with us 'monsters' to the Dragon Scales."

Tristan stalked away from them, heart pounding and limbs shaking. Styrax loped after him.

"Tristan, what on Sister Earth was *that*? This isn't like you! Did something—?"

"Not now, Styrax!" Tristan squeezed his eyes shut, trying to banish the image of the monster from his mind. Orange haze filled the darkness behind his eyelids. "I don't want your help!" His stomach lurched at the words, knowing they weren't true, but he couldn't get them to stop.

The monster in his eyes laughed.

TWENTY-ONE

Laire had retired to his room at the inn after his fourth bar fight in just as many days. His sword leaned against the wall in the corner, ruby eyes glittering in the candlelight. The stress and lack of sleep were finally edging Laire to his breaking point. If he wanted to get any information out of anyone, he had to remove himself before he turned everyone in the village against him.

He leaned back against the inn wall and shut his eyes, breath hissing through his mouth as he favored a fat lip and bruised eye. Laughter, tavern lights, and the smell of cooked meat bled through the floorboards and pounded against his skull. He could go down and try to enjoy a quiet drink away from everyone, but it was all too much. Too strong. Too loud. Too bright.

As he sat, he nodded off once, but immediately jumped to his feet and paced the room. Six days since he had seen Tristan. In those six days, neither hide nor hair had appeared to indicate where he might have gone. He'd simply vanished. Laire couldn't sleep now. He had work to do if he ever wanted to reinstate his family back into Osmen's good graces. There was a tavern full of people downstairs, ripe for the asking. Surely one of them would have seen a rogue

Ancient One traveling with a lost-looking human by now, especially considering how big and out of place Styrax was. Even magic-users had to stop for supplies somewhere.

But so many people had looked at him like he was insane when he had asked about them. No one had seen anything of Styrax or Tristan. What would make the people downstairs any different?

At least no one had seen an elf with a black sword, either. He could hope that she had faded into the realm of phantoms for good this time.

Laire rubbed his aching brows. It didn't matter how impossible the entire thing seemed; how horrifically he had botched this entire mission. He had already failed King Osmen once at the Dragon Scales. He couldn't fathom the king would be so lenient with his punishment again, especially when he had no collateral to bargain with. No. He could not fail again. For Vinea and Linae's sake, he would find Tristan. He had no other choice.

I had no other choice.

The words came so clearly to his mind that Laire whirled to the door. Bile rose to his throat and all the feeling drained from his face. He expected to see her there, covered in blood and traitorous, lying tears spilling from her wide, broken eyes.

She wasn't.

Laire sat on the bed, body numb and shaking. Exhaustion hit him like a runaway cart. Maybe he could take one night of rest. It would do him no good to drop dead in the middle of the road for lack of sleep. He closed his eyes and began to drift to sleep, but memories drew to the surface. Images of his men dead in their own pools of blood as relentless waves pushed and pulled at their bodies. Watching them get mowed down by a force that should not have known they were coming. A young woman wielding a black sword, meeting his white one blow for blow. Osmen's look of disgust as Laire told him he had lost the Vanguard.

Laire lunged from the bed and paced the room. No. *No.* He could not sleep. He would rest when he was dead. There was too much to do. He had to find Tristan. Had to bring that dark-haired wench to justice. She had made a fool of him once. He would not let her do it again.

His eyes lost focus as sleep threatened again. His sword swam in his murky vision. Whispers dripped from it like spiders on fine threads, crawling to the base of his skull.

Sleep, they whispered. *We will guide you. Rest, and trust in us.*

No. He couldn't do it. His ancestors had warned him time and again that the sword could not be trusted—that it drove mortals to madness. But he was so *tired,* and every avenue he had pursued had come up fruitless.

Not every avenue.

The whispers overwhelmed him. He collapsed back to bed and the inn was lost to him. Instead, he was outside a small cottage, surrounded by the brightest assortment of flowers and bushes he'd ever seen before or since. Vines embraced every corner and curve of the walls, reaching broad leaves for the dusty, sparkling sunshine. Purple wisteria shaded the doorway and windows. A child laughed. A woman hummed songs to herself, and the flowers leaned closer to listen.

Laire cried out and ran to the cottage door, his legs feeling hollow and leaden all at once. They had been here? This whole time? How could he have abandoned them? How could he have left a place so dear to him?

He burst through the door, expecting summertime and family and love. Safety. Happiness. But the golden sunshine was gone. The wisteria and flowers withered. The interior was nothing but wood tinged copper from the raging fire outside the window. It roared and crackled, spewing flames and screams and stark against the silver moon. Smoke billowed in through every crevice, coating overturned furniture and shattered glass. Faces formed and vanished in it, twisted in horror and agony. Fresh flowers spilled down the cottage table, their petals soaking up the crimson puddle on the floor.

Laire wanted to leave his body. Flee to anywhere but here. His heart thundered in his chest, and he couldn't draw in breath. He knew what happened next. He couldn't see it again. Not again. He tried to stop himself—tried to leave back the way he had come. But the door and windows had vanished. His only path was forward. As if moved by invisible hands, his legs moved, stepping toward a dark corner untouched by the flickering flames outside.

"Anise?" he asked. A shaking, hollow word in a voice so young he almost didn't recognize it. The screams from outside echoed the screams in his heart.

He heard her sobs before he saw her. Her dark hair pooled around her face and tucked behind her long, elven ears. She looked at him with those green eyes, once full of life but now shattered into millions of soulless pieces. She cradled a body so small—too small— closer to her. A boy, with her dark tresses and pointed ears, but Laire's strong jaw and blue eyes. The boy stared at his mother sightlessly, his mouth open in a silent scream. Blood dripped from her fingers onto the blade at her side.

"Laire, my love, I had no other choice," Anise said, choking on her tears. "I had no other choice."

"*No!*" Laire flung himself from his bed, heaving for breath, sweat pouring down his body as he trembled. The cottage was gone. The fire and screams and smoke had vanished. Anise and his son, Ivan, were gone. One taken from him, the other brought to grim justice by his own hand.

Laire found the nearest chamber pot and emptied his stomach. He sat back against the wall, chamber pot clutched to his chest, and sobbed. It had been so long since he had had those dreams. He had hoped they had finally left him in peace. But he should have known better. A man never forgets his son—never forgets the monstrous mother that slew him.

We remember, the whispers returned, dredging through his frantic thoughts. *That was the first time you wielded us. The first of your family to give us a taste of blood.*

Anise's screams echoed through his bones. He felt her warm blood spilling over his hands again as she collapsed against him.

A monster deserves a monster's end. We can help you again if you let us.

The buzzing, hissing words filled Laire's mind and drowned out his own thoughts.

Trust us again. Let us find the monster that once more threatens your happiness.

Laire was across the room before he realized it, the sword in his hands. He dropped the blade in shock, and the sound immediately stopped. Heaving, he paced in front of the sword a few times, not sure what to do. He had heard that voice before—first when Ivan had died, and second at the Dragon Scales—but it had never controlled him like that before. The thought raced like acid through his body. Was he becoming what his ancestors had warned against? No. *No.* It would not come to that. He gathered a corner of his tunic around his hand and went to pick up the sword again, but a booming voice from the tavern below interrupted him.

"I'm tellin' ya! Strange things are afoot in Caldrech village. Crops growin' almost overnight, and not a single one lost to critters. 'Tain't natural, if you ask me."

"Shut your mouth! You're eating, aren't you? That's all thanks to the crops from Caldrech. More than half the kingdom isn't as lucky as you are!"

Laire perked at the sound. It seemed too fortuitous. Surely, after days of searching, his hunt couldn't have been solved so easily. He stood and wiped his sweaty palms on his trousers, casting a last glance at the sword. "I don't need you. Not yet. You do not own me."

The sword said nothing. He couldn't tell if he was disappointed or not.

Shaking his head, Laire left the room. He had a job to do. It would be stupid to pass up that information. He went downstairs to see a man about Caldrech.

TWENTY-TWO

Vinea watched Sorren closely over the next few days, her heart breaking more and more for him with every step. He looked so much like his mother, with his rich, almost golden skin and dark, curly hair. He even had her spray of freckles across his nose. At one point, she had known his mother's same laughter and joy to shine through his eyes. But now, Sedick had stolen every ounce of that from him. He moved like a marionette on strings, awkward and without his own purpose. His expression never changed. He said nothing to her, not even when she asked to see Linae every time they stopped to rest. He was just an empty boy in an empty body, and Vinea hoped Sedick rotted for it.

After their days of travel, she could stand the silence no more. Once she finished her nightly viewing of Linae—she was sleeping, a rag doll tucked into the crook of her elbow and smudging her tear-stained cheeks—Vinea dabbed away her tears and faced Sorren across the campfire. "We've come a long way, haven't we? It's been a long time since I've been so close to Vastet."

Sorren said nothing. Only nodded.

Vinea pursed her lips. She removed a piece of jerky from her knapsack and offered half to him. He ignored it.

She huffed with exasperation. "You have to eat."

He pulled out a hard tack biscuit from his cloak and nibbled on it, teeth scraping against its rock-hard surface.

Vinea sighed and finished the half-piece of jerky. She stowed the other piece for when he got hungry. If she knew anything about teenage boys, she knew he would get hungry eventually. "Will you tell me about yourself?"

Again, he said nothing. Just gave her a fleeting glance before going back to his hard tack.

"Be careful, little one. It's rare that I don't get what I want. If you don't tell me, I'll just make it a game."

He still said nothing.

Vinea bit her tongue to keep from cursing Sedick out loud. Bad enough to steal the boy from his mother, but to steal any ounce of life he had behind those eyes was just...shameful. Monstrous. She had to believe there was something still there.

"Do you..." She cast around for something she remembered of him. She wished she had paid more attention back then. But she had been too focused on entertaining every avenue to have her own child than to pay attention to him. "...like dragons?" She remembered he babbled non-stop about them as a boy, raiding every library he could for more books on them. Didn't matter they were all extinct; he knew each one by heart.

Nothing. Not a flicker on his face.

"Do you have a family? A mother perhaps?" The two had been tied at the hip. Surely...

Still nothing.

A lump of frustration welled in her throat. "Will you at least tell me your name?"

"I have no name," he said. His voice had gotten so much deeper than the last time she had seen him, but he was still a child. "I have no interests. No family. All I have is my magic." He shot a small purple blast into the fire, which leapt a few meters higher before settling back down. "And my purpose. I am a sorcerer bound to my master. I serve Lord Sedick, and that is all."

Vinea reeled back at the unfeeling tragedy of it all, no matter how hard she tried to remain neutral for his sake. "Not even a name? How dare—?" The boiling, implacable rage rose so quickly in her that it cut her words short. How dare he? How *dare* he? She closed her eyes and vented her hatred through her nose. Slow and steaming. Sedick would pay his penance. She would make sure of it. Until then, she had a young sorcerer under her charge, and she would right his "master's" wrongs.

Vinea leaned over and grasped Sorren's hand. He flinched away from her touch and she let go, hurting with him. Another reason she would see Sedick to the Pit. "Would you like a name?" she asked, smiling despite herself. "It seems I am in the business of giving them out."

Sorren shifted away from her and refused to look her in the eyes. "I have no use for a name."

Vinea's heart shattered. "Everyone needs a name."

He looked doubtful.

"What if I were in the village and needed help? I couldn't just yell 'help, boy!' There are so many other boys there. Who's to say which one I called for? And by the time you all figured it out, it'd be too late!"

The barest ghost of a smile touched his face and then vanished again. Vinea almost cried happy tears. "You may call me something if it makes you feel safe."

"It does." Vinea studied his face, remembering a similar moment with Tristan all those years ago. She could have given him his true name back then—a piece that could have helped him build the whole—but she had refrained. For his safety and hers. She had regretted it ever since, wondering if she had done the right thing, or if she had just been a coward. At least now she could make it right with someone else.

"How do you feel about Sorren?"

A light flickered briefly behind his eyes, and Vinea's heart surged with relief.

"I think it's fine," he said.

And that was all she needed.

They sat in silence that way for a long time. Vinea's stomach grumbled and she pulled out her own hard tack, but could only manage nibbles without breaking her teeth. Sorren didn't speak again, but as the shadows grew longer and their surroundings grew quiet, Vinea noticed Sorren worrying at a silver stud in his ear. He didn't move otherwise, staring unblinking into the flames. No life in his face, but shadows flickering in his eyes.

"Sorren?" she asked gently.

He gave her a rigid look, all muscles tight through his shoulders and neck. Still no expression on his face.

Vinea tried not to be unnerved by the far-off, blank look that seemed intent to pierce to her very soul. She had to remind herself that it was not Sorren's fault. It was all Sedick's doing. She gestured to the earring. "What is that?"

Sorren's hand dropped to his side. "A gift. From my master."

"Oh?" Vinea took another excruciating bite of hard tack to keep herself from spewing a few unpleasant thoughts about his "master".

"Yes." Sorren touched the earring again. "Sometimes, I have these...thoughts. Images calling to me, saying I don't belong. And then these *monsters* appear. Horrible things with rows of teeth and large black eyes and—" A shudder ran through him, and his grip tightened around the stud. "Lord Sedick gave this to me to help. It clears my mind, and then I am able to serve him again. He is a merciful master."

Vinea snorted, and crumbs flew from her mouth. She choked them back, eyes watering, and composed herself. "Sedick is many things, but merciful is not one of them."

Sorren cocked his head at her. "What do you mean by that?"

Vinea sighed and put her hard tack away. "Nothing to worry

about." She studied him closely, looking for any sign of life. Nothing but cold emptiness. "What would happen if you took the earring out?"

A flicker of something. Fear. Hope. Desperation. But in the blink of an eye, it was gone. "I think it's time to retire now." He left her at the fire and curled against a tree, cloak wrapped tightly about him and the silver stud catching the shifting firelight.

Vinea chewed on her lip. She could remove the earring, and perhaps the Sorren she had known would return. But perhaps he wouldn't. Sedick might have made him too far gone. She wanted desperately to try either way—to see if she could free him—but she stopped herself. Sedick had made himself clear—any wrong move from her, and Linae would be in danger. She couldn't risk that.

She put out the fire and went to bed, guilt eating at her conscience as Sorren sat against his tree, staring out into nothing.

Sorren screamed. Long and loud and piercing.

Vinea jolted awake with a gasp, heart pounding in her throat and her body paralyzed for too many beats. What had happened? When had she fallen asleep? Sorren continued to scream.

When she got control of her body again, Vinea leapt from her bedroll. Sorren thrashed in his cloak, his magic spilling from him in a blanket of purple mist. Lightning arced through it, setting small fires ablaze on the dry undergrowth.

"Sorren!" Vinea ran to him, suffocating the fires with her skirts the best she could. "Sorren, wake up!"

He screamed again, clawing at the stud in his ear as tears poured down his face. "No more! *Please*, no more," he yelled to nothingness, his words garbled in sobs.

"*Sorren!*" Vinea knelt and clutched him to her, his magic singeing her skin and careening through her blood. "Sorren, *wake up!*"

Like a man pulling himself from tar, Sorren wrenched himself from his sleep in slow, painful increments. His grip on his earlobe loosened. He took a gasping breath, and his rigid body relaxed. The tears and purple mist remained, but they faded with every new heartbeat. "...monsters..." he muttered without opening his eyes. "...coming. Destroy my mind if I...I don't obey..."

"Shhh," Vinea drew him close and rocked back and forth, her arms shaking with horror. His tears soaked her shoulder. Sedick had done this to him. Sedick and the trinkets he forced on his subjects. The silver stud Sorren wore ground into her collarbone as he wept. She could take it out. Right now. Free him from Sedick's torture. But then Sedick's threat loomed over her, taunting her and paralyzing her best intentions.

Vinea ground her teeth as her own tears threatened to spill. She was just as much a prisoner as Sorren, and Sedick knew it.

"...mama-he's-he's got her. My punishment. Have to help...save her."

Vinea's heart turned to lead. She pried Sorren from her and held his shoulders. "Sorren, what about your mother?"

A tremor ran through him, and then his eyes opened, red and swollen. He blinked at Vinea uncomprehendingly.

"Sorren, what about your mother?"

His lower lip trembled, but no tears fell. "I have no mother," he said in a hollow voice. And then softer, quieter, an aside that breathed a little life back into his eyes, he said, "But I wish I did." He pulled away and drew his cloak around him again. Tremors ran through him that wouldn't stop.

Vinea sat in silence with him, feeling like a coward. Any words of comfort stuck to her tongue as her heart twisted into guilty knots. What could she possibly say to him when she refused to do the one thing that could actually help him?

Without looking at her, Sorren asked, "Will you...sing that song? The one you sang to Linae?"

Vinea tried to smile, but it was a miserable attempt. "Of course," she said. "And I will be here with you for however long you need." The words scraped like sand across her tongue, laced with acrid guilt.

The emotionless mask over his face did not change, but she saw relief chase away the clouds in his eyes. "Thank you," he said.

TWENTY-THREE

Laire shifted his weight from one foot to the other, careful not to disturb the wheat he crouched in. His stomach growled low and menacing, and a bubble rose to his throat. He choked the belch back and grimaced. Perhaps that fifth ale had been ill-advised. At least he hadn't gone for a sixth.

No matter now. What was done was done. Besides, it had nudged that farmer into loosening his tongue about the odd happenings in Caldrech. Fallow fields giving yield to enormous bumper crops. Sickly trees bearing ripe fruit overnight. Laire had a hard time believing any Ancient Ones would be stupid enough to use magic so openly and chalked it up to wives' tales, jealousy, or both. But he had to check either way. After a week of unsuccessful elf chase, he was desperate enough to follow any lead.

Crickets whirred in the tall grasses, calling to each other through the night. The noise drove like so many nails into Laire's already pounding head. He ground his teeth and pinched the bridge of his nose. Mother Night, maybe he *should* have accepted that sixth ale. He wouldn't have felt or remembered a thing.

Before Laire could burn the entire field down to shut it up, a glow rippled up the stocks of wheat. A warm, copper color that could have easily been mistaken for sunset light. If there had been any sort of sunset to speak of. Clashed against the moon's silver, the copper turned eerie, almost the color of dried blood. An image—only a flash —of another silver night painted gruesome copper shot through Laire's mind like a barbed arrow.

Laire clenched his hand around the hilt of his sword and peered into the night. It seemed that farmer hadn't been spewing wives tales after all. Somewhere out there, one of *them* lurked.

It took him a few moments of scanning before he saw it. A tiny figure swaying side-to-side, elbows at its sides, and palms faced upward. The only visible parts of its face were the copper rings around its irises. The wheat shuddered. New stalks appeared and old ones grew plump with kernels. The rapid growth sent hisses of strained stalks through the fields.

Laire set off silently through the wheat, staying downwind as best he could. He used cautious steps, crouched and almost invisible, picking up each foot completely so as not to scrape dust and rocks beneath his boots. He checked for rocks and twigs before letting his weight settle on the foot. His thighs and abdomen burned, but he pressed on. One careless tread spelled the doom of any hunt, and this was not one he intended to fail.

Ancient Races, particularly the small ones, were more skittish than most hares. Smarter than most hares, too, unfortunately. Laire couldn't get too close without the risk of scaring it. He'd lost too many trophies for that mistake. Let too many monsters get away. Instead, fifty paces away, Laire stopped and drew the serpent root from the pouch at his side. He wrapped it around a crossbow bolt and shot it into the night, just a hair's breadth away from the crea- ture. The pained squeal and soft thud were all he needed to hear. The fields' copper light vanished.

Laire straightened on his protesting legs and strode to his whim- pering catch. A sprite. A small creature—probably no taller than Laire's waist if it weren't squirming on the ground—that had the build of a young man. Tears of pain welled in its wide, black eyes and trickled down its freckled cheeks as it clutched the leg the serpent root had wrapped around. Gold flecks flashed in its mousy brown hair. A thick squirrel's tail wrapped around it like a security blanket, twitching in agony.

"Please, *please!*" it sobbed. "I've done nothing wrong! I've hurt nobody!"

Laire curled his fist around the creature's tunic and pulled it to face level. The sprite struggled against Laire to tear his grip away. It flailed its legs and dug its sharp, claw-like nails into Laire's forearm, its tail whipping around it in distress and its chest heaving with the effort, but all in vain.

"Let me go! I've done nothing!"

Doors creaked open on fading hinges and candlelight flicked amber tongues across the fields. Drawn by the ruckus, nearby farmers emerged from their homes and peered into the night.

Laire clenched his teeth. "This doesn't concern you!"

"Who are you?"

"Leave the fields alone!"

Farmers snatched pitchforks and hoes and approached, their wives ushering curious children back inside. "These are our livelihoods. Leave in peace and we'll forget this whole thing."

The sprite smiled in relief.

Laire tightened his grip on the sprite, twisting the chunk of tunic until it nearly choked it. "Do not think for a moment that you are saved," he hissed before turning to the farmers. "I am a General of the King's Men!"

"The King's Men?" The creature's face stretched in utter, petrified terror. "Sister Earth help me."

Laire ignored it. "Return to your homes before I declare you all traitors for interfering with King's Men business!"

The farmer's faces paled. Their weapons went limp in their hands, and they dropped eye contact, though some cast hasty, saddened glances at the sprite. "Forgive us," they said. Laire couldn't tell who they were talking to. They retreated to their families and shuttered their doors and windows.

A forlorn sob bubbled from the sprite's throat. It grimaced as the serpent root inched farther up his leg but looked at Laire with solemn resolve. "What do the King's Men want from lowly Barley Bushtail?"

Laire sneered at it and tossed it to the ground. It hit its head and tried to sit up in a daze, but Laire pressed the tip of his sword to its chest. "I'm looking for someone."

Barley shook its head, laughing in disbelief. "No one here but farmers. Can't imagine what you'd want with any of—"

Laire dug the tip deeper into its chest. "I will decide what I need." He waited a moment and watched for the gulp of fear and resignation that signified the sprite knew who was in charge. When he got that signal, he relaxed the sword by a fraction. "Ancient Races can sense when others of your kind are nearby. Have there been any that have passed through here recently?"

Barley's eyes widened. "How do you know that? No one should know but—"

"Brahmon," Laire said with a sneer, the word a dagger across his tongue.

Barley froze with a gasp. "You...you lived in the half-blood village? Then why work for the Flameslayer? Why go after your own kind if—"

Laire pressed his sword deeper. "*You* are not my kind."

A trickle of blood welled from Barley's chest. His face went white and he screamed in the pain only a cursed sword could inflict. "It hurts. It *hurts!*"

Laire withdrew the blade slightly.

"That sword," Barley tried to inch away. "I know that sword!" The color drained from his skin, and his body shivered with fever. "The Demon Queen's sword, made to steal souls and—"

Laire flicked the blade and traced a gash across Barley's cheek. Barley screamed again. His eyes nearly rolled all the way back from the pain. "I have no interest in whatever superstitions you ascribe to my weapon," Laire said. "All I know is it kills and kills well."

Barley's eyelids sagged. He bowed his head and said nothing.

"Have any elves passed through as of late?"

Barley swung his head from side-to-side with great effort. "None...that I've sensed. Only a sorcerer."

"That is *not good enough!*"

"P-please don't kill me!" Barley's face crumpled. "I'll do anything. Anything you want! These people depend on me! They have poor soil. If I don't help them, their crops will die! They'll starve!"

"And why do you care so much?"

Barley's face softened. "These people are good people," he said. "They may fear me, but if I can help them...no one deserves to go hungry."

The look on his face reminded Laire of a look he had once loved from someone that spouted grand dreams of love, coexistence, and happiness. White-hot rage welled in his chest. He smacked Barley across the face with the flat of his blade and sent him sprawling. "You say you would do anything to live?" The ale roiled in his stomach and burned the back of his throat. Instead of the sprite, he saw a woman with long, silky tresses the color of chestnut. He saw the blood on her shaking hands and the treacherous tears rolling down her face as she tried to explain herself, as she begged for her life. He kicked Barley's ribs. "You say you want to make the world better? Tell me this—" he put the blade tip at Barley's heart. "Can you bring back the dead?"

Any hope fled the sprite's face. "The dead must remain with the dead," it intoned.

The words rang hollowly in Laire's ears. They echoed with *her* voice as she cradled Laire's shattered world in her arms.

"It's one of the Three Ancient Laws. I... I *cannot* break it. It's impossible!" Each of Barley's words became more desperate than the last.

Laire hauled Barley up so their eyes met. "How sad for you, to be so helpless against a world that never loved you." He ran the sprite through.

Barley choked. Its eyes bugged from his skull. It fell limp, its eyes still wide as they reflected the moon's silver. Copper drizzled from its mouth. The crops withered in their fields, heads bowed low in grief. Laire's sword hummed a keening, eerie note as blood dripped from its edge.

Laire let the body drop. A tremor ran through the earth, likely an aftershock from the quakes that had plagued the front lines as of late. Laire cleaned his sword on the sprite's tunic and sheathed it. He left the sprite in the field in its own blood and stormed away. Once he was out of the villagers' earshot, he punched a tree until his knuckles bled and screamed. Another dead end. Another wasted night. He wasn't even sure he was on the right path anymore. All he knew was that Vinea and Linae's lives hung in the balance, and he was failing them. Again.

He drew his sword and swung it a few times against the tree, gouging massive wounds in the trunk before he fell to his knees, leaning heavily against the sword. His knuckles throbbed. A stitch in his side ached. "What am I supposed to do now?" he asked no one in particular. The gods. His son. Mother Night. Sister Earth. He didn't know. Didn't care. Just anyone that would listen.

I hear you.

The voice from the inn came again—buzzing, hissing, filling his mind until there was nothing left except for its presence. Laire was too tired to push it away again. The sword glowed sickly gray.

The blood sacrifices you have offered the many years you have wielded me are acceptable, the voice—the sword—said. *I will help you.*

"How?"

Go to Vastet. I sense blood there. It is there that you will find what you seek.

With no other options, Laire followed the sword's advice. Anise's words rang in his ears. *I had no other choice.*

TWENTY-FOUR

Tristan couldn't remember the last time he had slept. He stumbled through each day in a daze, barely able to hold his head up, limbs and mind numb and plagued incessantly by fear, hatred, and horrible monsters. They were there in his sleep, torturing and murdering loved ones and strangers alike. They were there behind his eyelids in the waking hours, grinning at him with their horrible, ragged teeth. And they were coming for him.

Destroy them all, a voice would hiss to him as he watched the others mill about him, casting glances his way as they passed. All he saw on their faces was the monster. The fear. The hatred. *Destroy them all before they do the same to you.*

That thought worried him the most, not the fear, not the monsters, but whatever lurked inside himself. He had tamped down those thoughts so far, but every sleepless night—every monster jumping from the shadows—brought him closer to losing his grip. He needed help; needed to get out. He could only keep the monsters, within and without, at bay for so long before they devoured him.

The only thing he could think to do was leave.

The perfect time came not long after he made up his mind.

Another day of hiking. Another stop. Another camp set up. Tristan watched Aspen and Ash, knee bouncing absently. He didn't unpack but deftly hid his knapsack behind him. The untouched journal weighed heavily in it, and he considered abandoning it, but couldn't fully bring himself to do that. Not yet.

In the monotony of pitching camp, Aspen stopped and looked at him. Glanced at his bounding knee. She looked about to say something, but Tristan broke eye contact to avoid the conversation.

Just go away. Leave me alone so I can get out of here.

From the corner of his eye, he saw Aspen's jaw clench and her shoulders tighten. She said something in undertones to Styrax. Styrax glanced Tristan's way a few times, his face grimmer with each word Aspen spoke. The conversation couldn't have been more than ten words, and then Aspen went back to work. A few minutes later, she and Ash left, one to scrounge for dinner, and the other to who knew where, toting her stack of crumpled, disorganized collection of hare-brained plans with her.

Tristan waited for three beats after they were gone and then swung his knapsack over his shoulder.

"What are you doing?" Styrax asked.

Tristan jumped. When had he gotten there? He turned to him with his shoulders thrown back, jaw firm. "I've made my decision."

Styrax tilted his head; folded his arms. "What do you mean?"

"Aspen told me to decide about traveling with them, and I've decided it's not worth it. I'm leaving."

Styrax watched him for ten counts, several emotions flickering through his face at once. His cheeks paled a few shades before reddening. He blew a slow breath through pursed lips and rubbed his brow. "Were you going to tell me about this, or just let me find out when you didn't come back?" The hurt in his voice was obvious.

Anger boiled in Tristan's veins. "I didn't tell you because I don't trust, you, Styrax! You *lied* to me! For *five years!*"

Styrax reeled back, hands up in a placating gesture. "I thought we talked about this already. You *know* I couldn't tell you."

"Just sounds like a convenient excuse to me," Tristan said, his gut twisting in knots. Why was he being like this? They *had* already talked about this, so why was it bothering him all over again?

Styrax furrowed his brows, the lines of his face hardening. "I can't figure you out, Tristan. One moment, you're my friend. The next, it's like you think we're all out to eat you."

Because you are! It took almost all of Tristan's willpower not to let the voice hiss from his mouth. Did he really think that? He couldn't be sure anymore.

"What about the Dragon Scales? Don't you need their help to get you there?"

"We're getting close. I could probably—"

Styrax held up a hand. "What I'm trying to say is that we are willing to help you if you just let us. If nothing else, you can at least trust me!"

No, you can't! Monsters, all of them!

Tristan gritted his teeth. "Styrax, I've made my decision. You can come or stay. That's your choice. But I'm going either way."

"Going where?" Aspen asked, in her infuriating way of finding the worst times to appear.

"Aspen!" Ash called from the trees. "Will you go to the village and grab a few things for me? Our pickings are slim for dinner."

Tristan smiled at Aspen, teeth bared in a too tight snarl. "To the village with you. Figured you could use the help." And the supervision.

Aspen raised an eyebrow. "Mm-hmm." She looked at Styrax, who shrugged. She waved Tristan off. "I'll be fine. I would hate to inconvenience you."

"Oh, no. I insist." Going to the village would be perfect. He could pick up supplies of his own and then slip away into the crowd. And he could make sure Aspen left the villagers safe and alone.

Aspen looked ready to protest, but she just sighed and rubbed her brows. "Fine. Come if you want. Stay if you don't." She left with no more fanfare. Tristan loped after her, hands clutched tight about his knapsack, hoping he actually knew what he was doing.

Aspen didn't say anything to him as they made their way to the village. Her steps were slower than usual, and her eyes hooded with dark circles beneath them. She had probably been up all night, going over her parchment over and over again like a lunatic. What could possibly be so important? What were her plans?

Monsters, all of them. Whatever they touch they'll destroy.

Tristan blanched at the thought. If that was true, then what were Aspen's plans for the village? "What are you planning to do?" Tristan asked.

Aspen rolled her eyes skyward. "Didn't you hear Ash? We're going to get supplies. I assume you like to eat?"

Tristan bristled. "Were you planning on starving me?"

"*What?* No, why—?" Aspen stopped herself. She pinched the bridge of her nose and furrowed her brow with a sigh. "No. Which is why we're getting supplies."

"Are you going to steal them?" Tristan asked.

Aspen splayed her hands with another roll of her eyes and kept walking. "Not my expertise. Talk to Ash about that sometime."

She's stalling—avoiding your questions. She's up to something.

"Ah, so you're just going to murder them and pillage their corpses," Tristan said with a sneer. That had to be it. Ancient Ones brought nothing but pain and anguish wherever they went. This war had started for a reason. Tristan's duty now was to minimize how many more victims magic would claim before it was over.

Aspen threw her shoulders back, spine straight as a blade, and stopped. She looked at him, lips pulled taut against her teeth. "It may surprise you, but even monsters carry spare change every once in a while." She jangled her coin bag for emphasis.

Why? Why did she insist on playing this game with him? He had *seen* her true form back when they were dueling. He knew the horrors that lurked beneath her facade, and it was time that she knew she couldn't get away with her charade any longer. "You don't have to put up an act."

Aspen threw her hands heavenward. "What *act* am I putting up?"

"I know what you really are. I've seen it." His voice dripped with venom. "You're a *monster*."

A flicker of hurt flashed across her face, but then was gone. She pressed her lips together and said nothing to him. They continued on.

They made it to the village without any incident, or any additional conversation of any kind. Tristan's stomach twisted itself into sickening knots the whole way there, waiting for her to strike him down at a moment's notice. He pulled on the golden ring around his neck and worried at his bottom lip.

A low rock wall lined the entrance to the village, and Aspen gestured to it. "I'll only be getting enough for me to carry, so I won't need the extra hands. You're welcome to wait here and keep an eye on things, or whatever it is you're planning on doing."

He gave her a tight mockery of a smile, trying not to let his relief show on his face. At last, he would be rid of her. He sat, examining his nails as his hands shook.

Aspen massaged the bridge of her nose and walked away. "The Pit have you, for all I care," she said as she left.

CHAPTER

TWENTY-FIVE

Sorren had lost track of how many days they had been traveling; he found he couldn't quite bring himself to care. Gone were the anxieties of trying to get back to Sedick in record time. His ear hurt less. His head hurt less, and he found he smiled sometimes when Lady Vinea talked to him. He knew Sedick could look through his eyes anytime he wanted to and wondered if Sedick could sense the change in him. He wasn't sure he cared. For once, he felt free and loved and taken care of. And it was all thanks to the woman that had taken the time to give him a name.

The smell of fresh baked pie wafted over to them, and Sorren's stomach rumbled. It smelled so good.

Lady Vinea laughed and straightened her sack on her back. "I'm hungry, too, and I think you and I have both earned the chance to have something fresh, and a warm bed to sleep in. Do you agree?"

Sorren grimaced at his thoughtlessness. "I don't know, my lady. We really should avoid other folks." Even though the food smelled amazing and the conversations from the village sounded warm and inviting. What would it be like to get a bowl of stew in a crowded tavern and listen to all the stories around him? To sleep in a soft bed with the breeze flowing through an open window?

Lady Vinea looked him in the eyes, a warm, soft glow of smugness on her face. She reminded him of another woman with dark coils of hair and bright eyes and...it was gone before he could finish the thought.

"If *you* are suggesting we stay in the forest, then we will stay." Vinea drew her knapsack closer. "However, if Lord Sedick the *divine* is saying we sleep outside on the ground when we could be perfectly happy on mattresses inside, then I will not have it," she said with a smile. "So, which is it?"

Sorren smiled back at her. "I suppose one night won't hurt."

Vinea nodded emphatically. "That's what I thought. Shall we?" She parted the trees and went to step toward the village. Suddenly, though, her entire body went rigid and she let out a gasp.

Sorren was on his feet in an instant. "What? What is it?"

Vinea turned back to him, branches snapping shut behind her, all smiles again, but there was a wildness in her eyes and no color to her skin. "It's nothing. Nothing to worry about. I just realized that maybe it would be best for us to stay here. Away from prying eyes and all—"

Sorren pushed past her before she could finish. Something was out there. Something that had frightened her. She had been too good to him for him to ignore that.

At first, he saw nothing. Just a squat little village hemmed in by small fields and a ramshackle stone wall that had seen better days. He scanned the fields first. Maybe she had seen a wolf, or, even worse, a saber? Sorren knew they frequented these areas. If that were the case, then it would be even better for them to stay in the village. Large groups of people were safe. But lone travelers were easy prey. Lady Vinea had to have known that. So it was something else. An enemy, perhaps? Someone she knew from her past? Or...

And then he saw him. Alone. Unprotected. Out in the open on a portion of the wall. Completely unsuspecting.

...kill him on sight...I don't care if it even takes your life to do it. Just kill him.

Adrenaline, magic, and fear collided into a dizzying concoction that raced through his body at the speed of fire. Flaring through his muscles. Searing through his bones. Orange-tinted hate clouded his vision. *Kill him.*

"Sorren, what's wrong?"

He didn't hear her—only a buzzing, faint and irritating, in his ears. He marched forward, the purple light of his magic curling around his arms. The wind roared around him, hissing and fierce, as he closed on his target. Approached his purpose, and whatever end it led him toward.

"Don't do this!" Someone threw themselves at him.

Without a second glance, he shoved them away, ropes of magic pinning them to the ground, and launched a flaming spell at the man they called Tristan.

TWENTY-SIX

spen looked up from the stack of carrots she had been perusing when she felt the flare of magic at the edge of her senses. The stall owner tried to question her, but she waved him to silence. And then the blast hit, followed by screams as flames erupted on the walls around the village, burning through the stone as if it were wood.

"Oh, merciful Mother Night," the stall owner said, his hand flying to the twine ward around his wrist. "*Magic.*"

Aspen cursed and drew her sword. "Leave your wares, find your family, and get out. I'll try to stop them."

The merchant looked at her, mouth agape. He didn't question her, though. He nodded his thanks and left, calling for his family as he ran. Aspen saw him safely away and then took off toward the initial blast. People screamed and ran past her, but all seemed relatively unhurt. Minor scrapes and burns as they patted out smoldering clothes and dragged themselves from collapsed roofs, but nothing life-threatening. No more explosions ripped through the village other than the initial one.

Aspen furrowed her brow. For someone to attack a small village like this was uncommon, but not unheard of. Those with power got bored and liked to harass those that couldn't defend themselves for a bit of fun. But that involved more widespread chaos. More injuries and overall destruction. This, though...the fire stayed in one place, almost like a barrier to keep something out—or something in. The affected area was small. Whoever had caused it must have been after something specific.

Aspen slowed as she neared the heart of the fire. The sorcerer's presence practically singed her eyebrows with how powerful it was. The magic swirling through the air hissed and fizzed across her skin and crackled in her ears. It filled her nose with the smell of lightning and smoke. How had she missed it before? It was like a feral creature unchained. She crept behind a building, trying to assess the situation before rushing in. The purple-tinged flames around her belched acrid smoke as the stone beneath them melted.

"What do you want from me?"

Aspen jolted with dread. She knew that voice. What was it about that thorn in her side that always drew trouble in? She peered around the corner to find Tristan backed into a wall, a little dusty and battered but otherwise unhurt, his face white as he watched the sorcerer approach.

"You-you're one of Sedick's men, right? Sorren? That's what Lady Vinea called you, right? It's not me you want! We're on the same side!"

The sorcerer continued to advance, mute and deadly. Aspen saw sweat bead down Tristan's face and carve tracks through the grime that had collected on his cheeks. "There-there's an—" He snapped his mouth shut. More sweat trickled from his brow. "I-what do you want? I can do anything." His eyes had almost gone cross-eyed, like he was fighting some sort of internal war. He clutched at the leather strap around his neck. Aspen almost thought she saw him mouthing the words *don't say it, don't say it, don't say it*. But then his eyes narrowed, his face contorted into something not his own. "There's an elf here. I can show you where she is if you let me go!"

Aspen's jaw tightened as her heart dropped to her stomach. So there were his true colors.

The sorcerer said nothing. Instead, the ground rumbled beneath him, and the cobblestones fractured in a straight path toward Tristan. Tristan leapt out of the way just as a cluster of dagger-sharp stalagmites erupted from the ground and nearly impaled him. He crashed into a stall, and the thing collapsed on him.

"Stop. Moving," the sorcerer said in a voice far too young. Aspen peered at him through the blinding haze of magic around him and reared back in shock. He couldn't be older than sixteen. He was still a boy, but his magic control was incredible. It moved and breathed like an extension of himself and changed forms as easily as blinking. One moment fire that singed the ends of her hair; the next a cyclone whirling debris at her at impossible speeds. A rare power like that could win wars. The signet flapping proudly on his cloak made her scowl. He had just been enlisted on the wrong side. Of *course*, he was one of Sedick's acolytes. But what was one of his followers doing here?

Tristan cried out and brought Aspen back to the task at hand. He had dug himself from the ruins of the collapsed stand but had gotten entangled in some loose rope and canvas. No matter how desperately he tried to pull free, he was stuck fast.

Aspen steeled herself. He was an arrogant prick and had just tried to bargain for his own life with hers, but she couldn't leave him here. Her conscience wouldn't allow it. "I really shouldn't be saving you, you ungrateful swine!" She leapt from her cover and raced to him, slashing through his bindings, and swung her blade up just in time to parry a blast of lightning from the sorcerer. It ricocheted off the blade and veered into a blacksmith shop, which exploded in a hail of straw and nails.

Tristan gaped at her. "You can *do* that?"

"Obviously," Aspen said through gritted teeth, fighting through the pain of the bolt's impact and the buzz it sent through her body. Her sword arm was numb, and she smelt burning hair from the follicles that had been zapped off. "But don't count on it working every time."

"What kind of useless trick is that, then?"

"*Really?* Maybe next time I'll just let him turn you to charcoal!"

The young sorcerer had gotten over his shock at having someone parry his magic, and he was now striding toward the two of them with purpose.

"Go!" Aspen said to Tristan, shoving him toward the village outskirts. "Run and don't stop! You're useless in a fight and *will* die!"

"He's not going anywhere!" The sorcerer conjured a swirling gale and hurled it at them. Aspen planted her sword in the dirt and held on for all she was worth. The storm raged around, turning dust into stinging projectiles that tore gashes into her skin. She shut her eyes against it as the wind howled in her ears and tightened her grip on the hilt, her sword swaying and groaning. *Don't break. Please don't break.*

The wind subsided, and she was still somehow standing. She spat dust from her mouth, pulled her sword from the ground, and kissed the blade, silently thanking her brothers for their superior craftsmanship. She looked for Tristan, but he was gone. Just like she had told him. A stab of bitterness still pierced her gut.

The sorcerer screamed in fury, and a concussive wave flared around him, leveling buildings. It slammed into Aspen with so much force that it threw her off her feet and forced all the air from her lungs. She skidded across dirt and cobblestone, tunic and skin shredding beneath her as she bowled through groups of villagers. A crumbling portion of the wall finally stopped her. Villagers lay sprawled around her, screaming in varying levels of pain and horror.

Pain throbbed through Aspen in waves. Her vision whirled in dizzying circles, her head pounded, her skin was on fire, and her ears rung. She clenched her jaw. *Get up. You have to get up.*

She did, just as the sorcerer came into view, magic swirling around him, eyes ablaze with fury.

Aspen dove behind a portion of the crumbling wall as a blade of magic sliced above her head and erupted into a building. Mortar and straw rained down around her. She threw her hood off to dislodge the debris. A woman stared at her, mouth agape.

Elf, she mouthed, and threw a rock at Aspen.

It hit Aspen's temple as another blast of magic roared past her. She dodged again, but the blast tore off one of her sleeves. Too close. Blood trickled down the side of her face. She needed to minimize her distractions. It would have been nice to have someone to control the crowd—Ash usually excelled at that—but she was on her own now. As long as her secret was out...

She slowed her breathing and let the barriers flung against her magic inch open. Green mist curled from her skin and washed over the ground. Rose vines pushed their tendrils from broken soil and rushed around the villagers, latticing together to form defensive domes around them. The people screamed, but at least they were safe and out of the way. Now she could focus on the real problem. The small vine she kept in her breast pocket erupted from its vial and swirled around her, growing into a wreath of rose vines.

The sorcerer stood in the middle of the square, fists balled and magic swirling around him. When she poked her head out from her barricade, he screamed and flung portions of the wall at her. She worked her way toward him, dodging and bashing at the biggest pieces with her sword. Every blow sent a shock of pain through her arm and shoulder. The wreath of rose vines lashed out to protect her from shrapnel. Exhaustion bore down on her like an anvil, and not for the first time she cursed it, and herself. If she could just get it under control...

But she could not, and there was no use wasting mental energy on it. She had no other choice than to use it. There were too many people to protect, and not enough man-power to do it without magic.

The sorcerer looked at her, chest heaving. The fury dripped from his face like hot wax, leaving cold, dead neutrality in its place. Aspen's stomach clenched. Something was not right here.

"I have no quarrel with you, elf," the sorcerer said in a voice that didn't sound like it should belong to him.

Aspen took in the surrounding devastation and the wounds she'd sustained from his onslaught. "I'm not sure I understand your definition of quarrel."

He ignored her. "Where is Tristan?"

"I don't know." She paced a few steps around him, trying to gauge if he had a blind spot or weak point. His eyes never left hers.

"Why do you protect him?"

Excellent question. "I protect the innocent, and you are hurting these people. Leave, and we will consider this matter settled."

"Not without my prize." He launched himself at her, fire spraying from his hands and feet.

Aspen braced herself for impact, wishing that once, just once, someone would actually take the offer and just walk away before it got ugly for her. She flung her hands out and her vines shot to the buildings on either side of her, building a framework with her as the center. The sorcerer collided with her, and her world went dark.

THE IMPACT ROCKED the entire village and knocked Tristan flat on his chest. His eardrums shrieked and skewed his vision. He gasped for air and struggled back to his feet, nauseous. He kept running, despite the screams and clash of steel and magic that charged the air so much that his hair stood on end.

Let them kill each other, the voice hissed. *It's what they deserve.*

Tristan couldn't agree more, feverish and shaking. The world would be rid of two monsters at once. Seemed the best situation for everyone. But something inexplicable kept him rooted to the spot. Something deep inside screamed at him to stop, to turn around. He had left something back there. Something irreplaceable.

More nausea. More terror. But not for himself. For Aspen.

Run and don't stop!

She had told him so herself. But there was an echo in those words —a loop repeating itself. Something his body remembered better than his mind. A dark night. Screams. The sound of arrows whistling through the night. Perpetual, ever clashing waves. And a sword—a piece of the night sky itself—held at the ready to defend him to the last.

The silver ring burned against his chest. *For evergreens and aspen trees.*

Monsters leapt from those memories, tearing and slashing at every precious fragment of them.

Lies!

They are nothing!

Phantoms. Sweet deceptions to gain your trust before they slaughter you!

Do not let them win!

Fight them!

The voices drove Tristan to his knees. So loud. Too loud! They forced the breath from his lungs and replaced it with fear. Piercing, deadly, all-encompassing terror. What could he do? He couldn't stay here. But would he be able to outrun them? No. His only option was to—

"Get up! You have to move!"

Tristan jerked from the hand that seized his tunic. Fight. He had to fight! His tunic tore. With a snap that thundered through his whole body, the strap around his neck broke off in the stranger's hands.

Pain cleaved through Tristan's mind and nearly split him in half. He collapsed, clutching his head and unable to draw breath. The monsters screamed. He screamed. Orange haze swallowed his vision and his mind. More monsters leapt from it, eyes spinning wildly in their heads.

Tristan laid there, frozen, eyes and mouth wide with horror. He couldn't move. Couldn't breathe. This was it. This was how he died.

And then a green mist appeared, forming a barrier around him. *For evergreens and aspen trees.* The words tumbled through the mist, battled back the haze, and seared the monsters and blinded their wide, unblinking eyes.

The monsters screamed and dug their claws like anchors into his mind. *We are not gone forever,* they snarled. *We will be back, and we will not give in so easily a second time.* They vanished, swallowed up in green mist.

"I'm...I'm sorry!" The well-meaning villager dropped the rings by Tristan and ran away.

Tristan instinctively gathered them and put them in his pocket. He laid there for a long time, sweating and heaving. Villagers ran past him, screaming, and dust and wood rained down around him, but he stayed put. His mind was...quiet. For the first time he could remember, there were no lurking monsters. No bitter voices. Just silence. The wind whipped through his tattered clothes, and the smell of rain and smoke clung to the air. The clouds swirled above, and he just watched them, marveling at the quiet.

And with that quiet came the realization of what he'd been about to do. He blanched, panic setting in.

"Aspen." He forced himself to his feet, staggering beneath the raging pain that split his skull. He hobbled forward a few steps, getting the feel of his wobbling legs beneath him again. A few more steps turned into a jog, picking up momentum until he was running full-tilt, dodging people and stacks of debris and walls collapsing. How could he have even entertained the thought of abandoning her? Aspen, who he had laughed with and shared secrets with. Aspen, who had listened without judgment, and had been willing to help in whatever way she could. And who, despite everything he had done, had *saved* him.

Now was his chance to return the favor.

Tristan skidded to a stop behind a still-standing wall and peered into the village square. Sorren was there, heaving in a crater of destruction. Domes of rosebushes peppered the square, untouched by the magic that had leveled the surrounding buildings. A net of them clawed their way up two parallel buildings, looking like they had once been connected, but now hung limp with their center missing. Where was Aspen? Had the sorcerer killed—

Tristan's heart clenched at the thought. No. She was fine. She was *Aspen*, after all. The most stubborn, indestructible person he had ever met. It would take more than a pre-pubescent wizard to take her down. Even if said wizard was one of the most powerful people Tristan had ever seen.

Sorren screamed and swept away, cloak billowing behind him. Tristan waited until Sorren was out of earshot before he scrambled through the crumbling ruins. "Aspen? *Aspen!*" He didn't dare raise his voice above a hiss as he dug through the rubble, looking for a corner of a cloak or a flash of a black blade. Instead, he found her crumpled against a tree, nearly knocked free of its roots, wheezing as she tried to stand.

"Aspen!" He ran to her and put an arm beneath her shoulders to help her up.

She grimaced and peered at him through squinted eyes, blood dripping down one side of her face. "Tristan?" She winced and coughed blood. "Thought I told you to...to leave." She tried to fight him off and stand on her own, but her knees gave way and he caught her again.

"You did, but I shouldn't have. Not to leave you to get yourself killed."

She peered at him more closely, quiet for an uncomfortable amount of time.

Tristan glanced behind him, and then back to her. "What?"

"I'm trying to figure out who...you are. You're not...the Tristan...I know. That one wanted me...dead," she said with a gargled, bitter laugh. Her eyes had no humor in them, but instead were clouded with pain. "He's almost got his...wish."

Tristan winced, guilt churning in his stomach. "I'm sorry," he said.

Aspen staggered forward a few steps, dragging Tristan along with her. "The villagers?" she asked.

Tristan heard them crying to be let out from their orbs, but didn't hear the distinctive cries of the wounded or dying—the wheezing, rasping last words as a soul drained from its body. He didn't know how he knew the difference. "Safe. Did you do that?"

She nodded with another wince, favoring her ribs.

"What were the other vines for?"

She scoffed to herself, which turned into another fit of coughs. "Myself. Tried to soften...sorcerer's impact. Didn't work so well." She sagged from the effort of talking.

Tristan helped her back to a somewhat upright position. "No more talking. Let's get you back to camp."

Aspen heard the footsteps before he did. Her eyes went wide, and she whirled, drawing her sword and shoving Tristan out of the way.

"Sorren, *enough!*" a shrill, frantic voice screamed.

Tristan smashed onto the cobblestone road before he could place where he had heard that voice before. Aspen stood over him, struggling to raise her sword as a flash of orange and purple illuminated the square. Tristan was blinded by the light, but Aspen's silhouette burned onto the insides of his eyelids.

The blast went wide. Instead of hitting Aspen square in the chest, right where Tristan's back would have been, it glanced across her side. Her body went rigid, and she dropped without a sound. Someone screamed.

Tristan gaped as steaming droplets of blood dripped from Aspen's side and pooled on the ground beneath her. She made no sound, but her breath was ragged and her face was fog-white. Her whole body trembled. She had...She had taken the blow for him.

Why?

Tristan cursed and scrambled to her without another thought.

"Aspen!" He drew her into his lap, even though she tried to fight him off and stand on her own.

"I'm fine," Aspen slurred, unsuccessfully batting Tristan's hands away.

Tristan caught her wrist. "No, you're not!" He couldn't keep the panic out of his voice. This was so beyond anything he knew. She was burning to the touch and losing blood fast. On top of that, black, infected veins fractured from the wound, turning the skin around them swollen and gray. He had to get her out of here, *now*.

Teeth set, Tristan scooped her into his arms, her head lolling against his chest, and ran as far and as fast as he could. He expected the sorcerer to come after them, but only heard screams of anguish. No one followed them.

His chest was about to burst and his legs were about to give out when the camp finally came into view. "ASH! STYRAX! HELP HER!"

Ash jolted away from her stew pot, and Styrax leapt to his feet at Tristan's scream. They stood there, frozen, as they took in Tristan and Aspen, uncomprehending.

"By the Architects, *Aspen!*" Ash moved first, dropping everything from her arms and rushing to them, face white. "Styrax, get the salve from my pack!" Aspen had lost consciousness sometime on their way over, but she tossed fitfully, mumbling nonsense as her eyes rolled in her head. "This is sorcerer blight! What *happened?*"

Tristan stood there on trembling limbs, heaving from his sprint. Sweat rolled into his eyes and down his back. His cheeks ached from his open-mouthed breathing. "I was attacked." He showed her Aspen's wounds. Ash immediately tore away that section of Aspen's tunic and pressed a clean cloth there to staunch the blood. Styrax brought her the salve she asked for. She slathered it over the wound and muttered in the Ancient Tongue, her irises glowing gray. "This is an extra strength salve for her back," she told Tristan. "It has the best shot of saving her from this." She wrapped more cloth around the wound, her eyes still glowing. "Tell me more about what happened."

"A sorcerer appeared out of nowhere and came after me. She-she took him on all by herself, and then—"

Ash grew still. She looked at Tristan, her face like granite as she continued to apply pressure to Aspen's wound. "Why was she all by herself, Tristan?"

Tristan stopped in his tracks, not sure why this was important to helping Aspen. "What?" He shook his head. "That doesn't matter right now. She's *hurt!*"

"It *does* matter!" The words sliced through him as clean as any dagger. Ash's arms shook as Aspen's blood covered her fingers. "You said the sorcerer attacked *you*. Why would Aspen have to fight him all on her own if *you* were there?"

The question hit like an arrow to his heart. He couldn't look her in the eye as nausea crept up his throat. He clutched Aspen tighter to him. "I...I left her."

"You *what?*" Styrax asked, his face white and his eyes wide with disbelief.

"You *left* her?" Ash watched Tristan for two beats. He saw all the trust, their friendship, disintegrate in an instant. Ash clenched her jaw and wrenched Aspen from Tristan's arms. She whirled to Styrax. "We need to be ready to move as soon as I'm done tending to Aspen. We don't know who will want to come after us. Clean up the trail of blood she left so we won't be followed."

Tristan tried to help her carry Aspen, but Ash threw her shoulder into his chest and shoved him away. "You touch her again, and it will be the last thing you do." She marched back to the tent.

The coolness in her voice froze a lump in Tristan's throat. "Ash, wait..." He followed her to the tent. He wasn't sure if he could make it up to her. Doubted he ever could. But he had to help Aspen somehow. He wouldn't leave her again.

Ash laid Aspen down, and then drew a dagger from her boot, brandishing it at Tristan with furious tears in her eyes. "I won't tell you again. You are not coming *near* her ever again. Do you understand?"

The lump swelled in his throat. This was not about him. This was about Aspen. She needed all the help she could get, especially after what she had done for him. "Ash, *please*. All I want to do is help."

Aspen grabbed a fistful of his tunic, eyes ablaze as she pressed the tip of her dagger into his throat. "I. Don't. Want. Your. Help. I'm sure Aspen did, and you abandoned her." She threw him out of the tent. "Come back in here and I'll put an arrow through your head."

Tristan staggered back a few steps to keep from falling over. He met eyes with Styrax. Styrax looked just as shattered as Tristan felt. Lips pressed together, hands rigid at his side, Styrax shook his head at Tristan, wordless, and went to his task.

Broken, humbled, and terrified, Tristan sat, bowed his head, and prayed to whatever gods would listen.

TWENTY-SEVEN

Vinea stumbled through the village, wrists and ankles raw and bleeding. Pain pulsed through them as quickly as worry raced in her heart. "Sorren!" She couldn't believe the destruction in the village. Houses and stonework in flames. People were buried beneath the rubble and others were trapped in latticed mounds of rosebushes. "Tristan!" This was not the work of a young boy. Not the boy that smiled and laughed and needed rescuing from nightmares and found wonder in the smallest of dragon scales. No. This was the work of men at war that were too cowardly to fight their own battles. And Vinea would see them pay for it.

Sorren. Tristan. She had to find them. She had to save her two boys before something horrible happened—before there was no coming back from whatever damage was done. Jaw clenched and body trembling from the shock of it all, Vinea pushed herself forward, one step at a time, cursing Sedick to the Pit and back. "Sorren, Tristan! Where are you?" Her heart hitched in her throat and tears welled in her eyes. "Please be all right," she said to herself. "You have to be. I will never forgive myself if—" The words died on her tongue. A sob welled in her chest.

There they were, through the crowds of wailing people and shambles of village homes. Both were all right. Both standing. Both *alive*.

Vinea picked her way to them, unable to speak through the lump of emotion in her throat. Tristan had his back to her, helping a young woman hobble away from the rubble. She contemplated calling out to him. What a reunion that would be. Far from the prying eyes of Lorate, she would be able to tell him *everything*. He could finally claim what was his.

And Sorren—sweet, beautiful Sorren. She would squeeze him senseless for the worry he had caused her.

He had gotten lost in the crowd somewhere, but then she saw him again. Facing Tristan, building a spell into being. A spell meant to kill.

A guttural cry ripped from Vinea and she sprinted for Sorren, skirts tearing beneath her as she stumbled over piles of uneven debris. People clutched at her, begging for help, but she ignored them. Help would come for them. But she was the only one that could save her family.

The earring. She had to get to Sedick's cursed earring. It glinted tauntingly at her as she ran for it. If she could tear it out, then this madness would end. Sedick would have no more power. She had been a fool to leave Sorren with it for so long.

"Sorren, *enough!*"

THEY WERE THERE, wounded and unable to fight. His master had made his purpose clear. He *could not* let Tristan live. No matter the cost. No matter who else got hurt. One shot was all it would take to end it. Growling, he built his magic in his palms. The spell whirled and snarled in a haze of orange and purple, the energy ripping through his muscles and tendons. He bit back a scream of agony and readied to release the spell.

"Sorren, *enough!*" Someone ripped the silver stud from his earlobe.

It was as if his brain ripped in two, one half shearing away from the other in shattered pieces. He shrieked and the spell ricocheted from his hands. His vision went dark. Monsters leapt from the shadows, howling at him.

You belong to us, boy, they said in Lord Sedick's voice, trailing orange haze. *You are nothing without us. You serve one purpose, and one purpose only. You are a killer.*

His chest and ribs felt as if they might cave on themselves. No. That couldn't be true. There had to be something else. There *was* something else. Warmth. A mother. Two of them. One dark and brimming with magic. The other light and soft, filled with kind words. "You are brave and strong, Sorren. You are more than what others tell you to be."

No, he wasn't. He was just a boy. A boy with nothing but the words of his master.

The other voice. Deep. Rich. Fierce. "Listen to me, my son. Whatever he tells you—whatever you think of yourself—know this: kingdoms have risen and fallen with the magic in your veins. You can be the greatest good this world has to offer. *Choose* what you will be, and your mother will support you in it."

Tears coursed down his cheeks. He had never heard that voice; not that he could remember. But his heart lurched at its sound, wanting to be everything it told him and more.

He surrounded himself in his magic, a barrier against the monsters, strengthened by the words. The purple light seared the monsters' bare flesh. They shrieked and retreated.

"I would rather be nothing than a killer," Sorren said, sending bolts of magic after them. *His* magic, and no one else's. "Be gone. And tell your master that I am no longer his."

They laughed, a hissing sound that grated on his ears and sent chills down his spine. "We do not give up so easily. Bask in your fool's freedom while you can. It will not last for long. You will pay your dues to the master, one way or another."

They left him and all light vanished. In that darkness, his mind cleared, and he was left with nothing but blessed, merciful silence. The orange haze vanished. His vision returned, and when it did, the world stopped.

Lady Vinea fell, eyes wide and mouth agape. She clutched her abdomen, fingers coming back bloody. A single silver stud tumbled from her hands before her eyes rolled back in her head and her body went still.

"Wh–What?" Sorren lurched to help her, but then saw his hands. Covered in blood. Not his. Hers.

You are a killer.

Killer.

Killer.

He screamed and collapsed next to Vinea, trying to staunch the blood. Burns covered her wrists and ankles. She had broken free of his magic. Tristan and the elf vanished, a trail of blood in their wake, but Sorren didn't care. He had hurt the one person that cared about him. "No, no, *no*, Lady Vinea, *please*. I'm so sorry. I'm sorry! I didn't mean it!" Healing magic. *Healing magic!* He knew healing magic. He put his hands over her wound and called his magic forth, but nothing came, only wisps of purple that leaked from his skin, thrown free by his emotions. Weak and useless, just like him. His magic was spent, all siphoned into the spell that had wounded Lady Vinea. "Oh no. *NO!* Not right now!" Sobbing, he screamed to anyone that would hear him. "HELP! SOMEONE, HELP HER, PLEASE!"

A few villagers shuffled forward, eying him and his leaking magic with distrust. He whirled on them, tears coursing down his cheeks. "Please, will you help her?" For all his power, all the magic the voice claimed he had, he was useless in this one moment, and for that, he couldn't help but feel that he had failed in everything.

"You are a…sorcerer?" one villager asked, careful not to get too close.

"Yes, yes. I'm a sorcerer for the King." He fumbled with his tattered cloak and flashed the king's crest sewn beside the fastener, fingers shaking.

They still didn't approach him. "Are you…alone?"

"Yes, I'm—" he stopped, realizing the hostility in their stances. Fists clenched. Shoulders thrown back. Eyes blazing. By Osmen's edict, all sorcerers bearing his crest were to be treated as captains and generals. They could demand anything they wanted from the common folk, and to be disobeyed meant treason. But he was young, without magic reserves, and on his own. If they were to enact justice for the destruction he had caused, no one would be able to prove anything. They would get away, free from blame, and he would be very, very dead.

He swallowed and straightened his shoulders as best he could. He took a few deep breaths, and the curling wisps of runaway magic sunk back into his skin. "Do you think I'm a fool?" he asked in his best impression of Sedick. "I am a sorcerer to the king and therefore the greatest weapon the kingdom has against the Ancient Races. Do you *really* think I would travel without a retaining force?" His lips and throat were dry. He couldn't swallow properly. It was a weak argument. He knew it, and they knew it. But he prayed that *someone* would buy it. Lady Vinea kept bleeding through his fingers. Much longer, and there wouldn't be any chance of getting her back. Nausea swam in his stomach and his head and chest throbbed. *Please. Please, please, PLEASE.*

With pursed lips, the villagers approached him. "Of course. We could not deny help to such an *honored* guest." They cast their eyes about the village; fires were still crackling through the shells of their homes. "Thank you for running off the elf that posed *such* a danger to our livelihoods. We are grateful for your protection."

Others muttered and cast dirty looks at Sorren. He pretended to ignore them, but the guilt shot straight to his core.

Several men gathered Vinea up between them. "We have healers that will help your friend, if you will allow us the honor."

Sorren's lower lip trembled, but he cast his head back as best he could to stare down the length of his nose at them. "Thank you."

They nodded and left. He followed them as they carried her to the healer's home, which had miraculously been spared from his rampage. With glowers and whispers to the healer, they slammed the door in his face and locked him out.

Sorren placed his hand on the door. "Thank you." His facade melted from his body, and he slid his back along the door until he was sitting, knees curled tightly to his chest. He rocked back and forth, humming Lady Vinea's lullaby to himself. Lady Vinea would be okay. She would be. She *had* to be.

TWENTY-EIGHT

The sword had not been wrong when it said it smelled blood in Vastet. Rubble filled the streets. The buildings that hadn't been demolished were scorched black or choked by the largest, wildest rosebushes Laire had ever seen. Villagers were hacking their way through cocoons of them or digging themselves from the ruins of their homes and shops.

Amidst the destruction, Laire jolted with anticipation. Only magic could have caused chaos like this. He glanced at his sword for reassurance, but it said nothing. Laire scowled.

Laire approached a man picking disconsolately through a pile of spoiled wares. "Pardon."

"No goods to be had here," the man's words were jagged with bitterness. "Best move along to Tribaine, though Mother Night knows we could use the money." He gestured to the swathe of destruction.

Laire handed him a silver piece. "What happened here?"

The man looked between the silver and Laire, wide and misty-eyed. He pocketed the money carefully. "An *elf* happened, sir. Tore through this place like a wild boar. Thank Mother Night a *sorcerer* was here to wreak even more havoc."

Laire fought the excitement from his face. An elf was a good start. A female elf was even better. "Was this elf with anyone?"

"A man, I think? I couldn't be certain." He looked Laire up and down. "You a bounty hunter?"

Laire tightened his grip on his sword. "Of sorts. Is there someone that could tell me more about the elf and who she was with?"

The man motioned to a squat building on the edge of town that had avoided the worst of the destruction. "Sorcerer's holed up there with a wounded friend. He could tell you more." He hesitated a moment. "Just...be careful. Sorcerer's may work for the king, but they're not like us other folk. I only trust him a little more than I can throw him, and that has a lot to do with the King's Crest and nothing to do with him."

"Thank you." Laire tossed him a gold piece and strode toward the sorcerer, anticipation growing with each step. Drawing him ever closer to his prize.

ALL THE BREATH left Laire's lungs when he caught sight of the woman in the bed, bandaged and unconscious. She looked so much like Vinea, but that was impossible. Vinea was back in Lorate, *safe*. But the more he looked, the less he could deny it. A cry leached from his throat and he ran to her, shoving a healer out of the way cradling Vinea in his arms.

"Vinea! What—Why-Why are you here? What's happened to you?" He brushed her hair from her face. She burned to the touch. "She has a fever! Bring cold water, NOW!" He looked up to see that his orders had been followed, and then saw the boy. Sedick's boy.

Fury erupted in his veins; his vision stained blood-red. "*YOU!*" He leapt across the room and snagged the boy by his tunic. "You did this, didn't you?" He shook him before he could answer and threw him across the room. Sorren laid there in a crumpled heap, and Laire was on him in a moment. Fists flying, feet whirling, he beat the boy into the wall. "You *dare* touch my wife? I'll break every bone in your body!" He couldn't tell if he was screaming at Sorren, or at Sedick. He would bury that weasel the next time he saw him. Not even his precious magic baubles would save him.

Sorren said nothing as Laire continued to rail on him. It took Laire a few moments to realize that the boy was *choosing* not to fight back. Somehow, that made him more enraged. "Stand up and *fight*, you worthless coward!"

"I won't because you're *right*," Sorren said past a fat lip and the blood draining from his nose. "It's my fault she's hurt." Sorren looked up at him, eyes hot with tears. "And I will do *anything* you want to make it right."

Laire took a step back, his knuckles aching and bruised. The boy remained crumpled, head down, submissive as a lamb. "*Anything* is a dangerous offer, boy."

"I mean it," Sorren said. "Lady Vinea—" A shuddering sob ran the length of his body. A flash of pain crossed his eyes, and he cradled his ribs, but he bit back any protest. "She was kind to me. She-she *cared*. And I hurt her. I have to make it right somehow."

Laire hissed and turned away, moving back to Vinea and stroking her hair with one hand while he clasped her fingers with the other. "You can start by telling me why, by Mother Night's good graces, you're both out here."

Sorren ripped a piece of his sleeve and dabbed at his nose. "Lord Sedick sent her to retrieve your sword for him."

Laire gripped Vinea tighter. "You're lying. Vinea hates the man. She would never help him, especially not to betray me."

"Sedick has...leverage over her."

Laire cast about for what that could mean. Leverage? What on Mother Night would convince Vinea to do *anything* Sedick asked her to do? "He has—" His face flushed white. He whirled on Sorren. "He *threatened* my daughter?"

Sorren looked at him with wide eyes. "N-No, sir. She's perfectly safe."

Laire didn't believe that for a moment. He believed *Sorren* believed that, but he had known Sedick too long. "I'm going to kill him." He kissed Vinea's knuckles, and they sat in silence for a while. Sorren chanted spells to himself and fixed most of the damage Laire had caused him. He left a black eye. Probably for Laire's ego. And it seemed his ribs still gave him trouble.

"The villagers say there was a fight. What happened?"

Sorren's shoulders slumped. "It was my fault. Sedick ordered me to kill Tristan. When I saw him, I—"

Laire's world spun to a complete halt. "You *saw* him?"

Sorren straightened himself. "I did, sir. An elven woman with a black sword was protecting him and then Lady Vinea—"

"No."

"Sir?"

But Laire didn't realize he had spoken. No. *No!* Not her again. *Anyone* but her. Not the same whelp that had taken everything from him at the Dragon Scales—the only victim that had survived a wound from his sword. She was the one person that could finish unraveling his last bits of hope for success.

The sword's hissing, buzzing laugh grated against Laire's ears. His hands shook and sweat pooled around his temples. Furious bile rose in the back of his throat. That elf—that *monster*—couldn't leave him alone. Not him. Not his best laid plans. And now she had nearly killed his wife. No matter how many steps he took forward, *she* always dragged him back. All his power, scheming, and training had failed him yet again.

But you will not fail again, will you, Laire? The sword asked.

Laire leaned into the sword's voice, his mind broken. He had no power of his own—never had. Only the sword and its power could help him now. He had no other choice.

He gripped the sword's hilt. *No, I will not. Not with your help.*

The entirety of the Ancient Races would pay for touching his family, even if he had to sell his soul to do it.

The sword's presence raced like lightning up his arm, flooding his mind with its dark embrace. Power swelled in his veins and ignited the world around him. Sights, sounds, and smells erupted in him like he had never imagined before. He heard the magic flowing through Sorren's veins—smelled the blood from Vinea's wounds. The entire world pressed on him at once with a riot of sensations that nearly knocked him from his feet. But then it faded as quickly as it came, only a glimpse of the sword's true power. It's words swirled in manic, all-consuming circles through Laire's thoughts. *Kill them. Kill them all. Let the Earth drown in their blood.*

Reeling but also somehow more calm and in control than he had ever been in his life, Laire turned to Sedick's boy. "Did you see where Tristan went?"

Sorren shook his head. "But I can help you find them. If you let me go with you."

Laire regarded the boy. His immediate reaction was a raging "absolutely not!" He had nearly killed Vinea. Why, by Mother Night, would he trust him with anything else?

But then the sword opened his eyes to the wells of magic swirling through Sorren. The boy possessed one of the most powerful magical bloodlines the world over—the magic of Malcolm Maprix. An asset like that was too valuable to take lightly.

"Fine," he said. "But the *moment* you step out of line, I will end you. No questions asked."

"I won't step out of line, sir," he said, drawing himself up to his full height. "I owe your wife, and by extension, *you,* too much for that. When would you like to leave?"

"Right now."

"Oh? And where are we going?"

Vinea's words pierced through the sword's hold on Laire for only a moment. Tears sprang to his eyes, and he whirled, nearly driven to his knees with relief. She was *alive!* "Vinea, my love." He held her to him, kissed her forehead, and thanked each and every known and unknown god. "I thought I had lost you!"

She put her hand on his chest and pushed away. "Yet you seemed perfectly happy to go running off to leave me behind just moments ago."

Laire recoiled from her vehemence. "Vinea, I would have made sure you were in expert hands. Always. You know *you* are my priority."

Vinea smiled at him, but the smile did not reach her eyes, which smoldered with pain and so much anger. "I'm not sure I know that anymore." She looked away from him to Sorren, who looked ready to burst into tears.

"Lady Vinea, I am so, *so*—"

Her features softened. A stab of jealousy twisted in Laire's gut. "It's not your fault, Sorren." She brushed the tears from his cheeks. Her lips tightened when she saw his bruised eye. "Perhaps you could leave the general and I alone for a moment?"

Sorren bowed, wiping his nose on his sleeve, and left. He shut the doors behind him.

"So, you're out to hunt down the last of my family, are you?" Vinea asked when they were alone. No preamble. No niceties. Not even a look his way. Just cold distance.

Laire's heart sunk into his gut. He sat at the foot of the bed. "You know, then?"

"Of *course* I know, Laire!" She rounded on him, her eyes alight. "I've known since the night you brought him back. How could I not? He looks just like my sister! Did you think I was *stupid?*"

Anger of his own rose to Laire's face. "I don't appreciate the accusations, Vinea. I didn't think you were *stupid*. I never have. I just hoped—"

"Hoped that I would turn a blind eye to you raising my nephew for slaughter?"

Laire blanched. Freezing heat sucked the feeling from his face. He looked at her with wide eyes.

Hot tears brimmed in her eyes. "I knew that, too. I overheard you talking with Sedick. What I'm baffled by is that you, *knowing* who I am and who my family was, would think I would ever let something like that happen!"

"I did it because I had to!" The words lashed out more sharply than he had intended, and Vinea flinched. He reached for her hand to soften the blow, but she snatched it away. "I'm doing what's best for us."

"I can decide what's best for me, thank you very much."

He flinched at the ice in her voice.

They sat that way, stiff and unyielding, for more time than Laire cared to admit. Where did they go from here? How could he make her see reason? Help her understand that this was all *for her?*

Vinea sighed, the fight draining from her body. She was so pale, her freckles stark against her drawn skin. Laire pulled her closer to him. He shouldn't have fought with her. Not now, with her so wounded. By the Architects, he had almost *lost* her. He couldn't bear it again. He had to be better.

"Whatever benefit you're seeking," she said into his chest. "Bloodshed is never worth it."

He squeezed her hand tightly and breathed in the smell of her hair. Despite being away from home for who knew how long, she still smelled of lavender. He knew what came next, and he had to take in every moment he could. "Unfortunately, I have no other choice."

He stood and walked to the door.

"LAIRE!" The hurt and betrayal in Vinea's voice nearly broke him.

No other choice. No other choice, his dead wife whispered in his head. His sword echoed the words.

"You have a choice." He heard her tears as she spoke but couldn't turn around. "You can either come home to me and our daughter, who *needs* her father, or you can continue on this blood mission. You *cannot* do both."

Laire turned the door handle. "Get some rest, my love. I'll be back to get you, and then we can all return to Monterro as heroes."

"I mean it, Laire."

This time, he stopped. He still couldn't bring himself to look at her, but he imagined the icy resolve burning bright in her brilliant blue eyes. The set of her lips. Her head held proudly. He had fallen in love with her fortitude and determination. And now it threatened to destroy him.

"If you walk out that door..." Her voice broke for a single breath, but then she brought it under control once more. "If you walk out that door, neither Linae nor I will be there when you return."

A single tear spilled down Laire's face, and he gritted his teeth against it. This was for *them*. Always had been. Always would be. "Then I'll have to find you again, won't I, your highness?" He bowed to Princess Vinea Vastir, the beauty of the Northern Hills, Second Sister to Queen Eden, and the woman that had stolen his heart. Without another word, he shut the door behind him.

Sorren waited for Laire outside. The way he couldn't make eye-contact with Laire betrayed him. He had heard every word between Laire and Vinea.

Laire ground his teeth until his jaw cracked. His fingers twitched around the pommel of his sword. "I suppose you have your own things to say?"

"No! I—" Sorren stopped and sighed. He shuffled his feet in the dust and fidgeted with his fingers. "Are you sure you want to do this? All I want is to help Lady Vinea, and if she doesn't—"

"She has no idea what's best for her!" Laire adjusted the belt around his waist, the sword's whispers crackling through his body. "Tristan is the key to regaining our old life, and that elf could ruin it all. She's threatened my family, and that cannot go unpunished." He leaned close to Sorren and gripped his ragged gray cloak in his fist.

"If you won't help me, then you are as good as an enemy. To me *and* my family."

Sorren bowed his head, shoulders tight. "Yes, sir."

Laire released him. He went to move past him, but Sorren stopped him again.

"There's something you should know." He pulled at a ragged hole in his ear. "I'm tied to Lord Sedick. Lady Vinea broke me free of the talisman that anchored his curse to me, but there could still be some of it lingering..."

"And what do I care for your problems with Sedick?"

"He ordered me to kill Tristan. That may still be in effect when we see Tristan next."

Laire cursed Sedick, imagining with barely bridled glee what it would be like to run him through with the sword Sedick so desperately craved. "Well, then, consider this your new curse," he said to Sorren. "If you kill Tristan and subject my family to failure again, I will kill you. Slowly. Painfully. And with no mercy." Without giving Sorren time to answer, he swept off, no longer caring if Sorren followed him or not. If that asset failed him, he still had his sword, and that had yet to steer him wrong.

TWENTY-NINE

Tristan watched the dead coals, letting the wind kick their dust into his face as Ash ministered to Aspen. His hands shook, both from cold and fear. Aspen had been so small, so *fragile*. Worn out body, spirit, and magic, and there was no telling if she would come back from that. And she had done it all for *him* when he had all but run away. He gripped his hands together, squeezing until his knuckles turned white. He would make it right. He had to.

But what if you can't? His mouth ran dry at the thought. *What if she dies, and it's all your fault?*

Styrax sat across from him, silent and grim. They sat that way for a while, not a word between them, and for once, Tristan had no inclination to break that silence.

"Tristan." Styrax clenched his hands, his gaze steely as he watched Tristan. His usual humor was gone, replaced with hurt and betrayal and fury and a desperate need to understand. "I have put up with a lot from you because I understood a lot happened all at once and it was hard to break the habits of Lorate. But *this*?" He gestured to Aspen's tent. "You have crossed a line that there may be no coming back from."

Tristan couldn't look him in the eye. "I know."

"Aspen could *die*."

"I—" Tristan's voice broke. "I understand."

Styrax rubbed his face and sat back. He studied his hands in silence for a while. "*Why*? What have we done to deserve this treatment?"

His voice sounded as broken as Tristan felt. He sensed the question referred to something greater than just their group. "I can only take responsibility for my own actions. You, Ash, and Aspen have done nothing to deserve the way I have treated you."

Styrax rested his brow in his hand and twiddled a stick in the dirt. "I'm not here to punish you. I just want to understand. The Tristan back there is not the Tristan I know. Please tell me why."

The lump in Tristan's throat seemed too big to talk around, but Styrax needed to know—*deserved* to know. "Styrax I-I think I'm a monster."

Styrax said nothing. Didn't agree nor argue. Tristan silently thanked him for it. He already understood so little of what was happening to him. Adding any further distractions would only make the problem worse. "There are thoughts...this *voice*...it tells me horrible things. To *do* horrible things. I see monsters everywhere I look, and lash out when there's nothing there." He looked into the fire, hands clenched so tightly his nails dug furrows in his palm. "It might be best if I...found my own way. I'm dangerous." He heard Aspen's skin tear. Saw the scarlet stains on her tunic. "To you and everyone else." Memories of the voice—of the darkness it sowed in his chest—haunted him. He feared he would lose his mind entirely if he left. But he feared what he would do if he stayed more.

"What happened, Tristan?"

Tristan's hands shook. "I-I almost *killed* Aspen. I—"

"No, not that. What made you go back to help?"

"I..." Tristan's mind went blank. "I don't know. It's like...I *knew*

Aspen for the first time. The voice was gone, and I didn't think. I just *did.*"

Styrax leaned forward, face earnest. "And what happened before that? Anything unusual?"

"Other than getting a thorough and well-deserved whipping from a child? No."

"What happened in that fight?"

"Does it matter?" Tristan leapt to his feet and paced. "What does that have to do with anything?" He pulled at his hair, reliving that moment over and over again—watching Aspen fall soundlessly, face as gray as fog. "He attacked me. Aspen saved me. And now she's sharing a bed with Death and it's all my fault!" He dropped to his log again and buried his face in his hands. Tears, bitter with guilt and remorse, wet his cheeks.

"Tristan," Styrax leaned forward, gaze piercing, face set with firm earnestness. "I know this may be a lot to ask of you right now, but I need you to trust that I'm asking these things for a reason."

Tristan took in a shuddering breath. He pressed his palms into his eyes, scrubbing away the overwhelm of emotions, and the images relented. For the moment. "I do trust you. Of *anyone* in this upside down kingdom, I trust you the most."

Styrax put a hand on his shoulder. "Then tell me."

Tristan did. He told him everything from the moment they entered the village to the moment he tried to keep the villagers off Aspen and failed. Every bitter, terrifying thought. Although it didn't make the situation any better, talking about it made it less...cursed? Less like he had imagined it all and was slowly going mad.

When he finished, Styrax sat back in silence for a long time. He stared at the stars as if they could speak. "Can I see the rings?"

Tristan nodded and fished the broken strap from his pocket. He hesitated for a moment. These had been the only things he'd ever had from before his memory. If anything happened to them...

He handed them over. He trusted Styrax.

Styrax took the first ring into his palm and left the other with

Tristan. He weighed it, turned it over in his fingers, and whispered a few words over it. It glowed green. A somehow familiar mist curled from its edges. Styrax stopped speaking, and the glow faded.

"What was that?" Tristan asked, his voice hoarse. A spell? A *curse?*

"A talisman," Styrax said as he handed it back to Tristan. "It's meant to protect you from those that would do you harm. It's weak, but the magic's still there." He looked Tristan in the eyes. "Whoever made this cared a lot about you." Styrax gestured for the other ring. Tristan handed it to him, still dangling from its strap.

Styrax gasped in pain the moment it touched him. He flung it to the ground and kicked a pile of dirt over it as he scrambled away. Tristan had never seen him look so horrified.

"What? *What?*"

Styrax looked at him with wide eyes. "You...You've had this *on you* for five years?"

Tristan nodded. He couldn't get words out. Not in the face of Styrax's fear.

"Tristan, that thing has been...*touched.*"

Any previous notion of what that word meant fled the moment Styrax said it like that. Tristan's tongue latched onto his cheeks in his dry mouth.

"A demon, a warlock...I don't know *what*, but there's enough dark magic in there to *kill you.*"

Tristan found his voice, weak and barely there. "But Laire said it was supposed to help me bring back my memories—"

"He *lied.*"

Tristan shook his head. No. He couldn't believe it. Not of the man that had saved him. Not the man that gave him a home. "No. It's Sedick. It has to be. He tricked Laire when he made it for me."

"*Sedick* did this?"

Tristan nodded again. What else could he do?

Styrax leaned forward with a puff of breath as if expelling some demon from himself. He rubbed his eyes. "Okay. This is a lot to take in. We'll revisit this whole Sedick thing later. Right now, do you understand what this means for you?"

Tristan simply looked at him, uncomprehending.

Styrax leaned forward, his face warm and soft. "It wasn't you thinking those thoughts and doing those things. It was a curse."

Tristan's heart leapt at the thought. "It...it wasn't me?"

Styrax shook his head.

"I'm not—" Tristan's voice choked and tears sprang to his eyes. "I'm not a monster? I'm not a danger to anyone?"

Styrax's eyes welled. "No. And I'm so sorry I didn't recognize the curse sooner, and that you had to suffer from all of that all on your own."

Tristan wept, all his fears washing out through those floods, and Styrax sat quietly next to him until he had no more tears to cry.

Aspen woke to an almighty crash, and Ash cursing under her breath.

Despite feeling like someone had thrown her to a herd of stampeding minotaurs, Aspen smiled. "Sweet Sister Earth, you'll wake the dead with that racket." It alarmed her at how much she *sounded* like the dead, rasping past chapped lips and horrific cotton mouth.

Ash sucked in a gasp that she nearly choked on and whirled. She gaped at Aspen for a moment with unabashed relief before she pursed her lips and quirked an eyebrow. "Then I will have done my job." Her eyes welled, and she swept Aspen to her, squeezing her until her ribs nearly collapsed. Aspen grimaced past the pain and patted her on the back.

After several long, excruciating seconds, Ash finally released her. She wiped the moisture from her eyes and brushed her hair away from her face. "*Sweet* Sister Earth, if you *ever* scare me like that again..." She shook her head, unable to finish the words.

Aspen patted her arm. "I'm sorry."

"I would certainly hope so! Stop. Putting. Yourself. In. Danger!" A punch to Aspen's leg punctuated each word. But softly. "A cursed back. Stab wounds galore. And now sorcerer's blight. *No more*, do you understand?"

"I said I was sorry!"

"You'd better *keep* saying it until I actually believe you!" Ash sat back on her hands, disturbing the pile of cooking utensils she had dropped. "You are so lucky we have Hemlock's miracle salve for your back. Otherwise, you wouldn't be here for me to yell at." She put a shaking hand to her face and smiled at Aspen. "It's good to see you." Her voice broke with emotion.

Aspen smiled softly back, choking back the unexpected lump in her own throat. "It's good to see you, too." She didn't want to dwell on how close she had come to being gone forever. How the faceless shadows had breathed down her neck and loomed over her head. The thought sent chills down her arms. She rubbed the gooseflesh away. "How's Tristan?"

Ash's face darkened. "Ah, yes. Him."

Aspen sat up straighter, grimacing at what that did to her body. Ash's tone reminded her of some...dark times for Ash. "What did you do?"

Ash threw her hands up. "Nothing! Although I definitely *considered* removing him from his limbs." Some of the tension left her body with a sigh. She tucked her knees to her chest and wrapped her arms around them. "There have been some...developments."

Aspen watched her with narrowed eyes. "What do you mean?"

Ash sighed again and scratched her scalp. "I suppose there's no polite way to say this." She gave Aspen a pointed look. "Tristan was cursed."

Aspen had nothing to say about that. She sat and mulled the thought over in her brain. It certainly made his lunatic antics more understandable. But how? And why? Her tired, ill mind ached at the effort to piece it together. "That doesn't make any sense," she said.

"Why waste the resources and energy? Surely there are other people that it would be of more benefit to curse?"

Ash leaned forward, her look earnest. "I could hazard a guess."

Her meaning evaporated the pained fog of Aspen's mind like a forest fire. She blanched. The world swayed, and she clutched at her blankets for balance. "No," she said. She couldn't tell if her voice came out hoarse due to misuse or fear. The tent walls threatened to collapse on her at any moment. Her throat ran dry and the base of her left thumb burned. Her scar writhed on her back. "It can't be..." she gulped. She couldn't get enough oxygen to her lungs. "*Him.* It *can't.* I told you already; he's not him."

Ash put her hands on Aspen's. "I know you don't want to get hurt again. I don't blame you. But there are too many," she waved her arms vaguely about her head, "*things* for it to all be just a horrible coincidence! Laire just *happening* to be in the same fort as Tristan? Tristan not remembering anything about his past life beyond *five years*? They never found the body, Aspen. There's too much evidence—"

"I *know* that!" Aspen's outburst wracked her body and triggered a coughing fit that tore through her lungs. All the better for it. It kept her from sinking into that night, watching his head shatter over and over again. She bit back tears and pulled her hand from Ash's. "What you call hurt, I call *torture*. Real, physical anguish I am trapped in every moment of my life. You think I don't *want* him to be alive? I have done nothing but dream and hope and pray for it since that night." She rubbed the mark on her thumb and ignored the pain in her back. "But all I'm ever reminded of is the horrible finality of that night. How irreversible my mistakes were. I watched it with my own eyes, Ash. Ro is dead. Gone forever. And I —" Her voice gave out on her. She bit her lip. "I have to live with that."

Ash looked like she wanted to say more, but refrained. Aspen saw her own pain mirrored in Ash's face and wished she could recant her harshness. But she couldn't. Choices were irrevocable once they were made. She rubbed the mark on her thumb. It reminded her of that fact every day.

Ash patted Aspen's knee, all her unspoken words tight on her face. *Trust. Believe. Try.* Aspen didn't have the strength to do any of it. Ash, blessedly, didn't say any of them. "I'm going to make you some food."

Aspen's stomach curdled at the thought. "I'm not—"

Ash pushed a finger to Aspen's lips. "I'm. Making. You. Food. You *are* hungry, and you *are* eating. Stay here and get some rest until I come back to get you."

She left Aspen alone with her thoughts. A dangerous place to be. They trembled through her body, reliving the nightmares. Her fingers twitched into the way she held her sword. Her scar ached. Crimson pools of blood spotted her vision while faceless specters hovered at the edges. Three men stood before her, each staring into her soul with lifeless eyes. They were gone. She knew it.

Another face swam through her memories, blurring the nightmares. A woman with dark hair and a scar across both eyelids. Aspen had tried to forget her. To push her aside as just a hopeful fantasy that had emerged amid her agony. The woman had offered too much hope. Had driven Aspen on too many feverish searches for a man she had watched die. But today, her words resonated in Aspen's bones and nurtured hope where it was not wanted.

I will help him.

Aspen pressed the heels of her palms into her eyes until she saw nothing but the stars they made. A single tear slipped down her cheek before she could catch it. She twisted her fingers into the hairs on her scalp and pulled. "He's gone," she said to her phantoms. "He's gone. He's gone, he's *gone*. No one saved him. And it's my fault."

But the woman's voice came again to her mind as it had that night so many years ago. *All will be well. All will be well.*

Aspen sobbed.

TRISTAN'S FIREWOOD clattered from his arms. He didn't know if he should laugh, cry, or faint at the sight of Aspen sitting by the fire with her cloak wrapped around her like a blanket.

"You're awake!" He picked up a few stray slivers of firewood and bustled to her. "We didn't know...I was worried you..." He shook his head and threw the wood onto the fire. Sparks fizzed into the night. "It doesn't matter. I'm just—" his voice cracked. He bit his lip and choked back the lump in his throat. "I'm glad you're all right." He sat across from her and smiled.

Aspen didn't look at him. She stared into the fire, a bowl of stew clutched in her lap.

Tristan's smile faded. Right. They weren't friends. He had been a monster and almost gotten her killed. He wouldn't be surprised if she never spoke to him again. He wouldn't blame her. He clenched his hands in his lap.

"I'm sorry for everything I did," he said.

Aspen slurped her stew and rolled the chunks in her cheeks.

"And I know that's never going to be enough. I mean, you nearly *died*! Why would words make any of that better?"

Aspen slurped again.

Tristan ran a hand through his hair. He was making it worse. Absolute, total disaster. "I wish there was a way I could make it all up to you, but I know there isn't. I was awful, ungrateful, bigoted, and just a monster. If there was any way I could erase all the hurt I caused you, I would in a heartbeat. And if you ever think of *anything* I can do to make it up to you, I would jump at the chance."

Aspen swallowed. Swished the last remnants of broth in her bowl.

Tristan's throat ached around the lump that had formed. He should have expected this. He *deserved* it. All the apologizing and begging in the world wouldn't fix the damage he'd done. But that didn't mean he still hadn't wished…He clenched his jaw. He couldn't expect that of her. "But if you choose to never speak to me again, that is more than I deserve."

He stood to leave.

"Aren't we fervent tonight?"

If the sky rained golden coins, Tristan could not have been happier than in that moment. He whirled to face Aspen, eyes wet with relief. "You're *talking* to me?"

"Considering my only other options are a stew bowl and the empty expanse of darkness, I would certainly *hope* I'm talking to you."

"But, *why*?"

"Because if I *were* talking to my stew, my sanity might come into question."

"Not *that*." Tristan couldn't believe he'd missed her sarcasm. "*Why* are you talking to me? You didn't say anything for a while, and I thought…"

"Most consider it rude to talk with your mouth full." She sipped the last of her stew, the gleam in her eyes wicked. "Plus, you were saying such nice things."

Tristan put his face in his hands, unsure if he should be relieved or irritated.

"Tristan."

He looked up. The humor had gone from Aspen's face. She looked at him with a soft intensity that made his heart trip in his chest. Aspen set her bowl down and leaned closer to him. The smell of roses and fall leaves wafted from her hair. Had he noticed that before?

"Ash told me about how you ran me all the way here, and that you were never far while I was recovering. I wanted to say thank you."

He bowed his head, his shoulders hunched. Sparks from the fire spat in his face, and he thought of all the times he'd done the same to

Aspen. "I don't deserve your thanks. You wouldn't have been hurt in the first place if it wasn't for me."

"I've had more people than I can count try to kill me," she said with a smile—a small thing that barely turned up the corners of her mouth—and the warmth of the gesture burned on his cheeks. "But none of them have ever come back to help me recover."

Tristan didn't know how to respond to that. "Is the number of your near-death experiences supposed to make me feel better?"

She stirred the ashes, their glow turning her skin to amber. "We all make choices we wish we hadn't. It takes a rare character to let go of their pride and try to fix things on their own." Her gaze darkened and her jaw clenched. "Ash also told me about the curse."

Tristan nodded. "Even with it, though, that's no excuse for how I—"

Aspen held up a hand. "I know. It certainly didn't help, though."

Tristan couldn't argue with that.

Aspen nodded as if acknowledging his acquiescence. "I've been doing some thinking since Ash told me. All of it is pure speculation, but I'd like to discuss those thoughts with you sometime when I'm not quite...so..." a yawn poured from her mouth, "*tired.*"

"I'd be honored." Tristan helped her to her feet.

She scrunched her nose and patted his cheek. "Don't be so sure. You don't know what I have to say yet." She headed off to bed.

"Aspen?"

She moaned in response. "Not even two steps and you're already pestering me again?" she asked.

"Last question, I promise."

"So you say, but we both know that's nothing but lies."

Tristan chuckled. "Last one before I let you sleep, then."

"Fine," she grumbled.

"Will you teach me how to fight?"

She eyed him carefully. "Are you sure you're ready to take lessons from a monster like me again?"

Tristan grimaced. "*Yes.* How many times do I have to apologize for that?"

"That's now two questions. And as many times as I say so." Her grin was wicked and *far* too excited. "Your training starts as soon as I have time." With that, she made her way back to her tent.

"And when will *that* be?"

"*Three.*"

Tristan winced.

THIRTY

Tristan collapsed, sides heaving and sweat pouring down his face as the sun set behind the mountains, painting the sky harvest gold. He had lost count of the days since they had left Vastet. Had been too tired to care. Aspen had gone right into training him, much to Ash's chagrin, every night when they set up camp, and every night she walloped him into exhaustion. "When I... asked you to..." he gulped in a breath of air and nearly choked on it, "...*teach* me...I envisioned you *teaching* me...not using me as a...a..." He cast around for the proper word.

"Sparring dummy?"

"*Yes.*"

"I'm fairly certain you bring the 'dummy' all on your own." Aspen sat next to him, a small smile on her face and hardly a hair out of place. Tristan noticed a faint sheen of sweat on her brow and that mollified him. Somewhat. "But, really, though, you're doing well. You already have the skills but are just out of practice, and the best way to get back into the game is some high speed, high stakes sparring."

Tristan flopped onto his back. "My bruises disagree." He studied his hands, though, pleased with the calluses forming at the base of each finger. He *was* getting better. Aspen landed fewer blows on him, and it had been three sessions since she could knock his sparring stick from his hands. He didn't know about *best way*, but it was something. "So, you think I was a master swordsman at some point?"

Aspen chuckled. "I wouldn't say *master*," she said. "But passable, certainly. You wouldn't have been able to hold your own in our first duel if you weren't."

Tristan groaned and covered his eyes. "Don't remind me. I was a horrific little know it all, wasn't I?"

"Yes." Aspen stood and helped him to his feet. "Now you're at least a little less horrific."

"Haha."

She patted him on the shoulder. "How about this? To make it up to me, *you* can take first watch tonight."

Tristan winced. "You drive a hard bargain." He took her hand and shook it. "But I accept." Their hands rested a little too long in each other, and Tristan gaped at them, warmth spreading up his arm. He realized what he'd done and dropped her hand, his face burning. "I better go, um...set up a post," he said. He marched stiffly away, telling himself that Aspen's cheeks were only pink from their workout.

One by one, the others went to bed except for Aspen. She stayed by the fire for a while, pacing and scribbling on scraps of parchment.

"Hey, if you're not going to sleep, I'll make you take over watch," Tristan said, face stern.

She rolled her eyes and finished a few scribbles. A few minutes later, though, she did finally pack up and disappear into her tent.

The fire faded to glistening coals. Tristan patrolled the perimeter and stirred the coals every now and again to keep them from dying out, but otherwise enjoyed the climate of the night air. It was cool without being frigid, the first bite of autumn taking hold, and the breeze stirred the pine needles around him in a whirring chorus that never quite turned to words. The coolness sat sharp and fresh on his nose and tongue, and he breathed it in deeply. For the first time he could remember, he was exactly where he needed to be. His blood flowed swift and energetic through his body, and his senses heightened to take in everything at once. He didn't know what the next moment would bring, but this one had peace, contentment, and purpose.

"Tristan."

Everything crashed around him in a single word. He whirled and saw a figure huddled in the dark. "Laire? What are you doing here?"

Laire emerged into the moonlight, looking more haggard than Tristan had ever seen him. Something manic shadowed his eyes. "I'm here to save you, Tristan," he said, clutching his sword like a lifeline. "Let's get you home."

Tristan cast a look at the tents, all dark and silent. "I—"

"Don't worry," Laire said. "I won't let them do anything to you ever again. You're safe."

"No, that's not—" Tristan shook his head and took a tentative step toward Laire, hoping that somehow he could make this man that had done so much for him understand. "Laire, I...I can't go."

A shadow crossed Laire's face. "Have they done something to you? Put you under a curse?"

"*No*! No, Sister Earth, nothing like that!" Tristan took a few steps closer and lowered his voice so as not to wake the others. If either party met right now, it could only end in disaster. "Laire, I will *forever* be grateful to you and Vinea for saving me, but here, with them, I'm finally getting close to discovering who I was. Who I *am*. I have these memories hovering around me, so close I can almost *taste* them, and I...I have to stay. I think this is where I belong."

Laire seized Tristan by the arm, so tight that bruises formed beneath his fingertips. Tristan jerked back in surprise. "It's a lie!" Laire said in a desperate hiss. "All a lie. Their kind will draw you in with promises of home and love and trust, and then will rip that from you and laugh while you crumble. They're *monsters*, Tristan. What do you think this entire war has been about?"

Tristan wrenched his arm from Laire and took several steps back. The hairs on the back of his neck stood on end. Something was not right. Laire was too manic—too desperate. What was going on? He had never seen this side of Laire before—dark, vengeful, and *dangerous*. How long had he been like this? "Laire, they're not like that. It's all just stories. They're dif—"

"Oh, they're *different,* are they?" Laire asked with a laugh that boiled from his throat, his eyes wild. He took a step toward Tristan. "They love you?" Another step. "They care about you?" Two more. "They're out to make your life the happiest it's ever been?" He was almost on top of Tristan now. Tristan had never noticed how *huge* he was. The sword at Laire's side seemed to glow a sickly gray. "Those are the same things I told myself when I married an elf years before I met Vinea."

Tristan recoiled. "You...you what?" Laire? *Laire,* of all people?

"Disgusting, isn't it?" he asked. He laughed again, this one thick and broken with emotion. "She bore me a son. I thought we were in love." His softened eyes suddenly ignited with rage. "And do you know what she did at the first sign of trouble?"

Tristan shook his head, speechless and dreading where the tirade ended. Laire was unhinged. There was no telling what he might do. Tristan's hand drifted to his dagger, wishing it were a sword. Could he defend himself if he needed to? Would a dagger be any use against the jagged sword at Laire's side? Was it too late to call for help?

No. No, he needed to handle this on his own. They had already done so much for him. He couldn't drag them into more danger just to save himself.

Laire didn't seem to see Tristan anymore. His eyes were glazed, lost in a memory Tristan couldn't see. "She murdered my son, Tristan. Said it was a mercy killing. Said she had no choice." He snapped back to reality. His face contorted into a horrifying mix of anguish and glee. "She left me no choice but to return the favor." He moved to seize Tristan.

Tristan dodged him, heart pounding. "I don't understand what happened to you, Laire, but I'm sorry." He leapt away from another swipe. "I won't go with you. I can't."

"This is why Sedick cursed away your free will," Laire snarled. "Too stubborn for your own good."

"W-what?" The world stopped. His heart stopped. He knew. He *knew.* "You knew about that?"

Laire's eyes widened when he realized his mistake. Tristan's heart plummeted, even as rage bubbled inside him. Laire had known. The whole time, he had offered *choices* and *purposes*, when he had been pulling the strings the whole time. "They were right about you," he said, breathless. "I wouldn't believe that you could do something like that. I played right into your plans, didn't I? Poor, trusting Tristan."

"Tristan," Laire said, slow and commanding. "They're influencing you. You and I need to leave *now*, and then I will explain everything." He moved closer.

Tristan drew his dagger, so puny against Laire's massive frame, but he didn't care. His arm shook with agonizing betrayal and white-hot anger. "*No.* I won't go anywhere with you, and if you take one step closer, I will slit your lying tongue from your mouth."

A purple-tinged fireball whizzed past Tristan's face and exploded against a copse of trees. Splinters shrieked past and forced the two men apart to shield themselves. The trees groaned and cracked as flames engulfed them.

Tristan took off toward the camp, putting as much distance between himself and Laire as possible, head reeling. But that didn't matter now. They had to get out. *Now.*

"You *idiot,*" Laire screamed. "What are you doing? We want him *alive!*"

Tristan turned to look, and his stomach dropped to his toes.

Sorren emerged from the trees, arms wreathed in his swirling purple magic.

Tristan filled his lungs and screamed, "GET UP! We have to leave! We're under attack!"

"NO!" Laire ran after him, and Tristan put on another burst of speed.

Aspen was out of her tent first. "Can't leave you alone for *two* seconds, can I?"

"Not *now*!" Tristan gestured to the men behind him, and her face went white. She drew her sword as Tristan dove into his tent. He seized Styrax by the ankle and dragged him out. "Get up! Grab what you can and *go*!"

Styrax flailed like a disoriented fish until he caught sight of the fire, and Aspen with her sword drawn. His eyes widened, and he scrambled to his feet.

Another explosion ripped through the camp.

"ASH!" The scream that tore from Aspen's throat was nearly inhuman. Their tent had gone up in flames, with Ash still inside.

"*Ash!*" Styrax tried to douse the fire, but it only seemed to encourage the purple flames. So, instead, he wrapped himself in a coat of water and dove inside after her.

Tristan watched on, frozen in place, phantom flames billowing in his mind, another blonde woman blurred by the smoke and heat. He didn't know her. But he knew she hadn't made it out.

Styrax and Ash emerged, coughing and covered in soot, but alive. Tristan could have cried. Ash limped on a twisted ankle.

Tears welled in Aspen's eyes. "Don't *ever* do that again," she said to Ash. Her shoulders tensed and she turned to Laire and Sorren, both charging, eyes alight. "Take care of her," Aspen said to Styrax, "I've got something else that needs to be addressed." She strode toward the two men, head and shoulders thrown back and eyes blazing. The very picture of a vengeance.

"*Aspen!*" Ash said. But she was already too far gone.

Laire stopped in his tracks, eyes wide. "*You.* I told you you'd made an enemy of a dangerous man."

"Oh? Perhaps you can point me in his direction." Aspen swung at him, and their swords locked in a rain of sparks. Aspen's back arched, agony flashing across her face, but she still pressed into Laire with the full force of her weight. Sorren leapt in to try to split them apart, his whole body glowing with magic.

Growling, Ash drew her bow and shot two arrows. One hit Sorren in the foot. He screamed and crumpled, tearing the arrow from the wound and sending magic into it. The other almost hit Laire in the thigh, but he knocked it away with his sword and roared.

"By the *Architects!*" Ash shouldered her bow. "C'mon. That noble idiot won't leave until we do."

Styrax scooped her up before she could protest and they took off, Ash still shooting parting shots over his shoulder to keep Sorren at bay.

"Does she always do that?" Tristan asked Ash as he raced alongside Styrax.

"*Every time!*" Ash threw her hands in the air and nearly smacked Styrax in the face. "There's going to come a day when she *can't* handle everything by herself, and then she really *is* going to wind up dead."

Tristan ducked under a low-hanging branch to avoid getting clobbered. Styrax wasn't so fortunate. He ended up with a face-full of the stuff and nearly dropped Ash. Tristan caught her, and he and Styrax carried her between them as they ran. Styrax kept spitting out twigs and leaves.

"Does she thrive off near-death experiences or something?" Tristan asked.

Ash shook her head. "You would think so, but no. She just...has other reasons for it."

Tristan was about to ask what in Mother Night another reason could be for such reckless, blatantly fate-tempting behavior, but Ash pointed to a rope bridge, spanning a long-overgrown ravine. Tristan heard the roar of rapids far, *far* below.

"We'll cross here and then cut the bridge once Aspen crosses. They won't be able to follow us."

"I'm pretty sure the sorcerer can fly."

"Then I can shoot him down," Ash said with too much of a smile in her voice.

Tristan thought it might be a good idea until they actually approached the bridge. Bird and rodent skulls decorated stakes near the bridge entrance and hung along the ropes on the first half, warning away any passersby. Each passing gust of wind, or a draft from the river below, made each dry board shriek against the ropes holding it together.

Styrax peered down the ravine as they got closer. He said nothing. Just looked. His grip tightened around Ash, who mumbled incoherently, mostly what sounded like a lecture for Aspen.

"Styrax, I swear by every piece of Mother Night's wardrobe, if you're thinking of going for a swim right now, I *will* leave you here!" Tristan said.

"There are naiads down there," Styrax said, his voice distant.

Tristan inched his right foot farther along the bridge and scooted the rest of his body over to meet it. "Is that a bad thing?"

"Only if you fall in," Styrax said in his same trance-like tone.

Tristan chuckled incredulously and stepped back. "That's it. I'm not crossing that."

Clashes and shouts followed behind them, closer by the minute. Purple flashes and screams of defiance.

"Don't have much of a choice!"

Before Tristan could process the words, Styrax seized him by the back of the collar and hauled him across the bridge at an unholy sprint.

"Hey! Hey wait!" Tristan tried to clutch the rope rails, but only got burns on his hands for the trouble. The bridge lurched drunkenly from side to side with every one of Styrax's steps. Tristan could have sworn he saw the supporting ropes fraying as they passed. The water seemed to rear up in anticipation, waiting to swallow them whole the moment the bridge gave way. Whispers and hisses curled hungrily in Tristan's ears, coming somewhere from the currents. Every few seconds, his feet dangled out in the open as he passed from one slat of wood to the next. His heart stopped every time. His life flashed before his eyes. At least, the past five years of it. It was a pitiful existence, really.

Miraculously, they made it to the other side without the bridge collapsing beneath them. Styrax heaved Tristan over the end of the bridge, where he landed in a grateful heap. He wanted to bury himself in the dirt, become one with it, just to know for certain he had actually made it back to its loving, *solid* embrace. He abstained. But only just.

Aspen, Laire, and Sorren exploded from the tree line. She darted in front of them like a hare before a pack of hungry dogs. Both men favored cuts on their arms, legs, faces, and chests, but neither were mortally wounded. Just enough to slow them down.

Tristan cupped his hands around his mouth. "Aspen!"

She whirled in his direction and he waved her toward the bridge. She immediately veered toward it. Sorren shot a bolt of lightning over her head. Laire followed it with a crossbow bolt.

Aspen sped onto the bridge with no thought to where her feet landed. Tristan watched in terrified awe as her toes barely scraped the edges of the wooden slats but somehow kept moving. Laire and Sorren stopped at the end of the bridge.

Tristan thought it was odd until he saw a purple glow. He watched in horror as Sorren sliced through one side of the rope bridge. The corner lurched drunkenly. The support post next to Tristan—now bearing all the weight on that side—screamed and sagged. In a blink, it tore free of the ground and shot past Tristan into the abyss.

"*Aspen!*" He lurched to the edge of the ravine, not breathing. She had fallen. She had to have. There was no way she could have held on. "ASPEN!"

"Not helpful!" she snapped. With nothing short of a miracle, she had caught hold of the edge of the listing bridge. Her arms trembled and sweat dripped down the sides of her face. Tired as she was, Tristan doubted she'd be able to hold on for long. "Quit your... crying...and do something helpful!" she panted, her teeth clenched and knuckles white.

"Don't do it, boy!" Laire shouted. "We need him alive!"

They all looked. Laire dove for Sorren, but it was too late. He'd already loosed his magic for another pass at the strained ropes. They snapped, the sound falling like a death sentence.

No time to think. No time to plan or move. "Aspen, *jump*!" Tristan said.

She did as quickly as if it were instinct. She twisted and pushed off the taut part of the bridge before it severed completely. Hanging free of any safety nets, the only thing she could do was reach for Tristan.

Too low. She was too low! She would never clear the edge of the ravine! By the look of grim resignation on her face, Tristan could tell she knew it, too. For the barest of moments, an orange haze floated across his vision, and he had the thought that he could just let her fall. But something else reared up within him, roaring in outrage and horror at the idea.

With hardly a pause, he dropped bodily to his stomach. He nearly knocked the breath from his lungs, but he didn't care. He snatched Aspen by the wrists. She slammed against the side of the ravine. One hand broke free. Tristan hooked his other hand beneath her elbow and caught her. Safe.

Tristan laughed, giddy with relief. "I can't believe that worked!"

"Yes, yes, it's all rather miraculous. Perhaps we can discuss it when I'm *not* dangling over the side of the ravine?"

Tristan moved to pull her up. A glint across the water caught his eye.

"Tristan—!" Styrax tried to call out.

Ash let an arrow fly. It slammed into Laire's crossbow, which was trained on the small of Aspen's back. Ash's arrow shattered the crossbow, but the bolt still released, careening wildly. It thudded into Tristan's collarbone and he jerked back in shock. He stumbled and fell to his knees, one of Aspen's hands slipping from his fingers. Aspen gripped his other hand with only her fingertips. The world slowed to a horrific halt as she slipped from his grasp. He tried to snatch her again, but he was too slow.

"ASPEN!"

He couldn't tell if the scream was his, or Ash's.

Aspen hit the water with a sickening splash and vanished into its depths.

Without thought to the consequences, Tristan broke the shaft off the bolt in his shoulder, tore off his boots, and dove in after her.

"*Tristan!*" Styrax's voice rang out and followed him into the depths.

Laire watched Tristan disappear into the ravine. Lost. Gone. Laire had failed. Again.

He whirled on Sorren, who straightened to his full height despite the fear in his eyes. "*You.*" Laire stormed to him, white, furious rage swelling in his veins. He grabbed Sorren by his tunic and threw him bodily against a tree. Sorren cried out, and Laire struck him on the jaw. "You stupid idiot! We need him *alive!*"

"I'm sorry! It's Sedick's orders! I can't break—"

Laire struck him again on his cheekbone. "You betrayed me! Your stupidity has lost them to us!"

"I didn't mean to! I—"

"Shut up!" Laire struck him over and over and over again. Blood and sweat mingled in a pool on the ground and in droplets spraying everywhere. Laire ignored the way it blinded him and the pain in his knuckles. Ignored the boy as he curled into himself and begged for relief. "It doesn't matter your intentions. You *failed*! You failed your country! Failed your family!" Laire wasn't talking to Sorren anymore. He didn't see Sorren cowering against the tree. Instead, he saw a younger version of himself. Cocksure and bold. And then broken and defeated. He saw his hundreds of men dead at the feet of an enemy he had been so sure he could defeat, all because a stupid girl hadn't died and warned the Rebellion with her last dregs of magic. He heard King's Osmen's words as he stripped him of his privileges and sent him to a putrid fort on the edge of nowhere. Watched Vinea choke back her uncertainty as she held their newborn daughter in her arms and become the backbone he thought he had lost. He couldn't fail them again.

And he couldn't let the monsters that had nearly taken them from him roam free.

He stopped, panting and heaving and realizing just how much blood had covered him. Sorren slumped forward, barely recognizable. But still breathing. Still conscious.

Laire grabbed him by his hair and pulled his face close until the whites of their eyes nearly met. "Cross me again, and villagers will have to sweep up your pieces." He let him drop and stood, kicking him in the ribs for good measure. "Get up. We have work to do."

THIRTY-ONE

The freezing impact drove the air from Tristan's lungs and made his body seize. He gasped and sucked in water. Precious air exploded from his mouth and he scrambled to the surface. He broke through in an explosion of water droplets, the world spinning around him in dizzying arcs of shadowed cliffs and green canopies. He had just enough time to cough out water and inhale one lungful of air before the current dragged him under again.

He tried to keep his eyes open to look for Aspen, but it was a hopeless endeavor. Silver streams of current churned the riverbed and forced silt into his eyes, nose, and ears. He kept his lips pressed together to prevent air from escaping, but as his chest expanded with it and nearly burst, and his limbs thrashed with the need for fresh air, he knew he was fighting a losing battle. He needed to suck in something. *Anything.* The dark depths of the churning water filled his vision. His ears rung. His lungs heaved for air.

Let go. Let go, something whispered to him through the current. *You can let go.*

Tristan wanted so desperately to do that—the water was so

warm, the voice so soothing—but he couldn't. Something waited for him... Someone...

Aspen!

He fought for the surface again, but a hand caught his ankle. Something glowed on his skin, and then a flash shot through the water. A voice screamed, and the hand retracted like it had been burned.

"He is marked!" that same voice said, now wracked with pain.

Tristan barely heard the words. His vision had faded to nothing but a pinprick of light. The last of his breath shot from his mouth in a riot of bubbles. His limbs had gone numb.

And then there was air! He sucked it in greedily, his feeling and mind returning to him. He opened his eyes and found himself encircled by a cluster of beings covered in algae-colored scales with golden waves of hair. They regarded him with weapons of ice clutched in their webbed hands, their golden eyes cold and hostile.

"We are the guardians of this river," one said in a language hardly discernible from the rush of the river currents. It bore its fangs in a snarl. "You bear the mark of our sister naiads." He gestured to Tristan's ankle, where a white, glowing hand print stood out in stark relief against his skin. "For that, we are duty bound to give you air, but do not mistake that for a welcome."

Tristan tried to wrap his head around what that all meant. He shook his head free of the questions swirling there. They didn't matter. He had to find Aspen. "What about my friend? Have you given her air?"

"Your friend serves a greater purpose. Our Life Giver is weak, but shall be no more."

Tristan's eyes widened and his heart plummeted. "What?"

They didn't answer him. Instead, they clasped their hands together and chanted in a language that sounded like the ripples of a mountain lake. The rims of their irises glowed white. The water churned around Tristan, and before he could so much as protest, they shot him from the river in a pillar of water and deposited him on the banks, sopping wet. Coughing and fighting against his drenched clothes, he scrambled to his feet and ran downriver. If they hadn't given Aspen air...he didn't know how long she had been down there. He didn't want to think about it, but an icy dread had already clawed its way to his chest.

The naiads had disappeared back into the depths of the river, and Tristan saw no sign of Aspen. She *had* to be there somewhere.

And then he saw it. A pale, white-green glow, almost indiscernible from the rest of the river—magic from Aspen, the naiads, or both. Either of them would help him find her. He dove in, not sure what he intended to do after that. The air the naiads had granted him returned around him.

Through the murk, a huge plant emerged, nestled on the river floor and swaying in time with the currents. Thorn-covered vines wove together in intricate knots and forests while fish darted between them. It glowed white-green, its thorns nearly blinding with the light, and emitted spores of light into the river currents. Tristan's gut wrenched as he realized what it was.

Serpent root.

As the thought entered his mind, a group of naiads appeared, each with a grip on Aspen's limbs. She had a curtain of air around her and struggled against her captors, kicking and biting where she could. However, anytime she would get a limb free, her air bubble disappeared, and the naiads forced water into her mouth until she was clutching at her throat, her stomach and cheeks bloated from the onslaught. When they had hold of her again, they granted her air again. Water poured from her mouth and nose as she struggled to breathe, but then she would look at them with that determined fire in her eyes and try again.

As the group approached the serpent root forest, one naiad began to pray.

"Oh, Life Giver that grants us the magic to live in these peaceful waters far from the chaos of the surface, we bring thee nourishment."

They draped a wreath of serpent root about Aspen's neck and shoulders. The vine came alive and buried deep thorns into Aspen's collar bone, glowing green with her magic. All the color drained from her face, and she sagged between the naiads, spitting curses.

"We bring thee this life and magic, so that thou mayest protect us forevermore." They moved as one and approached the serpent root forest. The vines glowed brighter and reached hungry feelers out for her. She tried once more to wrench free, but the serpent root around her neck glowed brighter and she seized in pain.

"Aspen!" Tristan's cry echoed in the water, filling the entire river. Without thinking, he launched himself from a rock and propelled straight for Aspen. One naiad reached out to stop him. He twisted away, and his hand brushed her arm. She shrieked. The sound amplified a thousand fold in the water and ricocheted off the river banks. Tristan clapped his hands to his ears, lights flashing behind his eyelids.

The naiad sobbed and cradled her arm. Red blisters coated her scaled skin, hissing and festering with heat as if she'd been burned. "He's been marked!"

While the naiads were distracted, Aspen broke free of her other captors, but not fast enough. They hissed in unison, and her air bubble extinguished itself. She flailed, her lips turning bluer and her skin paler by the moment. She tried to swim for the surface, but the naiads dragged her down by her ankle. The fight left her bit by bit as she writhed for air.

Tristan panicked. His vision blurred and his mouth moved faster than his mind. "That's right, I'm marked!" He spread his arms wide and puffed out his chest, trembling with fear and adrenaline. "I will burn anyone who dares to lay a hand on me!" He thrust his hand forward and the creatures shied away. "Release the woman and return her to me. After you have done this, I will let you leave in peace."

"He wishes for us to steal from the Life Giver—from our god and maker." They all narrowed their eyes to dangerous slits, spears of water forming in their hands. "We would rather be burned."

Tristan cursed. He'd pressed his luck too far. He shoved himself off a nearby rock as they threw their spears at him. The spears hissed by in a curtain of searing bubbles, but they missed him. He shot through the middle of the naiads, brushing his hands along their skin to keep them at bay. They wailed and swam backward, forming new weapons. He got to Aspen and tried to breathe air into her, but the bubble around him didn't reach her. He had to get her to the surface.

"He will kill the Life Giver!" One naiad rushed him, burying a watery dagger into his bicep and ramming his shoulder into Tristan's stomach. The blow threw Tristan into the river's depths, trailing blood and wheezing as he tried to catch his breath, and he let go of Aspen. Another naiad seized her again and swam her back to the serpent root forest. The other naiads closed in around Tristan, circling and snatching at pieces of him. They tore his hair. Scraped their razor-edged weapons across his cheeks. Ripped his clothes. Jabbed more watery blades at him. He dodged most of them, sustaining only a few nicks here and there, but they had set up a curtain of currents that was slowly tightening a noose around him. Soon, he would have nowhere to go. He screamed in frustration as Aspen was taken further from him.

"Even if we cannot touch you," one naiad said, "you will pay for stealing from the Life Giver." A spear scraped the skin along Tristan's ribs, and he cried out. The naiad smiled. "We will keep you here, trapped in your air, until you die of thirst surrounded by water. You will then join your friend in the blessed embrace of our god."

They threw Aspen into the serpent root forest. Tristan screamed.

A body crashed into the midst of the fray and sent the creatures scattering. The binding currents around Tristan vanished. Someone grabbed him through the curtain of bubbles that had appeared. A flash of blonde. A pair of gold eyes. The moment they made contact, though, they recoiled in shock, their hands burned.

The bubbles parted and there was Styrax, surrounded in swirling currents and gaping at his hand. "You've been marked!" He grinned at Tristan, relief flooding his face.. "I thought you had drowned!"

Tristan smiled like an idiot, tears of his own relief flooding his eyes. "You have the *best* timing!"

The naiads banded back together, more weapons forming in their hands as they glared daggers at Styrax. Currents formed around them again, steaming with heat and venom and fury.

"We have been told of you, traitor," they said. "A thief who steals from his maker."

Styrax's smile faded. Something dangerous—almost feral—darkened his eyes. All the lines tightened along his jaw and mouth. He swam in front of Tristan and faced the naiads, currents fanning around him like a shield. "Get Aspen. I'll keep them busy."

Tristan wanted to protest—he couldn't leave Styrax on his own, not after what had happened with Aspen in the village—but realized he didn't need to. The river surged around Styrax like a team of horses waiting to be given their head. He emitted pure power—a lightning storm ready to be released, and ten times stronger than any of the other naiads. Styrax seemed to be an element incarnate, and Tristan watched him in awe.

Trusting in Styrax's care entirely, Tristan turned his back on the naiads and swam for Aspen.

"We will not allow this!" the naiads bellowed. Something exploded through the water and the shock of it sent Tristan tumbling forward in a spray of steaming bubbles. He didn't look back. Styrax would have it under control. He knew it.

He propelled himself forward, straining every muscle through his shoulders and back. Water streamed around his face and ears, too fast for anything under his own power. Styrax had to have been helping him.

One naiad blocked Tristan's way, guarding Aspen as she was pulled deeper into the serpent root. More light spores erupted from the forest and the naiads' skin glowed a deeper green, the magic around it growing. Tristan didn't care. He screamed a battle cry and shoved his hands into the naiad's face. It tried to dodge, but he snatched it by the arm. It shrieked and tried to wrench free. Tristan put his palm over its face. Scales melted, scorched flakes swirling away in the currents. It howled and struggled, but then went limp. Tristan couldn't tell if it was alive or dead. He should have felt some remorse, but right now he didn't care. He needed to get to Aspen.

"You would steal our livelihood too, oh lonely one?" a naiad asked Styrax with a growl, bleeding from a head wound. "Was one curse not enough for you?"

"The traitor cursed to wander the world of men in an unnatural body. How does it feel to be the only one of your kind? The banished abomination?" They sent a crushing, swirling current of water at Styrax. He nullified it with a cross current, which also washed away a hail of ice shards aimed at his heart.

Tristan made it to the serpent root. All he could see of Aspen was a few strands of hair and one pale hand. The rest had been pulled into the heart of the forest. He picked up a sharp rock and dove in after her, cutting his way through the vines to get to her. The naiads shrieked as if he were brutalizing them. He saw flashes as they tried to break through Styrax's barrier, but he held firm.

"Kill another Life Giver and you will lose all hope of redemption. Your probation will have been for naught. Are you prepared to be alone for eternity?"

"Better alone than a murderer!" Styrax said, veins popping on his forehead as he battled off their attacks. "Tristan! Do you have her?"

Tristan slashed the last piece of the vine to free Aspen and wrapped his arms beneath hers. "Yes!"

"Hold on! When you get to the surface, run fast and far!" Styrax thrust his hand up, and Tristan and Aspen shot away from the naiads like an arrow, straight for the surface.

Tristan erupted from the water, Aspen gripped tightly to him. He lugged her from the water as it churned behind him with Styrax's and the naiads' magic. Tristan laid Aspen flat and blew into her mouth with all the breath he could give. He then thumped on her chest, trying to force the water from her. She didn't move. Didn't breathe. Only laid there, silent, as the glowing serpent root around her neck faded.

"ASPEN!" He wrenched the serpent root off her and threw it back into the river. It trailed scarlet droplets of her blood. He shook her and blew into her mouth again. No. No, no, *no*. He couldn't have been too late. She couldn't be...Not after everything she had been through —everything *he* had put her through. She was too stubborn for that. This wouldn't be the end. Couldn't be.

A sob hitched in his chest. "Aspen, *come on!*" He blew one more time, praying to the same gods that had saved her from Sorren's magic. The silver ring around his neck brushed against his arm, glinting green.

For evergreens and aspen trees.

Water erupted from her throat and nose and she gasped herself awake, rolling over to vomit out the rest of her ordeal.

A sob broke through Tristan's throat. He crushed her to him. She tried to say something, but he held her too tightly. "You're all right. You're *okay!*" he said, as much for himself as for her. That had been too close.

He let her go and they sat back, sucking in air. Shock crept through Tristan's muscles and made him shake. Realization began to set in, seizing in his veins and making his heart skip a beat. They had almost *died*. If it hadn't been for Styrax, they would have—

The river exploded. Styrax flung from the water and landed with a sloshing thump against the river bank. He shakily got to his feet and noticed Tristan and Aspen. His face paled with dread. "What are you still *doing* here? I told you to get away!"

The river separated from the riverbed, floating and undulating like a serpent, its hide glittering in the first rays of morning sun. Water roared around the riverbed as it drained into the floating current. Fish dropped from it like so many silver coins. The naiads glowed white at its heart, whatever words they were chanting spilling over each other in a waterfall of syllables. The snake lashed out. It missed Styrax and crashed into the ravine wall. The cliff face crumbled. Tristan flung himself over Aspen to protect her from the worst of it.

"What's happening?" she shouted, her eyes not quite focusing. She pushed him off her and stood with shaking limbs.

"Magic!"

"Helpful!" She drew her sword, still uncertain on her feet, and faced the river, ready to fight. Her eyes threatened to roll back in her head, and blood oozed from her clammy, gray-tinted skin. She was in no condition to fight, but she stood her ground anyway. Tristan moved to her side.

Before they could do anything, though, an arrow thudded into one naiad's shoulder. The river snake careered away, thrashing as the naiads tried to right themselves.

"Take that, you slimy murderers!" Ash called from atop the ravine.

They hissed in response.

Styrax unburied himself from the rubble of the cliff-side, eyes glowing and hair whipping about him in a non-existent breeze. A current swept Aspen and Tristan up and carried them up the ravine walls, Styrax close behind. The naiads screamed and shot the water snake toward them. It bashed against them, driving them deeper and deeper into the ravine wall with every blow, but Styrax's magic shielded them from all but bruises.

And then they were up and away, skating across treetops on Styrax's magic. Styrax had grabbed Ash, and they all fled as the river reared its vengeful head. The wind whipped through their hair and leached moisture from their eyes. Birds erupted from the trees, shrieking in alarm. Bolts of water followed the group, mowing trees down in deadly sprays of water and splinters. Styrax dodged the direct hits, but all of them sustained gashes from the flying wood. The water snake did not pursue them.

"You have killed us, traitor!" it screamed in many voices merged in one. "With our Life Giver starved, we will perish, just as your mother and sisters have!"

Styrax gasped as if they had shot him. The water currents continued to churn beneath their group, but they turned sluggish and muddy. The snake river receded beneath the treetops, hissing curses as it went. A thunderous splash marked its final resting place back in the riverbed, and then all fell quiet. After it had been gone for more than a few heartbeats, Styrax lowered them to the ground. He staggered away from them, clutching his chest.

Tristan ran to him, supporting him beneath the shoulders. "Styrax, what happened?" he asked.

Styrax shook his head and righted himself. "Hand me Aspen."

Tristan wanted to argue, but he knew Aspen needed the help. She leaned, glassy-eyed and sagging, against Ash, unable to stand on her own. Tristan and Ash helped her over, and Tristan watched both Aspen and Styrax in concern.

If Styrax noticed, he ignored him. He asked Aspen to open her mouth. She did so sluggishly, eyelids drooping.

"You almost drowned," he said. "There will still be water in your lungs, and we need to get that out."

Aspen nodded. Styrax's eyes glowed white, and two globes of water oozed their way out of Aspen's throat. Styrax flung them away. "Good, that should be every—" His legs gave way beneath him, eyes rolling back in his head. Tristan caught him before he could fall. Styrax snapped back to consciousness and nodded his thanks.

"That's all I've got," he said breathlessly, sweat dripping down his brow. "Might be good to start some fires and take off your wet clothes."

"No-no fires," Aspen said. She shook her head as if clearing cobwebs and straightened a little. "We still don't know where Laire and that sorcerer are. They might find us."

"Architects have them all," Ash said with venom, wiping sopping hair away from her face. "At least I got a good shot at one of them."

Styrax nodded. "Bundle up with everything dry you have. Naiad waters have a way of sinking into the skin if you're not careful. Could freeze you from the inside out."

They paired off and left for relative privacy. Tristan peeled off his sopping pants and went to lift his shirt off. A cry of pain wrenched from his throat as his wounded shoulder lit on fire, the arrowhead grinding against muscle and bone. The cold water had numbed it, and he had almost forgotten it was there.

"By the *Architects*, Tristan, what is that?" Styrax wavered to his feet and marched to Tristan. His eyes widened when he saw the wound. "*Sit down* and let me look at that shoulder!"

"Can I put trousers on first?" he asked with a weak attempt at a smile.

Styrax pursed his lips and nodded.

"We're all a sorry lot, aren't we?" Tristan tugged on a dry pair with some effort and sat down.

Styrax said nothing, but his dour expression deepened.

Tristan tilted his head back and shut his eyes, a wave of nausea washing over him. Mother Night, he *hurt*. "Are you sure you're up for tending this? You're pretty spent."

In response, Styrax cut Tristan's tunic off and knotted it. "Bite on this."

Tristan did, and Styrax dug out the arrowhead and what remained of the shaft. Tristan screamed and clenched his teeth through at least three layers of the tunic before he blacked out.

When he came to again, he was drenched in cold sweat, but the worst of it was over. Styrax wrapped a bandage over the newly stitched wound, his jaw clamped tight. Tristan had never seen him so *angry*.

"Styrax, what—?"

It was as if he had broken open a dam. Styrax whirled on him, eyes blazing. "What kind of stupid, *idiot* thing did you think you were doing, jumping into the river like that?"

Tristan leaned back from his fury. "I-I was trying to help—"

"And did you consider the fact that there may have been other people more suited to the task? People that weren't injured or could, I don't know, *breathe underwater*?"

"I didn't think about it, I just sort of did…it." Tristan let the words trail off. He knew he wasn't helping himself.

Styrax looked ready to implode. "You're right! You *didn't* think, which is exactly the problem! You could have *died*!"

"But I didn't! I was marked!"

"But you didn't *know* you were! I don't think you even really know what it means!"

"Well, what does it mean?"

Styrax tore at his hair. "It means you were stupid enough to tangle with naiads before, and somehow lived to tell the tale!" He paced for a few minutes, breathing deeply. It looked as if he was trying to vent his anger out of his body before he exploded again. Finally, he sat down, pulling at his hair and head hung low. "You exhaust me."

Tristan studied his hands, feeling like a child that had just been scolded. His pride rankled a bit, but he knew it came from a place of genuine care and concern. He couldn't fault Styrax for that. "Styrax, I'm sorry."

Styrax scoffed, but some of the tension left his body. "You should be," he said. He looked at Tristan, his expression vulnerable. "You're the only friend I've got left." His lip quivered slightly. "And, apparently, now the only family, too. Please be more careful with yourself."

Tristan wanted to ask what he meant by that—what the *naiads* had meant—but Styrax seemed too fragile for that at the moment. Both he and Tristan needed some levity.

"What about Ash?" Tristan asked so that he didn't have to address his own feelings. He had been *terrified*, and it was nice to know that someone would care if he was gone. "Seems like you and she are a little more than friendly, or at least you'd *like* to be."

Styrax buried his face in his hands. "I should have just let you drown."

Tristan chuckled, trying to ignore the terrified lump in his throat and his pounding heart. It had all been far, *far* too close. He and Aspen would have both been dead if not for Styrax. He leaned forward and patted Styrax on the shoulder. "Thank you for saving us, really." He wished there was a better way for him to say it—to convey everything racing through his mind. It sounded too trite. Too easy.

Styrax lifted his head with a small smile. Tristan saw in his eyes that he had understood exactly what Tristan meant. "You're welcome." He leaned back on his palms, watching clouds pass overhead. "Just don't make me do it again."

THIRTY-TWO

Aspen waited for the two men to finish talking before she approached. She needed to thank them for risking so much for her but didn't want to interrupt. She'd already been enough of a burden recently as she recovered from the sorcerer's blight. It made her smile, though, to hear how similar their conversation had been to a one she and Ash had had only a few weeks ago. She and Tristan would give Ash and Styrax consecutive heart attacks one of these days.

When they finished and sat in silence for a few minutes, Aspen took that as her cue. She knocked on a tree trunk to announce her approach. "Tristan, Styrax, I wanted to—" She stopped dead in her tracks. The morning sun carved Tristan in copper outlines, shirtless and baring a scar that covered nearly half his torso. And there, resting against his chest, was a ring she had thought she would never see again.

Aspen took a step back, chest heaving as visions swam in her mind. A young boy escaped with his adoptive father from Monterro's burning on the Day of Bluest Blood, covered in blisters and fire wounds across his torso. The boy healed as he grew, and the scars faded, but they had always been there. For all the years she had known him.

And that ring. That ring she thought had failed her—had failed *him*. She had to get a closer look, but she couldn't bring herself to move. Her heart floated somewhere away from her body, unmoving, fearful, and hopeful all at once. Her magic flared with her emotions, and she battled them both back.

"What—?" She had to swallow to get moisture back in her throat. "What does that ring say?"

Tristan looked at her, thunderstruck. He grabbed the ring. "I don't...I don't know." He tilted his head, his eyes piercing. Searching. "How did *you* know—?"

Aspen shook her head and took a step back. No. No, she couldn't do this. *Wouldn't.*

She nearly turned and ran, but Tristan grabbed her by the arm, desperate. Her eyes glazed over his bare chest, taking in the scars. The scars she had seen thousands of times. How? How could this be? He had *died.* She had watched it happen; she still heard the sickening crack of his skull being split in two every time she fell asleep. This couldn't be real. It had to be a dream. It *had* to.

And yet, Tristan's breath brushed warm and real across her face. His hand gripped tightly around her arm—strong and firm—did not feel like a phantom. She looked up into his face, not daring to hope.

He glanced at his bare chest and took a step back, his cheeks pink. "Aspen, you have an idea, don't you?"

Please don't ask that. She felt vulnerable. Naked. Completely exposed to the elements. "Have an idea of what?" she asked, her voice barely above a whisper. Tendrils of green mist bled from her skin.

"Back at the beginning, you thought you might have known something about me. You asked me about my scar." He brushed his hand over his scalp. "I called you a monster, and we never spoke about it again, but I—"

Aspen choked on the lump in her throat, tears dangerously close to spilling from her eyes. She looked away, cursing herself and begging her heart to stop pounding so fast.

His face softened. He touched her shoulders and crouched to her eye level. "Who did you think I was?"

She battled back her emotions and forced herself to be neutral. Unreadable. Locked her heart away. "That is a treacherous road, Tristan. I'm not sure you want to see where it leads."

He chuckled, some of it strained, some of it genuine. "I've already got people cursing me and out to kill me. I'm not sure it can get more treacherous than that."

She hesitated still, and he put a hand over hers. "Aspen, please. I've lived my entire life in the dark. If you could shine even just a little light—"

"Come eat before you freeze to death out there!" Ash called.

Aspen sucked in a deep breath, both grateful and resentful for the interruption. The logical side of her wanted to get it over and done with. The emotional side needed time to prepare and insulate. She pulled her hand away from Tristan's. Her magic stopped leaking from her as she claimed control of her emotions again. "Fine. After we eat. But don't say I didn't warn you."

Their meal passed in tense silence. It took every ounce of Aspen's willpower to keep her knee from bouncing anxiously. She felt Tristan's eyes on her—felt his anticipation buzzing through the space between them—as he sat beside her, but she ignored him until they had cleared away bowls and Styrax and Ash wandered off. Styrax whispered something to Ash, and they both glanced back expectantly before disappearing around a corner.

Aspen didn't know where to start—didn't *want* to start. But it was not only her duty to tell him; it was his right to know. He had more than earned it.

She leaned forward and wrapped her arms around her knees. She couldn't look at him. Didn't dare as she tried to fight the living nightmares away. "Five years ago, the last surviving Prince of Loralan died."

Tristan sucked in a breath. It seemed he'd already picked up where this was going. She dreaded the questions she was sure he had, but if she stopped, she feared she wouldn't get started again. She braced herself for the onslaught, but he kept quiet, so she plodded on.

"Hit over the head with a mace. No chance of coming back from something like that." She gritted her teeth to chase away the phantom images of that night. "But the Rebellion could never find his body. Rumors circulated across Loralan that he was alive in such-and-such village or holed up deep in the mountains or some other nonsense."

Tristan blew out a long breath and shook his head. "Seems anyone will try to profit off another person's fame."

"Exactly," Aspen said, cursing all those frauds again for never allowing her time to heal. She rubbed her arms and bit the inside of her lip. "Someone had to find out if any of the stories were true, and the Rebellion assigned me." She couldn't keep the bitterness out of her voice.

Tristan tilted his head and leaned forward, elbows resting on his knees. He gave her a look that Ro had given her so many times before—concern, care, and attention—and her breath caught in her throat. "Why you?" he asked.

A hollow pain flared in Aspen's chest. Screams ricocheted behind her eyelids as a body dropped, blood spilling everywhere. She clenched her jaw and bid the images gone. "Because he was my best friend." Her lower lip trembled and she lowered her voice. If she put any sort of strain on it, it would break out from under her. "And I watched him die."

Tristan fell silent. They both did. They listened to the water run by, the whisper of branches overhead, and Styrax and Ash's chatter as they washed dishes. Aspen tried to breathe it all in. The peace. The calm. The world as it should be.

Tristan let out a heavy sigh, running his fingers through his hair and his knee bouncing. Aspen watched a thousand questions flash through his eyes, but he settled on one. "Does that mean I was one of your rumors?"

A corner of Aspen's mouth quirked in a smile. Tristan never had been one for silence. Neither had Ro.

"We got a tip. From Lady Vinea."

"*Lady Vinea?*" He leaned back in hollow disbelief, blinking shock from his eyes. "Why would she do that? She's married to a *general*! And why wouldn't she tell me?"

Aspen shrugged. "I couldn't say. War makes people do strange things." She touched her knee to his, giving him a small smile and hoping it reassured him. It simply ached for her. "But I can't blame her."

"Why do you say that?" he asked her quietly as if the words caught in his throat.

"Of the countless people I have found, you are the only one I really, truly believe could be our missing prince." She rubbed the base of her left thumb as it twinged. She felt the lumps of the scars there. "And I would *never* say that lightly."

Tristan sat back. Aspen watched a myriad of emotions filter across his face one by one. Disbelief. Fear. Hope. Anxiety. Dread. Relief. All the same emotions that churned in endless knots through Aspen's stomach.

Tristan sat that way for a long time. Aspen didn't dare say anything. She might betray how much she wanted—*needed*—for him to be Ro. For him to end her five-year search. For her to have her best friend back. The man she loved and lost returned to her when she least expected it. But he had to be certain. Not for her. For himself. And so she waited.

After a while, Tristan steepled his fingers and leaned forward, resting his lips against the side of his hands. He sighed deeply and looked over at her, still saying nothing. The morning light turned his hair to blazing strands of amber and gilded his face in glowing copper. More thoughts raced behind his eyes.

"Tristan, if you think any harder about this, I'm afraid your head might explode." Aspen tilted her head and leaned forward, a small smile on her face, trying to keep it steady for him. "Just tell me. I'm more resilient than you might think."

Tristan rubbed his face. She saw the aching in his eyes already. "Aspen, I...I don't know if I'm who you think. I have no proof for myself. And I'm not sure I believe Laire would be that cunning for so little payout."

Aspen watched him, keeping her expression unreadable even as his words drove daggers through her heart. She should have known never to hope. It would only lead to more hurt. "Will you tell me if you do get proof, one way or another?"

"Of course."

She stood and smiled at him over her shoulder, her heart shattering to pieces and her knees wobbling beneath her. "Then that's all I can ask from you. Don't feel pressure to be someone you're not. Find out who you are, and I will accept it either way." She moved to leave.

"Aspen, wait, I—"

"It's all right, Tristan. I'm fine. Really." Aspen strode through the camp, back straight, shoulders back, head high, and heart crumbling with every step.

"How did it go?" Ash asked after her.

Aspen barely heard it. "Going...scout." The effort to form the words almost overwhelmed her. She just had to make it to the tree line. The trees beyond it. The clearing beyond that. Far enough away for no one else to hear her.

"Aspen!"

She ignored Tristan's cries after her and melted into the shadows. The moment she was free of prying eyes and ears, her knees collapsed beneath her. She hugged her ribs as shaking, ugly sobs tore through them. The crush of dead leaves, grass, and mushrooms swirled beneath her as the trees loomed over her. All sound ceased except for the roar of emotion in her ears. She couldn't breathe, couldn't move, could only drown in her spill of tears as her magic pooled around her in waves of agony.

"Sister Earth," she curled into herself, grinding her boots into the dirt. "Please-Please. I-I ca-an't." Her words came out in pathetic hiccups as she gasped for breath. "Not again."

Birds cooed, and the trees sighed. The setting sun pierced the canopy and warmed her back while a cool breeze whispered across her skin. Peaceful. Calm. A mockery of the chaos raging through her heart.

"Please," she could barely croak out the whisper. "If you've given him to me only to tear him away again, I—" She what? What would she do? Cry? Wither away? Keep marching on in this useless game of life? No. No, she would not. She had been beaten and broken before, far worse than this, and she would rise above it.

She gritted her teeth, cursed, and pressed her fists to the ground to force herself up. She swiped at her cheeks and brushed off her knees, jaw clenched tight. She paced the clearing, breathing in and out as long and even as she could, trying to force feeling into her numb, empty limbs. It didn't matter what she wanted. The world would move on, with or without her. She had a duty to fulfill. And she had promised to see it through. A chipped cup could still hold water. A broken-hearted body could still work.

"Aspen, there you are!"

Aspen froze. Her exterior nearly cracked again; currents of emotion fighting to break free. Why? Why *him*? Couldn't he have left her alone for even just a few moments?

She didn't look. Didn't move. Just melted into the shadows as she had done thousands of times before, waiting to be overlooked and forgotten about. Then she could be left in peace.

Tristan found her and touched her shoulder. "Are you all right? I —" He stopped when he saw her face. His brows furrowed in worry and regret. "Aspen…"

"I'm fine," she said on reflex, the words snapping like a released bowstring. To his credit, he didn't laugh, though he had every right to. The lie was so blatant. So ridiculously untrue. He could see it. She felt it in every fiber.

His face softened. He released his grip on her shoulder and sat down, back against a log. He left an open space for her but didn't force her to sit. "Is this about the…about your friend?"

Aspen shut her eyes and tilted her head back until the ends of her hair brushed her arms. "You know, I almost liked it better when you asked me pointless, mindless things."

"I mean, I could ask you if stars were really just fairies that flew too high."

Aspen kept her eyes shut, imagining a younger self, bantering with her best friend beneath a canopy of gold. "And I would say yes, only because you are far too trusting."

He chuckled. "That's fair. I am the one that asked a perfect stranger if I could come with her and her shifty cousin to some far off place that I *still* don't know is real."

Aspen scoffed, letting the sun dry her cheeks. A noose of guilt clenched her gut. "Do you regret it? Coming with us?"

"Not at all."

Aspen looked at him. Saw the clouds reflected in his eyes as perfectly as they hung in the sky. Her heart both writhed and warmed in her chest. She had seen that attentive look so many times before; she had watched that face as they had talked about everything under the sun, from the best strain of pea vines to the future and what they hoped to see in it. How could it be possible for him to be anyone other than Ro? But the doubt, the wounds that ached from so many other betrayals, still burned within her. She couldn't afford to trust anything to faith or chance. She would be torn apart otherwise.

She finally sat next to him, their shoulders barely brushing. She couldn't look him in the eye and instead studied the branches dancing in the wind—bobbing, weaving, and lulling her into a false sense of peace.

"I wish I could give you a better answer," Tristan said finally.

Aspen smiled slightly to herself. Never could stand the quiet.

"I know how important the prince is to the rebellion. And I gather he meant something a lot more to you, but…" Tristan ran his hands through his hair and puffed out an exasperated breath. Another gesture that ached with familiarity. "I don't know, Aspen. I've lived five years without a shred of idea who I was. I'm getting bits and pieces of something, maybe, but nothing substantial to go off. I don't want to be wrong. I don't want to disappoint you."

"You would be the first to care about that," Aspen said, amazed at the bitterness that still lurked in the back of her throat.

Tristan stewed on that for a moment, his jaw tight with remorse as he traced circles in the dirt with his fingers "It must have been difficult, getting your hopes up about finding the prince, only to have them crushed each time."

"It was." Aspen fought back the lump that had reformed in her throat. "It still is."

"I'm sorry to add to that."

Aspen gave him a smug look. "If it makes you feel any better, you are the one I hate the least."

Tristan snorted. "I don't know why. I was rotten garbage to you."

"Perhaps." Aspen bumped his shoulder. "But, from what I've heard, even rotten garbage can redeem itself every now and again."

He smiled at that, and they fell into silence again. Tristan studied his hands, twining and untwining his fingers. "Will you be angry with me? If I'm not him?"

Yes. Was her gut reply. But she couldn't be. She knew she couldn't be. Not with him. Not after everything they'd been through. "You can't help who you aren't." She stood and brushed herself. "But I want you to know, that whoever you *do* end up being, you're all right in my eyes."

Tristan gaped at her, moisture brimming in his eyes. He cleared his throat and rubbed the nape of his neck, his cheeks pink. "Thank you," he said with a small smile. "That means a lot more than I think you know."

CHAPTER

THIRTY-THREE

Their training continued over the next several days as an impenetrable anvil of obsidian, lightning-laced clouds drew further into view. Tristan continued to improve with every round of sparring with Ash and Styrax cheering him on, but he felt a slip in Aspen's focus. She slept less, toying over and over with her stack of parchment and glancing at the storm system every moment she could spare. Her anxiety was palpable, and Tristan felt it building in him as well. They were nearly to the Dragon Scales—the place he'd recover his lost memories. Or at least he hoped. Dread clawed through his mind as he realized that he had no plan for after they made it there. What if it didn't have the answers he was looking for? What if it had too *many* answers; ones he didn't like? What if he'd been a murderer? Or a cheat? Or someone that nobody cared about? The thoughts tightened in his chest until he couldn't breathe anymore.

But then Aspen would ask him a question, Styrax would joke about something, or Ash would make a face, and then all of his anxieties would quiet. It didn't matter who he was in the Dragon Scales. It didn't matter that he didn't have a plan in place for the aftermath. He would figure it out. And they would all be there to help him.

He had finally started to use the journal Aspen gave him as well. Ever since he had left the gold ring behind, his nightmares had stopped. No more monsters. But, also, no more of the hazy images that came with them. So, instead, he filled it with his day-to-day memories. If he found nothing at the Dragon Scales, at least he would have those to remember forever.

The sun shrank early behind the black wall of storm one night. It reached higher than Tristan could see—an impossible, swirling, endless, looming tapestry of a vengeful storm. Lightning arced across the billowing, pulsing black clouds in silver and purple. When he stopped to listen, Tristan heard the gales' keening howls that shaped the clouds beneath their clutches. The sky and earth rumbled in a dissonance that wracked his frame. His heart stopped pounding in his chest. They had made it.

Aspen called an immediate halt, her face tinged green. "We're here."

Ash dug out rations and Styrax settled in next to Tristan, watching the storm with careful, reverential awe.

"We're going into *that*?" As heroically as he tried otherwise, Tristan's voice cracked when he gestured to the Pit manifested.

Aspen set her knapsack down and rolled her neck and shoulders out. She flexed her back with a grimace, pointedly avoiding looking at the storm. "The storm will clear in the next few days. We'll enter the valley it leaves behind when it's gone."

Tristan watched the storm while a maw of dread ate his stomach. What in Sister Earth's name would convince someone to ever go into that madness? What had convinced *him* all those years ago?

Styrax bumped Tristan's shoulder. "You sure it's still worth it?"

Tristan chuckled weakly. "Ask me again when I see what 'gone' looks like."

Aspen cinched her sword tighter about her waist, her face set in grim lines. "The land's constantly torn apart near the entrance. I'll need to find a safe path now so we don't waste our precious clear-sky time." She cast a glance at Ash in an aside. "Considering how accommodating their last gatekeeper was, I imagine we'll need every precious second."

"I'll go with you." Ash jumped to her feet. She almost hid her wince when she put pressure on her injured leg.

Aspen didn't look at her. "No, you're still injured."

Ash laughed, a bark of incredulousness. "*You* are talking to me about injuries? General Everything-I-Touch-Tries-To-Kill-Me?"

Aspen rolled her eyes. "I'll be *fine*, Ash. I had an excellent healer."

"*I'll* be fine, too! It's only a twisted ankle!"

Aspen didn't argue, but still stubbornly refused to look at her cousin. Ash thwacked Aspen over the head with her quiver of arrows. "Aspen—Sister Earth, help me—I let you get away with *so much,* but going down there by yourself will not be one of them!"

Aspen whirled to face her in disbelief, eyes alight with indignant rage. "Did you just *hit* me with your quiver? Are we children, now?"

"*You're* certainly acting like one, you stubborn, infuriating—"

Tristan stepped in before he could help himself. If they let this go on for too long everyone would end up with bruises, both to body and pride. "What if *I* go with her?" he asked.

"*No!*" Aspen said with a flash of...panic?

Tristan put up a conciliatory hand. A smirk threatened at the corner of his lips. "Well, Sister Earth, if I'd be a *burden*—"

"No, no." Ash stopped him with a hand. "I think that's an excellent idea," she said. She raised a defiant eyebrow at Aspen.

Aspen muttered a curse and turned to leave pointedly without Tristan, but Ash caught her arm again. "It'll be fine. You're just looking around."

Aspen pressed her lips together. A look of regret weighed on her eyes. "I've heard that before."

Ash's face softened. "Aspen..."

Aspen touched Ash's arm. "I'll take him with me, but only

because we don't have time to argue." She adjusted her sword belt again with a sigh and looked at Tristan. "Are you ready?"

Tristan reared back. She was letting him go? Without a ten-minute argument beforehand? Strange, uncertain times were upon them.

He mutely dogged Aspen's heels as they left the camp's relative safety to approach the impenetrable mass of a storm. Only someone like Aspen would *ever* get him to be so harebrained and reckless.

Says the man that asked 'monsters' if he could travel with them.

"Stay close to me," Aspen said over her shoulder. "The winds change frequently. They can sweep you into the storm if you're not careful."

"Oh, great." Tristan couldn't help but wonder if he should have stayed back at camp.

Aspen clambered over broken ground and upended trees as if she had seen them a thousand times. Much as Tristan had expected to struggle, he kept pace with Aspen step for step. A...*something* pulled on his mind. Lingering. Achingly familiar yet distant all at once. Anticipation and dread roiled in his stomach. He had *been* here before. No mistake. Something about the way the trees twisted and the boulders split and the absolute silence save for the storm's omnipresent wailing created a feeling of déjà vu so complete he felt barely tethered to reality.

Tristan absently brushed the scar on his scalp. Something horrific had happened to him here, but he only felt the electric spark of excitement leap through his body. Would he finally, truly remember himself? If even a piece? Anything to get him on a path toward home and family and history.

"You still with me?" Aspen called over her shoulder.

Tristan blinked. He hadn't realized how far his daydreams made him lag. "Sorry! I'm coming!"

Aspen waited for him. When he got closer, she nodded to the monster storm. "Do you think you'll find what you're looking for down there?"

"I hope so, once the storm clears."

Aspen was quiet for a moment. She stopped and turned to him, face soft with empathy. "And if you don't?"

A pit dropped in Tristan's stomach. The thought of leaving the valley with nothing to show for it still filled him with dread. It made his chest and teeth ache. "I'm...I'm not sure," he said.

Aspen parted a cracked, low-hanging branch aside and motioned him through. "I won't pretend my opinion counts for much, but you are welcome to stay with us." She gave him a rare, small smile. "No matter who you end up being."

Tristan's heart thumped once, hard, in his chest before it stopped completely. "Thank...Thank you," he stammered. He didn't know what else to say. What *could* he say to someone that had freely offered him a home if he wanted it? Had he known how much hearing that from her would mean to him? Absolutely not. It pierced soft and deep and threatened moisture in his eyes. He blinked it back. "I'll consider that."

Aspen nodded once, satisfied. Only when she turned to proceed down the topsy-turvy mountain path did he notice her hands shook.

"Aspen, are you all right?"

She stopped and sighed, shoulders slumping. With a groan, she shook her head. "No, there's something—" A gasp of pain tore through her throat. Her back arched—nearly snapping her in half—and she staggered forward. "The sword—" she said, the word a gurgle in her throat. "Tristan, run!" She fell to one knee but drew her sword in time to parry a bone-white sword that had every intention of slicing her back to ribbons. Even with her miraculous defense, her spine still arched as if it had been hit. Her arms quivered. Somehow, she shoved the swordsman away. Barely.

"Laire!" Anger and fear stormed through Tristan in fiery knots.

Laire ignored him and lunged at Aspen like a wounded, trapped saber. The white sword hissed in a deadly arc. The air snapped around it as if recoiling from its touch. Aspen moved her sword to parry the attack, even as her back arched away from the blade. In that vulnerable position, she had no chance of stopping the blow. It'd slice clean through her.

"Aspen!" A noise somewhere between a grunt and a battle cry tore itself from Tristan's throat as he bunched his legs beneath him and leapt between Laire and Aspen. He faced the sword with the flat of his dagger and shoved his other hand to the back of his blade for support, fingers curled in, knuckles pressed against the metal. The white sword hummed a funeral dirge as it fell toward him.

"Tristan, *move!*" Aspen tried to lurch for him but crumpled.

Laire saved Tristan. He faltered in shock at Tristan's sudden appearance, and that hesitation dampened the power behind the swing. The sword's smooth edge clanged off Tristan's dagger and harmlessly deflected to the side, but the blow's impact sent a devastating jolt through Tristan's arm that left it numb and practically useless. Tristan staggered back, clutching his arm to his side. He maintained his grip on his dagger.

Aspen forced herself to her feet and leapt in front of Tristan. "*RUN!*" She shoved Tristan in front of her and they took off. "*Sweet Sister Earth, what were you thinking?*" she asked as she vaulted between boulders, checking over her shoulder for pursuit. "You could have lost your arm!"

Tristan knew about as much as she did. His body had moved on its own. He shrugged wryly, his breath ragged, but immediately regretted it when his arm shot agony through him. "Got caught up in the moment, I guess. It's been a while since I've been to a good sword fight."

"You *will not* stop me again!" Laire screamed. He barreled through the trees leapt for them. Aspen braced herself and took his blow head-on. Tristan jammed his shoulder into Laire's midriff. Air exploded from Laire's lungs and he flew back, tangling himself in the trees.

"That won't hold him for long. Be ready." Aspen dragged him away again, her brows furrowed in stern lines. "And you don't bring a *knife* to a sword fight."

"I'll remember that the next time I own a sword that hasn't been tossed into a river."

A small, reluctant smile tugged at the corners of Aspen's lips. "You do that. LOOK OUT!" She skidded to a stop, rocks clattering over down the edge of a cliff. She cursed and shoved Tristan away from the edge, stepping closer to him as her attention flicked between Laire and the surrounding trees. They were trapped. "Stay close to me," she said under her breath. "That sorcerer can't be far behind."

With Tristan's shoulders pressed against hers, Tristan realized how clammy Aspen's skin felt. Cold sweat beaded down her neck and back. "Are you all right?"

She let out a coarse, humorless chuckle. "Not particularly." She motioned with her shoulder to Laire, who had finally freed himself. "It's that cursed sword. It's what he wounded me with during a skirmish at the Dragon Scales five years ago, and now I can't get anywhere near cursed galatite without feeling like I'm getting torn open all over again."

Tristan's world ground to a halt. The edges of his vision blurred. No. No, it couldn't be. It couldn't have been so simple. Couldn't have been in front of him this whole time. He forgot how to breathe. "Did you say *five years ago* at the Dragon Scales?"

Aspen didn't have time to respond. Purple flames arced from the trees, and Sorren let out a battle roar that clashed against the thunder as he leapt from the shadows, encircled by tongues of lightning. The lightning thrummed through the air like thousands of bow strings released in sync. Laire joined him and charged. Aspen threw Tristan to the ground and met the attack head on. She caught Laire's blade on her own. Sorren's lightning missed her, but he drew a knife and stabbed her in the hip. Blood welled from the wound and trickled down her side.

Still holding off Laire, arms shaking from the strain, Aspen twisted her body and disengaged, kicking Sorren in the midsection. He folded like a broken marionette. His knife dropped from his hand.

Aspen kicked it to Tristan as Laire came at her again. "Tristan, take it!"

Tristan numbly wrapped his fingers around the knife's hilt and extracted himself from the skirmish. He stood shakily, trying to get his racing mind under control. He should have known. Should have put the pieces together the moment Laire had admitted to cursing him. But he had hoped that maybe something about that kindness, that home, hadn't been a lie.

Laire and Aspen charged each other, sparks flying from their blades and teeth grit in snarls. Flashes of images bombarded Tristan's mind with each spark that flew. They echoed the fight in front of him. Swords clashing. Hundreds of them. A night that roiled with screams and grunts and the steam of warm bodies and steaming blood. The trees rustling around him turned to the distant crash of waves. A familiar voice screamed his name. Blinding, twisting, crushing pain in his skull. He cried out and clutched his head as his brain twisted itself in knots, trying to fit the disjointed images into one cohesive whole.

"Tristan! *Tristan!*"

Tristan. Was that his name? He didn't know. Another name knocked against his skull, but he couldn't quite catch it. It sounded the same. Or maybe the voice calling it sounded the same.

"TRISTAN! Look out!"

Tristan snapped from his trance, but too late. His foot slipped on a loose rock, and he tumbled down the mountainside. Uprooted trees, fractured rocks, nettles, branches, and bushes—he hit them all on the way down. He lost count of how many times he blacked out from the pain.

He reached the bottom with a final thud. Dust billowed out around him. Groggy and still miraculously alive, he struggled to his feet. His body did not keep quiet about the beating he had put it through. Broken ribs. Twisted ankle. Splitting headache. He wheezed and groaned.

The wind howled through his ringing ears and plucked at his

clothes. Shards of rain pelted against his skin, and the air grew thicker and harder to breathe. Without even looking, he knew.

He'd fallen to the edge of the storm.

"Tristan!" Aspen barreled down the slope like a deer. Tristan had no clue how she kept her footing. Laire and Sorren weren't far behind, more magic following her down the slope.

When Aspen reached the bottom, she snatched Tristan's hand. "We have to get out of here!" she yelled over the howling wind. "I can't hold them off forever, and you're in no shape to help me!"

Sorren flung himself at Aspen. Still disoriented and reeling from his fall and the images flashing through his mind, Tristan tripped over his feet to avoid their tangle and fell flat on his back.

Aspen fell beneath Sorren's weight and landed on her chest, striking her jaw on the ground. Sorren drove another dagger through her shoulder, searing magic arcing across the blade, and anchored it to the ground. She tried to writhe free, her eyes clouded in agony, but to no avail.

"Aspen!" Tristan blinked back the images still flooding his senses and moved to get to her, but Laire seized him and hauled him to his feet.

Laire double-checked to make sure Aspen wouldn't interfere. She snarled at him, and Sorren, sitting on her back, smashed her face into the ground. Tristan instinctively moved to jump to her aid, but Laire tightened his grip on him. "You are a difficult man to catch."

Tristan balled his fists. "You didn't think that the night you dragged me from a battlefield, did you? The same night you wounded a young woman with a black sword on the plains of the Dragon Scales?"

Aspen froze in her struggle against Sorren and looked at Tristan, wide-eyed. Not breathing. The question she didn't dare ask was frozen on her lips. Laire said nothing, his face impassive, but Tristan saw the guilt build behind his eyes.

Ire flooded through Tristan. His limbs shook and his muscles spasmed in revolt against the skin that kept them caged. All the world disappeared except for Laire; the man that had kept him in the dark, lied to him, and made him believe he had no purpose and no place in the world, other than to serve the vision Laire had dreamed for him. The man he had told Styrax could *never* have been the one to curse or abuse him in any way. He gritted his teeth until he saw red and clenched his fists.

"Let me go," he growled.

Laire tightened his grip on his arm. "I can't do that, Tristan. You're sick. Once we get this all straightened out, then—"

Tristan twisted his arm out of Laire's grip and threw him bodily to the ground. Laire recovered quickly and charged at him. Tristan scooped up Aspen's fallen sword and parried Laire's attack. Before Laire could regain his equilibrium, Tristan went on the offensive and rained blow after blow. He remembered the training sessions he and Aspen had had over the past several weeks, but he also pulled on the knowledge he'd had long before any of that. The lessons learned from the vague figure of a man surrounded by a golden glow, radiating kindness and love and patience. The hours of forgotten hard work that had trained his body to a point where it no longer had to rely on lessons and memory; it felt and knew what to do on its own.

Sorren tried to leap in, more magic gathering around him, but Laire called him off. "We can still bring him home!" he said, his eyes manic. "He can still serve his purpose!'

"Go to the *Pit!*" Tears of frustration and anger welled in Tristan's eyes, accumulated over the past five years. He ground his teeth as he continued to pummel against the man that had kept everything he cared about away from him. The man that had touted family and bonds and loyalty. All he had ever wanted was to know who he was. He wanted the vague impressions—the feelings and images that were *almost* there—to become his again. He wanted to know about where he came from; who raised him, who he loved, and who loved him. But he knew nothing. The only person who had had any sort of link to it stood in front of him and, despite knowing how desperately he wanted—*needed*—to know, refused to tell him.

Laire had refused to even acknowledge he'd had a past to begin with.

Laire took one misstep—fumbled briefly over a dead branch that didn't immediately crack beneath his weight—and Tristan had him. He knocked Laire's sword out of his grip. Tristan pressed to his advantage and took three steps toward Laire. Laire backed away from the weapon to avoid getting skewered through the neck. Tristan planted the white sword, tip first, into the dirt. He motioned with his head to where Aspen still laid pinned beneath Sorren. "Move."

Laire hesitated. His attention darted between Tristan and the bone-white blade.

Tristan reared back his head and straightened his shoulders, his grip tight on Aspen's sword. "I command you to *move!*" His voice cracked over the group like a great boulder broken from its mountain to crush everything beneath it. Laire's eyes widened. He did as he'd been told, but fury radiated off him. When they got next to Aspen and Sorren, Tristan motioned with his sword arm. "Sorren, release her now, or I kill Laire."

"Don't do it, whelp," Laire snarled. "Release her, and we've lost him forever."

Sorren paled, his eyes darting between Tristan and Laire. "You have to go home to Lady Vinea," he said quietly to Laire. He removed the dagger without question.

The moment she was free, Aspen lurched and threw Sorren off her back. A swift kick to the head knocked him out cold. Tristan winced.

Tristan angled himself to become a barrier between Aspen and Laire as she gingerly regained her footing. She stood at Tristan's shoulder, not quite touching, but leaning toward him in case she needed additional support. Her breath came out pained and ragged. She sagged lower with every passing moment. Blood seeped between her fingers as she clutched at her injured arm. She needed medical attention. But Tristan couldn't leave Laire and Sorren. That would put them all in danger again.

"Tell me about that night, Laire." Tristan tightened his grip on the sword hilt. "Tell me about where and how you found me." He swallowed. "Tell me who I am."

Laire regarded him. "Careful boy," he growled. "Much more of this, and I won't be able to take you back alive."

"I'm not going back. *Never* again!"

Laire met his eyes. A shroud fell over them, gray and dead and dangerous. He said nothing.

Tristan pulled on the leather strap around his neck in aggravation. He was *so close* to the memories he'd ached to recover for ages. The key had been dangled in front of him, yet he couldn't quite reach it. "Where did I come from?"

Still, Laire said nothing.

Tristan stepped into him. He pressed the blade so tightly against the skin on his neck it drew blood.

"Tristan," Aspen warned.

Tristan ignored her, even though he knew he'd put himself in more danger by coming so close to Laire. "WHO AM I?"

Laire looked at him with nothing but pity and regret. "A fool." He lunged and latched onto Tristan's wrist. "You've given me no choice." He hissed. *"Betliaoter!"*

Someone screamed; not Tristan, but Sorren. He convulsed, agony and foam torn from his lips as he sobbed and clutched his head.

Tristan whirled on Laire. "What did you—" The words seized in his throat like hands strangling him from the inside. He collapsed with a gurgling gasp as Aspen's sword dropped from his hand. The voice he thought he had banished forever roared to life like some primordial beast from the Pit itself. It rampaged through his mind and tore away the tiny fragments of memory pieces he had collected, eating them until nothing but emptiness remained. It replaced those memories with fear, terror, and hatred. Blood, carnage, and shrieks for revenge with monsters prowling in the shadows filled him, gobbling his memories and smiling at his despair while they licked their bloodless, cracked lips. Every muscle in Tristan's body seized as he tried to curl away from the fear. Or hide. Or run. His body refused to do any of those things. He couldn't flee from his own mind, even as the monsters razed it around him. He choked on the smoke of his burnt memories and screamed at the fear and pain and loneliness and his inability to escape any of it.

Someone snatched him beneath the arms, their grip tight and cruel. He lashed out, seeing only the toothy, spindly-limbed, wide-eyed demons closing in on him, reaching with their knobby, hooked finders for his heart. He struck something hard, like a cheekbone. None of the monsters were fazed. Their grins widened and their bodies expanded. He was slowly, torturously losing himself, bit by bit, and he had no tools or means to stop it. He could only watch as his life went up in flames around him and danced away as ash in the wind.

"Just remember, I had no other choice."

With a heave, whatever had grabbed hold of him threw him into a wall of pounding water, suffocating wind, and roiling earth. And Tristan could do nothing to stop it.

THIRTY-FOUR

The world slowed to a stop as Aspen watched Tristan disappear into the storm. Her heart stopped beating. Her breath caught in her chest and expanded until she nearly burst. The screams. The blood. The pain and death and agonizing heartbreak. It all flooded through her again and rooted her to the spot. She had failed. She had failed again and had everything ripped from her. She couldn't stop it. Couldn't fight it.

"NO!" Aspen picked up her sword. Blood flowed from her shoulder and the earth swayed beneath her feet, but she bared her teeth and clenched her sword's hilt. No. No, she would not let it happen again. She would not lose anyone else ever again. "What did you do to him?"

Laire drew his sword from the dirt—the sword that had hovered on the edge of Aspen's mind every waking moment and in every tinge of her scar. He laughed, the sound manic and inhuman. His eyes blazed with madness. The boy he had brought with him writhed on the ground, clutching his head in agony as his mouth gaped open in a silent scream.

"He's gone." Laire clenched and unclenched his fist around the cursed blade's hilt. "My bargaining piece...my future. Their future. Gone. Just gone. All gone." He repeated the phrase in a manic loop. He paced two steps forward and one step back in an endless circle.

Aspen tried to inch around him, but anytime she had a clear path to the storm he lurched in her direction, tearing at his hair and giggling to himself. She couldn't get close enough to disarm him. The mere presence of his sword served well enough to ward her off. One step too close and she would be immobilized, and then her death would follow in short order. Her heart slammed against her ribcage, and her thoughts raced.

She planted her feet and breathed deep. *Think, Aspen. Think. Don't panic.*

Every moment in the storm exposed Tristan to more danger. She had to get to him, and quickly. She would do whatever it took.

Laire stopped his circles. His unbridled, manic energy had subsided. Instead, it focused on one point. Aspen.

Aspen's neck prickled. She had seen that look on the battlefield before. Had *felt* it in her own heart. The look of someone that had lost all hope, and would drag everything to the Pit with them.

"*You.*" He advanced on Aspen, his sword now sure in his grip. "It's always been you. You stop me. You get in my way. *WHY?*" He swung his sword for emphasis, too far to reach Aspen. "I just want to take care of my family! That night, you warned the rebels, didn't you? You couldn't just die. You had to be *noble.*"

Aspen backed away from him, teeth clenched. He was too close. Her back was aflame. She growled as she watched the distance widen between her and the storm.

"And now *this!*" Laire flung his arms wide. "I didn't have to destroy him. It was *your* doing. You destroyed my family's future!"

"*You* threatened *mine!*" Aspen spat with as much venom as she could muster. "*Your* choices led you here, not mine." Pinpricks of light danced beneath her eyelids, and her head swam. She didn't know how much blood she had lost. Her sword drooped farther every second. *Not yet! We can still fight!* "*You* all started this war.

Leave the Ancient Races alone and maybe the bloodshed and ruined lives can end!"

"You know nothing about me!" He bore down on her with more fury than Aspen had ever seen in any mortal. "You struck first!" He swung at her head. She glanced it off the flat of her blade. "You're all a poison on this earth and I will purge it of your stain!" A sweep at her stomach. She lurched back. "I won't let you touch my family again!" Blow after blow rained on Aspen. Lightning flashed each time their blades met.

Aspen bit her lip until it bled, battling the pain more than the man. Every flash of his blade was another memory. Another nightmare. Arrows flying through the eerily quiet gray-dawn morning. The wordless thuds of bodies falling beside her. Screams and blood and wishes for death. Her wishes. A monster with a blade of bone that should not have been there. Not unless someone had betrayed them. The man was surrounded by hordes, all bearing down on three resolute figures. Bearing down on the people she had been assigned to protect and lead. She had been the only one left. She would not let that happen again.

A battle cry welled from Aspen's stomach, fueled by the emotions she had trapped for so long—rage, fear, regret, pain, loneliness. She pushed back against her attacker and banished the paralyzing thoughts. She ignored the agony in her back and fought. Blow after blow after blow, she bent him back. She was not the girl she had once been. She had faced death and terror and loss and she had still somehow made it this far. She would not let this journey end here. Not when others needed her help. No matter how deeply her limbs shook and how much terror had taken root in her chest. Just one swing. And then another. Another and another and another. That was the only thing she could afford to focus on. Individual steps in an intricate, flowing dance.

Laire was unprepared. His eyes widened as he stumbled back under her constant onslaught. "You should be paralyzed! This sword's curse should drive you to your knees!" Aspen smelled the fear on his breath.

Her back shrieked in agreement as if it intended to tear itself in two. Aspen battled back the agony straining in her throat. "You are not the first one to tell me what I should be," the words cut through her clenched teeth. "And you will not be the last one I have proven wrong."

She did something absolutely, unquestioningly stupid. Ignoring feeling, ignoring logic, she barreled straight for him. A mad dash she had laughed at Tristan for. His smug face, if he could see her now, would be unbearable.

Laire had no time to react. He screamed when she cut a gash in his abdomen. He flailed at her, hugging his wound, and she knocked the sword from his hand. It skittered away, too far from reach for him to retrieve it.

Laire screamed again and kicked gravel into Aspen's face. She shut her eyes against it. Through the space between her lashes, she saw him throw his full body weight at her. She sidestepped to safety, her eyes still closed. Laire roared and whirled back to her. He lunged again and missed a second time. Mostly. He snagged a chunk of Aspen's hair and wrenched her head back. The cracks in her neck shot all the way through her skull and down her spine. She tore herself free—a chunk of her hair left in his fist.

Lightning arced from the storm system and struck between Aspen and Laire. They fell to their knees, blinded with ears ringing. Aspen forced herself to her feet again. Her sword buzzed. She swayed on her feet and desperately tried to blink the swimming purple, blue, and white stains from her eyes. Where was Laire? *Where was he?* She couldn't see him. Maybe he had been vaporized?

Someone plowed into her like a massive wagon horse. She plunged forward. Her ankle snapped. Her sword skittered from her hand. Meaty fists clenched around her windpipe.

"You were supposed to die that day," Laire said, breath putrid in her face. He grinned as Aspen tore at his hands. She couldn't get a proper grip. "This time, I'll make sure of it. I'll watch your life drain away, and then I'll break your neck for good measure."

Aspen's left hand continued to snatch uselessly at Laire's while the other reached for her sword. Too far. It was too far. Just a finger's width away. Blackness encroached on her vision. Her body buzzed and fizzed. Sleep crept through her bones.

No. *No!* Tristan! He needed her! He was caught in the storm by himself. She reached for the raging wall of gales, willing herself to crawl there. A gurgling, unintelligible sound fell from her mouth as tears slid down her face.

Laire leaned close. His words hissed in her ear. "He's gone. Even if you survived, and even if you found him, he'd still be gone. His mind has been destroyed, torn apart from the inside." He pushed his thumbs against her jaw and forced her to look at Sorren. The boy foamed at the mouth and mumbled unintelligibly, his body locked and spasming. "That is all that will be left of him. The only thing he'll be good for is death. I'll present him to the king as another offering. Another trophy. The pathetic end to the pathetic blood of King Salaith."

His words flew like flies through molasses in Aspen's mind. Something important was there. She knew it. But she couldn't force herself to grasp the meaning of his words, though he seemed to think they should have an effect on her. She'd already spent too much effort to keep herself conscious.

Laire hummed to himself. "But that's not something you'll need to worry about, is it?" He squeezed tighter. Aspen's eyes bugged out as her throat nearly collapsed on itself. She choked for air, but nothing came. "You won't have anything to worry about in the next few seconds. I almost envy you that."

A single pinpoint of light remained in Aspen's vision. She couldn't move her limbs anymore. Her body had given up. Maybe... maybe it was time she did, too.

Something hissed through the air and thudded with the unmistakable sound of an arrow to flesh. Laire screamed and jerked away.

Aspen's airway was free. She gasped and drank in the air as greedily as she could. Adrenaline fed feeling back into her body and she heaved Laire off her, scrambling for her sword. She hacked phlegm and spittle, her throat tense and shaking as if it had forgotten what air felt like.

Laire screamed again, this time as a challenge. Another arrow flew into his left shoulder. The first had already impaled the right. Styrax shambled as quickly as he could over the cliff's loose debris without plummeting as Tristan had. As he ran, his eyes glowed white. A pillar of ice froze around Laire and encased him from the shoulders down. He roared again but was no longer a threat.

"Aspen!" Ash stumbled down the mountain, slinging her bow over her shoulder. "Aspen, what happened?"

A lump formed in Aspen's throat. What had she ever done to deserve her cousin?

Her body desperately wanted to sink to the ground to recover. Her shoulder still bled down her side. Her broken ankle had swollen in her boot. Her throat spasmed. Her heart pounded frantically and her frame sagged with exhaustion. She was safe. She could rest.

But she couldn't. Someone else still needed her.

"Tristan." She clutched at her throat. She could barely raise it above a croaking whisper. "Tristan's in there. Help the boy. I'll be back."

"What?" Ash ran to her, still out of reach. "Aspen, wait!"

Aspen shook her head. She had no more time to explain. She turned. Ash screamed for her.

Aspen leapt into the storm.

THIRTY-FIVE

The wind railed against him. Thunder deafened him. Pillars of lightning robbed him of his sight. He sobbed and stumbled through the rain's icy claws as the monsters devoured his mind bit by bit. His name. His face. His *life*. All swallowed in ripping, rotting teeth.

The monsters only laughed. Their black eyes rolled in their heads as they leapt at him through the storm. They scoured wounds on his body as deep as the wounds on his mind. He tried to fight back, but they danced out of reach and cackled as they faded back into the storm.

He couldn't run. The winds buffeted him and forced him to his hands and knees to avoid being swept away. The rain and monsters pummeled him further into the dirt. He tried to call for help, but the gales snatched his cries away and forced them back down his throat. Trapped. Trapped by the storms. Hounded by relentless monsters. Imprisoned in a mind filled with nothing but a wasteland. Panic—thick and bubbling like molten tar—clogged his chest. Any breath he tried to take lodged in his throat and refused to budge. Faster and faster he tried to gulp in air, to no avail. His heart thrashed against his ribs.

The world faded around him in an orange haze. He clutched his chest and collapsed. An inarticulate scream wracked his body. Disappear. He wanted—*needed*—to vanish. No more pain. No more confusion. Only nothingness. He clawed at his chest to rip himself free. "Help," he rasped. To whom or what he didn't know. "Please help."

Something smooth and metallic settled into his palm, attached to a repaired leather strap.

For evergreens and aspen trees.

The words rippled through the core of his being. Green mist and orange haze both flooded his vision, curling and tearing at one another. His mind seared white hot, but the ring in his palm blossomed warmth and comfort from its surface.

He clutched the ring closer, desperately searching its battered edges as he curled into himself. "Say it again." He couldn't say why or how, but he *knew* those words. Echoes of...*something* whispered to him. He tried to understand them—tried to keep them in one place long enough to grab hold of—but they slipped through his fingers like silvery strands of a spider's web, broken and fleeting, but not truly gone, forever brushing his cheeks where he couldn't reach them.

The green mist swelled, as if strengthened by his plea. It swallowed the orange haze and battled it back. The silver ring glared white-hot, blinding him. The orange mist burrowed through flesh and bone as it tried to protect itself inside him. He screamed in agony. Green mist flared from the ring and forced the haze out of him. A garbled shriek escaped from it before the mist swallowed it, and it evaporated into star dust.

The green mist hung around him. It caressed his skin in a gentle coat. The storm's roar dimmed. The rain coursed around him but never touched him. The monsters screamed and retreated a few paces.

The mist brushed his eyelids, leaving kisses of cool dew, and swirled into a faded, swirling image. "I'm your friend, silly." A young girl's voice swept across his ears, aching in its familiarity. She swung a carved baton through the air and smiled at him. "So, I have to stick with you. For evergreens and aspen trees."

"Why for evergreens and aspen trees?" Another young voice. *His* voice. He mouthed blearily along with the memory. "Doesn't forever and always make more sense?"

"Not if you want it to sound cool!" She stuck out her tongue. "Besides, then it will just be between you and me."

The images faded, leaving him hopelessly alone again. "For evergreens and aspen trees," he said in a whisper. "For evergreens and aspen trees."

Every word caused the monsters pain. They hissed and gnashed their teeth, pacing around him but never drawing close. "Who are you to stand against the memory eaters?" they seethed, a thousand voices dripping over each other at once, mere shadows of a noise. "We are insatiable. We will devour you, mind and soul, until we starve ourselves off your empty past, present, and future."

Terror twisted in the pit of his stomach. He rubbed the ring beneath his thumb. The words he knew were there slowed the frantic beat of his heart. He didn't know how he would make it past the monsters, but borrowed courage made him want to *try*.

I want you to have this, a voice said.

The undulating storm around him changed in an instant to a forest gilded in sunlight. A young, dark-haired woman with olive skin and eyes the color of sun-kissed leaves held out the ring on its leather strap. "It's a talisman," she said. "To protect you from harmful magic. It...it also has our promise on it." A blush rose to her cheeks, and she couldn't quite meet his eyes. Her toe scuffed the ground. "If we ever get separated, you'll never forget where you're supposed to be. For evergreens and aspen trees."

He mouthed the words along with her. She handed the necklace forward. Someone with his voice asked, "Did you make this yourself?"

Her cheeks flushed an even brighter red. "Yeah." She looked at him with sudden fierceness. "You know my magic's not very good, though, so don't look for unnecessary danger to put yourself in, all right?"

The scene faded to murkier images, none as clear as the first, but each had the same voice. The same comfort, courage, and friendship. The same *love*. Sometimes she was a little girl with frizzy hair and pouty lips. Other times a teenager with a warm smile and fire in her eyes. She spoke those words every time. They spun in the air like a protective enchantment, *for evergreens and aspen trees.*

When the last image faded, his cheeks were wet with tears. The message, the girl, all resonated within his bones. He wanted it. Wanted the connection, the devotion, the ties to something other than the wasteland he inhabited.

A glint caught the corner of his eye. He tracked it and saw a glow buried in the mud a few feet away. More and more caught his attention, scattered through the storm like so many stars. As stark as silver flecks against a black blade. A breath hitched in his chest. He couldn't remember a more beautiful sight.

He slipped the leather strap with the ring attached back beneath his tunic and patted it against his chest. He battled against the wind to rise and collect the other glows, eager to see what they would show him.

But then he heard it.

A distant rumbling. The approach of thousands of feet. Shrieks and hisses and growls. Gnashing of teeth and gleeful howling. In the distance, on every side, droves of memory eaters poured in on their long, spindly limbs. Their wide, dark eyes rolled in their heads while lightning coursed across their backs. He had found the secret treasure trove of precious memories, and now, so had they. And they had come to feast.

They stopped as a collective whole. They waited, and they watched. His hair stood on end. The scathing raindrops and body-quaking thunder still wracked his body, but he couldn't see them, couldn't hear them. The storm, lightning, and oppressive dark had given way to a barren wasteland, swirling with dust and emptiness. The monsters said nothing, and neither did he. The quiet hung eerily on his ears. He only heard the breath in his lungs and the heartbeat in his chest. He glanced at the specks on the ground, glowing faint but warm. The moment he made a move, the hordes of monsters would come after him. How much were those tiny, almost inconsequential flakes really worth?

He clutched the ring around his neck. The gentle, precious words washed through his bones. *For evergreens and aspen trees.*

Before any more doubt could paralyze him, he barreled straight for the first flake. Something manic in him wanted to laugh. Stupid. *Stupid!* He almost felt *her* disapproving glare. That arched eyebrow and pursed lips. But he had no other choice. *Knew* no other choice.

The monsters shrieked as one—flaying the sky with the sound— and closed in on him. Their rampaging footsteps made even the ground quiver with fear. He scooped up the first shard of light. It held a single name.

Tristan.

One of the memory eaters screamed and toppled. The others trampled it beneath them.

Tristan recognized the name. He'd been called that once; he didn't know by whom. It didn't feel like *him*, but it was familiar. He pocketed the light and bolted to the next one. No time to pause. No time to listen and revel in the shard.

The race began. Each flake he collected, he stuffed into his pocket, already moving to the next before the other had even settled into place. Images, sounds, smells, and feelings all crammed into his head as they tried to organize themselves. A white blanket with a burnt corner, the foulness of tanning leather that somehow felt like home, rows upon rows of tender pea vines covered in red blossoms, the hum of a lullaby. *Hush now, my child, my young meadowlark.* Tristan ignored them all until he could safely gather the rest.

For every piece Tristan picked up, a memory eater screamed and died. Breaths were snatched from their throats and ribs protruded from their skin as they starved in moments. Their twisted bodies littered the outskirts of Tristan's vision as he continued to fill his pockets. The others had taken notice and slowed their pace. Tristan knew it would only be a matter of time before they figured out what was happening.

The time came much sooner than he hoped.

"Kill him. He will kill us all if we do not stop him!" A few at the front veered toward Tristan and directed the others to do the same, the flecks forgotten.

Only Tristan's complete and utter terror kept his feet moving. Adrenaline ate its way through his veins. He darted glances at the approaching horde. For every step he took, they took three. His lead shrunk in moments.

One of the leaders leapt at him, screeching with sadistic glee. Tristan dove for another memory shard. The memory eater's cry strangled in its throat. Its body fell slack and flattened Tristan beneath it. Its weight crushed the breath out of him, but he heaved it off into another group of monsters that all fell beneath it with snarls and whines. It gave him a moment to breathe, but only just. Others climbed over their fallen brethren and reached for Tristan with long, filthy claws. They snarled at him with their rows and rows of yellow, pointed teeth. Tristan snatched one of their bony wrists and flipped the monster over his shoulder. Three more swarmed to take its place. Their talons tore at his clothes and scoured deep furrows in his skin. One buried its fangs into his shoulder and narrowly missed his neck. Tristan screamed and tried to shake it off, but it only sunk its teeth deeper. Its black eyes reflected his contorted face back at him.

The other monsters took their opportunity and piled on top of him. They tore at his pockets to get at the lights. Tristan kicked and snarled and fought back, but it was a losing battle. There were too many.

One knee gave out first. And then the other. And then he fell to their crushing weight.

I'm going to die, he realized with a note of terrifying finality as they ripped more and more of him away. Clothes and skin flaked away in clouds of ash. The green mist bashed as many memory eaters away as it could, but even it was fading. A pocket tore open, and the glowing shards spilled beneath their feet. *I'm going to die here,* he realized. *No one will know and no one will care. What was the point?* He shut his eyes against the inevitable. A tear slipped down his cheek. *I'll never know who I am.*

"You are a *prince*," a soft voice said. Fierce. Loving. Desperate.

Tristan opened his eyes. Memory eaters screamed as they evaporated under a cloud of silver mist. The others retreated away, hissing and spitting. One of the memory shards floated from the ruins of his pocket. Its silver glow shone around him, forming a protective barrier against the monsters. Tristan rose shakily to his knees, collecting the fallen memories, and watched as the silver memory glided to his forehead and kissed it.

The wasteland disappeared, and he was a little boy surrounded by stone walls. Smoke billowed around him, flickering with sparks and the shadows of famished flames. Shouts and screams ricocheted through the corridors. None of that mattered as much as the sight of a golden-haired woman smiling at him. Blood trickled from the corner of her mouth.

"He's just a boy," she said, to someone outside his sight. "Leave him."

"The old rule must die," a deep, rumbling voice said, laced with a hissing undertone that did not belong to anything human. "*All of it.*"

"Mama!" Tristan said in a tiny voice.

"Shh." She hugged him to her and kissed his forehead. "You have nothing to fear. You are the sole prince of Loralan, now, and you have a mighty destiny. You *will not* die here. Live. For all of us."

She tightened around him for a moment, a gasp escaping her lips, and then she fell limp atop him. Fire engulfed the scene, and Tristan found himself back in the wasteland. More tears cut tracks down his cheeks, this time with a deep and longing ache for the mother he'd lost.

The memory eaters attempted to draw closer to him, but another fleck of light flew from his pocket. It joined the silver memory and emitted a wave of blue light that obliterated memory eaters that had inched too close. The others withdrew a few more steps.

The light settled on Tristan's shoulder and transported him to a forest swathed in gold. A man with kind eyes and a gentle smile placed a hand on his shoulder. "You are *my* son," he said. "I don't care what anyone else says. You may have been born to Salaith and Eden, but you are *mine*." He ducked to meet Tristan's eyes and raised his eyebrows. "Are you all right to be the son of poor old Gan the pea farmer?" he asked with a wink.

The images went away. Another light landed in Tristan's palm.

"You're my friend." The girl again! She grumbled while she dragged him by the hand through the same golden trees. "For evergreens and aspen trees, remember? You can't just wander off and never come back whenever you feel like it."

Another light. Another memory.

"You're the only friend I've got left," a sandy-haired man said. "... Please be more careful with yourself."

More images flooded Tristan's mind, each tied to a speck of light. They flew from his pockets and from every corner of the wastelands. More of the memory eaters fell as they came. The monsters attempted to flee but to no avail. The memory shards covered every spare inch of Tristan's body, interlocking in a protective chain-mail of light. They brought with them memories of tears, laughter, love, loss, fear, courage, success, and failure. Tristan basked in all of it. The pieces of his life locked into place. His wounds from the memory eaters healed themselves. His fear and fatigue dissipated to almost nothing. Every new shard sent a wave of magic and warmth through the wasteland. Blooms shoved their way through the dust. Mountains built themselves toward the heavens. Water sprung from the earth and washed the dead memory-eaters away. Soon, the wasteland gave way to a thriving paradise.

Trees sighed and laughed on the edges of rolling grasslands, passing messages between each other. Wildflowers bounced in whispered breezes. The bright blue sky dripped down the mountains' cliffs in sparkling waterfalls and fed glittering silver brooks and streams that laced their way through the landscape.

Tristan breathed it in. He savored the crisp air in his lungs. Peace settled over his once racing heart. The lights—in a nearly perfect cocoon around him—glowed brighter around him. The one place that remained dark was a single patch over the center of his heart— his name.

Across the grasslands stood the last memory eater. It sneered at Tristan, its claws latched over the last piece of light like the bars of a cage. Tristan approached it, the fear in him replaced by quiet confidence. He strode with shoulders thrown back, supported by dozens of silent, invisible hands born from the precious memories.

Tristan stopped a few paces away and met the monster's gaze. It watched him, pacing with teeth bared, for some time before it spoke.

"Are you sure about this?" it asked in a voice similar to Tristan's, but worn hoarse with doubt and terror and bitterness. "The moment this name is restored to you and you leave this place, you run the risk of it all being taken from you again."

"I know," Tristan said. He rubbed his thumb across the silver ring. "I'm willing to chance it."

The monster shook its head, growling with teeth bared. "*Why?* What could be so worth risking all of this?"

"I—" Tristan couldn't articulate the prismatic emotions and memories coursing through his body. Couldn't describe the warmth, comfort, heartache, and loss that all intermingled in a mosaic of *him*. Couldn't express how priceless they all were, and how they would be meaningless if he gave up on them now.

The creature grinned, its jagged rows of teeth dripping long ropes of saliva and its black eyes wide with triumph. "You cannot find the reason. So you must *stay*."

"I *can't*," Tristan said. He strode toward the monster, eyes fixated on the last memory it held. "There's too much waiting for me out there."

The monster danced away, claws closing like a vice around the shard. "And what about *in here*?" it screamed. "Do you want to risk losing all of this? Risk it being shredded and trampled by everything out there?" Its chest heaved. Spittle flew from its mouth, and its eyes nearly bugged out of its skull. Its nearly transparent skin trembled over its protruding bones.

Tristan set his feet and prepared for it to charge. Instead, it took a few paces back. Where Tristan had expected to see rage, he only saw panic and desperation. A wounded, broken thing that refused to be broken again. He softened.

"What are you afraid of?"

The creature looked at him with its wide eyes. Its grip around the memory loosened. The anger in its face slipped away, leaving something else in its place. Surprise. A creature that had never known care. "I fear nothing."

Tristan sat on the grass and crossed his legs. He said nothing, only watched.

The creature paced back and forth. It still clung to the light. "I fear nothing. I wish only to protect!" It whirled on him. "*You* put this place in danger! And for what? For *love?*" it laughed, a rasping sound that grated on Tristan's ears. "Where was your love—your friends, your family—these past years while you suffered alone? They never came for you. Never rescued you from your silent prison. But *I* was here." It spread its arms wide, the memory shard clacking against its claws. "I feared nothing—not the emptiness, not the silence. I protected what was mine, and I will continue to do so after everyone has abandoned us again." It sneered at Tristan. "I. Fear. Nothing."

Tristan remained silent.

The creature curled one of its thin lips. "You do not believe me?"

Tristan refrained from comment.

The monster scoffed. "Perhaps it is *you* that is afraid! Why else would you stall like this?" It gestured menacingly at the shard in its clutches. "Are you worried I will destroy this? This last piece of yourself? That you will never be whole again?" It grinned. "That would be poetic, would it not? To collect all those memories, only to lose the last, most precious one to a monster." It swung its arms around itself and took in the vista. "At least you would have all of this. For now. Until you left for the world out there. And then this place would be open to attack...again." The creature's voice cracked, every word quieter than the last. "They would abuse it. Destroy it. Tear it to shreds and use it like some old plaything. And then they would take it, again, and there would be nothing left. Nothing but emptiness. Again. And starving, horrific creatures like me." Its shoulders heaved, and it roared with broken, crushing sobs. "You would subject me to that again without a *thought!*" Tears rolled from its lidless eyes and dripped onto the shard as it held it tight to its chest. "We-we cannot survive that again. They will hurt us. They will take it. They will take it! Again and again and again! Nothing will be left! *NOTHING!*"

Tristan went to the creature and sat shoulder-to-shoulder with it. It cried and hiccupped and keened like an inconsolable child. The sound rippled across the plains and mountains and rivers, hushing everything in its mournful notes. Minutes passed. Years. Moments. Eons. Tristan didn't know how long he sat.

Finally, the creature shed its last tear and drew in a shaking breath. "We cannot do it," it said, hushed and terrified. "It will cost too much."

Tristan took in the expanse again and let himself feel everything this creature felt. All the pain. All the misery. All the pride and happiness and joy. "This place is beautiful," he said.

The creature nodded. "That is why we cannot lose it."

"Do you remember how we built it?" Tristan asked. "I don't."

The creature gave him a strange, suspicious look. It nodded again, slowly this time. "I remember every piece. Every blade of grass that grew, every speck of dust that built those mountains. I remember it all."

"Do you think we could build more?"

The creature wiped its eyes on its shoulder and nodded to a small pond. "I thought more trees there would be..." The creature froze. It looked at Tristan with narrowed eyes. "You mock my dreams."

Tristan shook his head. "Never." He smiled and patted its shoulder. "More trees there sound fantastic. And maybe a mountain or two more over there?"

"The only way we can do that is by leaving this place." The creature bowed its head with a heavy sigh. "You are sure about this, then?"

Tristan stood. "I am." He inhaled every scent, feeling, and memory he could. Everything the wretched creature next to him had tended.

"And nothing will stop you?" it asked, its voice small.

"No."

Silence.

"What...what will happen to me?"

Tristan looked at it—folded over itself, broken, shaking, and lonely—and his heart hurt for it. He knew this thing, deep down. He had felt it in his darkest, most vulnerable, and fear-infused moments. He couldn't abandon something that had been with him from the start.

He took the creature by the wrists and helped it to its feet. "Will you stay here and guard this place? Keep it safe when bad things come our way? You've kept me alive for this long."

The creature looked at him in disbelief. "You-You're not-you'll really let me—" its words tumbled out one over the other. It beamed as its chest filled with pride. Its teeth were still as sharp. Its eyes were still as wide. But they were somehow less horrifying now. "I will! I will do that! Nothing will get by me!"

"Only trees and mountains and pleasant changes?"

It grinned. "Yes." It extended its hand. "And I believe this will be the best place to start." It relinquished the last memory shard and ran into the distance, howling with glee.

The light settled into place on Tristan's chest. The name resounded through his entire being. Every floodgate of emotions and memories burst open and rolled and churned into one connected whole. He knew how the grass had grown. Knew how and when each mountain had been born and when the rivers had carved their paths through his mind. He never thought he'd have that again. That his past and future would connect so perfectly and completely, and that he could claim them both at once. He couldn't keep from smiling, even as he cried like a lost child that'd found his way home. Blinding light burst from the armor encasing him and enveloped the verdant space. It faded to warm feelings and a contented creature in the back of his mind, and he left with the sweet taste and sound of his name rolling over and over again through his thoughts.

CHAPTER

THIRTY-SIX

He returned to the storm, uncertain he'd ever left. Despite the horizontal rain pelting like darts into his skin, the howling wind doing everything in its power to strip the clothes and meat from his bones and carry him away, and lightning threatening to strike him down at any moment, he smiled. Bigger and brighter and more manic than he ever had before. His cheeks nearly split. Salted raindrops slipped into his mouth from his cheeks. He closed his eyes, tilted his head back, and laughed. He whooped to the heavens, competing with the wind and thunder.

He knew. He *knew*! He had a home—a family. Friends. A purpose. A history. A name. A full and proper name! Here, in the place that should have been his death, it had gifted him a new life. And a promise to keep.

He clutched the ring to his chest like a lifeline and attempted to stand. *She* was out there, alone in the storm. He had to find her.

With more of his body mass exposed, the wind nearly sucked him away into its abyss while simultaneously almost braining him with a flying tree. He flattened himself. Crawling would have to do.

He inched his way through the sludge, ducking pieces of debris flying at him and calling for Aspen. The wind snatched her name away the moment he uttered it, but he kept trying. He didn't know where he was going, but she had to be *somewhere*. She wouldn't have been able to wander far with her wounds.

A faint blue glow in the distance caught his attention. Hoping it wasn't the residue of lightning flashes in his eyes, he moved toward it, still calling Aspen's name. The closer he got, the more he saw the vague outline of a person bent double against the gales, dragging a black sword behind them. They held a glowing key before them like a lantern.

"ASPEN!" He threw caution, along with his sanity, to the wind, and ran to her, battling to stay grounded. All the childhood memories of her bubbled inside him like a great flooding fountain. *For evergreens and aspen trees.* He loved that girl. He loved his friend that laughed and cried and fought with him through everything, and he couldn't wait to tell her he had made it home. The moment he reached her, he enveloped her in his arms, holding her as close as he could.

Aspen shrieked as if the Pit itself had snatched her. She threw her shoulder beneath his chin, and when he reeled back in surprise, she jammed her elbow beneath his ribs. He happily released her. As she tumbled from his grip, Aspen drew her sword and swung to face him in one deadly arc.

"Aspen! Aspen, it's me!" he said. He threw up a placating hand, trying to cradle his injured jaw and ribs simultaneously.

For a moment, it seemed the wind had stolen the words away. Aspen's sword continued to train on him. Her attention darted back and forth, as if she didn't see him at all, but other monsters. Her entire body trembled with terror or pent-up fight. She blinked once, and whatever nightmare she saw seemed to fade. Her gaze focused on him. The sword drooped at her side. "Tristan?" she asked, almost listlessly.

He shook his head. "Not Tristan," he said. He took her face in his hands, his grin returning. "I'm back. Aspen, *I'm* back, and I—"

"Tristan!" The film over her eyes subsided. She pulled him closer and checked him over, hunched against the rain. "Are you hurt?"

"What? No, Aspen, I'm trying to tell you. I—"

She forced him to look her in the eyes. "Tristan, *are you hurt?*"

"I'm not Tristan, I'm—" He grabbed her hands.

"I don't care *who* you think you are right now! Are. You. *Hurt?*"

"Aspen, I'm *fine!*" He smiled at her, tears running anew down his cheeks. He wiped a sopping strand of hair from her face. "You don't have to search anymore. It's me. It's Ro."

The tears. The smiles. The relief. He waited for her to mirror everything that wanted to burst from his body at once.

Instead, she took a step away from him, back rigid against the wind. Against the fear in her eyes. She might have run completely if he didn't have hold of her hands. "Tristan, if you're lying—" She took a breath that hitched in her throat. Her lower lip trembled. The rain pelted her skin mercilessly. "If you're not certain, I *will* break, and there will be no coming back from that."

He stepped to her and pressed her to his chest, hoping to dispel every fear he could. "I won't let that happen. I'm real, and I'm here." He kissed her temple and withdrew the silver ring beneath his tunic. He put it in her hand and closed her fingers around it. "For evergreens and aspen trees."

She rolled the ring in her hand, fingers brushing the engravings. She cupped her mouth, choking back a sob and a laugh all at once, and looked at him, eyes shining. The storm seemed to stop at that moment, chased away by the joy on her face. Tristan's breath fled. It was like watching leaves change from gold to silver—like coming *home.* Tears poured down his cheeks as he smiled. "I'm sorry I've been gone for so long."

Aspen mirrored his smile, her face aglow.

It was then that Tristan realized the bruises around her neck. Blood poured from her shoulder and a new gash had welled on her temple, and she leaned on a crooked ankle. Horror and fury and guilt raged through him in a wash of emotion. He gripped her by the arms, his heart in his throat. "Aspen, are you all right?" *Stupid* question. Of course, she wasn't all right! He had to get her out of the storm. *Now*.

Aspen's smile faltered. "I'm—I'm all right. I'm fine," she said, her voice fading and pain shadowing her face. The blood drained from her cheeks. "Just so long as you're-you're safe."

She collapsed, vomiting blood.

THIRTY-SEVEN

Sedick screamed and threw a bangle at one of Laire's trophies. The bear's head exploded and rained stuffing across the office. "May they all rot in the PIT!"

Sorren was lost to him—destroyed by the word meant only to obliterate Tristan. Not that Sedick cared for Sorren—he had betrayed him too many times—but the information he provided was invaluable. He'd seen every twist and turn and knew the players by name and face now. He'd been wary when Sorren had joined forces with Laire, and now it appeared to be with good cause. His "eyes" were gone. And by the looks of it, so was the prince. And the sword. He cursed again. There was nothing left for him now. He barked at the bangle, and the rest of the stuffed bear shredded to pieces.

"What are you doing to papa's things?" Linae demanded in her sniveling, imperious voice.

Sedick rolled his eyes and snapped a finger at his guards. "Bring the girl. If her father returns, we'll trade her for the sword. We're going to Monterro."

"I'm not going without mama and papa!"

Sedick ignored her. One of his men scooped her up, and she shrieked, pounding against his back.

Sedick rubbed his temples. He had to get back to Osmen before rumors spread and incriminated him in this disaster.

"Let me go!" Linae scrabbled at Sedick's hand as they marched through the lower levels of Monterro castle. "Papa! Mama! Help!"

Sedick pinched her wrist in his fingers. "No one's coming for you." He unlocked a plain wooden door and flung Linae inside. A sliver of light through a crack of a window illuminated a frail, dark-skinned woman as she darted from the shadows. Golden shackles glinted on her wrists.

She scooped Linae into her arms and whirled on Sedick. "Where is Sorren?"

Sedick ground his teeth at her shrill demand. It pounded in his already throbbing skull. He ignored her and went to close the door, but she shoved her foot in the door. "SEDICK! WHERE IS MY SON?"

"Silence, Milaia!" He backhanded her, the crack echoing through the small room.

Milaia took one step back. Linae looked at them both with wide eyes, silent tears pouring down her face. Milaia stroked Linae's hair and cuddled her close to her chest. "He will not touch you. Not while I'm here," she said, her eyes never leaving Sedick, burning with the hatred she had held for him the moment he had made her his wife. At one point, that fire had made him wild with desire. Now, it only made him pity her.

"Where is *my* son?" she asked again.

"He was my son, too. And *you* ruined him!" A cruel, bitter grin spread across his face. "And now he's lost to both of us."

Milaia's legs collapsed beneath her. "*NO!*"

Sedick slammed and locked the door behind him. Milaia slammed her fists against the door, shouting muffled curses through it. He rubbed his temples and made the trek back up to the throne room.

He swept past the guards—flashing his crest for access—into the king's audience hall. The white walls nearly blinded him, but he blinked past the pain and pressed forward, stepping around the pools of brown bloodstain the servants could never scrub out. Even twenty-five years after The Day of Bluest Blood, the slaughtered royal family could not relinquish their grip on the castle. Sconces scorched the walls black, and limp drapes framed the gray sky through their lofty windows. The world seemed as miserable and bitter as Sedick felt.

King Osmen sat upon his crystal throne beneath the pinnacle of the vaulted ceiling. Mute light fell from the single, circular glass pane above and haloed him in silver. "Sedick," he said, his soft voice carrying across the hall in an ethereal echo.

Sedick bowed, his sleeves dripping across the gray tile and brushing the last brown vestiges of King Salaith, cascading down the steps to the throne. "My lord, I am afraid I bring ill tidings."

"I cannot remember a time you have brought me anything else."

Sedick bits his tongue, smoldering. He knew that was not true. *Osmen* knew that was not true. How many secrets had he loosed from unyielding prisoners? How many battles had he ended before they started because he could get an enemy to talk when no one else could? He breathed slow and deep. It would not do to lose his temper now. Although he and Osmen shared no love between them, Osmen was a means to an end. So, for now, Sedick had to play the part.

"Speak," Osmen said finally.

Sedick rose and met the king's gaze. "The prince escaped Laire's fingers. Laire left his post to find him and I have it in good faith that they are now both lost to us. The Golden Grove massacre will be without its key player." He bowed again. "I am sorry to report Laire's failures yet again."

"As I recall, Sedick, you were also at Lorate. You did nothing to stop this?"

"I voiced my opinion that we should have killed the boy the moment we found him, sire, I do not see—"

"But *I* was not in concurrence, Sedick. I am King, and you are my servant. You carry out all *my* orders, no matter your personal allegiances."

Sedick flinched, but kept his mouth this time. Further argument would do him no good. "What would you have us do about the Golden Grove, sire?"

"Lay them waste, as we planned," Osmen said with a dismissive wave. He settled back in his throne and looked through the window. Boredom slumped against his shoulders. "Leave no survivors on either side. This kingdom needs a blood sacrifice to galvanize it into action."

Sedick dropped low and backed away. "Of course, your majesty. Long may Loralan conquer."

"And far may it fall."

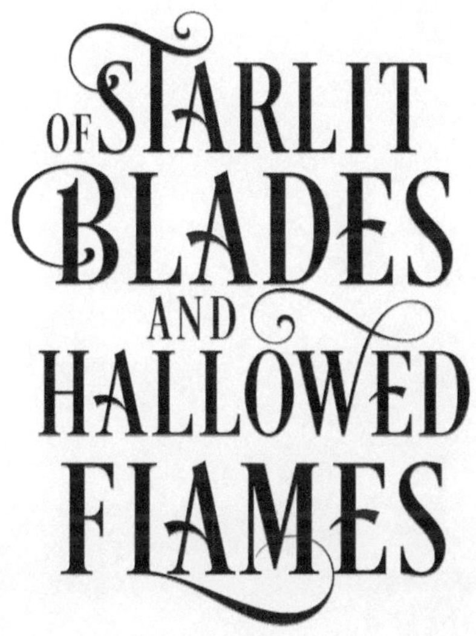
THE SONGS OF LORALAN
OF STARLIT BLADES AND HALLOWED FLAMES
A.L. LORENSEN

ACKNOWLEDGMENTS

I started this book fourteen years ago at the ripe old age of eleven. When I wrote those first few lines in shaky cursive, surrounded by my mountain of stuffed animals, I never could have imagined all the wonderful supporters and amazing people I would come across because of it. I could write an entire novel (or twelve) in acknowledgements alone and still not do justice to the people that have been instrumental in the development of this book and my life in general.

I will mention a few key players here, but I will have you all know that if you ever had a kind word for me, some gentle encouragement, gave a really spectacular hug, or were just an awesome human in general, you had a hand in this book. Thank you for everything. It means more than you know.

Dad, thank you for showing a bored little girl something productive to do with her time. Thank you for being just as excited about the things I wrote when I was six as you are about the things I write now. Thank you for encouraging my creative endeavors, and for pushing me to be my brightest and best self. I'm still working on that, and I think I always will be.

Ryan, my dearest love, thank you for enduring my "almost done"s and "someday"s and "oh-my-gosh-I'm-the-worst-writer-in-existence-and-I'll-never-get-anything-done-ever"s. You have all the grace and patience of a saint. You inspire me—to be better, to be kinder, to be truer to myself. Thank you for believing in me, for loving me and all my quirks, and for always reminding me to get my writing done. My productivity and creativity reached new heights the moment I married you. I would never have gotten this far without you.

Miranda and Morgan, my sisters of choice, I'm not sure I can say anything here that hasn't already been said. You have been through it all with me. From midnight alfredo in our hobbit holes to now, what I way we've come. Thank you for being you, and for being my go-to hype-women.

Moms (*all* of you amazing women that have chosen to claim me in some way, shape, or form), thank you for teaching me faith, patience, perseverance, and grace in the face of adversity. You modeled those traits as if you were born to them, and I hope to one day live up to your examples even in some small part.

To the people I chased throughout my life, shoving pages upon pages of fuzzy ideas and half-baked manuscripts at you, begging for feedback and validation, *thank you*. Thank you for tolerating me, for humoring me, and for genuinely doing your best to find something kind and encouraging to say to me. It was a rough task, but I hope it was never a thankless one. I thrived off every single note, edit, and comment. Someone was *reading* my work and had enough of an interest in it to help me be better. I hope I *am* better. It is all thanks to you.

Cassandra Caswell-Stirling, Jen Boles, and Aria Carpenter, my *incredible* editors, thank you for saving my manuscript when I was ready to burn it and making it more polished and beautiful than I could have ever done on my own. I can actually read it now without wanting to gouge my eyes out.

Timea Schweiger, thank you for making all of my cover design dreams come true. I find every opportunity I can to show it off.

My readers, thank you for picking this book. Thank you for picking me and allowing me to occupy some of your time. I hope it made your day brighter. I hope it was the escape you needed at the time. I hope you read it often. But even if not, thank you for giving it a chance.

About the Author

A. L. Lorensen has had a lifetime passion for writing and the art of storytelling. She graduated from Utah State University with a Bachelor of Science in Social Work and maintained her writing on the side. A. L. mainly writes fantasy, but has dabbled in fiction, mystery, comedy, and anything else that may strike her fancy. *For Evergreens and Aspen Trees* is her debut novel.

A. L. Lorensen currently resides in Logan, UT with her husband, their cat, Muse, and their many, many bookshelves. If you would like to keep in touch with A. L. Lorensen (and get a free short story), you can join her newsletter at www.allwrites.com.

facebook.com/allorensen.writes

instagram.com/a.l.l.writes